FOR ALL TIME,

FABIO

"YOU SHAME ME, VIKING!"

"There will never be shame between us, Reyna," Viktor replied fiercely. "I will know your body, and you will know mine, and we will both glory in the intimacy and discovery."

He caught her face between his hands as he spoke in a mesmerizing whisper. "We are already linked, Reyna. Linked in our souls. You must feel it, because you are part of me. Our being together is pre-ordained, inescapable. You belong to me."

"Why do you say I am yours?" she asked warily.

He was silent for a long moment, then whispered, "Because I have loved you in another life . . ."

Praise for *Rogue*

"The lovemaking is scintillating and adventurous.
Fabio fans will devour this unusual passion-packed story."

Rendezvous

Viking

by

Fabio

in collaboration with

Eugenia Riley

AVON BOOKS ◆ NEW YORK

VIKING is an original publication of Avon Books. This work has never before appeared in book form. This work is a novel. Any similarity to actual persons or events is purely coincidental.

AVON BOOKS
A division of
The Hearst Corporation
1350 Avenue of the Americas
New York, New York 10019

Copyright © 1994 by Fabio Lanzoni
Photograph courtesy of Fabio
Published by arrangement with the author
Library of Congress Catalog Card Number: 94-94322
ISBN: 0-380-77048-2

First Avon Books Printing: November 1994

AVON TRADEMARK REG. U.S. PAT. OFF. AND IN OTHER COUNTRIES, MARCA REGISTRADA, HECHO EN U.S.A.

Printed in the U.S.A.

RA   10 9 8 7 6 5 4 3

I dedicate this and all my works to Women—
the guardians and teachers of love for all humankind.

This author gratefully acknowledges the contributions of Eugenia Riley, without whom this book would not have been possible.

Acknowledgments

Special thanks to Peter F. Paul, my friend, partner, and manager, who has dedicated his indefatigable energy and creativity to working with me, and for creating a new superhero, Thorr, in my image, for the first time joining the male and female perspective in one superhero.

Special thanks to my friend and partner Eric Ashenberg, whose business management and friendship have been invaluable in ensuring the success of our "phenomenon team."

Thanks to Hero Entertainment and Stephen Brind for making it possible for my fans to support my television and movie activities through a NASDQ public company.

Thanks to Steve Raimondi for launching *Fabio's Healthy Bodies*, a fitness lifestyle magazine that communicates my health and fitness philosophy to millions of readers monthly.

Thanks to Bonnie Kuhlman, my international fan club president, and to all my fans around the world who have given me the fulfillment of knowing that my message of self-esteem, romance, health, and fitness have brought some joy and happiness into their lives.

Thanks to Romance Alive, and Beverly and Marshall Blonstein, for their contribution in making my work available on audio tapes around the world.

PROLOGUE

IVAR THE INVINCIBLE SWUNG HIS BROADSWORD, DEFENDING HIS BE-
loved wife and his people from the barbarians who lived
across the fjord.

The battle between the two Viking tribes had raged for
hours on the frigid shores of Iceland. The mighty Norwegian
Ivar blocked with his shield and hacked away at his mortal
enemy, Grundar the Barbarian, leader of the rival Danish
tribe. Ivar's tunic dripped with blood; his tall, magnificent
body was covered by gouges and punctures. He felt weak,
dizzy, close to death.

The huge, cross-eyed Grundar screamed curses and
chopped at Ivar with his broadsword, knocking off his
horned helmet. Even as the Viking struggled to retaliate,
Grundar's blunt-edged weapon slammed Ivar's side, not
penetrating the chain mail, but stunning him, robbing him
of breath. Ivar watched Grundar raise his broadsword high
overhead to rive him asunder. He heard his wife's scream of
terror in the background.

Her cry mobilized him; he caught an excruciating breath,
raised his own sword, and thrust powerfully at Grundar. With
an agonized gasp, the huge Dane crashed, dead, to the
beach.

A lull fell over the battle. Spotting their slain leader, the
other Danes fled in the wake of arrows and spears cast by
Ivar's men. At last dizziness staggered Ivar and he fell to the
ground, tasting sand in his mouth.

1

"Ivar! No! No!"

Gentle hands rolled him over, and he looked up to see Gerda, his magnificent bride, hovering over him. With reality swimming in and out, he thought of how beautiful she was— imprinting on his memory her sleek blond hair, soulful dark brown eyes, and lovely, smooth features. He realized he was surely dying now; he could hear the voices of the Valkyries summoning him to the Hall of Odin. He felt a stab of sorrow that he would never know the wondrous fruit of his dear wife's body—that they would never have a child together, that his legacy would die in Midgard on this day.

By now Ivar's warriors had regrouped. They, as well as the women, sank to their knees around their fallen leader, all beseeching the gods to save him. Gerda drew her fingers through Ivar's long blond hair. With tears streaming down her cheeks, she grasped his battered hand and kissed the bruised knuckles.

"Ivar! I implore you, do not die!"

"Gerda, my love," he whispered back. "On this day I must leave you and my people—"

"Nay! Nay!" she pleaded.

"But take heart, my love. 'Tis a day of great victory for our clan. Our homeland has been saved from Grundar's treachery."

"Because of you, my lord. You cannot abandon us now!"

"My mission on Midgard has been completed," he assured her solemnly. "Now I must rise to greater glory in the hall of slain warriors."

Gerda clutched his hand to her heart. *"Nay! Tell me 'tis not true."*

"I must go, my love. A moment ago during the battle, I felt a heavenly Valkyrie maiden tapping me on the shoulder."

"But how can I live without you?" she cried. *"You promised me a child—"*

"I know, but mayhap we will meet again in another world," he said tenderly. "And you must promise me that tonight you and my people will launch me to Valhalla in my burning longship, in the tradition of the great Viking king, Viktor the Valiant."

"Ivar, please, I cannot—"

"But you must, my love. I am bound to fight and feast anew in the meetinghouse of the dead." He squeezed her hand and stared into her eyes in a poignant moment of love and communion. "Promise me."

She shuddered with exquisite sorrow. "Verily, I promise."

"We will meet again, my love," he vowed.

As he drew his final convulsive breaths, Ivar felt blessed by Bragi with a skaldic verse befitting a dying warrior, and in his failing voice he recited it for Gerda and his people:

> Reign of my heart
> Be ended.
> Love of my life
> Know peace.
> I rise on wings of honor
> To feast at Odin's table.

Gerda leaned over and tenderly, tearfully, kissed the lips of her dying husband . . .

ONE

"CUT!" YELLED THE DIRECTOR.

The familiar voice propelled Marcello back to awareness, and he shook his head to gain his bearings. When he acted, he often worked himself into a trancelike state, totally integrating his own psyche into that of his character. Blinking, he saw the California beach, the towering dark cliffs, the blinding lights, the cameras on tracks and dollies, the production people scurrying about, securing equipment and moving cables.

Then he spotted Monica. Dressed in her Viking-woman costume, she knelt beside him, grinning, reaching out to wipe sandy grit from his chin. He winked back at her. She was the love of his life, both in reality and in this movie.

"Not a bad job of dying, big boy," she teased. "I noticed you had our newest production assistant in tears."

Marcello sat up eagerly. "You mean the blonde with the ponytail and the red halter top?"

"Beast!" she cried, showering him with a handful of sand.

"Hey, you two, cut it out!" called an imperious male voice. "We're too far into this production to lose our star to temporary blindness."

They glanced up to see the director, Irving Hartman, approaching with the cinematographer, Harold Schindle, at his heels. Both men were middle-aged, balding, bearded, and wore thick-lensed glasses. Privately the crew referred to them as "the Compulsive Clones."

Shaking off sand, Marcello popped to his feet and tugged Monica up with him. "Well, Irving?"

The director's grin was broad. "We got a wrap this time."

"Thank God," said Marcello feelingly. "After twelve takes, it's high time."

"If you hadn't run into the Steadicam on the ninth take, we could have wrapped long before now," teased Harold.

"The Steadicam operator ran into me," Marcello said indignantly. "I was right on the mark, and he stepped into my frame."

"That's right, the mighty Marcello never makes mistakes," Monica put in drolly.

Marcello rubbed his side and grimaced. "I'm going to have to go home and soak this bruise in the hot tub."

"Shouldn't you have the doctor look at that?" Irving fretted.

"Naw."

"Superheroes like Marcello don't run to the doctor every time they stub a toe," Monica quipped.

Harold winked at her. "You'll help Marc work out the kinks, won't you, babe?"

Monica smirked.

"Are you sure you're ready for tomorrow's shoot?" Irving asked Marcello. "I'm still nervous because you won't allow a stuntman to do the burning-boat scene."

"Nothing to it," Marcello assured him. "Besides, it's the last scene in the movie, so if you lose me in the inferno, you'll still be ready for post-production, right?"

"I just don't know," the director muttered, scratching his head.

"Hey, Irv, why don't you worry about something of consequence, like whether the skies and the wind will cooperate tomorrow?" asked Harold.

Irving eyed the ominous heavens. "Lord, if we have to cancel the final shoot, the producer will have a stroke. We're already way over budget."

"Perhaps we should all beg Thor to hold his temper in check," said Marcello. He leaned over, picked up Ivar's helmet, and stared cynically at the horns. "You know, when we shoot the launch to Valhalla tomorrow, it will be the one time during the entire filming that these horns will be authentic."

Irving rolled his eyes. "Are we back to that again?"

Marcello frowned. "I take my craft very seriously."

Irving flung his hands wide. "So who cares whether or not Vikings actually wore horns, for heaven's sake?"

"I care," said Marcello earnestly. "Vikings wore only plain helmets, never horned ones, during battle. Horns were reserved for religious or ceremonial occasions—or for Valkyries to wear. Now I ask you, do I look like a Valkyrie?"

"Whatever you are, sweetie," Monica remarked, looking him over greedily, "you sure as hell ain't no Valkyrie."

Marc grinned and plopped the helmet on her head at a jaunty angle; she saucily wrinkled her nose at him.

"Quit worrying about being so authentic," advised Irving. "It's too late now, and anyway, we wouldn't dream of depriving your adoring female audience of every possible embellishment."

"Besides, guys, I can testify that Marcello does have horns—and a tail," Monica teased.

As Irving and Harold laughed, Marc shook a finger at her. "You and I will deal with that at home, minx."

Monica feigned horror and pressed a hand to her ostensibly trembling bosom.

Irving laid a hand on Marcello's shoulder. "There are a few pointers I want to give you about tomorrow's shoot; then we can all meet back at the studio to see the dailies." He nodded toward Monica. "You coming to the studio, Monica?"

"Sorry, guys." She handed Marc back his helmet. "I have an appointment I can't miss."

Marc winked at her. "See you at home, babe."

She in turn winked at Irving. "Keep him away from the red halter top."

Irving laughed. "Sure thing, Monica. See that Marc rests tonight, will you?"

She turned, tossing her smooth blond hair. "As soon as he works his kinks out," she quipped over her shoulder.

Four hours later, after stopping by the studio to review the rushes with Irving, then working out with his personal fitness trainer at his club, Marcello headed home. With the sun roof open on his gold Ferrari, he drove out of Hollywood and took scenic Laurel Canyon Boulevard up into the Hills. The spring breeze felt cool on his face, and the setting sun gilded the houses and trees with a pristine glow. After the brutal day he had put in, he felt tired but fulfilled. He was eager to get home, play with his dogs, and sink into the hot tub. *I must be sure to pull Monica in for a little recreation—and retribution,* he added to himself with a wicked grin.

As he rounded a curve, a trio of hitchhiking, teenage girls shouted and waved at him. Marcello wagged a finger at them and grinned as he drove past. They should know better than to be out on the highway hitching rides. The world had become so dangerous.

Marcello was a man who had always felt somewhat out of step with the modern world in which he lived, almost as if, through some quirk of destiny, he had been fated to exist in the wrong time. Born Marcello Lazaro thirty-two years ago in the ancient city of Venice, he had been raised in the northern Italian countryside, in a fifteenth-century villa that had once been a monastery. Just as he had always been enamored of the history, culture, and majesty of northern Italy, he had also felt as if he belonged in an earlier age. As a small boy, he remembered being fascinated when his mother told him tales of his Norwegian ancestors, of how he had acquired his blond hair and blue eyes from the Viking warriors who had invaded southern Italy in the ninth century. By the time Marc was in college, his fascination with ancient times prompted him to join a medieval reenactment society and spend many weekends at joists and war games.

How ironic that he was playing a Viking now. Even in his movie roles, he almost invariably played a man of another age.

Marcello had come to America ten years ago, seeking fame as a movie star. His background in construction and architecture had helped him there. A job as a grip on a movie set had led to roles as an extra, then a few bit parts, and finally his first big break: co-starring as a desert sheikh in a swashbuckling tale about British colonial days in Egypt. The role of the sheikh had catapulted Marcello to overnight stardom as "the new Valentino," and his subsequent roles—a Caribbean pirate, a medieval knight, a Byronic rogue—had reflected his qualities as an eternal hero. On every talk show on which he had appeared, the inevitable comment was, "You look as if you've stepped out of another time."

Perhaps he had. His feelings of being misplaced in the present age had increased five years ago, when he had lost his family. Marcello drew a heavy breath at the memory. He had been in the south of France shooting a film when his mother, father, and sister had chartered a small plane to come visit him on location. Tragically, their plane had gone down over the Alps.

Now his family consisted of his dogs, and more importantly, of Monica, whom he had met three years ago. He thought of the dream he kept having about them lately, a haunting, poignant, surreal vision. In it, he saw himself and Monica on the shores of Iceland. He was holding his just-born son in his arms, and he was weeping, as all the Viking peoples around them bowed in tribute. Marcello was convinced that he saw himself and Monica in Iceland because of the movie they were making. To him, the dream signified that it was high time for him and Monica to marry and start a family of their own.

They had lived together for over two years. A year ago, they'd had a terrible fight and had almost broken up after Marcello asked Monica to marry him. At twenty-three, she just wasn't ready to settle down, she had argued; her career wasn't as established as his. She had begged him to give her one more year, and he had agreed.

That year was up now, and Marcello was ready to collect on a solemn promise.

At a crest just off Mulholland Drive, he wheeled his car into the driveway of his one-story Mediterranean villa. He hopped out and strode toward the front door, passing pots filled with blooming geraniums. As soon as he put the key in the lock, the dogs began barking out on the patio. He smiled at the sound as he went through the deserted foyer and picked up his mail. His housekeeper, Mrs. Nowotny, had likely already gone for the day.

Marcello gave his mail a cursory glance and put it back on the credenza. He stepped down into the den, which had a brown, Saltillo tile floor, beamed ceiling, and stone fireplace.

He enjoyed this room with its accoutrements of earlier times. He and Monica frequently skied in Taos, and they had made numerous side trips to Santa Fe, where they had purchased many of the objects decorating this room—painted wooden figurines of tigers, birds, and dogs; Navajo rugs, pottery, and baskets; and Southwestern art.

Continuing to the kitchen, Marcello strode to the patio doors and unlocked them. His three huge Great Danes vaulted in and jumped on him, all but knocking him down.

"Beasts!" Marcello cried, affectionately petting Geronimo, Apache, and Blitz. The three followed him, yapping exuberantly as he went to the pantry and pulled out two cans of dog food. He filled the double dish Mrs. Nowotny had cleaned, added water to another bowl, and took both dishes out to the patio. The sleek dogs eagerly followed, barking with gleeful anticipation.

He set the dishes down, and as the dogs ate with relish, he strode toward the edge of the patio, flexed his sore muscles, took a deep breath, and looked out at the spectacular view of Los Angeles and the surrounding hills. Hummingbirds buzzed at the feeder hanging from the patio cover. The evening was clear and cool, without the usual smog. The nectar of blooming spring flowers laced the air.

Marcello enjoyed his property—the lot was large, providing a feeling of seclusion. Two sides were walled for privacy, and the back was outlined in wrought iron to afford a view of the canyon and the city. Here he could enjoy the panorama, yet feel safe from his sometimes overzealous female fans.

Feeling a throbbing of pain in his side, he went over to the hot tub beneath the patio cover and stripped off his jeans, T-shirt, and briefs. He settled into the hot, bubbly water with a sigh. Ah, that felt good . . .

Having Monica here would make it heaven. He wondered what was keeping her. She had mentioned an appointment, but where, and with whom?

Marcello had planned to propose to Monica again the day after tomorrow, once production was completely wrapped up and the cast party was over. He had already made dinner reservations for their special, romantic evening. But now, sitting in the hot tub and missing her, he wasn't really sure he could wait two more days before speaking his heart. This appointment of hers—which was taking too damn long!—left him feeling threatened and off-balance . . .

He knew she had arrived the minute he heard the dogs squeal and race toward the patio doors. He grinned as he heard her belting out an intimidating expletive, then the dogs whimpering and scampering off.

She came to stand before him, looking very sexy in her white blouse and slacks and tinted sunglasses, her blond hair whipping around her shoulders. His gaze moved over the classical, angular lines of her face—the smooth brow and high cheekbones, the delicate nose, the wide mouth and strong chin.

He greeted her in mock-surly fashion. "Did you hurt my dogs, woman? If so, I'm going to beat you."

Looking down at Marcello, Monica whipped off her glasses and glowered, even though it was difficult for her not to smile. He appeared so sexy in the hot tub, with the golden muscles of his arms and chest gleaming with moisture, his bright blue eyes fixed on her intently, and his damp hair clinging to his corded neck.

"Hah!" she retorted. "You know I've never touched a hair on the head of those mangy mutts. When are you going to teach them to quit trying to sniff my crotch?"

Marcello threw back his head and laughed. "I must say I admire their taste. They only want to be your friends, Monica. But you won't give them a chance."

"I have no interest in getting friendly with those depraved beasts."

"Then why don't you come closer and get friendly with this depraved beast?" he suggested devilishly.

Now Monica had to smile, although inwardly she felt uncertain and a little sad. Despite Marc's teasing tone, she realized increasingly what his invitations to intimacy truly meant. Though he hadn't broached the subject yet, she was well aware that the year's reprieve he had granted her for her career had ended. She had been dreading the day when he would demand that she deliver on her part of their bargain. Monica feared that what Marc wanted from her at this juncture in her life might be more than she was prepared to give. Still, when he took her in his arms, she was too often tempted to surrender all of herself and more. The power this sexy, magnetic man held over her was both exciting and unnerving.

She stalled for time. "What are you doing languishing in the tub so long, anyway? Was the battle scene today really too much for you at your advanced age?"

His suddenly ferocious expression promised revenge. "Get your smart ass into this tub and I'll show you what too much is, woman."

She could no longer resist his charm, or the sexy things his words, his eyes, were doing to her. "I'll go change into my bikini."

His gaze smoldered and his voice came out very husky. "No, don't change. Just take it off."

That invitation proved irresistible. Monica's fingers trembled as she began stripping off her clothes. Marc's gaze never left her, and the heat reflected there scorched her senses. Wearing just her panties and bra, she dangled a toe into the tub.

Marc eyed her sleek body greedily. Monica was five ten, strongly built and beautiful, with long, shapely legs that felt heavenly wrapped around his waist—as they soon would be, he promised himself. It was so odd, he mused. After almost three years of intimacy with her, he wanted her more than ever. He often wondered if her elusive qualities only increased his hunger for her. He did so long for a child to bind their lives together and bring them closer. Indeed, the image of the beautiful baby they could have together made him impatient to get started.

Monica stepped down into the tub, shrieking with laughter as Marc grabbed her, pulled her in with a splash, settled her on his lap, and kissed her. A moment later, she kneaded his tense shoulder muscles with skillful fingers.

His eyes shut, Marc groaned his delight. "Ah, baby, that feels so good. Your touch is heaven."

"I aim to please," she whispered.

After several exquisite moments, Marc opened his eyes, smiled tenderly, and caressed her soft cheek. "Where have you been, angel?"

Stiffening slightly in his arms, she glanced away. "I had drinks with Wally."

Marc's content expression faded to a scowl, and his large hand cupped her chin, turning her face toward his. "Wally again? And you were gone so long. I'm starting to get jealous."

"Marc, he's my agent." Tentatively, she added, "And he had news."

"Oh?"

She ran her fingertips over his muscled chest and smiled. "Why don't we save it for later?"

Marc undid her bra. "Fine," he said with an urgency that both thrilled and unsettled her, especially as she glimpsed the darkly passionate expression on his face.

He leaned over and took her nipple between his teeth. She moaned. He worried the turgid peak and held her close. She dug her fingernails into his shoulders and panted with pleasure. He nibbled at her shapely throat and began sliding off her panties. Eagerly she straddled him. His fingers began working their magic between her thighs, caressing and probing. She gasped sharply and chewed her bottom lip. He kissed her hungrily, drowning her moans with his hot, demanding tongue.

"I've missed you today, darling," he said huskily, running his hands over her back and bottom. "Even though we're together on the set, it's not the same, you know. Sometimes I can barely keep my hands off you. I miss having you close like this."

"Me, too," she murmured, panting, her mouth on his smooth shoulder.

"What are you thinking, Monica?"

Meeting his searching gaze, she ran her fingertips over his face and powerful shoulders. "Of how beautiful you look, all wet, muscled, and hard. All mine."

"Anything else?" he whispered, pulling her fingers to his erection.

She caressed him, enjoying his ragged moan, her own body throbbing at the very thought of his hardness inside her. "Of the way you make me feel."

"Yes?"

Though her expression mirrored regret, she spoke honestly. "As if you want things I'm not quite ready to give."

"You're right. I want it all, angel."

"That's what I'm afraid of," she said ruefully.

Marc thrust into Monica with a powerful stroke. She cried out and frantically sought his lips. Her hands coiled into fists on his shoulders, then uncoiled. Her hips rode his, taking all the passion he could give, and giving back in full measure.

A moment later, he pulled his lips from hers and gazed into her eyes, feeling obsessed to see just what he was doing to her. Her fevered gasps and the desperate desire etched on her beautiful face excited him beyond reason. He continued to observe her enraptured response and listen to her ragged cries, until both succumbed to another drowning kiss.

"You're right, it is too much," she panted against his mouth. "And I want it all, too."

Marc tightened his arms around Monica's waist and gave her everything.

TWO

AFTER THEY MADE LOVE, MARC SLIPPED ON HIS JEANS, AND Monica went off to change into shorts and a tank top. They puttered around the kitchen, Marc preparing angel hair pasta with scampi, Monica throwing together a Caesar salad. They opened a bottle of white wine, heated up some French bread, and ate heartily at the kitchen table, sharing anecdotes about their day on the set and discussing tomorrow's final shoot.

"Are you going to be ready to leave with me for Big Bear Lake on Saturday?" Marc asked her.

All at once she appeared wary, and set down her fork. "I'm not sure, Marc. Can I let you know for certain after the cast party?"

He scowled. "Monica, we've been planning this vacation for months. The contractor called yesterday, and the cabin is ready."

She reached out to touch his hand. "I know you're excited, sweetie, after you designed it yourself and all."

"We both need a break," he argued. "You promised me we could have two weeks completely alone together."

She flashed him a guilty smile. "I know I did, and I hate to renege—"

"You never have enjoyed the country as much as I do," he accused.

"Can I help it if I'm a city girl? Still, I was so looking forward to our trip, but—"

"Does this have to do with your news?"

14

She sighed. "Marc, why don't we wait until shooting is finished?"

"Meaning that when you tell me, we're going to have a fight?" he demanded.

They were staring at each other tensely when the phone rang. Monica jumped up and grabbed it, as if supremely grateful for the intrusion. Marc heard her say hello to her best friend, Lisa. She took the phone into the den and spoke in hushed tones.

Gathering up the dishes and stacking them in the sink, Marc wondered what the two friends were gabbing about. He couldn't hear the words, but Monica's tone sounded urgent and excited.

He felt intensely disappointed that she was hedging on the trip to the mountains. He loved the outdoors and nature, and it was there he often found his peace. Spending time together in the cabin he had designed himself was important from another perspective, too. Marc's father had been a renowned architect in Venice, and Marc had gotten his degree in architecture before he had turned to acting as a career. The cabin at Big Bear Lake was the first design of his that had actually been constructed, and he had supervised the project closely from start to finish. Although Marc enjoyed L.A., the mountain retreat was where his heart truly lay. To him, the cabin would be his and Monica's true home, the place where they would start their family.

Why was she trying to back out of going there with him?

While Monica completed her conversation and went to take a shower, Marc finished tidying up the kitchen. He wandered into the bedroom, heard the shower still running, and considered joining her, then vetoed his own impulse. They would have their talk first. He was through waiting, and they really needed to clear the air.

He heard the shower stop, and a moment later, he wandered into the dressing area. Monica was sitting at the dressing table, wrapped in a thick white towel, her damp hair hanging down her back. The glow of her skin and the delectable, fresh-washed scent of her enticed him, and normally, he would have ripped off her towel and carried her to bed.

But not now. Her gaze met his in the mirror, and he watched her quickly, nervously, shut a drawer.

Marc leaned over and opened the drawer—

"Marc, no!" she cried angrily.

But it was too late, as he was already staring at the half-used packet of birth-control pills. His gaze flashed back up to meet hers in the mirror, and her guilty eyes darted away. He slammed the drawer shut and left the dressing area.

"Marc!"

She followed him into the bedroom, and he turned to regard her with hurt and anger. "Do you know what today is, Monica?"

"May eighteenth?" she replied in a small voice.

He stared her straight in the eye. "Do you remember what you promised me, a year ago in early May?"

"That I would marry you?" she whispered miserably.

"That we would marry and start a baby," he finished meaningfully. "How can I get you pregnant if you're still taking those damn pills?"

She offered a contrite smile. "Marc, I'm sorry."

Unmoved, he crossed his muscled arms over his chest. "I had intended to wait to discuss this until filming was complete." He smiled tightly. "Actually, I wanted to make it very romantic—I've already made reservations at Spago—"

"How sweet," she put in.

"But now I think we cannot wait to address this." He jerked his head toward the night table. "Why don't you see what I've left for you in the drawer?"

Sighing, she went over to the nightstand and opened the drawer. Pulling out a velvet-covered jeweler's box, she bit her lip. "I think I'm afraid to open it."

"Open it."

With trembling fingers, Monica flipped open the small black box, then gasped as she stared at the dazzling diamond solitaire ring. She blinked back tears, shut the box, and set it down.

Her expression was fraught with ambivalence as she turned to him. "Marc, the ring is gorgeous, but I can't accept it right now. I think we need to talk."

"*Sì*, we do."

Watching Monica go to the closet, drop her towel, and put on a teal-blue silk caftan, Marc struggled to rein in his roiling emotions. They went out onto the patio adjoining their bedroom and reclined on chaise longues—sitting widely apart, as wary as strangers. The view of the lights of L.A. was dazzling, the night filled with romantic scents and sounds. Yet both Marc and Monica wore morose, abstracted expressions.

"I didn't want to tell you this until after we'd wrapped up tomorrow," she began hesitantly. "I was afraid my news might spoil your concentration."

"Believe it or not, Monica," he remarked cynically, "there are more important things in life than this damned movie. Have you found someone else?"

"No! No, of course not!" she denied, appearing crestfallen.

"Then don't you love me anymore?" he asked in pained tones.

Her beseeching countenance met his. "Of course I love you. I think now more than ever."

"Then what? You promised me a year ago that if I would just wait, you would marry me—"

"I know, but that was before—"

"Before what?"

She drew a convulsive breath. "Before I had drinks with Wally today."

"Go on."

"There are still a few details for Wally to settle, but—"

"Yes?"

She broke into a smile. "Marc, I got the part."

"You mean the role of Stephanie in *Winds of Destiny?*"

"Yes." Earnestly, she whispered, "It's my big break."

"Congratulations," he said tightly.

"You don't sound very sincere," she accused.

He gestured in exasperation. "Well, what do you expect me to say? You know my next project is filming in Wyoming, and you'll have to be in Monte Carlo for six months! What about our plans—our family?"

"*Your* plans," she corrected him heatedly.

"Oh, so now they're *my* plans?" he shot back.

"More yours than mine."

"Explain that."

She was silent for a moment, her face mirroring her inner struggle. "You have never really listened to what I wanted, or taken our differences into account."

"Then what has our time together been about? Just sex?"

Her anguished gaze met his. "You know it's much more than that."

His eyes were bright with emotion. "Monica, you promised me over a year ago that you would marry me and take enough time off for us to have our first child."

"I know I did, but things have changed," she argued passionately. "Your career is firmly established, but mine still isn't. This opportunity won't wait."

"Nonsense. You are talented enough to always have a career. You just don't want to put us first."

Monica made a frustrated sound and rose. Crossing her arms over her bosom, she muttered, "You mean I won't put what *you* want first. I don't hear you offering to give up your next project. Why is it your desires and your career must always take precedence over mine?"

He stood, strode over to her, and touched her arm. "Every relationship demands compromises—"

She turned toward him angrily. "What have you given up, Marc?"

"I've waited for almost three years for you to be ready to marry me and start our family," he responded fervently.

She shook her head. "My God, you're so retrograde," she said with irony.

"What do you mean by that?"

"You think your life will be perfect if you just have a faithful little wife and a family."

"Oh, so now I must listen to this women's-liberation crap?"

"Crap!" she repeated, outraged.

Marc was not deterred. "Family is very important to me, Monica. I will not apologize for feeling as I do. And if that is being retrograde, then I'm proud of it."

She flung her hands outward. "But don't you understand that you can't replace your parents and sister, or assuage your guilt over losing them, through having a baby with me?"

That remark touched a raw nerve. Furious, Marc muttered a curse and stalked off toward the pool.

Monica followed, reaching up to lay a hand on his rigid shoulder. "I'm sorry."

After a moment spent struggling with himself, Marc turned to her and spoke vehemently. "I'm not just trying to replace my family or lessen the guilt. Of course I felt terrible pain when my parents and sister died in the plane crash, but no one can ever replace them. The truth is, I'm thirty-two now, ready to settle down and have my own family—just as I know my parents would have wanted for me."

"Why can't you understand that I'm not at that settled stage yet?" she demanded. "Why can't you wait for me?"

His expression was poignant as he reached out to stroke her cheek. "Monica, I've waited too long already." He smiled wistfully. "Do you remember when we met?"

"Oh, yes," she whispered.

"The minute I laid eyes on you at the premiere, wearing that sexy black dress, I knew you were the one for me. I knew I wanted us to marry."

In a low voice, she pleaded, "Marc, it's only six more months—"

"Then what? Won't there always be another opportunity, another excuse to keep us apart? Can you deny it?"

Regretfully, she shook her head. "No. But is it fair that I'm the one who has to sacrifice, to take time off to have our child? To have my career disrupted and possibly derailed at this critical stage?"

"You don't want my children?" he asked, his expression wounded.

"No—I mean, yes, of course I do," she replied with obvious turmoil. "But not now. It would mean giving up too much."

He stroked her cheek. "Unfortunately, darling, I can't have our baby for you. And if you see our future together as such a burden, then obviously you don't want it as much as I do."

She was silent, blinking at tears in her eyes.

Quietly, he asked, "How long will it take, Monica?"

"I don't know," she said.

"What we have is so good, babe," he whispered intensely.

"I know. Before we met, I dated a lot of guys, but I've never known anyone like you." Her voice broke as she whispered, "I really do love you, Marc—"

"But evidently, not enough," he cut in bitterly.

"Perhaps not," she conceded. "Though I do want to build a future with you. Only right now I can't make you any promises."

"And I have to have a commitment—now."

"Then we're at an impasse, aren't we?"

"Sì."

She brushed away a tear. "Aren't you even going to say you're happy for me?"

His smile was sad. "You got your big break, darling. I hope it will be worth it to you."

Marc went inside and checked with his answering service, then returned some of his phone calls. He and Monica didn't speak for the balance of the evening, both silently reviewing their scripts for tomorrow's shoot—albeit each had much difficulty concentrating. Although on one level Marc could understand Monica's point of view and the ambitions driving her, he still felt very hurt and betrayed that she had refused to honor the commitment between them. How could they ever hope for a future together if her promise to him had meant so little?

When they finally went to bed, they lay back-to-back, not touching. Several times during the night, Marc ached to pull Monica into his arms, especially when he felt her shuddering and feared she might be crying. But when he finally turned and touched her arm, she stiffened, and he realized that for her, surrendering right now would indeed be giving up too much.

Could he compromise further? The tight emotion welling in his chest said otherwise. He simply loved Monica too much to accept being less than number one in her life. The alternative—living with her while they both led separate lives—was unbearable.

Marc remembered the glorious dream of him and Monica together, of him holding their firstborn—the dream that seemed to mock him now. His eyes stung with tears as sleep eluded him.

THREE

DRESSED AS IVAR THE INVINCIBLE, WITH THE WIND BILLOWING about his tall, muscled body, Marcello stood next to his director on the shores of an isolated beach in Malibu. Around them, technicians and production assistants rushed about, preparing equipment for the day's shoot, while the second assistant director tried to line up a group of extras in the background.

In less than ten minutes, director and crew would begin filming the movie's final scene. Although the blazing boat sequence was supposed to be shot at night, the brooding morning skies—along with some post-production assistance from optical effects—would suffice to lend an illusion of darkness. The overcast heavens were a definite stroke of fortune, yet a brisk wind blowing in off the Pacific threatened havoc with the entire production, and especially with the lighting equipment. Off to one side, Harold Schindle was all but tearing his hair as he instructed a group of grips and gaffers on the placement of delicate lighting grids and the positioning of the reflectors and screens that were continuously battered by gusts.

At the edge of the surf was beached the tall Viking longship that would soon bear Ivar the Invincible's slain body to Valhalla. Dark, sleek, and powerful, its prow and gunwales beautifully carved, the ship gleamed with its snapping bright blue sail and gold figurehead of a Valkyrie. Next to the longship waited a powerboat onto which a grip was mounting the

camera that would follow the Viking vessel out to sea. Facing
the ship on the shoreline was a second camera on a crane,
with the cameraman and assistant already in position on their
perches and busy adjusting the lenses. Up on the cliff, a third
camera was mounted on a helicopter that waited to take off.

Marcello had already spent hours this morning in makeup
and wardrobe before getting last-minute instructions from
Irving. But the brisk, wet wind threatened to undo all the fine
work of the makeup artist, hair stylist, and wardrobe mistress.
Marc's thick hair whipped about his ceremonial helmet and
shoulders, his blue silk tunic billowed around his torso, and
the gold brooches of animal figures that held the garment together were already tearing gouges in the fragile fabric. His
prop sword snapped in its sheath against one legging-clad
thigh. To add to the frustration, Marc and Irving had to shout
to hear each other over the roar of the waves.

Irving gestured nervously toward the prop and special-
effects technicians who were making final preparations for
the funeral pyre on the longship. "Marc, I wish you would
give up this insane decision to film the burial scene yourself.
It's still not too late for us to substitute a stuntman. I'm worried about those waves, and the flames could easily rage out
of control in this wind."

"If you want to feel truly safe, we needn't film the launch
to Valhalla on the ocean at all," Marc pointed out smugly.
"Vikings usually launched slain warriors by setting their
hafships aflame in burial pits."

"So we're dealing with Mr. Authentic again, are we?"
Irving snapped. "Where's the excitement in a burning burial
pit, I ask you?" Abruptly, he grinned. "But this time I got
you, kid." Cupping a hand over his mouth, he yelled, "Script
assistant!"

A thin, harried-looking young man rushed up with the
script in hand. During filming, Marc had become acquainted
with Chris Stennett, a graduate student in anthropology hired
as a production intern to help the script supervisor and the set
and costume departments ensure the authenticity and continu-
ity of the historical props and costumes from scene to scene.

"Yes, sir?" Chris asked, adjusting his glasses.

Irving jerked his thumb toward Marc. "Inform our superstar that the launch to Valhalla is authentic."

Stifling a smile, Chris pulled a notebook from his back pocket and began flipping through it. "Hi, Marc. Let's see, I have all those details written down here somewhere. Ah, yes . . . in Norse mythology, Balder, god of light, was slain by an arrow through the heart, and he was launched on the ocean in a burning boat."

"Ah, but Balder was launched to Hel, not Valhalla," Marc pointed out.

"I give up," said Irving in disgust.

Meanwhile, Chris was grinning. "Yes, you're right there, Marc. But that's not all I've discovered through my research. There was a King Sigurd of Sweden and also a King Haki of Norway who embarked for the afterlife in this same manner—as well as a Norse king, name unknown, who had his men launch him to Valhalla on the ocean in a burning boat, right after he was mortally wounded in battle."

Marc nodded. "Very good. So there is ample precedent. I like it when we all do our homework. But you have no name for this Norse king?"

"He was Viktor the Valiant, of course," Irving put in slyly, and all three men laughed.

Chris turned to Irving. "Actually, sir, I must commend you on the authenticity of your props and costumes. I've found most everything to be accurate, except for the horned helmets worn by the warriors in the battle scenes. You must understand that those were used mostly for ceremonial occasions."

At this comment, Marc shook with mirth, while Irving yelled good-naturedly at Chris, "You're fired, kid!"

As the white-faced young man glanced at Marc, he quickly reassured him. "Don't worry, Chris, Irving doesn't mean it. He just hates being wrong."

To Chris, Irving added, "Yeah, and get the heck out of here before I change my mind! Good grief, I'm surrounded by *experts!*"

Chuckling, Chris dashed back to his place near the script supervisor.

"Didn't I warn you about those horned helmets, Irving?"

Marc chided, adjusting his own. "They are going to ruin us yet."

Ignoring the comment, Irving was scratching his jaw and scowling at the longship. "I'm still worried about you being strapped down in the midst of those flames."

"No problem," Marc assured him. "The special-effects supervisor told me the fire will never get within two feet of my precious flesh. You just concentrate on getting all the camera angles right so it will *look* like I'm being consumed by flames. With three angles in the shoot, I just don't see how we can miss."

Irving grimaced at the brooding heavens. "Unless it starts raining and we have to cancel before we can get a wrap."

Marc glanced upward. "At least with all these dark clouds, it will be easier for the special-effects people to make the cliffs look like basalt."

"What the hell is basalt?"

Marc grinned. "Volcanic rock—it's what Iceland is made of. Didn't you know that Iceland was created from volcanoes that spewed ashes and basalt up from the ocean floor?"

Irving waved him off. "Whatever."

Marc stared at a flock of passing birds. "You may have some difficulty making those gulls look like puffins—unless you dress them in tuxedos, of course."

"You just watch your ass in that boat and remember we start filming *Fort Laramie* in June," Irving responded tersely.

Watching the uptight director rush off to consult with the sound mixer, Marc shook his head. He spied Monica off to the side in her gold Viking dress; the hairdresser was trying to smooth down her blond locks, despite a lack of cooperation from the recalcitrant wind.

Marc stepped over to join them. "You can't make her any more beautiful than she already is, Gretchen," he teased the stylist, winking at Monica.

"You're probably right, Marc—and, anyway, I give up," the exasperated woman replied. Then with a cry of dismay, she darted after a helmet that had sailed off the head of one of the extras.

"Alone at last, angel," Marc murmured. "Are you ready to bid your proud warrior the proper tearful farewell?"

As he reached out to smooth down her hair, Monica smiled tensely. "You will be careful today, won't you?"

"Have you been listening to Irving stewing about the scene?"

She glanced around. "I don't have to. The wind, the waves—the fire. I know it must be very dangerous."

He shrugged, then smiled. "You know, as a tribute to a slain warrior, Vikings used to sacrifice a slave girl, then launch her to Valhalla in the longship, beside the fallen fighter. You're still welcome to come with me."

"Do I sense an olive branch being extended?" she asked.

"Maybe."

She stared at him wistfully, then shook her head. "Oh, Marc. You want me to come with you, but on your own terms. A sacrificed slave girl would suit your retrograde instincts just fine.'"

"So I'm still this caveman type you keep referring to?" he asked darkly.

She looked him over and sighed. "And damned appealing in spite of it—or maybe because of it. I just know it would be a shame to change you."

He stepped closer and whispered huskily, "Then you're not volunteering to come with me on my next voyage of discovery?"

"I can't, Marc," came her tremulous response.

They stared at each other for a long, anguished moment; then he brushed a tear from her cheek with his thumb. "Try not to cry too much for Ivar, angel. It will ruin your makeup."

She bit her lip. "Marc—"

"Yes?"

"After the cast party, I'm planning to go home and pack my things."

He frowned. "Is that really necessary, Monica?"

Her face mirrored resignation and regret. "Yes. Otherwise we'll just be postponing the inevitable. I need to get on with my life, and you need to go find that right girl who can give you what you want and need"—she paused, braving a smile—"on your next voyage of discovery."

Marc cupped her chin in his hand. "I've already found her," he whispered intensely. "But she isn't ready for me."

They stared at each other poignantly, only to jump apart as an assistant director yelled, "Places, people! Now!"

Watching Marc frown and turn to start off, Monica touched his arm. "Can we at least part as friends?"

He assumed a pleasant expression. "Sure. No hard feelings. Shall I shake your hand?"

"Will you kiss me?" she asked plaintively.

With a groan he complied, hauling her soft body close and kissing her lips so passionately, so thoroughly, that soon some of the crew began hooting taunts in the background.

"Hey, Marc, save it for the Valkyries in Valhalla," yelled a grinning Chris.

The two moved apart, both smiling self-consciously amid all the curious eyes focused on them.

"Break a leg, handsome," Monica said, her voice strained and hoarse.

He fondly touched the tip of her nose. "Break their hearts, angel. After all, you always do. Especially mine."

He turned and walked away. She almost called after him, then stopped herself.

With the wind still whipping about him, Marc held onto his horns and strode over to the longship, where the special-effects technicians were finishing up and gathering their gear. "Are you guys going to barbecue me today?" he asked drolly.

"Don't say that, Marc, it's not funny," replied Stan, the special-effects supervisor.

Chuckling, Marc climbed inside the ship, which the prop people had already piled high with the typical bounty a Viking warrior took with him to Valhalla—food, ale, jewels and riches, weapons and implements. He moved toward midships and lay down on the narrow funeral bed lined with animal hides. A grip strapped him in, hiding the bindings beneath his tunic.

Closing his toolbox, Stan instructed Marc urgently, "Just remember, the mixture we've used for the fire is in a special reservoir running along the inner perimeter of the bulwark. It will ignite when Monica and the extras apply their torches."

"Then I'll become a human hot dog?"

Stan glowered. "You'll be far away from the flames. And

besides, you know damn well this compound produces little heat or smoke—"

"You mean I won't roast like a marshmallow or need to wear a gas mask?"

"Knock it off, Marc. Like I said, it ain't funny. You may smell a little smoke or feel a little heat, but basically, you'll be okay. Believe me, our entire special-effects department worked overtime to make this funeral pyre a fail-safe design. With all the fireproofing we've done, it's highly unlikely that the boat itself, or the sail, will become engulfed in flames before shooting is finished."

"I'm greatly reassured," rejoined Marc dryly.

"We'll be in the boat right alongside you with the cameraman. If the wind or the waves get too wild, we'll intervene immediately with the fire extinguishers. And we'll be there to put out the fire before you know it."

Marc nodded solemnly. "Fine, guys. Despite all my joking, I have to compliment you on doing such a conscientious job."

"Sure thing, Marc. Break a leg."

The technicians left. Hearing the commands of the first assistant director preceding the take, Marc concentrated on relaxing. As he and Irving had already decided, he knew he need not get "into" Ivar's character this morning, but should instead focus on effecting a proper death trance. He took deep breaths, let soothing images of clouds drift across his mind, and centered his thoughts on remaining utterly calm and still. Distantly, he heard the shouts of director and crew, the low roar of the powerboat motor, the buzzing of the helicopter as it took off overhead. Nearby, a bell rang and a slate snapped shut.

Along the shoreline, an assistant yelled, "Action!" Marc heard the extras weeping, and knew from previous rehearsals that Monica and the others were coming forward for the funeral ceremony, some with lighted torches, others bearing gifts for the gods that they began piling into the stern of the longship. The low chanting of their prayers told him the moment would soon come for them to launch him.

He heard Monica's tearful voice cry: "Farewell, proud warrior." Then flames hissed around the prow, and he knew the

torches were being applied. He felt the extras pushing the
ship out onto the waves.

With eyes still tightly closed, Marc could hear Monica's
wails of grief, the cries of the extras, and the sizzle of the
flames. He could feel the warmth of the fire around the bulwark, and the mighty waves tilting and buffeting the ship.
The technicians had been right, he realized. This was almost
pleasant. There was some heat, but the smell was far from
overpowering, and the roller-coaster motion of the vessel was
strangely soothing. He relaxed even more deeply and felt
himself drifting off to sleep. Soon, he thought distantly. Soon
the others would awaken him . . .

Suddenly Marc jerked awake, gagging on smoke. Feeling
flames lick at his feet, he fumbled frantically with his bindings, somehow managed to unstrap himself, and jumped up,
gasping for breath and choking on curses. Blackness enveloped him from all sides—except for the ship itself, which
now resembled a blood-red, raging inferno!

Where on earth was he? Why was the ostensibly "fire-
proof" ship suddenly burning like the flames of hell, and
where were the technicians to put out the blaze?

Totally disoriented, Marc gazed around him. It was truly
night, the wind was howling like a demon, and he illogically
felt both burning hot and freezing cold. Everything was
different—frighteningly different. The longship was emitting
thick clouds of black smoke that choked off his breathing,
and monstrous flames were gorging their way toward him at
midships. He looked up in horror to watch the entire sail ignite in a burst of red right before his eyes!

Marc had no additional time for observations. Realizing he
would be consumed next, he coughed out a quick prayer,
leaped through the flames, and dived into the ocean with a
mighty splash. Had he not been immersed, he would have
shouted from the shock of landing in water more frigid than
the bottom of an ice bucket. Struggling against cramping
muscles and a powerful undertow, he surfaced, shuddering violently and gasping for air. Frosty oxygen stabbed his starved
lungs like slivers of ice. He battled the powerful currents,
knowing he could not survive long in the subarctic water—

God in heaven, where *was* he? What had happened to him?

Then, like a miracle, the smoke cleared ahead of him and he spotted a murky shoreline just beyond. Among outcroppings of black rock loomed people with lit torches emblazoning the night. Of course—it must be Monica and the extras! He swam desperately toward them, growing weaker with each stroke against icy, turbulent waves. His entire body felt numb from his struggles. After what seemed an agonizing eternity, he was able to stagger out of the surf, shivering fiercely—

At last Marc was afforded a closer look at the group on the beach. What was this? All of these people were strangers, dressed in alien-looking costumes of wool, flax, and leather! The air remained as frigid as the ocean had been.

Then Marc blinked as he spotted ice caps in the distance. Ice caps? Basalt rock? *Dio del cielo!* Had he landed somewhere in Scandinavia? But that was impossible, wasn't it?

He began to tremble in earnest.

"King Viktor!" cried one of the strange men. "You are alive after all, our faithful jarl!"

King Viktor? Why in hell did this man call him King Viktor? As he watched in bewilderment, the bizarre group, which seemed to number over fifty, rushed toward him. Many fell to their knees, amid weeping and exclamations of joy.

"King Viktor! Thanks to Odin for returning you to us!"

"Our leader has come back from Valhalla reborn!" cried another.

"The gods have surely blessed our jarl with a bite from one of Idunn's rejuvenating apples!"

Marc, teeth rattling and body heaving from the cold, remained mystified. Where was he, and who were these demented characters babbling on about Odin and Idunn's apples? Did these idiots actually believe he was Viktor the Valiant, returned from Valhalla? Had the cast and crew played some kind of joke on him?

"What in hell is going on here?" he demanded.

Even as he spoke, the strangers shrank away in fear and stared off into the distance.

"Wolfgard!" one cried.

"The berserkers have returned!" yelled another.

"Get the women and children back to the village!" shouted a third.

Pandemonium broke loose. The women and children fled screaming into the black night, while the men drew out broadswords, spears, and axes, then advanced menacingly toward Marc.

He was horrified. "Holy Mother, save me!" Wild-eyed, he began backing away.

The men appeared flabbergasted by his retreat. "Jarl! You are going the wrong way! Come fight with us!" cried one of the warriors.

"In that way lies death!" warned another.

Hearing harrowing battle cries behind him, Marc whirled and understood what the men had referred to. A hundred yards beyond them along the shoreline had landed a mighty Viking dragon ship. And a huge tribe of ax-wielding, sword-swinging, arrow-shooting barbarians was swarming onto the beach, heading straight toward *him!*

FOUR

"Kɪɴɢ Vɪᴋᴛᴏʀ! Lᴇᴀᴅ ᴜs, ᴡᴇ ʙᴇsᴇᴇᴄʜ ʏᴏᴜ!"

"Help us, or we shall perish!"

Hearing the pleas of the warriors behind him and watching the barbarians continue to swarm off their ship with its figurehead of a fire-spitting dragon, Marcello had no more time for hesitation. Whether he was on earth, in heaven, in hell, or a thousand years back in time, he did not know. He only knew that these people needed him—*his* people needed him. And in that moment—for that moment—he became their leader. Relying strictly on instinct, he unsheathed his sword and led the charge.

"To battle, men!" he yelled and leaped forward, his clan of warriors close on his flanks.

An arrow whizzed by Marc's cheek as he and his followers ran forward to confront the invaders. In the distance, he spotted a silver-haired, bearded giant leading the opposition.

Within seconds, the warring parties collided. The impact was horrendous—broadswords banged against shields, arrows pierced chain mail, and cries of agony rent the air. Marc got his first taste of battle as a huge, bearded marauder loomed before him.

"Die, son of Hel!" the warrior cried, wielding his broadsword high over Marc's head.

Marc raised his own weapon to block the blow—only to feel the rubber sword buckle like a kite in a wind. A look of horror gripping his features, he just managed to lunge aside

31

before his assailant's weapon would have split open his skull. He winced as he heard the broadsword thud into the earth.

Meanwhile, his adversary was laughing—actually laughing! "Viking, you carry the toy of a child!" he scoffed.

Marc realized the man was right. The sword he had brought with him from location was no match for an actual Viking warrior's iron broadsword! *Dio,* this was no movie! He was back in *real* Viking times, with no more than a movie-set understanding of the challenges he faced!

Further thought was postponed as Marc watched the aggressor heave his broadsword back like a baseball bat and prepare to lop off *his* head! *Santa Maria,* this character was becoming a nuisance! And only a brilliantly timed duck kept Marc from becoming King Viktor the Headless! Knocked off-balance by the failed blow, his opponent staggered, appearing baffled by Marc's foil. Marc seized the advantage, delivering a stinging kick to the groin that sent the man dropping to his knees with a shout of pain.

Shivering and gasping for breath, Marc glanced around to reconnoiter the action. The battle was a nightmare scene, like something out of Dante's *Inferno.* Spears flew, lethally sharp arrows screamed through the air, and warriors hacked at and bludgeoned one another with swords and axes. Worst of all were the sounds—the crash of weapons striking, the moans of torment, the harrowing shouts of bloodlust that seemed to rise straight from the madness of hell.

Then suddenly, amazingly, Marc spotted Monica swinging her battle-ax in the distance! At first he was certain his eyes had deceived him—but no, it was truly she!

"Monica!" he cried.

If she heard him, she made no sign, but continued to do battle with a ferocious, huge warrior. He stared at the tall woman in fascination. She was Monica, all right, complete with sleek body and long blond hair. Yet she was dressed not as a Viking wife but as a Valkyrie, in chain-mail tunic, short, tight leggings, and iron helmet.

Was she a Valkyrie? Had he arrived in Valhalla after all? The possibility was unnerving, electrifying. Still, his heart welled with joy at the sight of her.

Marc worked his way toward the woman, dodging arrows,

spears, and swords. At last he loomed in her path. "Darling!
I am here!" he cried.

The woman turned to him, at first shrinking back and staring at him as if she had just seen a ghost. Then her lovely
features twisted with rage and indignation. "Viking!" she
screamed. "How dare you return to torment us! How dare
you call me beloved! I *hate* all Vikings!"

And then she raised her huge battle-ax high over his head!

Dio, what madness was this? Had Monica lost her mind?
Was everyone else here a crazed maniac as well? Were they
all obsessed with carving him asunder?

Watching the terrifying ax begin to fall, Marc leaped back.
The weapon narrowly missed him, chopping into the ground
with a sickening clunk. Enraged, the Valkyrie who so resembled Monica yanked and grunted until she had heaved her ax
from the frozen earth. Then she swung it high and charged at
Marc with a bloodcurdling howl.

This time, Marc was almost too horrified to react. In the
nick of time, two of his own company lunged between him
and the Valkyrie, with disastrous results. The warrior woman
sliced the sword from one man's grip, almost hacking off his
hand in the process, then chopped her ax into the shield of
the second. On her smooth, powerful upswing, she bashed
Marc on the side of his head with the flat of her weapon.
Marc reeled, seeing stars as the two warriors collapsed,
groaning, at his feet.

Marc could only stare, stupefied, at this unholy terror who
appeared to be both Monica's twin and her antithesis. Then—
horror of horrors!—the Valkyrie wielded her ax high one
more time and aimed straight for his head!

Mercifully, a voice in the distance yelled, "Retreat!" Just
as Marc jumped out of range, the Valkyrie lowered her
battle-ax and grinned at him. "We meet another day, Viking!"
she said. "I will anticipate once again the pleasure of slaying
you." She whirled around and raced with the others back to
the dragon ship.

Trembling violently, Marc collapsed to his knees, pressing
a trembling hand to his throbbing temple. For the moment, he
felt too stunned even to think.

"Jarl, we have won the day!"

"You have helped us repel the berserkers!"

Marc stared incredulously at the group of two dozen or so warriors looming over him. Most of the men were of medium, stocky build, fair and heavily bearded, and dressed in iron helmets, chain-mail byrnies over leather tunics, dark leggings, and soft leather boots. In the background, several other men were gathering the wounded onto travois. One of the younger men came forward and draped a coarse woolen blanket around Marc's trembling shoulders.

"Where in hell am I?" he managed to grind out. As a horrifying possibility again dawned, he added, "Don't tell me this is Valhalla?"

The men roared with laughter.

"You jest, jarl," said one burly fellow. "You well know that this is your island, your kingdom of Vanaheim."

"Vanaheim? Are you sure you don't mean Anaheim?"

At his astounded query, the warriors glanced at one another in puzzlement.

Then a second man explained. " 'Twas to Valhalla that we launched you tonight, jarl. But now you have returned from the dead to save us from Wolfgard's treachery in our hour of need."

Before Marc could comment, another voice shouted, "Yea, you have brought great triumph for the people of your clan! May all pay tribute to King Viktor!"

Utterly mystified, Marc watched most of the warriors sink to their knees around him, make weird signs with their hands, and start droning a chantlike litany. Good Lord, had he landed in a lunatic asylum?

"What are they doing?" he asked the burly one.

"Swearing fealty to you, jarl," replied the man as he, too, knelt and followed suit.

Watching the mumbling, gesticulating group, Marc was flabbergasted. These people thought he was their king? At the moment, he didn't feel equal to being king of the clumps of seaweed still clinging to his leggings!

"Good Lord, I can't believe this is happening!" he muttered as the chanting stopped. "I must have lost my mind!"

The large man stood. With a puzzled scowl, he inquired, "Mayhap you mislaid your wits in Valhalla, jarl."

"Mayhap your ordeal by fire and the rigors of returning from the dead have befuddled you," suggested another.

"Now wait just a minute," snapped a very disoriented Marc. "You say we are on Vanaheim?"

"Yea, jarl."

"Where in hell is Vanaheim?"

Again the men laughed. "By ocean, two days south of Iceland, jarl," said a voice from the ranks.

"Iceland?" Marc could not believe his ears. "How in God's name did I end up in . . ." He paused, his temple throbbing, the pain unleashing a new wave of confusion. "What did I just call it?"

"Vanaheim," provided a helpful voice.

"Yes. Vanaheim."

"Do you not remember, King Viktor?" asked the burly man. "Ten winters past, you and Eirik the Red were outlawed from Iceland. Eirik sailed north to discover Greenland, and you took the sea lanes south to Vanaheim."

"I left Iceland with Eirik the Red?" Marc repeated in a stupefied voice.

"He was your kinsman, jarl."

"Are you guys kidding me?"

The men stared at one another uncomprehendingly.

"Did Irving hire you to play a joke on me?"

More baffled looks followed; then a voice called out, "We know nothing of this Irving, jarl. Did you encounter him in the hall of the dead?"

"Good grief, what is happening to me?" Marc cried, clutching his head, which was splitting with pain and uncertainty.

He gazed at the dark, alien landscape—the tundra, the moors beyond, the ice-capped mountains in the distance. Heaven help him, this was no joke! He was definitely not in California anymore!

He ran a hand through his drenched hair and groaned. "Unless someone has engineered the most Machiavellian hoax in all of history, I think I have just been flashed back in time a thousand years."

"What did you say, jarl?" came a perplexed query.

"Do you suppose it had to do with my being launched to Valhalla like Viktor the Valiant?" he muttered to himself.

"So at last you remember who you are?" someone asked eagerly.

"Not exactly," grumbled Marc.

"Jarl, we must get you back to your hall," said the large fellow. "Wolfgard could return, you are wet and trembling, and you will surely catch your second death if you remain here." Sheepishly, he added, "And verily, jarl, although I mean no disrespect, your mind is not as it should be."

"No kidding," quipped Marc.

One of the warriors stepped forward. "Yeah, jarl, Orm has spoken the truth. Take my cloak."

Marc was too cold and exhausted to argue as the man slipped a smelly, shaggy wool cloak over the blanket. With his help, Marc heaved himself to his feet.

"Which way?" he asked, starting off to his left.

The warrior grabbed his arm to restrain him. "To the north, jarl. You are heading toward the west, where the great fjord lies."

"Oh." Pivoting and proceeding with the others in the direction he presumed was north, he asked, "Are we safe now?"

"Yea," answered the one named Orm. "Wolfgard and his forces have retreated across the fjord. We left behind several warriors to stand as sentries should he return."

"Who exactly is Wolfgard?"

"The leader of the clan that attacked us."

Marc mulled over this, remembering the battle. "Ah, yes. You mean the huge fellow with the silver beard?"

Orm grinned, displaying crooked white teeth. "So you remember, jarl. Five summers after our tribe settled here, Wolfgard also was outlawed from Iceland. He sailed here and settled across the fjord with his people. There has been a blood feud between our tribes ever since."

Marc tried to digest all this, then asked carefully, "Who was the woman with him?"

"His stepdaughter, Reyna the Ravisher."

"The Ravisher?" Marc said.

"We call her the Ravisher after Ran the Ravisher, the sea

siren who lures brave Viking warriors to Hel," explained Orm. "Reyna hates all Vikings."

"So she informed me," Marc remarked ruefully. He frowned. "But if she hates all Vikings, why does she ride with a Viking clan?"

A man directly behind them explained. "Reyna is a French captive, jarl. Years ago, she and her mother were kidnapped by Wolfgard's forces and brought to Iceland. Wolfgard did Reyna's mother a great honor by making her his bride instead of his concubine—and thus Reyna became Wolfgard's step-daughter. But the female has always been a hellion, neverthe-less."

"She despises Wolfgard and all his people," said Orm. "Methinks she tolerates her own tribe only because to attack them would mean her death."

"Smart girl," muttered Marc.

"Instead, the Ravisher now wreaks her vengeance on us. She is an ogress, that one, and for years has tried to kill you, King Viktor."

She wanted to *kill* him? Oh, Lord, Marc thought. He hadn't gone to Valhalla. Like Balder, he had been launched in his burning boat straight to Hel!

While Marc continued his trek over the tundra with his new companions, Reyna the Ravisher huddled against the mast of her stepfather's ship, mulling over the last few moments and her bizarre encounter with Viktor the Valiant. As the only woman allowed to fight with Wolfgard's forces, Reyna did not normally leave a battle feeling this shaken, but tonight had been quite different. In some ways, she felt as confused over her brief moment with Viktor as he had seemed during the ep-isode. Why had he greeted her with that strange word, "Dar-ling," followed by, "I am here!"? What had possessed her enemy to speak to her in such a familiar manner? Despite her show of bravado, Reyna had felt jarred by the very sight of him, and somehow seared by his words—

For she knew something about Viktor that the others of Wolfgard's company did not yet know. Although for most of her life the main focus of Reyna's existence had been revenge against all Vikings, Viktor's strength and bravery had secretly intrigued her. Even as she had battled him, she had also watched the enemy jarl closely during various raids Wolfgard had led against his clan. Earlier this eve, when Wolfgard had attacked Viktor's tribe for the first time, Reyna had noted the rival chieftain growing weaker during the battle, and she had presumed he was near death when Wolfgard had at last ordered the retreat. Later, her curiosity getting the better of her, she had returned to the enemy beach alone to see if her suspicions would prove true. From a safe distance she had watched Viktor's tribe launch him to Valhalla in a burning boat—and she had felt far more affected over his death than she ever would have dreamed.

By the time Reyna had navigated her small boat back up to Wolfgard's wharf, her stepfather was gathering his forces for a second surprise attack on Viktor. Why Reyna had not immediately informed Wolfgard of Viktor's demise, she did not know. Mayhap 'twas due to the confusion of launching the second attack, or because she despised Wolfgard and felt no true sense of loyalty to either clan, or because she feared her stepfather's warriors might guess of her longtime, secret fascination with Viktor. Whatever the reason, Reyna had kept her peace—

Then they had launched the second attack, and Reyna had discovered that Viktor still lived! Either that, or he had returned from Valhalla a god! Was he truly a god now? Although Reyna was a Christian, she held a healthy respect for the pagan traditions. Verily, in some ways Viktor had seemed a different man in their second encounter—clean-shaven and far more beautiful than she had remembered, especially when he had smiled at her with such fierce joy and devotion—

Reyna shuddered at the memory. The very sight of him had sent a powerful shiver straight through her, and had spread throughout her soul a sense of dawning recognition—almost as if she were seeing him for the first time, yet somehow already knew him. How could such contradictions be, unless he was a deity now?

'Twas a puzzlement. Indeed, at the time, Reyna's confusing, traitorous response had prompted her to fight her own feelings by attacking Viktor viciously. She had summoned every iota of her hatred and rage toward all Vikings. Yet she had not been able to bring herself to kill him, and even now she felt too overwhelmed by the encounter to share what she knew with the others.

No matter. If the idle talk she oft heard from her stepfather's warriors was true, Wolfgard had a spy in Viktor's camp, a traitor who would soon inform the chieftain of his enemy's "resurrection." In the meantime, Reyna was determined to learn more about this new, baffling Viktor, but only so she could defeat him with due haste, and never again have to deal with such perilous feelings ...

FIVE

Marc and the small group of Vikings trudged across the frigid, windswept tundra, beneath the glittering stars of a vast, black heaven. By now a thousand questions were bombarding Marc's overburdened mind. What had happened to him back in the present? Had he been killed in the stunt and somehow become reincarnated into the past? By being launched to Valhalla in the tradition of Viktor the Valiant, had he sailed through some mystical door in time to dock in the real Viking world? Had Viktor the Valiant even existed back in the Dark Ages? How he wished he could remember, from his brief conversation with Irving and Chris, whether Viktor the Valiant had been real or simply a legend. And how he wished he could utter that classic, comforting line, "This is only a movie." But unfortunately, he had just *been* in a movie that had now become frighteningly real—and yet jarringly different from the fantasy in which he had starred.

And what of this Reyna the Ravisher, who seemed the physical reincarnation of Monica, but evidently had no awareness of him? True, she had appeared shocked when she first spotted him in the battle, but that might have been because she presumed he had just returned from the dead. Why was she here? Was she really Monica in disguise, playing some sort of game, or did she truly not know him? Marc suspected the latter, and he remained stunned that this bloodthirsty vixen was determined to dispatch his soul to the

Viking Hel. It was almost as if God had decided to play a gigantic joke on him.

Despite his confusion, one thing he did know—and again instinct came into play. For whatever reason, he was no longer Marcello. He had jumped back into the life of another man, perhaps even an ancestor of his. Now he *was* Viktor the Valiant, a real Viking chieftain living in real Viking times and involved in a real—and very dangerous—war with a neighboring clan. Intuition also argued that he must not tell these people of his former identity or whence he had truly come. They would assume he was deranged and might even kill him. In fact, for the sake of his own safety—and sanity—it might be best if he started thinking of himself as Viktor, their king and leader.

Marc—now Viktor—felt his thoughts grow fragmented as a distant motion danced across his peripheral vision. He glanced off to the east to note three dark wolves stalking them, their hulking forms outlined by the full moon. To his horror, even as he stared at them, the beasts perked their ears, growled, then broke into a run—heading straight toward him!

Alarmed, he turned to the others. "Wolves—we must hurry!"

His men only laughed.

The wolves howled like fiends and raced across the tundra, swiftly closing the distance.

"They're attacking! Run for your lives, men!" Viktor yelled.

He leaped into a run, and it took him a moment to realize he was the only one fleeing—that his men were still laughing in the background! Were all these people lunatics? Had they no regard for their own safety? He lunged on, fighting agonized muscles, heaving frigid breaths into his lungs—and all the while the monstrous beasts were charging closer and baying like demons!

At last he heard the hiss of their breathing. A hard, lanky form crashed against his back—then another, and another, and he was hurled painfully to the frozen ground. Flipping over with a grunt, he yanked his forearms upward to protect his face from vicious teeth and sharp claws, fully expecting to be devoured alive by these hounds from hell. Yet in the next instant he heard soft whimpers, felt a rough tongue licking his face and playful teeth chewing on one of his fingers.

In the meantime, his warriors had gathered around him and the wolves and were roaring with mirth.

"What is going on here?" Viktor demanded, sitting up, only to be knocked down again as two of the frisky beasts leaped against his shoulders with their forepaws.

"Jarl! Do you not recognize your pets?" inquired one of the men.

"Pets!" Mystified, Viktor was at last able to sit up and hold the three rambunctious animals at bay. "These are my pets?"

"Yea, jarl. They have come to play."

"Play?"

Several of the men chuckled; then Orm explained. "Verily, this is the manner in which all of you cavort, amid much growling, chasing, chewing, and rolling about on the tundra."

With a scowl of lingering suspicion, Viktor eyed the wolves. Having expended their initial exuberance, all three now stood around him, watching him expectantly and panting with their tongues hanging out, sending up white puffs into the icy atmosphere. They were really magnificent creatures, he mused, with plump bodies, silver fur, fluffy tails, light faces and eyes. He reached out tentatively to pet the nearest one. The animal wagged its tail and licked Viktor's hand. Giving in to impulse, he hugged all three, and they responded with more licks and affectionate sounds. For the first time since he had arrived in this mystifying netherworld, he felt a moment of true happiness and bonding.

"What are their names?" he inquired of the men.

"You are petting Hati, the female," Orm answered. "She is named after the wolf of creation who chased the moon."

"The males are Thor and Geri," added another. "Named after the god of thunder and one of Odin's wolves."

Grinning, Viktor stood, and clucked softly to the animals. "Very well. Let us all move on, then."

With the wolves following closely at Viktor's heels, the men continued across the tundra. Soon they came to a huge longhouse with walls and roof composed of thick turf. Smoke curled from a hole at the center of the roof. Surrounding the longhouse were several smaller outbuildings of similar design; in the distance sprawled a small village.

"That is my home?" Viktor asked, jerking a thumb toward the large house.

"Yea, jarl."

Most of the warriors bade their jarl farewell, but five of them, as well as the three wolves, followed Viktor inside. As soon as they moved through the carved door into a crude foyer, Viktor began choking on the heavy odors of smoke, spoiled food, hay, and dirt. A smoky lamp Viktor assumed was filled with whale oil provided the only scant light.

He blinked at the men through smarting eyes. "My God, it's like a burning trash heap in here. Haven't you ever heard of ventilation?"

"Nay, jarl," answered all five in unison.

Viktor rubbed his eyes. "Do you have any idea how harmful it is to inhale all this smoke?"

The men exchanged bemused glances.

Suddenly Viktor felt bone-weary, and his pounding head threatened new waves of befuddlement. "Never mind. We will discuss this tomorrow."

"You do not wish to convene your war council tonight, jarl?" one warrior asked.

"What is that?" Viktor said.

"Whenever Wolfgard attacks, you discuss the outcome and plan future strategies with your war council."

"And I suppose you men comprise my war council?"

Five heads nodded. "We are your retainers, jarl," one man answered.

Viktor forced a smile. "I'm sorry. I seem to be forgetting myself ever since I returned from the dead. I haven't even asked you your names."

"We understand," replied Orm. "I am Orm the Bold, and the others will be pleased to state their titles to refresh your memory."

"I am Svein the Sagacious, your blood brother," said a tall, handsome blond fellow with twinkling blue eyes and a small, pointed beard.

"I am Rollo the Robust," added a brown-haired, brawny man with hazel eyes.

"I am Ottar the Good," said a fair, reedy lad.

"I am Canute the Cunning," said a tall, bearded, blond giant with a heavily scarred face and an eye patch.

Viktor shook the hand of each man in turn, prompting more perplexed looks. "I am most pleased to meet all of you, gentlemen. However, if you will excuse me, I don't think I am quite up to hosting a war council right now."

"As you desire, jarl," answered Svein. "After all, 'tis not every day that a warrior sails off to meet Odin and lives to remember it. You must tell us your story once you recover your wits."

"I may indeed, but you will never believe it," quipped Viktor.

"Think you 'tis wise you remain here alone, jarl?" asked a dubious Ottar. "We are fearful of your state of mind."

"Believe me, so am I." Viktor grimaced and rubbed his temple.

Canute pulled forward a young, blond wench who had just come forward to join them. "Iva will see to your needs tonight," he said gruffly. "In the morning, your housekeeper, Helga, will prepare your repast."

Viktor smiled at the servant. Short, blue-eyed, with her flaxen hair in braids, she was staring at Viktor agog, and appeared to be no more than sixteen. "Hello, Iva."

"Master, you are alive!" she cried.

"So it appears."

"But how can this be?"

"You tell me," Viktor replied dryly.

"Yea, slave, your master has returned from Valhalla," Canute informed the wench with a menacing frown. "And now you must atone for your own cowardice."

Watching Iva shrink back in fear, Viktor asked, "What cowardice?"

Canute's scowl deepened. "Iva was selected as the virgin to be sacrificed with you and launched to Valhalla, but she ran away to the mountains and hid with the elves. Mayhap you should now beat her dead for her treachery, jarl."

Hearing the slave gasp in terror, a bewildered Viktor replied irately, "Beat her? For not wanting to die? Never."

Surprisingly, the giant laughed. "Then you will find a more

befitting punishment, eh?" He jabbed Viktor's side with his elbow.

"Punish her?" repeated Viktor.

"I think our jarl needs his rest," Orm said to the others. He nodded sternly at the wench. "See you watch over our master carefully, slave, or I shall thrash you myself. Our jarl is much confused at the moment."

"Yea, master," said Iva, curtsying.

"We will seek your counsel in the morning, jarl," added Svein, and the men trooped out.

In the wake of their departure, the young woman was staring at Viktor with reverent eyes. "Master, how may I serve you?"

He cleared a raspy throat. "I don't suppose you have a bottle of Evian stashed somewhere."

She stared up at him blankly.

Viktor glanced from the slave to the eager wolves wagging their tails. He coughed again. "Is there anywhere in this house where the smoke isn't thick enough to choke on? I'm already developing a raw throat and a very nasty headache."

Iva smiled and took his hand. "I will show you to your bedchamber, jarl."

She led him through several poorly lit chambers, then behind a wooden partition to an area furnished with a high-backed chair, a sea chest, and a crude, narrow bed covered with animal pelts. At once the eager dogs bounded up onto the bed, their large bodies covering most of it.

Viktor glowered at the trio. "Now wait a minute, beasts! Where do *I* sleep?"

Iva giggled and squeezed his hand. "You can share my chamber, jarl. 'Twould be an honor now that you have returned from the dead."

Viktor jerked away and glowered at her. "You! But you are so young."

"Nay, master, I am the eldest virgin in the tribe, an adult for four winters now. 'Tis why I was selected to be sacrificed and launched with you—and I do regret my cowardice."

Viktor received this information in consternation. His headache was not improving at all!

To the wench, he said sternly, "I don't care if you are the

oldest virgin in the tribe. You may not offer to share your chamber with any man, not until you are at least eighteen winters old. Is that clear?"

"Eighteen winters old?" she repeated, crestfallen.

"And married," he added.

She smiled, displaying charming dimples. "Wed? But slaves do not marry, jarl."

He scowled. "I can tell already that there are going to be some big changes around here."

"But, jarl—"

"Am I the boss here or not?"

"The boss?"

"The master."

She lowered her gaze. "Yea, you are master."

He smiled. "Then go to bed, Iva."

She trudged off.

Eyeing the three huge wolves occupying his sleeping place, Viktor drew a heavy breath. *Dio,* he still felt chilled to the bone, and utterly exhausted! He removed the wool cloak and blanket, his chain-mail tunic and soaked garments. Shivering, he strode to the bed.

"Move over, beasts," he scolded, gently pushing them away from the center of the cot. "Wherever in Hel I have landed, I am whipped. This journeying through time is not all it's cracked up to be. I feel as if I've just lived through every one of those thousand years."

Somehow, Viktor managed to wiggle under the pelts and squeeze himself between the wolves' bristly bodies. He groaned as the monsters again licked and chewed him. His "pets" were loyal and winsome, but his head was still smarting from the Valkyrie's blow and the acrid smoke, and he felt utterly drained from his struggles against the frigid ocean— not to mention the emotional shock of what had just happened to him! Given all he had endured, he was hardly in a frolicsome mood.

He had been plucked from his cushy existence in the twentieth century and thrust back to the savage Dark Ages, complete with a raging blood feud and a Valkyrie determined to kill him. He had sailed through a door in time to land smack in the life of Viktor the Valiant—and God only knew what would happen to him tomorrow.

Across the fjord in her own bed, Reyna the Ravisher tossed and turned. Why could she not stop thinking about Viktor the Valiant, reliving their bizarre encounter, and even wondering if he now thought of her? Mayhap he had not returned from Valhalla a god at all, but some sort of warlock who now perversely tormented her.

Whatever the rhyme or reason, Reyna knew she could ill afford to become even more intrigued with her enemy. Viktor was no different from the other brutal barbarians who had carried her off as a child, taken her freedom, destroyed her life, and caused the deaths of her mother and baby brother. She would not rest until she had killed *all* Vikings, and she would not let this odd bewitchment with Viktor the Valiant deter her from her goal.

Tomorrow she would journey across the fjord and infiltrate his territory. Tomorrow she would slay him . . . Mayhap after she had assuaged her curiosity a bit more.

SIX

"GOOD MORROW, MASTER."

The following morning, Viktor first encountered his house-keeper next to the open hearth in the large chamber at the center of the house. The woman was stirring bubbling gruel in a huge iron pot suspended by a tether over the stone fire pit. Viktor rubbed eyes that smarted from the acrid smoke.

He had been awake for most of an hour, and the reality that he was actually living in the Dark Ages continued to sink in on him. If this experience was some sort of dream—or a nightmare!—he certainly was not waking up.

The wolves had roused him well before dawn, and he had let them out for a run in the cold blackness before proceeding back to his bedchamber. In the sea chest, he had found some of the former Viktor's clothing—a coarse white tunic and leather jerkin, brown leggings, and soft leather boots. The garments had fit him well, and he had completed his toilette with only a polished silver tray to serve as a mirror. He had shaved his face with some sort of loathsome, stinging soap and a crude razor, and had raked order into his hair with a primitive comb carved of whalebone.

Viktor had explored the house, surveying several partitioned-off rooms in which various female thralls had greeted their returned jarl with a combination of reverence and shy smiles: in one cubicle, he had marveled at spinning and weaving; in another, he had scrutinized buttermilk and cheese being processed, and butter churned; in a third, he had watched dough being kneaded, and vegetables chopped for a stew.

Now he had come face-to-face with the housekeeper—a tall, thin, middle-aged woman with silver-streaked hair flowing from beneath a dark house cap, and sharp, thin features that did little to enhance her leathery face. With interest he eyed the two brooches holding together her brown garment: one seemed ornamental, a combination of iron filigree and small stones of amber; the other gave evidence of her station, since it was shaped like a ring and held a variety of small household implements: keys, scissors, needles, a small knife, and a couple of tiny leather pouches.

"You must be Helga," he murmured.

"Yea, master," the woman replied, lowering her gaze. "Canute the Cunning informed me you have returned from Valhalla."

"I suppose it's the talk of the village by now," Viktor quipped.

The woman stared at him blankly. "You are hungry, master?"

Realizing he was indeed famished, he clapped his hands and smiled. "Yes, rising from the dead does give a man one hell of an appetite."

With a perplexed frown, Helga picked up a soapstone bowl and ladled some gruel into it. Grabbing a spoon, she took the repast to a nearby table.

Following her, Viktor settled his large body into a high-backed chair that was supported by beautifully carved wooden pillars. He lifted the rather misshapen, roughly finished iron spoon and took a bite of the hot cereal. The porridge seemed to be a bland corn mush, and though it was far from tasty, at least it was edible.

Helga placed before him an iron tankard containing a smelly, lumpy-looking white brew. Viktor grimaced. "What is that?"

"Whey, master. You drink it each morning."

"There is nothing else?"

"Yea, there is ale—or buttermilk."

"Ah, buttermilk sounds good," he said.

The housekeeper shrugged and trudged off with the tankard. Momentarily she returned with a different chalice containing a portion of thick buttermilk that Viktor found palatable, if tepid.

As he ate, Viktor examined the chamber in greater detail. Like the other rooms in the house, the central hall had a soaring ceiling composed of thick panels of turf supported by stout wooden beams. But here the resemblance to the other chambers ended. Whereas the cubicles he had explored this morning had contained only floors of packed earth, this central eating hall had been built up on a platform of light, smooth wood, save for the sunk-in fire pit. Viktor sat at a long table with a plain, scarred top, yet the high-backed chairs surrounding it were, like his, throne-style and beautifully carved with etchings of warriors, horses, and odd writing symbols Viktor guessed were runic characters. Against both walls rested long benches with dark leather coverings. Above the benches hung tapestries—intricately woven, colorful panels depicting Viking warriors battling dragons, elves, ogresses, and trolls.

Obviously, Viktor mused, this chamber served as both dining hall and council chamber. It was doubtless here that Viktor the Valiant met with his kinsmen to feast or plan battle strategies. Although the surroundings were attractive, Viktor's eyes and throat still felt raw from the haze of smoke, grease, and stale food—especially with the large, hot, smoky fire pit at the center of the room. The fact that his head was still throbbing from his encounter with the warrior woman's battle-ax last night only exacerbated his malaise. Assuming he remained here in the Dark Ages, he must insist that the servants air out this rancid longhouse—and he must teach these people how to properly vent their fires.

After breakfast, Viktor ventured outside. The day was chill but not unpleasant, and actually, it was a relief for him to escape the acrid interior of the longhouse. He took several deep, bracing breaths of cool air, and judged the temperature to be in the low fifties.

For the first time, Viktor examined his surroundings by full daylight, and the reality that he was very, very far away from twentieth-century California struck him profoundly. His eye scanned the panorama—the mountains in the distance with their gleaming ice caps, the craggy foothills, and closer, the vast, gently sloping tundra carpeted with mossy grass and a few brave, stunted silver birches and willows. He knew that a mighty fjord carved the land to the west and that rocky cliffs and the beach stretched to the south, but otherwise he could not gauge this island's boundaries. However, like Iceland, Vanaheim must be quite large, he mused. Judging from the rock formations, he presumed the island had been born from ocean volcanoes, from basalt rock, just like Iceland.

Closer to view were sprawled all the accoutrements of a crude farming village of the Dark Ages. Viktor the Valiant had obviously been both a chieftain and a gentleman farmer. Most of the outbuildings and cottages were smaller versions of the longhouse itself—primitive structures composed almost entirely of turf, with wooden doors and support beams. Viktor spotted storage sheds, vegetable gardens and haystacks, and small cottages with yards of caked dirt, where women boiled laundry and children played with primitive toys made of rocks and sticks. One large building on the edge of the settlement appeared to be a barn—chickens, pigs, and cows roamed the fenced yard. Just beyond the small village, several men tilled the fields with oxen-drawn wooden plows.

Viktor shook his head and smiled cynically. He was off living in another age, all right. Logic declared that he should feel horrified to be wrenched so suddenly from his safe, established existence in the twentieth century—and, on one level, he still felt disoriented and bemused. But in another sense he felt challenged and intrigued by the possibility of living in a time that would test his physical strength and mental abilities, a time in which he would live or die by his own wits and fortitude. And oddly, the nagging feeling of displacement he had known in his "other" life was somehow absent here.

Where did Reyna the Ravisher fit into this picture? Again he recalled his dramatic—and frightening—encounter with the Valkyrie last night. It was so strange, he mused, how she so resembled his love back in the present, yet she had no awareness of him as someone *she* had known and loved.

What of the real Monica in the twentieth century? Did she miss him? Did everyone there assume he had died in the burning-boat scene? *Had* he died? He wasn't sure. However, as much as he missed Monica, as much as he hated the thought of causing any confusion or pain to those he had left behind, he recognized that his life back there had become meaningless once he had lost Monica and the chance to have a family of his own. Here, by contrast, he found possibilities, particularly the primitive challenge of the warrior woman, Reyna, who intrigued him greatly.

If only he could get to know her before she killed him!

Viktor was thinking of exploring further when the man he recognized as Svein stepped out from between two buildings and strode eagerly toward him. "Good morrow, jarl. How fare ye this day?"

"I'm starting to get my bearings," replied Viktor.

Svein frowned and scratched his blond head. "You speak so strangely, jarl. Could it have to do with your ordeal?"

"Look, can I level with you?" Viktor asked.

"What is it you need to level, jarl?"

Viktor laughed. "The truth is, I could use a friend right now."

"Verily, we are friends," replied Svein indignantly. "Do you not recall the ceremony five winters past that made us blood brothers?"

Viktor shook his head. "So we are indeed blood brothers, you and I?"

"Yea. We mingled our blood in a most sacred ritual. Afterward, we feasted until dawn, shared the same women on our benches, and sacrificed a slave to Odin to honor the occasion."

Viktor went pale at this last revelation.

Svein gripped his arm. "Jarl, you are staggering and white as a spring lamb. Has some malaise possessed you?"

Glancing around to ensure that no one else was within earshot, Viktor confided, "Svein, ever since I have returned from Valhalla, I remember nothing of my life here."

Svein raised a thick brow. "Naught at all?"

Viktor fabricated an explanation for Svein. "It is as if my memories of Vanaheim are on a slate that has been wiped clean."

Svein nodded grimly. "The others and I already suspected

as much. We spoke of this affliction after we left you last night. Yea, jarl, you seem as lost as Thor without his hammer."

Viktor chuckled. "Well put."

Svein thoughtfully stroked his jaw. "Your retainers and I have decided there must be a reason for your odd state of mind. Mayhap Odin wishes you to make a new start. Mayhap you must give up your memory and learn anew to better lead our peoples, just as Odin gave up his eye to gain greater wisdom."

"You know, that could be true," remarked Viktor, struggling to hide a guilty grin. "At any rate, I need your friendship now more than ever."

Svein bowed from the waist. "I am entirely at your service, jarl."

Viktor gestured expansively. "You must explain everything to me—the workings of this farm, our society—and you must tell me in greater detail how we all came to live in Vanaheim in the first place."

"As you wish, jarl. Come along, and we will begin your lessons."

The two men started off, striding down a lane flanked by outbuildings. Viktor smiled as several young boys bounded across their path, prodding along half a dozen squealing piglets.

"As you know, you are leader of our clan," Svein explained. "You settle all disputes and make all decisions affecting the entire tribe."

"This I understand. And I take it all of the clan lives here in the village?"

"Yea, most are here, save for the herdsmen who are gathering the lambs up in the meadows."

Svein motioned for Viktor to follow him inside a small hut. The interior was sweltering, and at once Viktor recognized a blacksmith's forge. The walls were hung with everything from swords, spears, and axes to jewelry and helmets. In the center of the building stood a giant, muscled, sweaty man clad only in a sleeveless jerkin and filthy leggings. He held a bellows, and the hard muscles of his arms gleamed as he stoked a fire in a stone pit. Not noticing the newcomers, he set down the bellows, grabbed a set of tongs, removed a plank of red-hot iron from the fire, and carried the glowing metal over to an anvil. With a look of intense concentration gripping his bearded face, he began loudly hammering the iron.

"Eurich!" called Svein. "Our jarl has come to visit you."

Eurich glanced up and grinned at the visitors. He put down his hammer and stepped forward, bowing. "Jarl, we are so gladdened to hear you have returned from the dead."

"Thank you, Eurich." Viktor glanced around the building. "You have an impressive operation here."

Eurich scowled. "Canute told me you lost your sword last night in the battle."

"Ah, so I did." Viktor grinned at the memory.

Eurich crossed the room and took an iron broadsword off a rack. He strode back to Viktor and solemnly presented the weapon. "For you, jarl. I have been working on this for you since Autumn month."

Viktor could only gape at the beautiful implement. Long, broad, and heavy in his hands, the weapon was a masterpiece of pattern-welding, numerous layers of iron overlaid with steel to form a tapestry of coiled, spitting serpents along the blade. The hilt was plated with gold and jeweled with rubies and amber. Viktor had no idea that such magnificent workmanship was even available in the Viking age.

He nodded solemnly to the man. "Thank you, Eurich. I am deeply touched and honored to accept your gift."

The blacksmith beamed. "The honor is all mine, jarl."

"How do you get your materials?"

"We dig bog iron in the hills, jarl." Eurich winked at Svein. "The gnomes help us. Then I make use of the gold, silver, and jewels the men bring back from their raiding voyages."

"Very good." Viktor frowned. "By the way, do you know anything about constructing chimney flues?"

His expression blank, Eurich shook his head.

"We must have a long talk about this matter soon."

"Yea, jarl."

Svein and Viktor left the forge and headed toward a long, narrow structure whose double doors were open. Once he was inside, staring at a row of crude stalls scattered with hay and smelling of manure and oats, Viktor realized he was in a primitive stable.

He raised a brow at Svein. "Why did you bring me here?"

"Mayhap you will want to become reacquainted with your horse, jarl."

"Ah, yes."

Svein led him to the second stall, where a thin, dark-haired, saturnine-looking man was busy grooming a short, stout gold horse. He turned to eye the newcomers warily.

Svein told Viktor, "Jarl, this is your stablehand, Nevin."

Viktor nodded to the man, who had dark eyes, a sharp, prominent nose, and a receding chin. "I am pleased to meet you, Nevin. It appears you are doing a splendid job of caring for the animals."

The man's features did not soften as he bowed and spoke with constraint. "We are pleased you have returned from the dead, jarl."

"Nevin's twin brother is our village skald," Svein remarked. "Quigley recites verses at our feasts. Sometimes Nevin is enlisted to help serve ale when the war council meets, since no females are then allowed in the chamber."

"I shall look forward to seeing you again, Nevin—and to meeting your twin," said Viktor.

With a curt nod, the stablehand left the stall.

"A rather sullen fellow," Viktor muttered.

"Not all of our slaves take kindly to captivity," replied Svein.

"I suppose not, especially considering that *we* took them captive. Am I not right?"

"Yea, jarl."

As the little horse neighed, Viktor laid his sword against the wall. He stepped up to the animal, which affectionately nudged his arm. The horse was smaller than those he was accustomed to in the present, but appeared very strong and stocky, with a shaggy mane and hooves, and striking light gold eyes.

"A fine specimen," he said, petting the horse's thick mane. "What is she called?"

Svein grinned. "*He* is named Sleipnir, after Odin's steed with eight legs."

"And how did I get him?"

"At a meeting of the Thing—"

"The Thing?"

"Each summer, an assembly of all of Vanaheim is held at Haymaking month. Three summers past, Sleipnir won the stallion fight, and his owner presented him to you in tribute."

"Stallion fight?"

"Yea, jarl."

Viktor did not want to press for details.

"You will take Sleipnir for a run soon?" Svein asked.

Viktor rubbed the horse's muzzle. "Of course. As soon as we finish up our tour. I'd like to see the moors for myself."

"Very good, jarl."

Back outside, Svein gestured toward the small cottages and fields beyond them. "There are the homes of the karls—"

"Karls?"

"The farmers. Each owns a small plot of land, and most have thralls—slaves—to work the fields for them."

"And the rest of the island?"

"Very little is habitable. As you know, Wolfgard lives across the fjord, and we do not venture into his territory, except to raid. Beyond our moors and foothills are steam geysers and boiling mud, where Jotuns and trolls lurk to pull brave warriors down to Hel. And in the vast distance there is Surt, spitting forth vengeance at his mountaintop."

"Surt?"

"A volcano named for the fire demon."

"Ah. Has the volcano ever erupted?"

Svein shook his head. "Not since we have lived here. Surt sputters and fumes most every summer, but he keeps his peace as long as we maintain our distance—and sacrifice a slave girl to him at Sowing time."

Viktor felt his heart lurch at this revelation. He certainly had his work cut out for him here with these pagan, barbaric people! "Where do we get all these slaves, anyway?"

A proud grin lit Svein's face. "Why, when we go a-Viking, jarl. We capture males and females in Ireland, Wales, Scotland, the Shetlands, and France."

"And you show them no greater respect than you would an animal slaughtered for food?" Viktor asked tensely.

Svein's countenance darkened. "Slaves are property, jarl. They have no rights. They are frequently lazy, and must be beaten into obedience." Abruptly he chuckled. "The women we keep submissive in more pleasurable ways."

Viktor was stunned. "You mean you take the women against their will?"

Svein shrugged. "A slave is not allowed to deny the will of a freeman. Similarly, when a slave outlives his usefulness, he is destroyed by his master, or driven to the back country to die of exposure."

Staggered by Svein's glib description of such sadistic practices, Viktor almost protested, then bit down an impulse to soundly denounce the abominable custom. He realized that, to a Viking, such an attitude was normal, practical, and not cruel. Although he intended to see to it that there was no such wanton destruction of human life while he was jarl, Viktor knew that he could win the trust of these people and change their overall mind-set, only slowly. He also realized he was needed here—badly needed—by a people immersed in a feudal, savage way of life. Perhaps there had been a purpose, a divine design, in his journey through time after all.

"Tell me more about how all of us came to live here. You say we came here from Iceland?" He frowned. "I seem to recall one of the others mentioning I was outlawed there."

Svein nodded. "Yea. You were a member of the tribe of Eirik the Red. Eirik killed one of his neighbors without good cause, and when the neighbor's brother slew your brother, you killed five more of his kinsmen, and then refused to allow your family to pay blood money."

"Good Lord—was I that bellicose?" asked Viktor.

Svein's features twisted in perplexity before he answered noncommittally, "Mayhap. Afterward, the Icelandic Althing ruled that both you and Eirik should be declared fuller outlaws."

"What does this mean—fuller outlaws?"

"No man was allowed to shelter you, and any man was free to kill you without fear of retribution."

Viktor whistled. "That's pretty extreme. Then what happened?"

"Since there were warring factions within Eirik's own clan,

you and he decided to split your kinsmen. Half the tribe fled north with him to Greenland, while the others followed you south to Vanaheim."

"And what of Wolfgard? How did he come to join us here?"

"He, too, was outlawed from Iceland—for stealing sheep, and for fornicating with the wife of a neighboring chieftain."

"A nasty fellow, eh?"

"Yea. And ever since Wolfgard took residence with his kinsmen across the fjord, our clans have battled."

"How often do these attacks occur?"

"Sometimes there is peace for months on end. At other times Wolfgard may attack twice in the same day, as he did last eve."

"So we must be prepared," said Viktor grimly.

"Yea, jarl. But do not fret. We have stationed sentries along the fjord in case the berserkers should return."

"Good strategy."

Sternly, Svein continued. "However, you must also be ready to lead us, jarl, even though you have lost both your memory and likely your battle skills, based on what the others and I observed last night. But no matter. We practice warfare most every afternoon, and we will gladly train you, and quickly so. For it may not be long before Wolfgard's forces attack again, and you must be prepared to lead the charge with all the courage and skill of Viktor the Valiant."

Viktor half shuddered at the thought of the deadly abilities he would need to lead his warriors into bloodcurdling mêlées such as had occurred last night. Of course, if he were to remain here, he would have to learn to defend himself. Beyond that, could he somehow teach these warlike people to be more peaceable—not just his own clan, but Wolfgard's tribe as well? He considered the prospect and concluded again that first he must better gain his bearings, learn about Viking society, and earn the trust of his own clan.

As the two men headed back toward the longhouse, a curious thought occurred to Viktor. "Tell me, Svein, do I resemble my old self?"

Svein eyed him thoughtfully. "Before, jarl, you had a long beard. Mayhap you lost your beard with your memory in Valhalla. Otherwise, yea, you appear to be just the man we knew."

"How exactly did I die?"

Svein snorted a laugh. "Even that you have forgotten?"

Viktor nodded.

"You died yesterday at eventide, after the first battle against Wolfgard's forces."

"Ah, yes. So I would have."

"You repelled the invaders, but were horribly bruised and punctured. Only moments after the berserkers fled, you expired. We launched you to Valhalla at nightfall."

Just like in the movie! Viktor thought with awe and amazement. "Then when Wolfgard's forces returned, they did not know I had just returned from the dead?"

"Nay. I think not then, as you still clung to life when the first battle ended."

"But Reyna seemed to know," Viktor muttered, as if to himself.

"The Ravisher knew of your resurrection?" Svein asked with a raised brow.

"Perhaps," Viktor murmured, still lost in thought.

"Whether or not she had knowledge, I predict word will spread quickly throughout the realm." Svein clenched his jaw. "Indeed, we have suspected for some time that there is a traitor in our midst, a knave who has been secretly giving information to Wolfgard."

"You don't say?"

Svein's blue eyes gleamed with vengeful triumph. "But this time, mayhap the traitor will aid our case."

"In what way?"

"By telling of your feat, jarl, and thereby putting fear in the hearts of our enemies. Never before has a warrior defied the Angel of Death and descended the Rainbow Bridge back to Midgard. I am certain you will inspire great awe and fear among Wolfgard's clansman."

Viktor nodded. "Let us hope so. Otherwise we don't have a lot else to bank on right now, do we?"

Svein clapped a hand on Viktor's shoulder. "Do not worry. We will hone your skills. And soon we will have a great feast to celebrate your return from the dead. We will drink mead, sacrifice lambs, and ravish wenches until dawn."

"Drinking mead, sacrificing animals, and ravishing women?" Viktor repeated with a wan smile. "My, I can hardly wait."

Svein nudged Viktor with his elbow and chuckled. "If the mead is strong and Loki is about, we must pray we do not become confused and sacrifice the wenches and ravish the lambs."

Viktor was rendered ashen-faced and utterly speechless.

Svein threw back his head and laughed. "I am jesting, jarl. Can you not see the humor of it?"

For once, Viktor responded in a purely pagan vein. "Odin help me if I ever do."

Up on the tundra well above Viktor's village, Reyna the Ravisher rode her black pony, galloping among the spring's first brave wildflowers. She enjoyed her reckless forays onto her enemy's side of the fjord—not only so she could spy on the rival clan, but also because the jaunts gave her a feeling of power and freedom. In all honesty, she had to admit that curiosity about Viktor the Valiant had in large part spurred her adventure today—as well as a determination to slay him.

Reyna also savored being away from her hated stepfather's village, where she was endlessly goaded by his arrogant warriors, and where her only friends were her half brother, Ragar; his kinsman Harald; and her servant, Sibeal. On this side of the fjord, Reyna could actually feel safer, as well as more feminine and lighthearted. Here she lost herself in the natural setting; she played with her ice fox, Freya, and visited her good friend Pelagius, the Christian hermit monk who lived high in the hills. Here on these moors, she secretly indulged a different side of her nature, the part of her that was woman, not warrior, the essence of her that remained innocent and virginal, that missed her stolen childhood and the country of her birth.

For soon enough, the glaciers would melt and the spring rains would render the fjord too swollen to cross. Then Reyna's sojourns would cease. But for now, she could still ford the river at its most narrow neck above Wolfgard's village. She could unleash her more fanciful side while toying with her enemies—and perhaps gaining new insight into the baffling Viktor the Valiant, the man who had arisen from Valhalla's flames last night. That knowledge would give her the power to destroy him, she vowed.

At the sudden sound of hoofbeats approaching, Reyna reined in her horse and quickly took refuge in a stand of birches. Then, as if her very musings had summoned him, she watched Viktor the Valiant appear over the horizon on his yellow horse and gallop into the valley beneath her. Unaccountably, Reyna's heartbeat quickened at the sight of him. Viktor appeared magnificent, his golden hair tangling behind him in the breeze, the muscles of his arms and legs rippling as he rode the stallion with total ease. He appeared as carefree and happy as she often felt when she rode here, and she experienced an unexpected twinge of affinity with him.

That pang of feeling brought shame and anger in its wake. What was happening to her? By all rights, she should pull an arrow from its quiver and slay Viktor now, and yet ... Just as had occurred last night, Reyna felt uncertainty swamp her, and she could not bring herself to destroy such a magnificent creature. What if Viktor was indeed a god now? Would she be doomed to Hel for smiting him?

Mayhap Viktor did possess supernatural powers. How else could she explain the feelings he aroused—this strange excitement, this throbbing in secret, forbidden places where a virgin should never feel such wicked yearnings—and *never* for an enemy!

How could she want so badly to kill him ... yet long to get to know him better?

SEVEN

VIKTOR ENJOYED HIS RIDE ON THE TUNDRA, ALTHOUGH HE EXPErienced a strange, nagging feeling of being watched. Before returning to the village, he spoke with the sentries stationed along the fjord, and felt relieved when they reported having seen no further hint of the enemy. One of the men mentioned that the attacks almost always came at night, or late in the day. Still, Viktor was well aware that Wolfgard might strike again at any moment, and he had no time to waste in preparing to lead his warriors. Of course it would be far preferable to convince the warring factions to lay down their arms, but he still had to keep himself and the others alive in the interim.

He spent the next few hours exploring the village, feeling more of a sense of excitement, belonging, and, especially, challenge at being thrust back so far in time. His conviction deepened that he was meant to live at this moment in history. He thought frequently of Reyna the warrior woman and wondered when he would next encounter her—hopefully, when he was better prepared!

That afternoon, Viktor joined half a dozen of his men in combat practice. The seven gathered on a rise above the village. As two of the company, Canute and Rollo, prepared to battle each other with iron shields and wooden practice swords, Viktor glanced around the landscape. They stood beyond the fields on the cool, windswept tundra; the ground was covered with soft, mossy grass, and a few white

Balderblooms were beginning to peak upward in anticipation of summer. Overhead, a flock of plovers, trailed by a few awkward puffins, sailed across the clear blue sky.

Although the scene appeared pastoral, reminders of the brutal times in which Viktor now lived loomed close at hand. Beneath them, closer to the village, stretched the cemetery— row after row of graves encircled by rocks, or marked with crude, lichen-covered stone tablets etched with runes. There, two thralls were digging a deep burial pit for a warrior, Sigfred, who had died from wounds inflicted in last night's battle. Svein had told Viktor that, since Sigfred had died in bed, he could not be launched to Valhalla in the tradition of warriors lost in battle—and that alone seemed all that aggrieved these people regarding their comrade's demise. Staring at the yawning pit, Viktor frowned. More and more, he sensed that part of his purpose in being flashed back in time was to teach these hostile tribes how to live together peaceably.

Additional changes would be needed here as well, he thought. For instance, it troubled him greatly that slaves were being forced to dig the graves. So far, he had seen many in the village who were kept in human bondage. Even now, on a craggy abutment above, two thralls were digging up iron ore, while opposite them to the east, a third was attending a large outdoor smelter.

All at once Viktor was needled by a prickle of anxiety. Why did he have the feeling that a fourth set of eyes was watching him covertly from somewhere in those nearby rocks? It was the same spooky sensation he'd known earlier while riding the tundra, as if he were being stalked by some unseen person. He pondered the odd intuition for a moment, scanning the rocks for any signs of life. Then the sounds of banging and striking returned his attention to the combat practice . . .

Up in the hills, from behind a basalt outcropping, Reyna the Ravisher was intently watching the combat practice. She had trailed Viktor for much of the day, her curiosity and fascination with the Viking only increasing. Now she would find out for certain how skilled a warrior he was after having returned from the dead. During their clash last night, he had seemed strangely disoriented, inept, not his usual savage self at all. Had his clumsiness been a ploy, or had his journey to Valhalla truly befuddled him?

Reyna picked up a small rock and smiled. Mayhap she could have some fun here as well, disrupt the men's practice a bit, hit Viktor over the head and knock him to the ground. That might prove diverting, she mused with vindictive pleasure. Far safer to defeat her foe than to try to deal with the unsettling, intense feelings he continued to arouse.

But first she would watch him and learn what she could . . .

Viktor watched Rollo crash his sword against Canute's shield. On Rollo's upswing, Canute raised his own mock weapon high and smashed Rollo's shield. The two men whacked and lunged at each other for long moments, until Rollo grew fatigued. Canute promptly seized the advantage, knocking the sword from Rollo's hand. The one-eyed giant howled with triumph, heaved his wooden broadsword high, then lowered it slowly on top of Rollo's head in a symbolic gesture of slaughter. While the other warriors cheered the victor, Rollo bowed on one knee in acknowledgment of his defeat.

A huge grin splitting his scarred face, Canute turned to Viktor. "Jarl!" he called out arrogantly. "I challenge you next."

Even as Viktor considered the dare, Svein hastened to protest. "Canute, you are not playing fairly. Our king lost his memory and forgot his warrior skills in Valhalla. We are all well aware that you are our fiercest fighter. For King Viktor to take up your challenge would result in an uneven match."

Canute winked at Viktor. "Do not worry. I shall be gentle with our delicate lamb."

The other warriors roared in laughter, while Viktor scowled. As King Viktor, he had all but established himself as a laughingstock with his men; he realized he must assume a role of leadership and work toward commanding the respect due his station. If he was to make changes on Vanaheim, he must convince his men to take him seriously.

"I will accept the challenge," he said solemnly.

As Viktor started forward, Svein touched his arm. "Jarl, I warn you to take care. Canute is ruthless."

Viktor nodded and confided in low tones, "If I am to rule here, Svein, I must earn the fealty of my warriors. Even if I am defeated, there will be dignity in having tried. Moreover, I must learn to fight as well as the rest of you if our tribe is to successfully repel future attack by Wolfgard's forces."

Svein nodded resignedly.

Viktor stepped forward. Ottar rushed up and handed his jarl the iron shield, wooden broadsword, and leather helmet that Rollo had just abandoned.

"Make us proud, jarl," the lad said with a grin.

Viktor was tempted to roll his eyes. He put on the leather helmet, lifted the broadsword with his right hand, and tried to balance the heavy, awkward shield with his left.

Canute watched him, his shrewd eye gleaming. "Whenever you are prepared to begin, jarl."

"In a moment," muttered Viktor.

He had had little instruction in sword fighting, other than some brief fencing lessons to prepare for his swashbuckling movies—back in that already hazy, distant time when he had been Marcello Lazaro. Still, recalling his training, he held the shield braced against his chest while practicing striking and parrying motions. He danced about, lunging, then retreating, blocking the blows of an imaginary opponent.

He stopped amid the hooting and huzzahs of his men, then glanced around in perplexity to see them all holding their sides and rocking with amusement.

"What is so funny?" he asked the nearest one, Orm.

"What are you doing, jarl?" the grinning man replied.

"I am practicing swordplay."

The warriors slapped their knees and split their sides with mirth.

"Will you kindly let me in on this joke?" Viktor snapped.

"We do not play with our swords, jarl," answered the insolent Canute. "We deliver thrusts, body strikes, hatchet strokes, and sideways hits to knock the shield from our opponent's hands."

"I see," muttered Viktor. "Then you must depend on brute strength rather than dexterity, and on inflicting blunt, massive blows, causing your attackers to die of internal injuries rather than mortal cuts."

The men glanced at one another, utterly bewildered.

"We have wasted enough time, jarl," rejoined an impatient Canute, smiling with cruel relish. "Come give me your worst."

Viktor gritted his teeth and, extending his sword and tightly holding his shield, lunged at Canute. The one-eyed warrior deftly sidestepped him, knocked him across the shoulders, and sent his weapon spinning out of his hands and him hurtling to the ground. Viktor spit out a mouthful of dirt and moss amid the loud jeers of his men . . .

Above the men, Reyna stifled her giggles with her hand. Viktor the Valiant truly was a clumsy ox, for the other warrior had knocked him to the tundra as if he were a helpless babe.

Reyna had overhead one of the men say that Viktor had lost both his memory and his warrior skills in Valhalla, and such appeared to be the case. What a strange god he was, if he was indeed a deity now. His behavior was amusing, but this did not change Reyna's determination to defeat him—especially since she felt so threatened by much about him that she could not understand. She lifted the rock and waited for the best moment to strike . . .

On the ground, Viktor bravely bit back a groan, heaved himself to his feet, and retrieved his sword and shield. Canute stood mocking him silently, feet braced widely apart. Three more times Viktor attempted to attack the huge warrior; three more times Canute battered Viktor across his back or shoulders and sent him crashing to the tundra.

After his third spill, Viktor rolled over to feel the tip of Canute's wooden sword pressed to his throat. "Are you prepared to admit defeat, jarl?"

"It appears I must."

"Were we on a battlefield," the warrior said gloatingly, "I would now be carrying your head on the tip of my sword."

In the background, the warriors chuckled. His patience exhausted, Viktor shoved aside Canute's weapon and struggled to his feet. These barbarians knew much about savage force, he mused, but little about dexterity or strategy. Staring the grinning brute in his eye, he made a swift motion with his foot, locking his ankle around Canute's, yanking forward, and sending the unprepared giant crashing down on his stout buttocks. The stunned warrior glowered in befuddlement while Viktor's men stamped their feet and shouted their approval.

"I suppose it's a good thing we aren't in battle now," Viktor replied with a cocky grin.

Amid a bellow of rage, Canute surged to his feet. But again Svein intervened, stepping between Canute and Viktor before the one-eyed giant could retaliate.

"Our jarl has had enough practice for today," Svein said decisively.

"Sly trickster!" bellowed Canute.

He was still glaring at Viktor when suddenly a rock came sailing over the small group and hit the one-eyed giant squarely on the forehead. With a shout of pain, Canute once again tumbled to the ground, while all the other warriors stared around them in astonishment.

"What the hell—" muttered Viktor.

His words were cut short by the sound of thundering hoofbeats. He and the others jerked around, only to watch in awe and horror as Reyna the Ravisher abruptly burst upon them astride her black pony. The Valkyrie screamed an exuberant battle yell while using the flat side of her sword to knock several warriors off their feet like so many felled ninepins, leaving a chorus of grunts and groans in her wake.

Viktor was so taken aback by Reyna's sudden charge, he barely managed to leap out of range as her horse bounded past him. Beyond the group of disoriented men, she reined in her mount and turned to grin sadistically at Viktor.

"Viking!" she cried. "Next time my aim will be better."

With amazement, Viktor watched the hellion salute him, then gallop off. He almost grinned. He simply could not believe her audacity. Reyna was utterly magnificent—and equally ruthless!

Then Viktor's attention became diverted as a furious Canute staggered forward, his arm yanked back as he prepared to hurl an ax into the girl's retreating back.

"No!" Viktor cried, grabbing Canute's wrist to stay him.

"Why say you nay?" demanded Canute, struggling with Viktor.

"Because we do not kill women—nor do we slay anyone

with an ax in their back. That is not the way of courageous warriors."

Evidently Canute thought differently, for he wrenched his wrist away and hurled the ax into the ground. Spitting at Viktor's feet, he stalked off. Viktor heaved a sigh of relief as the men dispersed, frowning and muttering to one another about Reyna's bizarre attack.

Looking concerned, Svein stepped up to Viktor. "Jarl, you are unharmed?"

He nodded. "That was amazing. Has Reyna attempted this type of stunt before?"

Svein stroked his beard. "Methinks she has previously spied on our village, but never has she behaved quite so brazenly." He nudged Viktor with his elbow and grinned. "Mayhap she is intrigued with you now that you have returned from the dead."

"Hah!" scoffed Viktor. "Evidently, she meant her rock for my head and not Canute's."

"Yea, so it appears. Nevertheless, Canute is not pleased that you stayed him from killing the Ravisher."

"Then let him sulk—for I can think of no act more cowardly than to slay a woman in such a brutal manner," Viktor retorted passionately.

Svein's expression grew grim. "Again you are right, jarl, but I must still warn you not to turn *your* back on Canute."

A tingle of alarm pricked Viktor. "Are you saying the man's loyalty may be questionable?"

"You spoke the truth earlier. You must earn Canute's respect anew, and that of all your warriors. Beyond that, jarl, I must warn you that Canute would hardly be aggrieved to assume your place."

Viktor grew silent, lost in troubled thought. Could Canute be the traitor in their midst whom Svein had mentioned earlier?

And was Reyna the unseen shadow that had stalked him all day? He grinned. There, at least, he already knew the answer. He could even hope that perhaps Svein had spoken the truth, that Reyna might well be as captivated with him as he already was with her.

EIGHT

Several days passed, and Viktor did not again encounter Reyna. He became better acclimated to life in the Viking world. It was a busy time for his people. Sheep and cattle were brought down from the uplands to graze near the village. Oats, barley, flax, and vegetables were planted in the fields by the thralls. Viktor's men busied themselves with various manly tasks, such as the critical gathering of food. They hunted for seals or fished; Viktor grew accustomed to seeing racks of cod drying in the sun. The men also gathered seabird eggs, and introduced Viktor to the daredevil ritual of puffin hunting, in which the men would stand on the high cliffs overlooking the ocean and hurl out nets on long tethers to catch the plump fowl as they swirled about their nests. The first time Viktor watched Rollo totter on a precipice and fling out his net at a passing bird, he was amazed that the man did not go sailing off the cliff to break his neck on the treacherous rocks below.

Although Viktor demurred when his men offered to teach him the intricacies of catching puffins, he did welcome their instruction in ice fishing and in hunting with a bow and arrow. He particularly enjoyed riding his shaggy horse, Sleipnir, across the tundra. Frequently his wolves trailed behind him, howling exuberantly in the crisp spring air. At moments such as this, Viktor was increasingly convinced he really was meant to be here—at a time when he could connect with the primitive man in himself, lead his people to a better life, exist

in harmony with the elements . . . and find the woman of his
dreams!

While the men attended to their duties, the Viking women
occupied themselves spinning, weaving, sewing, processing
dairy products, cooking, and minding children. Viktor suspected they also gossiped, and they seemed especially fascinated with him now that he had returned from Valhalla.
Whenever he passed a group of wenches working in the longhouse, or a gathering of wives enjoying the mild weather in
the village, the females inevitably tittered and stared at him.

As time passed, Viktor wondered why Wolfgard did not attack again. When questioned, Svein explained that their enemy was likely occupied with the same arduous tasks of
sowing crops, driving cattle down from the moors, repairing
buildings ravaged by winter, and preparing for lamb-shearing
time. Nonetheless, the village remained alert to the potential
danger, and Viktor kept sentries posted along the fjord.

He practiced self-defense daily with his men, readying
himself for his next encounter with Wolfgard and company.
More than ever, he realized he had journeyed back in time ill-
prepared for the rigors of Viking combat. During the sessions,
the other warriors, particularly Canute, continued to hurl him
to the ground and batter his pride. At first, trying to land a
kick or engineer an over-the-hip throw against a Viking warrior was like practicing ballet against a bulldozer: Viktor met
with an occasional success; but more often, given the brute
strength of his warriors, he became intimately acquainted
with the wildflowers on the tundra. Still, as the days went on,
Viktor's skills did improve slowly but surely, just as his men
laughed at him less often. Over time, he was even able to
teach his warriors a few of the self-defense techniques he remembered from his movie career.

Two decidedly modern conveniences of the Viking village
fascinated Viktor: the saunalike steam hut where the men
bathed, and a separate bathing house that had been built over
a natural hot spring. He spent many luxuriant moments bask-
ing in the hot spring, Jacuzzi-style, soaking out muscle kinks
from the day's ride or combat practice. Sometimes he grew
sad as he recalled such pleasurable moments spent with
Monica back in the present. But more and more, he realized

that his life with Monica was never meant to be—and now it was the prospect of having a warrior woman luxuriating beside him in the warm, bubbly water that stirred his senses.

He repeatedly wondered when he would see Reyna again. Since the day she had disrupted combat practice, he had not spotted her spying on his village, although at times he had again sensed that he was being watched. Reyna was clearly a barbarian, yet the memory of her beauty and strength, even her savagery, continued to haunt him. She was Monica, yet she was reborn, all primal woman, and so intriguing. The thought of taming her ferociousness into spirited passion tantalized him.

One cool spring morning he took a long ride on Sleipnir, traveling well above the village, up into the moors. At noontime, he paused on an outcropping of basalt to have his lunch of fish and bread, while his horse nibbled on nearby grasses. He was soon taken aback as he saw a woman ride into the meadow below him. It was Reyna, on a small black horse. So she had ventured once again into his territory! A certain perverse pleasure filled him as he realized that now he might spy on her just as she had previously snooped on him!

Not wanting to alert her to his presence, Viktor tied his mount to a shrub and hid himself behind the abutment. He thanked the gods that his wolves had been off chasing rabbits when he had left this morning, or they certainly would have given him away now by charging after his enemy.

Actually, he did not want to risk another encounter with Reyna until he better understood her and had planned an appropriate strategy—and greatly improved his own warrior skills, he thought ruefully. Even so, his greatest challenge would likely be protecting himself from her barbarism without hurting her.

He studied her eagerly as she dismounted. As before, she was dressed like a man, in a tunic, short leggings, and soft leather boots. Like Monica in the present, she had magnificently long, shapely legs, and her partially bared arms were lovely as well. A headband restrained her long, thick blond hair.

He wondered why she was here. Was she hoping to spy on his people again, or did she simply seek to be alone? His curiosity was soon assuaged as she knelt and whistled softly. A moment later, to his amazement, Viktor observed a small, snowy-white arctic fox creep out from behind a basalt boulder and rush to her side. An exuberant Reyna fell to the turf and petted the little fox affectionately; within seconds, the two were rolling about and cavorting among the wildflowers.

Viktor watched, captivated, unable to believe his eyes. Reyna's tinkling laughter drifted up from the tundra, along with the lively, chirping barks of the little vixen. Reyna no longer seemed a savage, but was as gentle, carefree, and happy as a child.

So this brutal warrior woman had a soft spot in her heart after all. How he wished they were not enemies, that he could join in her joy and laughter.

After a moment, she got up, went to her horse, and rummaged inside a knapsack. She brought back several eggs for the fox to eat, and petted it as it happily devoured the treat.

Viktor could only shake his head. Reyna was clearly much more than a brutal savage. Indeed, he was now deeply convinced that she was the woman of his dream, the woman of his destiny. She was all natural woman, and he wanted her. He felt stunned by the depth of his feelings toward a woman he had seen only three times and had never even touched—

Or had he? Perhaps he *had* loved Reyna in another life—a life she hadn't even lived yet. Perhaps he was encountering her now at a point in her spiritual progression when she was truly ready for the type of relationship he so desired. The prospects were mind-boggling! Although Viktor didn't fully understand all the mysteries and complexities of space and time that had wrenched their souls apart, then brought them back together again, he did know he already felt a strong spiritual and physical bond with her. They had much in common, including their love of animals and the outdoors. He yearned to play with her and her fox on the wild, vibrant tundra. He wanted her laughter, her loyalty, and the love of her proud heart. Yes, that hard-won love would be more valuable than all the gold or jewels in the world. For here was a woman without career objectives who could give him the babies he so dearly wanted. The very thought of building a family with her in this raw, primitive setting excited him immensely. And if that was being retrograde, then so be it.

He watched Reyna rise and return to her horse, grabbing a bow and throwing a sling with a quiverful of arrows over her shoulder. With her fox standing nearby, she began shooting the arrows into the trunk of a birch tree, aiming the swift missiles with deadly precision. Viktor grimaced as each sharp projectile thudded home. Obviously, before he could love this woman, he had to divest her of these troubling homicidal tendencies. When he had tamed this glorious wild creature without breaking her, and had unleashed the more gentle and feminine side of her nature, that would be the true victory.

Once she finished her practice, she bade her fox an affectionate farewell, then mounted her pony and galloped off toward the north. Intrigued, Viktor mounted Sleipnir and followed her from a safe distance.

The landscape grew increasingly craggy and bleak. Viktor spotted several steam geysers shooting into the air, and watched an eerie fog rise from a lava tube. Why was the girl venturing so high into the hills, so far away from civilization, when logic argued that she should be heading back home, toward Wolfgard's village?

He soon had his answer as Reyna stopped beside a rushing stream—where a strange man was crouched, evidently praying, in the water. Viktor could tell little about the man other than that he seemed gaunt and heavily bearded, and knelt motionless, his hands laced before him as the water rushed over him. Viktor was flabbergasted by the sight. Was Reyna acquainted with a madman? He quickly halted his horse, dismounted, and took refuge behind a stand of stunted willows.

By now Reyna, too, had dismounted. Viktor watched her approach the bizarre man and frantically wave her arms. He heard the muffled sounds of her distraught pleas.

A moment later, the man climbed out of the stream, shivering violently, water sluicing off his long beard and dark robe. Viktor saw Reyna rush to her horse, grab a blanket, and drape it around the man's shoulders. She handed him some sort of crude staff, and knelt at his feet—

Viktor watched the man make the sign of the cross over

Reyna as she bowed her head and pressed her hands together in an attitude of prayer.

Dio, the girl was a Christian! Viktor was stunned, and more intrigued than ever.

Was the man a priest? he wondered. If so, what on earth was he doing here on a pagan Viking island, and what was Reyna's connection to him?

Back at the village, during dinner with his blood brother, Viktor asked Svein about the priest, wisely leaving out any mention of Reyna.

"While I was riding in the mountains today, I spotted this odd, bearded character praying in a stream," he remarked as the two shared a repast of mutton and ale.

Svein snorted, wiping grease from his whiskery chin with the sleeve of his jerkin. "Mayhap you saw Pelagius."

"Pelagius? Who is he?"

"An Irish hermit monk who lives in the hills."

Viktor scowled. "He is Irish? What is he doing here on Vanaheim?"

Svein bit into a chunk of mutton. "Ever since St. Brendan made his curragh voyage to Iceland in the fifth century, Irish monks have come here to the North Country, hoping to convert pagan Vikings to Christianity."

"How fascinating. Have they met with success?"

Svein shook his head. "Verily, most go mad and become hermits—just as Pelagius has done."

"Is that why his behavior is so outlandish?"

"Yea. You would be well advised to avoid him, jarl, as do the rest of our warriors. He is truly demented, that one, and the men fear his curses."

With a bemused smile, Viktor sipped his ale. So Reyna the Ravisher had a partner in crime who was every bit as unique and potentially dangerous as she was.

At sunset, Reyna the Ravisher sat leaning against the front wall of a small hut not far from her stepfather's village. In her arms was cuddled her special friend, one-year-old baby Hamar. Hamar's mother, Inga, was resting inside, as she oft did when Reyna offered to watch the baby. The young boy was cooing softly and playing with the iron bracelet on Reyna's wrist.

Reyna felt content here with the child, away from the village, safe from curious eyes and the possible contempt of her stepfather's warriors. She had felt relatively secure today on her enemy's moors as well, when she had played with her fox, Freya, and visited her good friend Pelagius.

Yet a small frown puckered her brow. Oddly, while in Viktor's territory, she had not felt quite as protected from prying eyes as she did now. Indeed, she had experienced an uncanny feeling of being watched. Several times she had glanced behind her, only to find no one there. Still, she could not help but wonder if Viktor the Valiant might sometimes spy on her just as she had watched him. Was it possible she had roused his attention, his curiosity, after the day she had hurled a rock and invaded his combat practice?

Reyna smiled at the memory of sending half a dozen Viking warriors crashing to the tundra like so many toppled toys. Yet on that occasion, as previously, she had been unable to harm Viktor directly—ultimately, her rock had struck another warrior's head, whether intentionally or by accident, she was not sure. She had told herself she simply wanted to toy with Viktor a while longer before slaying him, but in her heart she suspected otherwise. As for the Viking himself, he had just stood there intently watching her ride away, prompting a strange surge of confusion and perilous excitement within her.

Why did the Viking invariably arouse such odd and disconcerting feelings? And what if he *had* seen her today? The possibility that Viktor might have glimpsed the more feminine, vulnerable side of her was unnerving and frightening, for Reyna had never dared to reveal her more gentle side to any man, save for her beloved half brother, Ragar.

Surely Viktor had not seen her. Surely—

Reyna yelped as baby Hamar yanked on her hair and crowed loudly, as if proud of his own mischief. Glancing down at him as she gently disengaged his strong little fingers from her locks, she found the round-faced cherub cooing up at her unrepentantly.

"So you are impatient for my attention, are you, little one?"

The baby gurgled in response. Reyna took his little hands between hers and clapped them together while chanting a made-up rhyme about pigs and roosters dancing around a barnyard. She and Hamar often played this little game, which delighted him. He laughed in glee and tried to mimic some of Reyna's sounds. When at last he tired of their game, she ruffled his hair, nestled him close, and kissed his soft cheek. He turned his adorable face up to hers and yawned contentedly, prompting another surge of tender feelings inside her.

Would she ever have a beautiful child such as this—a baby of her own to love? The question saddened her, for Reyna knew that as long as she was trapped on this godless Viking island—where violence was a way of life and she considered all men her enemies—she could never take a husband.

Still, observing the boy's blond hair and blue eyes, Reyna was reminded once again of Viktor. Her enemy might one day have a son much like Hamar, she mused, and the image of Viktor the Valiant as a father filled her with an unexpected primal excitement.

She tugged her wayward thoughts to a screeching halt and scolded herself sternly. What was wrong with her, that she kept succumbing to tender fantasies of her enemy? Why could she not shake her fascination with the hated Viking? If she did not better guard her own thoughts, next she would be envisioning herself as the mother of Viktor's children! Not only was he her bitterest enemy, but any son of his would one day be impelled to become a warrior—just as poor little Hamar would someday be forced to take up arms against his Viking enemies.

Reyna sighed. At least she could take heart from the fact that Hamar was happy now. Reyna had known such bliss once, when she was a tiny princess in her beloved homeland of Loire. She missed that existence and longed one day to escape Vanaheim to return to the country of her birth.

She rocked the baby in her arms and hummed the poignant strains of a lullaby she recalled from her own early childhood. When she again kissed Hamar's soft cheek and felt his tiny fingers curl trustingly around her own, she found herself fighting an unexpected tear.

Later, Reyna crept inside the hut and lay the child down beside his sleeping mother. Forcibly turning her thoughts away from all that was soft and gentle, she considered launching another spying mission across the fjord tonight. More knowledge of Viktor might help her conquer her enemy—before he seized upon this troubling weakness in her to engineer her own defeat . . .

NINE

THAT NIGHT, THE LONG-ANTICIPATED FEAST TO HONOR VIKTOR'S
return from the dead was held at his hall. He and his retainers
gathered at the long table, with Viktor sitting at the head in
his throne-style chair, and his three wolves resting at his feet,
chewing on the scraps the men tossed them.

By now Viktor was aware that several of his retainers were
married, but no wives had been allowed to join the men tonight. Helga was also absent, and a bent crone Viktor had
never seen before was serving the men their bread and mutton stew. The pathetic, hunched creature wore a hooded mantle and ragged mittens; she mumbled to herself as she passed
with her bowl and loaf of bread. The unfortunate thrall must
also be near-blind, Viktor mused, since she kept missing the
men's plates and spattering their hands or arms with stew, or
tossing slices of bread into their laps.

Aside from the female, Nevin, the stablehand, assisted his
twin brother, Quigley, the skald, in replenishing the men's oxhorns with mead. Studying the two male thralls, Viktor
thought he had never seen a more different set of twins:
whereas Nevin was thin, sallow, and taciturn, Quigley was
round, jovial, and effusive. Pouring the mead, the skald
amused the warriors by extemporizing poems, spinning amusing yarns of Viking life, and improvising tales of the Norse
gods.

As the gathering grew rowdier, Viktor realized that his
kinsmen much preferred their heady libation over the food,

and that the word "feast" was actually a misnomer for a drunken brawl. At the same time, he had to wonder what was more harmful—the alcoholic beverages his warriors swilled so freely, or the diet so rich in fat and cholesterol that the Vikings consumed daily. He frowned. In addition to his other duties here, he would need to develop programs both for reforming drunkards and for unclogging their arteries through establishing more healthful diets.

At least with the coming of milder weather, he had convinced Helga to air out the longhouse and to do most of her cooking outside; consequently, the chamber was no longer as smoky. Viktor had also spoken with Eurich about constructing a chimney, but he had quickly realized that the forging techniques necessary for manufacturing a large stovepipe were nonexistent here in the Dark Ages. Instead, he had focused his energies on designing a chimney made of stone and whatever style of mortar he could improvise. With Svein's help, he had already begun to gather rocks for the project.

A roar of lewd laughter drew Viktor's attention back to his men. The talk had become loud and boisterous as several warriors tried to top each other with accounts of their sexual prowess.

"When I did service with the Varangian guard in Constantinople," announced a grinning Canute, "I seduced three of the Emperor's wives in their beds at the harem—and none was the wiser."

"Think you we are amused?" scoffed Orm. "Your feat is as naught. Remember when we all went a-Viking three summers past?"

"You are telling of the time we raided the Irish monasteries, took the monks as slaves, and plundered the illuminated manuscripts?" asked Svein.

"Yea, and that is far from all 'twas plundered," bragged Orm. "I had all four of the monks' embroideresses, I did! Before 'twas over, a few of *their* garments needed stitches."

Amid howls of laughter, Rollo jeered, "Why, a *boy* could tame four embroideresses. Recollect you the time we raided the Shetlands? I fornicated with five hefty milkmaids—one after another, and all on the same stool."

"Did the stool break?" asked Canute.

" 'Twas the wenches who were well broken," answered the arrogant Rollo.

Bawdy laughter all but shook the walls.

"Was their butter sweet?" called a voice down the table.

Rollo grinned. "Yea, and their milk 'twas like honey."

Amid new bellows of mirth, Ottar announced proudly, "Our jarl can best you all. Remember ye the time at market, when he single-handedly slew a band of six brigands who tried to rob us?"

"Yea, and afterward celebrated by bedding six women all in the same night?" added Svein.

The men rocked with laughter, while Viktor smiled wanly and wondered just how depraved his predecessor and namesake had truly been. He watched the old crone pass again, and as he smiled, she hurled a slice of bread at him. Catching the missile, he muttered a thank-you, and the woman grunted before moving on.

As much as Viktor's ears had been scorched by his men's tall tales, his eyeballs were not spared. Soon several other servant women ventured in, listening to the exaggerated stories and tittering to one another. Rollo and Orm quickly grabbed the comeliest two females and bore them, giggling and squirming, to the benches along the wall. There, the warriors brazenly hiked up the wenches' skirts, unfastened their own leggings, and copulated with the women openly, grunting with pleasure and wrenching earthy cries from the slaves. Their kinsmen cheered them on and the skald recited a bawdy verse.

Viktor was horrified, and would have intervened on behalf of the women except that the wenches, far from appearing abused, seemed to be thoroughly enjoying themselves, shrieking with delight and moaning with abandonment as they bounced on the laps of the lusty warriors. After Rollo and Orm finished with them, they handed the females over to Canute and Svein, who took over with huge grins, quickly unfastening their own leggings. Again the women, far from protesting, seemed to relish the public coupling. Viktor felt stunned that even his blood brother seemed to see nothing wrong with such reprehensible behavior.

When Canute finished with his female, he shoved her aside and grinned at Viktor. "Take her now, jarl."

"No, thank you," Viktor snapped back.

"Did you leave your prick with your memory in Valhalla, man?" roared Canute.

As several other drunken warriors guffawed, Rollo taunted, "Perhaps Loki cut off our jarl's manroot with his beard."

Viktor made no comment, glowering silently at his obnoxious, inebriated companions. He was thanking the gods that the appalling display of fornication had ceased when the young servant, Iva, ventured in with a small lamb.

Canute jumped up, his hand on his sword hilt. " 'Tis time for the sacrifice, jarl, and to drink our toast to Odin."

As an appalled Viktor lurched to his feet, the other warriors rose solemnly. Iva placed the pitifully bleating lamb into Canute's arms.

Watching Canute carry the lamb to the table, set it down, then unsheathe and raise his sword, Viktor felt the color drain from his face. "You are not going to kill that lamb!" he protested.

While Canute hesitated, scowling, Svein explained. "Jarl, we must make a sacrifice to Odin for returning you to our fold, else the All-Father will be displeased."

"You are not going to please Odin by slaughtering a helpless, innocent lamb," Viktor retorted. "Furthermore, I will not allow it."

As the other warriors glanced at one another in bemusement, Canute snorted his own contempt. "Our jarl has returned from the dead with the spirit of a woman."

At this blatant insult, the other warriors grew tense and hushed, and an enraged Svein hauled out his sword and pointed it toward Canute. "Insult our jarl again, son of Loki," he yelled, "and I will dispatch you to Hel."

With a disgusted curse, Canute sheathed his sword and grabbed the lamb. He swept around the table and shoved the bleating animal into Viktor's arms. " 'Tis true," he said with biting cynicism. "We are all well aware that King Viktor is valiant no more. Our jarl prefers the company of a lamb to the company of a woman."

Canute retreated to the laughter of all the other warriors—

save for a white-faced Svein and an openly anxious Ottar. Viktor realized that what little respect he had earned from his men was rapidly crumbling, yet he would not see a helpless animal butchered just to increase his own esteem with his warriors. Holding the lamb—which still quivered and bleated, as if it sensed its pending, terrible fate—he regarded the entire company sternly and unflinchingly. Maybe he could use the superstitions of these men to turn the tables, he mused.

"I learned much while I was in Valhalla," he told the others while petting the lamb to calm it. "I learned to respect all of God's creatures."

"What is this 'God'?" demanded a fiercely scowling Rollo. "Do not tell us our jarl has returned from Valhalla a Christian?"

The men shouted jeers.

Viktor did not waver. Once the taunts had subsided, he continued to speak slowly and vehemently. "Even Christians must be respected, as well as all things created by the All-Father. In Valhalla, I learned that Odin is no longer pleased with animal or human sacrifices."

The others grumbled among themselves and glanced around in uncertainty.

"Then what does Odin desire from us, jarl, if not a sacrifice?" Rollo asked.

"A poem," Viktor quickly improvised. "And a solemn toast to mark my return."

The warriors considered this in frowning silence; then Svein grabbed Quigley by his tunic and said gruffly, "Compose a poem, skald, or know the displeasure of your master."

The dark-eyed, bushy-browed little Irishman smiled nervously and came forward to stand near Viktor. He began spilling out several stanzas of verse as the warriors listened in reverent silence:

> *Our great King Viktor*
> *In glory slain,*
> *Plucked from the World Tree*
> *Defending his peoples,*
> *Along Bifrost is sent*
> *To dwell with the Valkyries*
> *To feast by Odin's side.*

And now the All-Father in his wisdom
Is pleased to grant
Life anew
To our courageous jarl.
We welcome King Viktor
Back from the halls of the dead
To lead his kinsmen to triumph anew
At Midgard's gates.

May all give thanks to Odin.

As the skald finished, the warriors lifted their oxhorns for the solemn toast, several of them calling out, "Hear, hear!" Shifting the lamb to one arm as he took a sip of mead, Viktor was beginning to feel as if the crisis had been averted when suddenly he saw Canute grab Iva and carry the slave to a bench. The thrall did not resist as Canute settled her on his lap, but her eyes were bright with terror as she turned her young, stricken face to silently beseech her master.

Pausing only to dump the lamb into the arms of the astonished skald, Viktor rushed over to confront Canute. "Release the female at once."

Canute, who was preparing to bury his face in the slave's bosom, scowled up at Viktor. His features were florid with drink, his voice ugly with belligerence. "What say you, jarl?"

"I say let the slave go."

Canute toyed with a copper brooch on Iva's shoulder and spoke with contempt. "Not until I take my ease with her."

"You have already satisfied your lust with a willing woman," Viktor argued. "Why force yourself on Iva? Can you not see that she is terrified?"

Canute only grinned. "Yea, she trembles like a fearful little sheep, but I will have her docile as a lamb in no time."

Behind them, several warriors laughed ribaldly, the lamb bleated, and Viktor's wolves growled as they, too, picked up on the tension. Still Canute held the wench captive.

"This is wrong," Viktor protested. "Iva is barely grown."

This time Rollo spoke up behind them. "You speak in error, jarl. The female is sixteen, well past the age when any

Viking woman may be taken as wife, and any slave as concubine."

Viktor turned to face down the others. "Then there will have to be some changes around here."

The men grumbled to themselves and eyed their jarl with resentment.

"Yea," mocked Canute from behind Viktor, "we can all use a new king, one with the courage of a lion and not the cowardice of a lamb."

This diatribe brought murmurs of alarm from the men. Svein rose, again wielding his sword, and yelled at Canute, "I warned you not to insult our jarl, son of Hel!"

New sounds of distress filtered through the ranks. But even as Svein rushed over to defend his jarl, Viktor held up a hand to stay him. "I will handle this, my blood brother." He turned back to Canute and spoke with barely repressed violence. "I said, let the wench go."

Canute snorted in disdain. "Is our jarl too much of a coward to watch me bed her?" He reached for the female's skirts.

Viktor's hands restrained Canute's before the latter could budge the hem of the slave's skirts even an inch. His eyes glittered with rage. "You will release her now, you pigheaded bastard!"

As the wolves again growled menacingly in the background, an enraged Canute shoved the girl aside. Iva threw Viktor a grateful glance and hurried off.

With an enraged roar, Canute staggered up to confront his jarl. "You would deny me the hospitality of your house?"

"I will deny you the right to rape a frightened sixteen-year-old."

From the table young Ottar spoke up. "King Viktor is right. If the female is not willing, she should not be forced."

Still furious, Canute yanked his sword from its scabbard and pointed it at Viktor, while the other warriors watched with mingled horror and fascination. His single eye glittered with fury as he sneered, "And I say I shall have her, or you will eat my broadsword, Viktor the Valiant."

The two men stood tensely confronting each other, Canute with his sword raised, Viktor with his hand on the hilt of his own weapon. Then, even as the drunken giant would have

charged, inspiration, however feeble and illogical, struck
Viktor.

"Tell me how you lost your eye," he said.

For a moment Canute merely stared at his jarl, appearing
both disarmed and confused. From behind them, the other
men began to laugh, rendering Canute more befuddled than
ever.

From the ranks Orm called out, "Yea, Canute—tell us the
tale."

" 'Tis the saga we all love best!" Rollo added.

As the excruciating seconds trickled by, several other warriors encouraged Canute with comments of their own.

Viktor glanced back at Canute and realized his request had
proved a brilliant diversion, for suddenly even the volatile giant threw back his head and laughed. A moment later, Canute
replaced his sword in its scabbard and faced his jarl with a
broad grin, as if the life-and-death confrontation of the previous seconds had never occurred.

"Why, I battled a polar bear on an ice floe that drifted
down from the North Country," he related proudly.

"Yea, Canute, tell us, pray!" yelled Ottar.

"The fearsome beast clawed out my eye before I slew her.
I recovered my eye and would have replaced it when we
glided ashore."

"Yea—now tell the best part!" shouted Orm.

"But Loki was about making his mischief, disguised as a
raven. He stoke my eye and flew off, hiding it in the well of
wisdom with the All-Father's eye."

As all the warriors cheered, Viktor clapped a hand on
Canute's shoulder. "A splendid tale, my friend."

Svein joined in with, "Yea, Canute has the heart of a
dragon."

"And the courage of Thor!" added Orm.

"Let us all toast to his bravery," said Viktor.

In the end, Canute's pride and arrogance were his undoing,
for he was pleased to gloat, strut about, and accept the acco-
lades of the other warriors as they saluted his feat. Once everyone was again settled down, swilling mead, Viktor heaved
a huge sigh of relief. Never underestimate the power of a

good story, he thought wryly, and filed that bit of wisdom away to use another day.

Afterward, a jovial climate prevailed as the men followed up on Canute's triumph with tall tales of their own. Several of the warriors related sagas of bravery in battle, embellishing the tales, as Canute had, with bits of mythology. When Viktor's turn came, he spun his own fantasy about his brief hours in Valhalla, telling of how he had kissed all the Valkyries and melted their warrior-woman hearts, and how he had outdone the mighty glutton Thor by single-handedly eating three whole oxen while at Odin's table, and how, while traveling back down the Rainbow Bridge, he had battled three trolls and an ogress with more than a hundred heads. His men listened with expressions of awe and reverence, occasionally making fascinated comments.

By the time the gathering was starting to break up in the wee hours, the warriors were glassy-eyed from many rounds of mead and smiling with fond memories of the storytelling. It was then that a distraught-looking Helga abruptly burst into the dining hall. Viktor noted that she appeared quite disheveled, her clothing rumpled and bits of straw protruding from her hair.

"Master!" she cried. "There is a spy in your midst!"

While the drunken warriors stared dumbly at Helga, Viktor managed to ask, "What do you mean, a spy?"

"Earlier this eve, as I journeyed toward the dairy, Reyna the Ravisher waylaid me, tied me up, then hid me in the stable. I only now managed to get free."

Several warriors gasped, "The Ravisher is here!" and looked around in horror.

Viktor surged to his feet. "Reyna is here? Where?"

Helga, too, glanced around in confusion. Then rage twisted her leathery features as she spotted the old crone. "There!" she cried, jabbing a forefinger toward the woman.

Viktor's men shook their befuddled heads and stared at the bent thrall. "But you can't mean—" Viktor protested.

He was never allowed to finish his sentence. Indeed, he observed what next happened with his mouth hanging open. The supposedly feeble old crone suddenly reared back to her full, menacing height and uttered a roar of rage. Like an ogress rising from Hel, she tossed back her hood to reveal the triumphant features and long blond hair of Reyna the Ravisher!

" 'Tis the Ravisher!" yelled one of the warriors.

"Slay her!" shouted another.

"Reyna!" cried Viktor.

Chaos erupted. At first, Viktor could only watch in amazement. All of his drunken warriors struggled up at once to pursue the intruder—but they succeeded mostly in staggering around and bumping into one another. Meanwhile, Reyna did not miss a beat. Observing the warriors advance, she yelled a blood-chilling battle cry and exploded, spinning out of the hall like a whirling dervish, fists flying and feet kicking. At least half a dozen warriors crashed to the floor in the wake of her savage blows. Several stumbled after her, only to grunt, groan, curse, and crash into one another again.

It was all over in a heartbeat—indeed, Viktor was shocked that Reyna did not leave behind a vapor trail while bursting out of the chamber. At last he sprang into action and chased after her, his wolves at his heels. He did not catch sight of her again until he was outside the longhouse. She was riding off on her pony, a lit torch in her hand.

"Reyna! Reyna, stop!" he yelled.

Near a haystack, she reined in her horse, grinned at him—then hurled the torch into the hay!

"No!" he screamed.

Viktor's plea came too late as Reyna galloped off, laughing exuberantly. He could have cheerfully throttled her—if he did not so admire her courage and ingenuity.

He heard Svein's distraught voice behind him. "Jarl! Jarl, the haystack is burning!"

"No shit," he muttered under his breath. "She's like a mischievous vixen loose in a chicken coop—and *we're* the chickens."

More confusion followed as the rest of the inebriated warriors staggered outside and tried to douse the flames, once again stumbling into one another. Tempers flared and curses spewed forth as everything and everyone seemed to get drenched, except the fire itself. Ultimately, the haystack was lost, but luckily, no other structures caught fire.

When the last ember died, when Viktor at last trudged into his chamber with his wolves, he found Iva sitting on a chair.

She rushed up to him. "Master, what has happened?"

He waved her off wearily. "Oh, only an unholy terror on the loose and a lost haystack. No big deal." He glowered. "From now on, no females will be admitted to the feast without a thorough background check. No exceptions."

Iva frowned in utter confusion.

Remembering Canute's earlier aggressive behavior toward the girl, Viktor flashed her a concerned smile. "Are you all right?"

She thrust herself into his arms. "Yea. Thank you for saving me, master."

Viktor gave the slave a fond hug before stepping back to gaze into her eyes. "You are certain you are unharmed?"

She nodded. "I was frightened, but you were so brave to battle Canute for me, even though our customs dictate that slaves have no such rights to be defended."

"Such unjust rules must be changed," said Viktor.

She regarded him wistfully. "I have decided that you are right, master. I am too young to be with a man."

He smiled. "Smart girl. In fact, after tonight, I have concluded that I may be too young to be with a woman."

She wrinkled her brow in new puzzlement.

He chuckled and tugged on one of her pigtails. "Never mind my ramblings. As for you, perhaps when you are older, I can help you make a good marriage." He scratched his jaw. "By the way, what do you think of young Ottar? You know, after you left the room, he rose to defend you."

"Did he?" Wide-eyed, Iva smiled. "I find him quite comely, jarl. But a slave cannot marry a freeman—and certainly not one of your kinsmen."

Viktor scowled. "Well, we shall see about that. You are not going to remain a slave for long."

"You would free me?" she asked in an awed whisper.

"In due course. But for now, let's keep this our secret. Agreed?"

She nodded happily.

"Now, get to bed."

She curtsied and left him.

Viktor crawled into bed among his wolves. What a night! To think that Reyna had actually infiltrated the feast, that she had been there all the time, brazenly spying on him! She seemed to be playing a teasing cat-and-mouse game with him.

Why did she continue to venture onto his side of the fjord? Had she come to learn how better to defeat him? Or was she truly as intrigued with him as he was with her?

He prayed the latter was true, since he definitely had a tiger by the tail with this woman. Following the episode tonight, he felt even more impatient to be with Reyna again, to catch her next time *before* she got away, to begin his life with the woman of his dream—although taming this fierce, ingenious Valkyrie would doubtless require even more effort than reforming his own people!

All in all, he definitely had his work cut out for him here on Vanaheim. These people lived in a society bound by barbaric traditions they considered perfectly normal. He was disturbed by their belligerent, feudal attitudes, and particularly by the way they treated their slaves—as property they could ravish, abuse, or destroy at will. Could he win the trust of these people and change their attitudes before real harm was done? He would have to, he vowed, or he would die trying. As long as he was jarl and had breath left in his body, he would not see a woman raped, a slave slaughtered, or an animal sacrificed.

As Reyna rode toward the fjord crossing, she found her triumphant smile fading to a look of sober contemplation. She had learned much about Viktor the Valiant tonight—mayhap more than she had wanted to know. She had discovered that he would not allow his men to abuse women or animals—most peculiar behavior for a supposedly ruthless Viking. She had watched him behave with kindness, wisdom, even fair-mindedness. And when she had ridden away, she had glimpsed him staring at her again with an unsettling combination of irritation, amazement, and admiration. He had called her name with an intensity that had tempted her to return to him.

Thus her knowledge gleaned tonight, far from helping her

defeat Viktor, only made him seem all the more mysterious and appealing. The frightening bond, the mystifying pull she felt from him, had grown even stronger. If she did not take greater care, she might soon be enticed to *like* her enemy!

Enough! she thought with a surge of righteous anger at herself. No matter how pretty, no matter how seemingly gentle, Viktor was a Viking, and no Viking could ever be trusted. It was high time to slay her enemy, before she became hopelessly entrapped in her own reckless, foolish game. And this time, by Loki, she would *not* let her weaker, feminine instincts get in her way.

TEN

Vɪᴋᴛᴏʀ ʜᴀᴅ ꜰɪɴᴀʟʟʏ ᴅʀɪꜰᴛᴇᴅ ᴏꜰꜰ ᴛᴏ ꜱʟᴇᴇᴘ ᴡʜᴇɴ ꜱᴛʀᴏɴɢ ꜰɪɴ-
gers gripped his arm and shook him. He jerked awake to see
Svein hovering over him, holding a lighted whale-oil lamp.
His kinsman's features were fraught with alarm.

Beside Viktor, the wolves sensed the tension, and Geri and
Thor growled. Viktor automatically petted the animals, murmured soothingly to them, and sat up.

"What is wrong?" he asked Svein.

" 'Tis Wolfgard!" Svein cried. "The sentries have spotted
our enemy and his company making their way down the fjord
in their dragon ship."

"Damnation, he really is a pest, isn't he?" Viktor muttered,
raking a hand through his disheveled hair. "What shall we
do?"

"If we hurry, jarl, there is still time to man our longship
and stay him in the fjord before he can land and attack."

Viktor scowled. "Is such a move preferable to mounting a
land assault? We could hide out along the cliffs and ambush
him and his company as they come ashore."

Svein scowled in obvious disapproval. "A Viking warrior
does not hide from his enemy like a woman, jarl."

Viktor groaned, again realizing that these men had little, if
any, knowledge of modern battle strategy. He had been cast
back to ancient times, when a man lived by brute strength
alone. Here, again, he might be able to effect some changes,
but for now, what mattered was protecting his people.

"Very well, Svein," he conceded, heaving himself to his feet. "We will sail out and prevent Wolfgard from landing. Rouse the other warriors."

"I have already set Ottar to the task."

"Good. Saddle our horses, and I will meet you at the stable."

Viktor hastily prepared for battle. He donned a jerkin, leggings, and boots, threw on his chain-mail tunic and iron helmet, grabbed his broadsword and shield, and rushed out into the frigid night.

Moments later, he and Svein were galloping their horses across the tundra toward the fjord, navigating through the windy night by moonlight. By the time they descended to the wharf, Viktor could already spot lighted torches on the longship and his men preparing to set sail. The dark ship appeared about eighty feet in length, and was magnificently curved from stern to bow; a delicate frieze, pattern-welded in gold, climbed its high prow, culminating in a figurehead of Tyr, god of the sword. Several smaller craft were moored nearby, from sailing vessels to sleek rowboats.

The two men dismounted, then hurried down the wharf and up the gangplank. They boarded, joining Canute and Rollo at midships.

"Are you prepared to defeat Wolfgard's forces, jarl?" asked Rollo.

Viktor nodded grimly. "We shall defend our own, and see to it that Wolfgard and his men do not set foot on our land."

"Jarl, are you truly prepared to lead us?" asked a clearly skeptical Canute. "This is no time for false pride, and I would be pleased to volunteer to serve in your stead until your skills improve."

Viktor and Svein exchanged a quick, meaningful glance; then Viktor shook his head firmly. "I shall lead." He cupped a hand around his mouth and called out, "All hands, prepare to set sail!"

The oarsmen took their places, and at Viktor's signal, the men dipped their oars into the icy, rushing water. The ship glided away from the dock with only a token groan of timbers. At midships, several stout warriors raised the heavy mast, snapped it into its housing, and then unfurled the glorious blue-and-white square sail. The mighty longship tacked into the wind and, with the help of the oarsmen, made its way slowly against the current, up the swiftly running fjord.

Viktor stood at midships overseeing the various activities and scanning the water ahead of them. In the darkness, with the wind howling and the deep forge flanked by high cliffs of black, craggy basalt, he felt almost as if they were sailing into hell.

"Do you see it, jarl?" asked a tense Svein at Viktor's side.

Wishing he had a pair of binoculars, Viktor squinted into the distance and spotted wan lights blinking to the north of them. "Wolfgard?"

"Yea."

"What do we do when he maneuvers closer?"

"Our custom is to shoot burning arrows to retard the advance of an enemy. But do not be surprised if Wolfgard grapples onto us and we are forced to fight at close quarters."

"Damn—you would think he enjoys such barbaric mayhem!"

Svein appeared astonished, raising an eyebrow at Viktor. "But he does, jarl."

Viktor ground his jaw, his sense of apprehension increasing as the two ships moved into close range. Sizing up the approaching vessel, he realized Wolfgard's *drakar,* or dragon ship, was much larger and heavier than his own longship; Wolfgard had the advantage of size and power, but Viktor would excel in maneuverability and speed.

At his order, a half-dozen archers moved to the bow. They lit arrows that had been dipped in tar, and began shooting the flaming missiles toward the approaching vessel. Soon Wolfgard's forces were returning the barrage, leaving Viktor and the others to dodge the razor-sharp slivers of fire, to pull arrows from the mast and bulwark to prevent the ship or sail from catching on fire.

Viktor grimly watched the *drakar* glide closer, on a collision course with his own longship. The decks of Wolfgard's vessel were filled with howling, arrow-shooting, spear-waving barbarians, while their leader stood near the mast, his arrogant visage held high, his silver hair whipping about his face, and his arms proudly crossed over his chest. Viktor searched the decks for Reyna. He did not spot her, although he realized she could be hidden behind the bulk of dozens of warriors.

Anticipating the imminent mêlée, he was left with a sick feeling in his stomach. He hated the thought of bloodshed, but knew he must protect his people.

The two vessels continued toward the inevitable impact, almost as if they were all playing a tenth-century game of chicken, Viktor mused. Finally, he was the first one to yield. At the last moment, he shouted an order to the helmsman to tack to the east. The vessel veered hard to starboard, compelling Viktor to grab the mast to keep from being hurled to the deck. Although a head-on collision was avoided, seconds later, the two vessels crashed alongside each other with a mighty bang and a screech of scraping timbers.

Clinging to the mast on the tilting deck, Viktor heard the battle yells, watched the wicked tentacles of grappling irons sail through the air to lock his vessel with Wolfgard's—and then the battle began. Dozens of Wolfgard's shrieking warriors swarmed onto his ship, hurling spears, shooting arrows, and chopping powerfully with axes and swords.

Quickly recovering his equilibrium, Viktor unsheathed his weapon, lifted his shield, and began to fight alongside his men. At once he encountered a huge, bearded warrior with a frightful ax. The man roared a battle cry and chopped at Viktor's shield. Viktor managed to block the blow, and was amazed that the shield did not buckle beneath the heavy, sharp ax. He retaliated with his broadsword, striking his opponent's ax and shield, although not managing to wrench either implement from the warrior's hands.

The giant heaved a cry of anger, raised his ax, and charged Viktor again. Shielding another blow, Viktor heard his men fighting in close quarters around him—the crashing and striking, the screams of pain and bellows of rage. Even in the coldness, the metallic, sickening smell of blood was already heavy in the air.

Viktor managed to sidestep his opponent as the warrior again lunged with his ax. Narrowly escaping the lethal blade, Viktor knocked the man hard across the shoulders with his shield and sent the attacker, groaning, to the deck.

Viktor had no chance to catch his breath. A new warrior

lunged in front of him, dancing about like a lunatic, crying out like a demented animal, and swinging his broadsword crazily. The man's eyes were rolling wildly in his gyrating head. With alarm, Viktor realized he must be confronting one of the dreaded berserkers, madmen who went into homicidal rampages during battle. He managed to dodge or parry the ferocious blows, even though his opponent's frenzy, feral eyes, and deranged screams were horrible to behold. At last, with a mighty heave, Viktor knocked the broadsword from the berserker's hand. When the man bayed his animal yell, then fled back toward Wolfgard's ship, Viktor wisely chose not to pursue him.

Catching his breath and looking around him, he spotted Wolfgard in the distance, clashing with Rollo. Watching Wolfgard strike the side of Rollo's head with his broadsword and Rollo stagger, Viktor started to go to the warrior's aid. But before he could proceed three steps, Reyna, the Valkyrie woman, abruptly leaped into his path with her broadsword raised.

Her smile was cruel, her body taut and ready for the charge. "We meet again, Viking," she sneered. "And so soon."

Viktor had no time to respond as she prepared to lunge with her broadsword. For a moment he couldn't decide what to do. It went against all his principles to hurt a woman—assuming he could even gain the upper hand over this demon from hell. He was left with the sole choice of defending himself as best he could without hurting her.

At her powerful thrust toward his midsection, he blocked with his shield. His successful foil only enraged the Valkyrie, and she struck and banged at him with greater wrath. During the tense seconds that followed, Viktor shielded himself again and again from Reyna's savage blows. But as much as she provoked him, he would not raise his sword against her.

The Valkyrie soon caught on to Viktor's unusual strategy and became more maddened than ever. "Fight, son of Nidhogg!" she screamed, advancing, magnificent in her fury, striking and charging at him with murderous resolve and staggering strength. Still Viktor refused to do more than obstruct her vicious blows.

Even as Viktor was weakening beneath her relentless assault, Wolfgard bellowed out the call to retreat. In a rush, the enemy warriors began to flee for their own vessel, ungrappling as they clambered over the linked railings of the ships.

At Wolfgard's command, the Valkyrie paused to stare at Viktor with an odd intensity—as if she were contemplating how best to slay him. Then, before he could react, she brought the blunt side of her sword crashing down on top of his head. Tottering from the blow, Viktor realized that she was toying with him—telling him in no uncertain terms that she could kill him anytime she chose.

"Farewell for now, Viking!" she shouted with ill temper, and turned to flee with the others.

At first, still reeling dizzily, Viktor could only watch her. Then anger mobilized him. He chased after her, caught up with her just as she was trying to clamber over the railing, and managed to grab a shapely ankle. Even as she yelled and kicked, struggling to shake free of his grip, the warmth, the softness, of her bare skin excited him. She soon managed to extricate herself, but not before Viktor had pulled off her ankle a copper bracelet fashioned in the image of two coiled, spitting serpents.

Wolfgard and his company cut the remaining lines and drifted away up the fjord. At the railing, Viktor watched them in silent fury and slipped the Valkyrie's bracelet onto his wrist. Then he spotted her on the deck of the other vessel. She was standing there proud as Loki's daughter, staring at him with contempt. Outrage prompted him to respond with equal disdain. He grinned, held up the wrist sporting her ankle circlet, and blew her a kiss. For Viktor, watching the ire flare on the Valkyrie's face when she saw the stolen bracelet was worth all the hell he had just endured. Satisfaction filled him at the thought that another of Wolfgard's harass-and-retreat raids had been repelled.

But his sense of victory was short-lived as Svein called out behind him, "Jarl! Come quickly!"

Viktor rushed to midships to find his men gathered around two fallen, blood-covered warriors who lay ominously still on the deck. Viktor glanced with alarm at Svein.

"Jarl, Sigurd and Magnus are dead," he confirmed grimly.

"Dammit!" Viktor exploded. He glanced from the corpses to his other warriors, most of whom appeared bruised or wounded. "Is anyone else badly hurt?"

"Nay, jarl," Svein answered. "The rest of us were battered, but will recover—"

"That will be scant comfort for the families of Sigurd and Magnus," Viktor cut in. "What a terrible waste. What in Hel started this feud anyway?"

The men glanced at one another in uncertainty.

Then Canute mused aloud, "Was it not the result of the dispute five summers past, when Wolfgard stole the beached whale that washed up on our side of the fjord?"

"Methinks the feud began after Wolfgard's warriors kidnapped three of our female thralls," said Orm.

"Nay, you both speak falsely," interjected Rollo, rubbing his battered head. "The feud ensued after Wolfgard's warriors desecrated our graveyard and broke several memorial stones."

"Nay, nay, you are all in error," contradicted Ottar. "My father informed me the feud started out at sea, when Wolfgard and his men slipped up beside our longship, then cut loose our nets and stole our fish."

"Well, which version is true?" demanded an exasperated Viktor.

Following another awkward silence, in which the warriors glanced at one another in obvious puzzlement, Svein answered sheepishly, "Jarl, no one can remember."

Viktor was incredulous, his hand slicing through the air as he spoke with barely repressed fury. "You mean to tell me you have been fighting Wolfgard's tribe for five years, yet you can't even remember what started this war?" He gestured toward the corpses. "These men are dead, and you do not even know why? What kind of fools are you, to sacrifice husbands and fathers over an insult no one can recall?"

At Viktor's diatribe, the warriors grew shamefaced and sullen. They went off to nurse their wounds or attend to duties on deck. Svein remained by his jarl's side.

Viktor's blood brother nodded toward the corpses. "Jarl, we must have a proper funeral for Sigurd and Magnus at the wharf."

Viktor was bemused. "You are suggesting we launch them

to Valhalla in a burning boat along the fjord, instead of in a flaming pit?"

"According to the custom of our tribe, a burial on water is the only fitting tribute for a warrior slain in battle," Svein explained. " 'Twas how we sent you to the afterlife, as you will recall."

"Right," Viktor muttered, too preoccupied to appreciate this bizarre custom that so closely paralleled the one in the movie he'd starred in. "Very well, then. We'll launch them on the fjord."

Farther up the fjord in Wolfgard's *drakar*, Reyna stood trembling near the bow, staring grimly at the cliffs ahead, furious with herself. Behind her, Wolfgard and his warriors were cheering one another over the purported victory against Viktor, but Reyna hardly felt in a celebratory mood. She had just been afforded the perfect opportunity to slay her enemy . . . yet at the last moment, she had gone soft and again spared his life!

Equally strange, even as she had attacked Viktor with her broadsword, he had refused to strike back. Was it his seeming inability to hurt her that had compelled her to spare him? What was this bewildering power he held over her?

And what was even more unnerving was that when she had fled, Viktor had touched her for the first time, grabbing her ankle and seizing her circlet . . . His thievery had left Reyna enraged, but also deeply jarred and daunted, as if Viktor had stolen her independence and now claimed that inner essence of her for himself. And that was not all that had been plundered, for his warm touch had seared her flesh, causing heat to streak up between her thighs and penetrate that secret, virginal part of her.

The memory all but blinded her with rage and confusion. Was the Viking a god or a demon, her savior or her tormentor? Whatever Viktor the Valiant was, he threatened her on every level. She was involved in a struggle not just for her life, but for her very soul . . .

Following the funeral rite of Sigurd and Magnus, Viktor stood on the wharf with Svein, both men silently watching the blazing funeral boat drift down the fjord, tacking southward toward the cold Atlantic.

Viktor reflected on the purposelessness of the two men's deaths, and struggled against his feelings of anger and frustration. Something had to be done, he mused; this insane war could not continue. If he didn't act soon, women and children were bound to die, as well as warriors.

Adamantly, he muttered to Svein, "This feud must end."

"What course of action do you propose, jarl?" asked a skeptical Svein.

Viktor's expression was resolute and unyielding. "I shall go to Wolfgard's village and reason with him, man to man, to end the conflict."

Svein appeared horrified. "Jarl, you *have* lost your mind! Such a move will mean certain death for you! You will be slaughtered if you venture so foolishly among Wolfgard's clan."

"Do not try to dissuade me," Viktor snapped. "My mind is made up."

ELEVEN

"JARL, THIS IS MADNESS! YOU MUST NOT GO TO WOLFGARD'S village alone!" Svein declared.

"It is the only way," Viktor replied.

That afternoon, after all the warriors had been refreshed by a much-needed nap, Svein was still arguing with Viktor as the two men, followed by half a dozen warriors, strode down the wharf toward the longship on which they had battled Wolfgard during the night.

"Jarl, Wolfgard has no conscience," Svein asserted. "The man is ruthless, without honor. He is a renegade and an outlaw. Last summer, he refused to attend the Thing—"

"Not the 'Thing' again?" Viktor inquired with a scowl.

" 'Tis an assembly of all Vanaheim held each summer, in the tradition of the Icelandic Althing. There, misdeeds are aired and grievances settled. During the gathering at Haymaking Month, Wolfgard and his clan refused to appear to hear your charges of continued, unwarranted attacks on our people. The council declared Wolfgard a fuller outlaw—not that it has made any difference. His people shelter him, and he goes on raiding, terrorizing, and killing our people at will."

Sternly, Viktor rejoined, "Whether the man is an outlaw or not, you know what they say . . . 'If Mohammed won't go to the mountain . . .' "

"Who has so said?" inquired a perplexed Svein.

"Never mind."

The party ascended the gangplank to the ship. Svein and

100

Viktor fell grimly silent as the oarsmen maneuvered the long-ship out into the fjord, while two warriors hoisted the large sail.

Standing at the railing, watching seals frolic in the turbulent waters ahead, Viktor fingered the copper bracelet that he still wore on his wrist—the trinket he had wrenched from Reyna the Ravisher's ankle last night. What a study in contrasts this woman was—part gentle female, part brutal savage. Remembering how he had covertly observed her just yesterday on the moors, playing with her fox and later praying with the monk, he wondered how any woman who considered herself a Christian, who loved animals as she did, could slaughter other human beings without hesitation or remorse.

Yet Reyna the Ravisher seemed the least of his worries as he considered the coming confrontation with his enemy. Would he survive the afternoon or be slaughtered by Wolfgard's warriors the minute he arrived in the enemy camp? Perhaps he *was* being reckless and foolhardy, but after the senseless deaths of Sigurd and Magnus, he was also at his wit's end, and desperate measures seemed called for.

Svein joined Viktor at the rail. He pointed to the opposite shoreline, where a crude wharf was met by a path that carved between low cliffs of black basalt. "That is the path to Wolfgard's village. You must follow it for about one hundred ells."

Viktor frowned. "What is an ell?"

Svein held his hands wide.

"Ah, a yard."

Svein scowled in equal perplexity, but made no direct comment. "Remember, jarl, that we shall await you on the opposite bank. Signal to us when you are ready to leave—or if you need help."

From the meaningful lift of Svein's brow, Viktor judged that his blood brother considered the latter possibility far more likely. He removed the wide leather belt holding his sword and scabbard and handed the entire apparatus to Svein.

"Guard this for me until I return."

Svein's mouth fell open. "You are braving the lion's den unarmed?"

"Should I try to lift my sword against dozens of armed

fighters?" Viktor stared grimly at the narrow path that might well take him straight to Hel. "Arriving in Wolfgard's village minus my sword may well be my only defense."

Svein's gaze beseeched the heavens. "May Odin help us all, and may Loki keep his distance today."

"Amen," Viktor concurred with a wry grin.

The helmsman maneuvered the ship up to Wolfgard's wharf. Although several small craft were moored there, Viktor noted that Wolfgard's *drakar* was missing, and he figured some of the village men might have taken the ship out to fish on the ocean.

Viktor disembarked and waved to his crew, watching them push off into the deep, rushing river to await him on the opposite bank. He eyed the steep path with a feeling of impending doom. For a moment he considered turning back, then vetoed the impulse. He was a man of reason, not violence; surely if he gathered all his wits and courage, logic could somehow prevail today.

Viktor started up the crude trail, and was surprised when he met with no resistance—no posted sentries, and only a circling red-tailed hawk in the clear skies above to note his passage. He wondered why Wolfgard's security was so lax. Perhaps his enemy had been the aggressor for so many years that he had grown complacent and careless, no longer expecting an assault from the rival tribe. And since most Viking raids occurred under cover of darkness, perhaps Wolfgard did not think daytime sentries were needed. Viktor mused that he could easily have led a sneak attack today—but such was not his way. During such an invasion, he knew he would be unable to stop his men from succumbing to their Viking instincts and brutally slaughtering the other tribe. This in all conscience he could never allow.

As he crested a rise marked by two stunted birches, he at last spotted the village sprawled in a stark valley below him. A ramshackle collection of shacks surrounded a larger longhouse he assumed was Wolfgard's abode. Even at this distance, Viktor saw the foul haze from the Vikings' fires and smelled the acrid smoke rising from so many roof vents.

He took a deep breath and began descending the trail. As he approached the outskirts of the hamlet, he was still not ac-

costed, though he did attract curious glances from several
thralls who were out tilling the fields with oxen-drawn plows.
Soon he proceeded down the filthy main street, sidestepping
slops and garbage, wending his way past scurrying chickens,
pigs, and dogs and scampering, dirt-smeared children. Along
with the ever-present smoke, the odors of rotting food and
human excrement assailed his nostrils. He caught the wary
looks of several women who sat in their open doorways, obviously having escaped the smoky interiors to sew, grind
corn, or nurse babies in the afternoon air.

Toward the center of town, not far from the longhouse that
he assumed belonged to his enemy, Viktor at last attracted
real notice. Three men leading horses spotted him striding
past the central well. Viktor knew his game was up when he
saw expressions of angry recognition spread across their
bearded, ugly faces.

He summoned all his bravery in facing his enemies. "Good
day, men. I would speak with your jarl."

He might as well have been trying to reason with Loki.
Within a split second, the three charged him, roaring with
rage.

"Seize him! 'Tis Viktor the Valiant!" cried one.

"We are under attack!" shouted the second.

"Kill the evil hound of Hel!" bellowed the third.

As the men moved in to grab him, Viktor knew better than
to resist. Although at first his attackers seemed puzzled by his
lack of aggression, his stoicism in no way diminished the
fury they unleashed on his person. Two of the men restrained
him while the third slammed Viktor's jaw with doubled-up
fists. The burst of agony was so intense that Viktor would
have collapsed had the others not held him. Soon four other
savages converged on the square to join in the mêlée, punch-
ing Viktor viciously. He found himself being battered from all
sides as the warriors shouted angry deprecations.

"Cursed whoreson! How dare you sully our village!"

"We shall roast you in your own juices, evil son of Loki!"

"Die, prophet of Hel!"

The brutal pounding continued, and Viktor could do nothing to stave off the stunning blows. Pain exploded on his
face, in his head, on his back, on his chest and arms—

everywhere. He realized—too late—the foolhardiness of his expedition, and wondered how long he would live beneath the savage beating. Reality was swimming in and out when he was surprised to hear the sound of a familiar, emphatic feminine voice.

"Halt, my stepfather's warriors!"

The hammering continued.

"I say halt, sons of Nidhogg!"

At last, grudgingly, the warriors backed off, save for the two who still restrained Viktor. Viktor blinked away the blood trickling into his eyes and spotted Reyna standing beyond him wearing an expression of haughty triumph. Next to her stood the white-haired, bearded giant Viktor recognized as Wolfgard.

"Why do you bid us halt, Reyna?" one of the men demanded belligerently.

Sneering at Viktor, she advanced a step. "Mayhap it amuses me to kill this mongrel myself. Surely such a filthy dog is not worthy enough to sully a great warrior's blade, Egil."

The one named Egil grinned, his ego obviously soothed by Reyna's apt remark. He nodded to the others. "Yea, we are content to allow a woman to kill this craven."

The men howled with laughter. One of the warriors restraining Viktor held up his captive's wrist. "Look, the evil coward wears your bracelet. Shall we remove it for you?"

"Yea, by slicing off the whoreson's hand!" added another.

Amid roars of bloodlust, Reyna shook her head and smiled contemptuously at Viktor. "Nay, do not trouble yourselves. The ornament of a woman suits this mongrel well, methinks. And verily, I do not wish the trinket returned after his vile skin has sullied it."

The warriors succumbed to new torrents of mirth.

"Kill him now, Reyna!" one urged.

"Yea—make it slow and painful, and let the entire village watch!" heckled another.

"Show us your contempt for him!"

"My contempt?" Reyna repeated with a vicious smile. "Yea, I shall demonstrate that now."

The others watched avidly as Reyna stalked toward Viktor.

He ground his aching jaw and regarded her with smoldering fury, but the little vixen was undaunted. Taking in her purposeful stride and scornful visage, he wondered how many seconds it would take her to kill him. But instead of drawing out her dagger and slitting his throat as he would have expected, she paused before him, looked him over insultingly, then spit full in his face.

The other warriors bellowed laughter, while Viktor trembled in anger and affronted dignity and glared at the sadistic shrew. He might not be a violent man, but the triumphant smirk on Reyna's face filled him with black rage. How could he ever have thought of this hellion with affection? How could he have felt the slightest affinity with her? For the first time, he found himself feeling just as a Viking warrior must feel when his honor was besmirched. He vowed that this devil's daughter would live to regret her contempt.

Meanwhile, Reyna was strutting around the circle of men and gloating over her victory.

"Kill him now, Reyna!" a voice yelled.

"Yea, cut out the bastard's intestines and burn them before his evil eyes!" taunted another.

Reyna turned to address the man. "That I choose not to do, for this cur is beneath killing. Mayhap we should make him a thrall and yoke him as we do our oxen to plow the field."

This suggestion was met with loud hurrahs and comments of approval until a deep, commanding voice yelled, "Silence!"

As Wolfgard came forward through the ranks, the entire group, including Reyna, fell ominously quiet. Wolfgard's pitiless gray eyes fixed on Viktor. "Bring the prisoner to my longhouse," he ordered gruffly. "I shall speak with this dimwit. His bravery intrigues me." He paused to smile cruelly. "Or mayhap 'tis his stupidity."

"Enemy, I present my stepdaughter, Reyna, and my son, Ragar. I would have you meet my clan before you meet your death."

In Wolfgard's longhouse, Viktor managed to nod to the sensitive-looking young man named Ragar, who sat to his right. To Reyna, across the room, he murmured cynically, "I do believe I have already had the pleasure."

Wolfgard laughed, and Reyna sniffed with contempt.

Sipping the ale his host had just given him, Viktor took a moment to thank the gods he had survived the past few moments. The small group had gathered somewhere near the center of the jarl's crude dwelling. This home lacked the accoutrements of Viktor's abode; Viktor, Wolfgard, Reyna, and Ragar all sat on a barren floor of packed dirt, their bodies encircling a central fire pit dug directly into the earth. Thick smoke scorched Viktor's eyes. In the background near the door loomed two fierce warriors who stood guard, their fingers resting on the hilts of their broadswords.

Reyna seemed disinterested in the proceedings as she sat with long legs crossed and sipped her ale. By contrast, Ragar, who had just nodded to Viktor with surprising courtesy, sat waiting for his father to speak, an expression of respect sculpting his finely sculpted features.

Viktor could see a familial resemblance between Ragar and Reyna in their strong chins, high cheekbones, brown eyes, and blond hair—although Reyna's mane was long and straight, while Ragar's locks were short and curly. Recalling Reyna's cruel behavior outside, when she had spit in his face, Viktor wondered how Wolfgard could have ended up with two such different offspring. But then, if memory served him, the two siblings shared only the same mother; Reyna was not Wolfgard's blood kin—and Odin only knew from where she got her savage, sadistic streak.

As for Wolfgard himself ... Viktor carefully studied his adversary. Wolfgard was a massive man who appeared to be in his late forties. Nevertheless, he was hard-muscled and tanned; even in the cool weather, he was dressed Spartan-style, in a sleeveless leather jerkin and tight brown leggings. He wore a gold ring carved with the face of a snarling wolf, a bracelet of ivory, and a necklace of crude, rectangular amber beads strewn with bronze-and-gold charms depicting the Norse gods and Thor's hammer.

Wolfgard's face was craggy and battle-scarred; the blunt nose jutted at a crooked slant, and Viktor suspected it had been broken more than once. Staring into the man's remorseless eyes, Viktor fully realized that he was alive now only because his presence amused his enemy; when he no longer proved diverting, he would likely be summarily executed.

As Viktor had expected, his host spoke directly to the issue. "What brings you to my village, Viktor the Valiant? Are you a hero—or merely a fool?"

Viktor replied firmly, "I come to seek the peace with you."

The room erupted into raucous laughter—only Ragar did not join in.

"You come on a fool's mission, then," Wolfgard scoffed. "I had heard you lost your memory when you returned from Valhalla. Now it seems you have misplaced your wits as well."

With the guards guffawing in the background, Viktor said stoutly, "I disagree. Seeking an end to the hostilities through reason, rather than brute force, is the height of intelligence, in my opinion."

Wolfgard waved him off with a sneer. "Do not seek to trick me with your claims of logic. This feud is too long-standing to end at your whim, Viktor the Valiant. There are blood bounties involved."

"Can you tell me what started the dispute in the first place?" Viktor asked.

Wolfgard pondered the question with a grimace.

One of the guards called out, "Jarl, did not the feud begin when Viktor's men stole the polar bear pelts we had stored away to sell at Hedeby?"

"Nay, nay," argued the other guard. "The feud started when Viktor's men set afire one of our hafships."

"I think you are both wrong," remarked Ragar. "I remember my kinsman telling me the conflict ensued when King Viktor refused permission for a woman of his clan to marry one of my father's warriors."

"Well, which is it?" Viktor asked Wolfgard.

He shrugged. "It seems no one can recollect."

Viktor flung his hands wide. "So we are all to fight a life-and-death struggle over a slight no one can remember?"

"It means naught how the feud started," Wolfgard snapped. "For 'tis a matter of honor now. By Odin, the only way for peace to come to Vanaheim is for you and all of your clan to leave."

"But why must it be this way?" Viktor reasoned. "My tribe settled this island first, did they not?"

Wolfgard snorted in contempt. "Yea, but you sought to expel my clan soon after we arrived. Clearly, there is not room for both our peoples on this island."

Viktor shook his head in mystification. "I can't believe I'm hearing this. You talk as if you stepped right out of some bad B Western. Are you saying that one of us must get out of Dodge by sundown?"

"What is this 'Dodge'?" Wolfgard asked in puzzlement.

Before Viktor could attempt a reply, Ragar intervened. "Father, perhaps our guest has spoken with some prudence. Would it not be wise to end the slaughter? Can our peoples not find some way to live together in harmony?"

"Bah!" Wolfgard glowered fiercely at the boy. "You have the soul of a woman, my son. I should have abandoned you at your birth, you were so feeble. But I listened to your mother's pathetic wails, and I took pity on you, because I had waited so long for an issue of my loins. Do not disgrace me again by speaking up in cowardice to our enemy!"

Ragar, appearing much chastened, lowered his gaze. "Yea, Father."

Viktor glanced at Reyna, who in turn was glaring at Wolfgard. He noted that her fingers were clutched tightly on the hilt of the dagger at her waist, and her brown eyes burned with anger. Had Wolfgard's diatribe to Ragar roused her wrath? Did she feel protective of her half brother?

Wolfgard turned his attention back to Viktor and chuckled. "Ah, children—what a bother they are. This one"—he paused to jerk his head toward Reyna—"has the heart of a lioness, but no respect for her jarl. This one"—he nodded toward Ragar—"is weak and puny, just like his mother."

All at once Reyna, who had been so explosively silent, bolted up with dagger drawn and faced her stepfather in a rage. "Slight my brother or my mother again, old man, and I will gut you like a fish and string your entrails from the mast of your dragon ship!"

Wolfgard's visage clenched with fury at this affront. "Sit down, stepdaughter, and save your spite for our enemy, or I shall cut out your vile tongue!"

With obvious reluctance, Reyna complied, while still staring murder at him.

Shaking his head, Wolfgard spoke to Viktor. "As I said, no respect for her jarl, that one. I would have slit her throat long ago, but there is no honor in killing a woman. Moreover, she does fight well for her jarl." Wolfgard winked at his guest. "Mayhap she will dispatch you for me soon, Viktor the Valiant."

Viktor wisely offered no reply. "You still haven't explained why we cannot settle this feud peaceably. I know there are remedies in our society—such as the Thing that meets in Haymaking month. Can we not air our grievances? If you persist in feeling slighted by our clan, perhaps some recompense can be arranged for you—"

But Wolfgard only laughed. "You misunderstand me, enemy. I want no blood money."

"Why not?"

Wolfgard's gray eyes glittered with vengeful pleasure. "Mayhap because I savor this feud too much to give it up."

For a moment Viktor was too frustrated to reply. Damn these Vikings and their bellicose ways! He knew there were warriors among his own tribe—particularly Canute, Rollo, and Orm—who would wholeheartedly endorse Wolfgard's bloodthirsty attitudes.

"Do you not agree, Viking?" Wolfgard pursued with a shrewd twinkle in his eyes.

"Speak for yourself," came Viktor's terse reply. "I prefer us to live in accord, without violence."

"Tell me, Viktor the Valiant, have you come here today for any purpose other than to babble about peace like a woman?"

"As I have already informed you, I consider ending the feud to be our most pressing and critical issue here on Vanaheim."

"Bah!" jeered Wolfgard.

One of the guards again spoke up. "Jarl, how say you we dispose of this loathsome dog? You have been patient with his ravings long enough. Verily, the men are eager to draw and quarter him."

While Viktor struggled not to show fear at the harrowing suggestion, Wolfgard eyed his captive cannily. "Yea, mayhap we should now put down our enemy. 'Tis true his ramblings no longer amuse me—and his screams might prove diverting."

The guards started forward wearing sadistic grins, and Viktor feared he would be rendered dogmeat at any second. Then, mercifully, Ragar spoke up.

"But, my father, if you kill the jarl of your enemies, who will lead his forces against you?" he asked with inspired logic.

Wolfgard hesitated, scratching his bearded jaw and frowning. Viktor tossed Ragar a grateful look, and felt heartened when the boy smiled back.

In the nick of time, Wolfgard held up a hand to halt the advancing guards. He nodded to Ragar. "Yea, my son, for once you have uttered a grain of truth." He shifted his scowling visage to Viktor. "We will release you unmolested this time, Viktor the Valiant, because your stunt amuses us—as does the possibility of continuing our feud. But do not attempt such a foolish feat as to venture among us again."

"Believe me, you have my word," Viktor agreed dryly as he rubbed a bruised arm.

Wolfgard chuckled. "Now we will toast to my beneficence, and to your good fortune. Then you may be on your way, Viktor the Valiant, to fight me another day." Cupping a hand at his mouth, he yelled, "Sibeal, bring ale!"

"Another round is not—" Viktor began.

" 'Tis required and traditional," Wolfgard cut in brusquely. He pounded a fist in anger. "Sibeal! By the mischief of Loki, where is that lazy Irish thrall?"

Ragar offered, "Father, I would be honored to—"

"Do not insult me by volunteering to do woman's work," Wolfgard said furiously, glaring at his son. He jerked his head toward Reyna. "Stepdaughter, go fetch us more ale."

Reyna stared haughtily at her stepfather and did not budge.

Wolfgard's face darkened to a menacing red as Reyna continued to defy him. "Do it, or I will see you beaten dead!"

Still she did not obey, though her fingers again moved to the hilt of her dagger as her rebellious gaze never left her stepfather's.

In an explosion of rage, Wolfgard surged to his feet, wav-

ing a fist and sputtering, "Daughter of Hel! I will strangle the
breath of life from you with my bare hands!"

Reyna came to her feet with a sadistic smile that sent a
chill along Viktor's spine. The two faced each other down in
a murderous silence, Wolfgard's hand moving to the hilt of
his sword, Reyna's fingers still gripping the haft of her dagger.

The charged moment ended as a tall, attractive woman
with long, graying black hair swept in bearing a keg of ale.
She addressed Wolfgard half frantically. "Master! I have
brought your refreshment. Forgive me, for these old bones
move slowly. But, yea, I am pleased to serve you now, master."

For a moment the enraged giant stood his ground. Then,
still glowering at Reyna, Wolfgard resumed his seat. After a
moment, Reyna sat down, though her contemptuous gaze remained riveted on Wolfgard. The tension in the room eased
somewhat as the slave refilled the oxhorns of her master,
Viktor, and Ragar. Although his frown remained formidable,
Wolfgard did appear calmer after several gulps of ale.

Hoping to soften up his host further, Viktor inclined his
head toward Reyna. "She is a spoiled little brat, isn't she?
Even though you are my enemy, I must say my sympathies
are with you, man."

Wolfgard snorted. "The man who could tame her—now,
that man I would listen to."

Hearing Wolfgard's words, Viktor felt as if a light bulb had
just clicked on inside his head. He stared intently at Reyna,
and she gazed back at him with icy disdain. The girl was behaving like a haughty little bitch, and suddenly Viktor was
itching to put her in her place—and warm her up a bit!

He turned decisively to his host. "Give her to me," he suggested rashly. "I will tame her, if you will stop the feud."

At Viktor's reckless suggestion, Wolfgard threw back his
head and laughed, as did the sentries at the door, while Reyna
appeared only amused by Viktor's proposal.

"You will tame her?" Wolfgard mocked. "You would be as
helpless as Freya when pitted against Loki's evil."

"Then what do you have to lose by giving me the chance?"

Viktor reasoned. "You know the girl is a thorn in your side—"

"Yea," Wolfgard cut in with a nasty grin, "and 'twould be tempting to make her a thorn in *your* side for a time, enemy."

"Then why won't you let me have her?" Viktor demanded.

Wolfgard regarded his belligerent stepdaughter, his lips twisting into a sneer. "Because I will not ease the way for you, Viktor the Valiant. Nor will I simply give my stepdaughter to you, however defiant the vixen may be." He paused, a look of shrewd calculation creeping into his gray eyes. "But mayhap I am amenable to a bargain of sorts."

"Yes?" Viktor said eagerly.

Wolfgard's canny gaze narrowed on Reyna. "If you want this Valkyrie from Hel, come take her. Tame her, and make her give you a son. On that day I will end the feud."

Viktor stared at the still-emotionless Reyna. How cool she was to betray no fear, to appear not the least bit threatened as two powerful men negotiated over her fate. Doubtless she felt certain she could defeat either of them with ease—indeed, Viktor was afraid Reyna's confidence might be entirely warranted.

"Do we have a pact, then, Viking?" Wolfgard asked.

"Yea," Viktor answered, his gaze locking on the obstreperous Valkyrie. "I will make Reyna my bride."

"What say you?" asked Wolfgard with an astonished scowl.

"I said I'll wed the little witch," Viktor snapped back.

A triumphant grin spread across Wolfgard's ugly face. "Ah, now you have made the stakes even more interesting, enemy. You will wed my stepdaughter, and the sea will boil up ere next spring, will it not?" He rocked with laughter. "Let us toast to your folly, then."

Viktor and Wolfgard made a toast on their agreement; then Wolfgard, mellowing over his ale, chuckled and confided, "You have a hard task before you, Viktor the Valiant. I must warn you that Reyna is a woman already once divorced."

Viktor smiled nastily at her. "So I am getting a soiled dove?" Saying the words, he thought he detected a spark of anger flaring in Reyna's eyes—and he felt most pleased.

"When she was fifteen summers old," Wolfgard explained,

"I wed her to my fiercest warrior, Thorstein the Terrible. That night, when Thorstein tried to claim his husbandly rights, this Valkyrie all but castrated the poor fellow. The next morning, she strutted about the village in his pants—thus effecting their divorce."

"Nice girl," Viktor murmured. "I take it Thorstein is terrible no longer?"

Wolfgard nodded morosely. "Now he is a beaten and humbled man, good only to weave baskets or churn butter with the women."

At this, Viktor spotted a gleam of vindictive triumph in Reyna's eyes. Oh, the little termagant! The Valkyrie had played a cat-and-mouse game with him long enough, he decided. Now *this* cat was ready to pounce! Still holding her gaze, he vowed silently, *It will be different with us, Reyna. You will rebel, but I will tame you—with a gentle hand, I hope, but with a firm one if necessary. Fight me if you will, but you will be mine and I will win your love. For we are meant to be together, you and I.*

As expected, Reyna showed no fear, no response at all, to Viktor's silent message.

Wolfgard gestured impatiently. "Now be gone and return to your village, Viktor the Valiant, before I—or my men—choose to be much less generous with your fate."

Viktor thanked Wolfgard for his hospitality and quickly took his leave. Under escort by the sentries, he left the enemy camp convinced that he had found a way to end the feud—and to bring the woman of his destiny into his life . . .

Back at the longhouse, Wolfgard lingered by the fire, rubbing his hands together in glee. Oh, he was such a clever man, and Viktor the Valiant was so stupid. The man had just made a fool's bargain. For Wolfgard was well aware that no mortal man could ever tame his Valkyrie stepdaughter. Indeed, the task was beyond even himself. But in this particular battle, Wolfgard would manipulate Reyna's brutal talents and inbred hatred well; in the end, she would do her jarl proud by making Viktor the Valiant's life a living Hel. Wolfgard intended to allow Viktor to capture Reyna with ease, for his enemy's supposed victory would actually be his defeat.

Then a small doubt prickled at the back of Wolfgard's mind. What if Reyna should reverse strategies just to spite her stepfather, and give her allegiance to Viktor and his people to bring disgrace on her own clan? This treasonous possibility made Wolfgard's blood boil; then he dismissed the idea with a rueful laugh. Verily, he doubted the Ravisher would betray him, as much as she clearly despised Viktor.

Still, if the girl should dishonor him, his spy who lived among Viktor's clan would so inform him—and he would then see to it that the little bitch was quickly put down. Either way, victory would soon be his, and in any event, it would be a vast relief to rid himself of Reyna.

TWELVE

WHEN VIKTOR THE VALIANT SET SAIL ON THE FJORD, A HELP-lessly seething Reyna watched him covertly from atop the high basalt cliffs. She had trailed the Viking and two of her stepfather's warriors who had been assigned the task of escorting Viktor back to the wharf. More than once during the journey, Reyna had felt tempted to shoot an arrow into Viktor's broad back. But she well knew such was the ploy of a coward; instead, she would fight this arrogant Viking face-to-face, then slaughter him for having the gall to declare that he could capture and tame her. She would ensure that Viktor died before he ever got close enough to touch her, much less gentle her.

In the space of an hour, Reyna's attitude toward the Viking had evolved from grudging curiosity to smoldering fury. Viktor might have intrigued her before, but now he had laid claim to her, declaring she would become his possession, his chattel. Reyna had promised herself many years ago that *no* man would ever own her, or carry her away against her will, a fate she had been forced to endure as a child. Thus Viktor now threatened her life, her future, her independence . . . and Reyna felt near insane with outrage and affronted pride.

A blight on Wolfgard as well for agreeing to the Viking's nefarious scheme! Recalling her stepfather's conversation with Viktor, she clenched her jaw. How had Wolfgard dared to offer her up as some sort of bounty to end the feud!

Watching the guards turn away from the wharf, Reyna

hastily took her leave, lest she be spotted, and headed back down the path toward the village. A doubt rose to niggle at her. Given the depth of her ire toward Viktor, and her anger toward herself for foolishly sparing his life so many times, why had she chosen to save him again today by intervening on his behalf? Although it galled her to admit it, she knew in her heart that she had admired his courage for brazenly venturing unarmed into the enemy camp. With all her daring and boldness, Reyna would never have attempted such a feat. Viktor the Valiant was either a fool or the most fearless man she had ever known.

Verily, he *was* a new man now that he had returned from the dead! Wolfgard's warriors oft acknowledged this when they whispered among themselves about the gods having blessed Viktor with supernatural powers. He also seemed different physically, and today she had noticed those changes at closer range. He appeared taller, more muscular, his features more regular and pleasing. His blue eyes burned bluer and more vibrant than ever, and reflected an uncanny sensitivity, even a magnetism, that both unnerved and drew her. Even his blond hair, more shiny and thicker than before, tantalized her. Perversely, she had wondered what it might be like to touch that rich silk.

She cursed under her breath. The Viking had definitely stirred some forbidden sensual twinge in her, and she knew she must battle the traitorous impulse with all her might. There was no room in her hardened heart for the softer feminine pursuits of love, marriage, and children. She *must* gain her revenge against all Vikings—and now Viktor had placed himself squarely between her and her goals by declaring he would take her to wife.

Not that Reyna was ignorant of the carnal, after having lived almost all of her life among these decadent Vikings. She remembered an incident that had occurred when she was fifteen. Wolfgard and his warriors had been feasting when she had stepped into the dining hall at precisely the wrong moment, just as Egil, sitting on a bench, had unsheathed his ugly, swollen member while an unfortunate female thrall knelt at his feet, shuddering in anticipation of the depraved act Egil had commanded. Reyna had eyed the unfolding scene in horror; spotting her, Egil had brazenly invited Reyna to ride his prick, while the other warriors had howled with ribald laughter. Undaunted, Reyna had only smiled cruelly back and hurled her dagger between Egil's spread thighs. To her immense satisfaction, she had frightened the crude bastard witless, nicking his balls and rendering him flaccid, and sending the other warriors into gales of bawdy mirth.

All of the warriors had learned an important lesson that night. Although they had continued to heckle Reyna, none had dared try to molest her—and no man had ever taken her innocence. Even when Wolfgard had married her off to Thorstein, she had quickly made mincemeat of that fat, obnoxious pig.

And Viktor the Valiant would *not* become the man who breached her maidenhead, even though no other warrior had ever evoked in her the taut, forbidden longing that Viktor stirred, especially today, when he had stared at her with such burning intensity. Damn those pretty blue eyes of his! Reyna had then spit at him out of fear that Wolfgard's men might otherwise guess her treasonous feelings toward their enemy. She needed to kill the Viking quickly—before this weakness he inspired in her robbed her of all strength as a warrior.

Near the center of the village, Reyna encountered two of her father's kinsmen, Bjorn and Dirk, both of whom grinned at her nastily and called taunts.

"It appears our little ice princess will shortly become a bride," teased Bjorn.

Dirk eyed Reyna with a sneer. "Yea, the little bitch will spread her legs for our enemy, but keeps them tightly locked against the warriors of her own tribe. I ask you, milady, is that fair?"

Not at all amused, Reyna drew her sword. "Foul-mouthed pigs! I spread my legs for no man! And I will lop off the head of any bastard who dares to say I will ever become Viktor the Valiant's bride!"

As the two men laughed with bravado, three other warriors joined in on the harassment. "I say the little Valkyrie may have finally met her match," snarled Garm.

"Yea, and shall we ease the way for our enemy and taste the wench first ourselves?" goaded Egil.

"I do remember our jarl saying last winter that any man who can wrestle Reyna down can have her," jeered Leif.

As the menacing company began to converge on Reyna, she again wielded her weapon. "Back away, you cravens! 'Twill take more than five of you puny cowards to set me down!"

Still the men advanced amid leers and insults, and Reyna began to doubt she could indeed hold five warriors at bay. But the tension mercifully eased when Ragar, with his friend and retainer, Harald, stepped into the midst of the altercation.

Ragar scowled at the men. "What goes on here?"

"We are but teasing your sister," retorted a belligerent Egil.

"Leave my sister be and attend to your duties, my kinsmen," replied Ragar sternly.

"Do you seek to defend her, boy?" Egil scoffed.

The husky Harald drew out his sword. "Yea, your future jarl will defend his sister, and so shall I."

Faced with resistance from both the highly skilled Harald and the equally fearsome Reyna, the warriors grumbled to one another and stalked off.

"Thank you, my brother," Reyna said afterward, expelling a sigh of relief. She nodded toward Harald, a handsome man of twenty-one with green eyes and fair hair. "And I owe a debt of gratitude to you as well, my brother's kinsman."

Harald bowed to Reyna, flashing her a devoted smile. "I am forever at your service, milady."

"I do not know why Wolfgard's warriors have all at once turned so ugly toward me," Reyna remarked. "Usually they are loath to provoke me this way."

"Yea, your status appears to have changed, my sister," Ragar muttered worriedly. He nodded to his kinsman. "Let us exercise our horses later, my friend. If you will kindly excuse me, I will speak with my sister."

Harald bowed and took his leave.

Ragar touched Reyna's arm. "Sister, let us walk."

She nodded, taking his hand. They headed out of the village and up the hill toward the cemetery—the graveyard where their mother had lain for five summers now, beneath a pagan rune-stone. Reyna glanced at Ragar. Her half brother's resemblance to their lost mother, and not to Wolfgard, had always been a source of perverse satisfaction to her. Ragar possessed their mother's finely boned nose, along with the brown eyes and the blond hair that curled about his handsome, angular face. But Reyna was dismayed to note his deeply troubled expression—the grooves surrounding his sensitive mouth, the scowl lines marring his normally smooth brow.

"Speak your mind, my brother," she urged.

Ragar flashed his sister an apologetic smile. "I feel our father behaved imprudently today in the council chamber, agreeing to this treacherous bargain with Viktor the Valiant."

Reyna spoke bitterly. "Yea, albeit I am not shocked to see Wolfgard acting like the coward he is."

Ragar did not comment on her diatribe. "Think you Viktor the Valiant could succeed in capturing you?"

Reyna made a sound of contempt. "Do not insult me by presuming he could!"

Ragar's expression remained anxious. "Nevertheless, the very possibility that you could end up Viktor's bride has stirred the wrath of our warriors. They feel insulted that our father has given Viktor license to seize you, instead of letting one of them take you to wife."

Reyna smiled maliciously. "Ah, so that is why Egil, Garm, and the others were harassing me with greater venom just now."

Ragar nodded solemnly. "Their pride has been affronted, and I am worried for your safety, my sister. If only you would wed Harald. He is a fine man and would treat you as his queen—"

"He is Viking!" cut in Reyna fiercely, dropping Ragar's hand.

"I am half Viking, my sister," Ragar responded in a wounded tone. "Surely you do not hate me, or Harald—"

Reyna touched his arm in reassurance and slanted him a conciliatory smile. "No, my brother, you well know how much I love you. As for Harald, given his devotion to us both, I must allow that I like and respect him."

"Then why . . ."

"He is Viking," she repeated, this time with more regret than spite. "I shall never wed any Viking. Besides, he is not Christian."

"Reyna, he tried," Ragar pointed out with forbearance. "Many times he journeyed with us to the hills, to hear Pelagius preach, translate the Gospels, and teach us our prayers. Ultimately, he could not reject his own heritage, or the pagan tradition of his people. Verily, has he ever betrayed our secret to anyone? And consider all those years he helped you develop your warrior skills, hidden away from the others. Did he ever once forsake your trust and reveal to Wolfgard and his kinsmen that you were training as a warrior?"

Reyna had to smile as she recalled those many clandestine practice sessions, when Harald had taught her how to strike with her sword or ax, to block with her shield, and his endless patience with her initial clumsiness. "Yea, I will admit Harald has been a true kinsman to us both, and has guarded our secrets as he would his life," Reyna conceded quietly. "Were I to marry any Viking, 'tis Harald I would take to husband. But you well know that marriage is impossible for me."

Ragar shook his head. "Why can you not stop hating, my sister?" he asked sadly.

They were approaching the highest point of the cemetery, where their mother lay buried. Reyna pointed ahead to the grave with its covering of moss and outline of stones. "There is the reason! You well know Wolfgard drove our mother to her death. Afterward, he broke the wooden cross I placed to mark her passage—"

"Reyna, my father is pagan—"

"He is an evil dog!" Reyna interrupted venomously. "The whoreson threw the pieces of her cross at me—a blasphemy that Pelagius assures me will doom his soul to hell! How can you forget that he was responsible not only for our mother's death, but also for the murder of our baby brother? How can you not despise him?"

"Can I hate my own blood?" Ragar cried.

Reyna's brown eyes gleamed with hurt and anger. "I am your blood, and so was Alain, whom your own father abandoned to die!"

Ragar's features reflected an exquisite struggle. "But my father's heritage also flows in my veins, as does yours. I can abhor nothing that is so much a part of me. Besides, I long ago came to the conclusion that life is too brief, too fleeting, to poison it with hatred."

At their mother's grave, the siblings paused to make the sign of the cross, as Pelagius had taught them. Ragar moved off to pick a few bright wildflowers from the tundra, then returned to place the bouquet at the foot of the stone. Both brother and sister grew morosely silent, staring at the runestone with its pagan characters and covering of lichen.

After a long moment of quiet reflection, Ragar asked, "Shall we return to the village now?"

Reyna's voice came out choked. "Nay, I shall linger for a time with my mother."

Ragar gestured helplessly. "Reyna—"

But the bright tears in her eyes stayed his words and he could only stare at her in anguish, for this was one of the few times in his entire life that he had seen his implacable sister display such raw emotion.

"You were not there, Ragar," Reyna said fiercely. "You never saw your father's cruelty, his treachery. As for me, I can never forget. *Never!*"

Twenty summers past, Reyna of Loire had been born a princess on a tiny island just off the western coast of France. Her mind still held misty memories of Loire—of rolling wooded hills and meadows strewn with wildflowers, of her happy life with her beloved mother and father, the King and Queen of Loire, in their majestic stone castle. But that idyllic existence had been shattered when Reyna was but three summers old. The hated Vikings had come a-plundering: sacking the castle; killing her father and most of his knights; taking Reyna, her mother, and the other remaining citizens as slaves.

None of these atrocities had devastated Reyna quite as much as the cruel fate that had befallen her infant brother, Alain. Even now she wiped a tear at the memory. Alain had been born only days before the Vikings came, and Reyna had fiercely adored her tiny brother. Her mother, Blanche, had clung to her squalling infant after the Vikings had killed her husband and taken the castle. But the villain Wolfgard, upon spotting that the baby had six toes on his right foot, had declared Alain de-

formed and unfit to live, and had ordered his men to abandon
the infant in the countryside.

Never would Reyna forget her mother's heart-wrenching
pleas for Alain's life as Wolfgard callously dragged her away
from the pitifully wailing infant. Reyna's soul still rang with
the sounds of Blanche's nightmarish shrieks of grief as the
unfeeling Wolfgard had refused to relent, taking Blanche and
Reyna away in his dragon ship. At that moment three-year-
old Reyna, too traumatized to cry out herself, had vowed in
her heart that no matter how long it took, one day she would
become a mighty warrior woman and wreak vengeance on the
cruel Wolfgard and all his clan.

Reyna and her mother had been borne away to live in cold,
desolate Iceland. Blanche, a frail creature, had been unsuited
either to the rigors of the voyage or to the hard life that had
awaited them in the North Country. But Blanche, like her
daughter, had been most beautiful, and Wolfgard had lusted
after Reyna's mother, just as he had after most of his female
thralls. On Iceland, the chieftain had done Blanche the
"honor" of making her his bride instead of his concubine.
Reyna had been elevated to the status of the jarl's stepdaughter and allowed to live at the longhouse with her parents. Yet
her malice toward Wolfgard had only increased as she had
watched him break and subjugate her mother, beating
Blanche repeatedly and betraying her with other women. At
times when Reyna had heard Wolfgard bellow drunkenly at
Blanche, or even strike her, she had tried to intervene, racing
into her parents' chamber, pummeling at Wolfgard's legs with
her small fists. But the cruel Wolfgard would only laugh and
kick Reyna across the room, leaving the child doubled up in
agony and her mother frantic with worry. Once Wolfgard's
rage had been vented, mother and daughter would try to comfort each other, while Reyna vowed again in her heart that
one day she would grow up, learn to fight like a man, and
carve out Wolfgard's blackened heart.

A year after their capture, Ragar had been born to Blanche.
When the puny baby was laid naked at Wolfgard's feet, in the
pagan tradition, the jarl again seemed tempted to reject the infant as he had spurned Alain. But this time, either Blanche's
pleadings had reached Wolfgard, or he had found himself un-

able to abandon the child of his own loins. Ultimately, he had scooped up the child in his tunic, thus effecting his acceptance of his son, and Ragar had been duly baptised according to Viking custom and allowed to live.

Even though it had galled four-year-old Reyna to know that Wolfgard's blood flowed in the veins of her half brother, she had also been well aware that the baby shared a blood bond with her and Blanche, and she had been unable to resist loving Ragar from the very moment of his birth. She had lavished on him all the devotion and affection she had never been able to give Alain. In a sense, Reyna had gotten her revenge on Wolfgard by ensuring that Ragar grew up with a gentle spirit and not a warrior's hardened heart. And the fact that the new baby had brought the frail, defeated Blanche a fleeting joy had gladdened Reyna. But this happiness had turned to bitterness when Blanche's wasted body had finally joined her spirit in death, five summers past, soon after the clan had been outlawed to Vanaheim. Reyna had then vowed that no man would ever break and subjugate her as Wolfgard had oppressed her mother, and she had pledged to take up her mother's duties with Ragar.

Thanks to his sister's devotion, Ragar had matured into a thoughtful, sensitive young man. Reyna recalled an incident that had occurred when Ragar was twelve summers old. Wolfgard's warriors had tried to teach Ragar to shoot birds with a bow and arrow. The boy had run away, sobbing, refusing to kill such innocent creatures. Although the warriors had been amused by Ragar's squeamishness, the jarl himself had been shamed and enraged by what he considered his son's disgraceful conduct, and he had decided to beat the "cowardice" out of the boy. But before the first blow could fall, Reyna, from a distance, had drawn out her slingshot and hurled an iron hammer at her stepfather's head. The missile had bounced off Wolfgard's forehead, inflicting a stunning blow that had rendered him unconscious for so many moments that his warriors had feared their jarl was dead. As the men hovered around Wolfgard, Reyna had unobtrusively slipped up to join them, picking up the hammer and hiding it in the folds of her garment.

When Wolfgard had at last regained consciousness, with a

huge goose egg on his forehead and a rage for revenge burning in his heart, he had dispatched his warriors to find the villain who had dared to attack him. But neither the assailant nor the iron object that had struck Wolfgard could be found. Of course, no one had suspected sixteen-year-old Reyna of the misdeed—no Viking worth his salt would ever admit that a mere female could best a skilled warrior. At last Reyna had suggested to the puzzled warriors that Thor must have chosen to protect Ragar; that when Wolfgard had tried to beat his son, Thor had hurled his mighty hammer, Mjolnir, in warning; and that afterward, the magical hammer had rejoined Thor in Jotunheim, where the fearsome god of thunder was busy battling trolls.

The stupid, superstitious Vikings had believed Reyna's pagan invention! She smiled in vengeful pleasure at the memory. Never again had Wolfgard dared to raise a hand against Ragar, fearing retribution from Thor himself. Only Ragar had realized the truth, but being loyal, he had not spoken out against his half sister. The incident had greatly increased Reyna's confidence in her ability to use the warrior skills she had secretly practiced for many years with Harald. Soon afterward, Reyna had asked her stepfather to allow her to ride with the other warriors on their raids against Viktor the Valiant's tribe. At first, Wolfgard had scoffed at Reyna's suggestion; in bravado, he had told her she could become a warrior only if she could first take down three of his fiercest fighters in combat practice.

Reyna had, of course, realized that Wolfgard intended to teach her a lesson and put her in her place. But she had turned the tables on him—taking up his challenge, then promptly defeating three of his strongest fighters. Thus the jarl had been forced to honor his word and allow her to ride on their raids.

Since then, Reyna had so distinguished herself in battle that at times she had spotted a gleam of pride in Wolfgard's gray eyes, as if the jarl took pleasure in the fact that she brought him triumph, whereas Ragar never could. Of course, Reyna's spirit railed at the very thought of her bringing the loathed jarl any sense of victory, and she longed to kill him in those moments. Still, she was no fool; she knew that to attempt to slay Wolfgard before the moment was right would only cause her own death. So, in the meantime, she vented her spleen on the enemy tribe led by Viktor the Valiant. Even though in all good conscience she had to admit that the continuing feud was more Wolfgard's fault than Viktor's, after all, a Viking was yet a Viking. In her heart, Reyna saw herself as bringing down the wrath of God on a pagan, lawless people.

And, by her mother's sainted memory, she would live for the day when she defeated all of Wolfgard's warriors and carried his despised head on a pike.

THIRTEEN

WHEN REYNA RETURNED TO HER CHAMBER IN WOLFGARD'S longhouse, her Irish servant, Sibeal, was waiting for her. Sibeal rose from her chair and laid down one of Reyna's nightdresses that she had just finished mending. The slave was dressed in a garment of long gray wool held together with a thrall's set of plain iron brooches. Yet her sagacious green eyes and aristocratic features bespoke that, like her mistress, Sibeal was of noble lineage. Although her skin was lined, her mane of long black hair streaked with gray, Sibeal was still lovely, her wisdom only enhancing her magnetic appeal. Tonight, her intelligent countenance mirrored deep concern.

"Reyna, you were gone so long," she murmured in her lilting Irish brogue. "Did you journey again to the hills, lass, to study the Scriptures with Pelagius?"

Reyna shook her head. Sibeal, a Christian herself, knew of Reyna's and Ragar's covert visits to the Irish hermit monk; she carefully guarded their secret.

"Nay, not today. I visited my mother's grave."

Sibeal, who had been taken slave several years before Blanche died, solemnly made the sign of the cross. "May God rest her soul. Still, you must take care with these long absences. Wolfgard may grow suspicious."

"I care not if he does," Reyna scoffed, plopping herself down on the pelt-covered bed. "Yea, I should be delighted to see the jackal try to put me down."

Sibeal sighed. "You are so full of spirit, lass. But let not your courage lead you astray. If Wolfgard knew you were Christian—much less that Ragar follows our faith—he would soundly thrash us all."

Reyna's gaze narrowed. "One day I shall fashion a cross tipped with spearheads and drive it through his evil heart."

Sibeal gasped. "Such malice, child! The God of Jehovah does not wish you to harbor such hateful thoughts in your heart toward your kin."

"After Wolfgard broke the cross marking my mother's grave and hurled the pieces at me?"

"He practices his own faith, pagan though it be. You will not serve your God well through smiting your stepfather."

"Then what of our God's great flood, and the vengeance He visited on Sodom and Gomorrah?" Reyna countered.

Sibeal shook her head. "You concentrate too much on the dire prophecies of the Old Testament. You need to refresh your spirit anew with the Gospels of love as recorded by the prophets. You must learn to forgive, my girl—"

Reyna snorted with disdain. "There is no room in my heart for forgiveness or love—and well you know it, woman."

Sibeal raised an eyebrow in reproach. "Then the state of your life—and of your heart—is sad, indeed, lass."

Reyna grew moodily silent, watching Sibeal move about, tidying up the room. At last she spoke her mind. "What think you of Viktor the Valiant? Was it not odd that he ventured among our clan today?"

"Yea, most odd." Sibeal was thoughtfully quiet for a moment. "He is a different man since he has returned from Valhalla."

"So it appears," Reyna replied grudgingly. "And now my hated stepfather has given him leave to come take me."

Repressing a smile, Sibeal turned to Reyna. "And how does that sit with you, lass?"

Not daunted in the least, Reyna made a flippant gesture and spouted, "I shall take Viktor down with ease, gutting his innards and gouging out his eyes, whenever he dares to appear here."

Sibeal still fought the smile that tugged at her generous

lips. "After Viktor the Valiant made his visit today, I had a vision about him."

Her eyes suddenly wide, Reyna sat up; Sibeal was blessed with second sight, and Reyna was invariably fascinated by her imaginings. "Tell me, I implore you. Please say a druid will curse his pretty face with warts and boils aplenty."

Sibeal shook her head regretfully. "You do not want to know of my prophecy, lass."

"You will tell me," Reyna insisted.

The servant regarded Reyna solemnly. "This will chafe badly, lass, but now I know your destiny lies with Viktor the Valiant."

"How know you?" Reyna demanded, her eyes gleaming with challenge.

"In my vision, I saw the two of you at wedding." Sibeal sighed. "And 'twill be soon, lass, I reckon."

As the servant watched carefully, a series of emotions flashed across Reyna's proud face—first disbelief, followed by denial, and then anger. She charged up from the bed with fists clenched.

"You lie!"

By now quite used to Reyna's rages, Sibeal spoke calmly. "Nay. Viktor the Valiant will soon become your husband."

"Bah!" Reyna scoffed. "And what do you know of my destiny, in any event? Have you become privy to messages from the Norns?"

Sibeal merely chuckled. "Why, milady, do you mean to say you hold with such pagan nonsense? That you, a Christian, now believe in the goddesses of destiny?"

"I believe in no goddess or god, save for the Almighty Jehovah," the girl retorted. "Now leave me, foolish old woman, before I abandon what remains of my patience!"

Sibeal smiled wisely and left.

Afterward, Reyna paced her small chamber and cursed under her breath. She felt far more annoyed with herself than with Sibeal. For so many years the thrall had been a most faithful retainer, almost a second mother to Reyna. Sibeal had not deserved such a tongue-lashing, not after her mistress had bidden her to speak her mind freely. Later she would seek out Sibeal and beg her pardon. Mayhap she could pick a few

Baderblooms from the tundra to appease her adviser and friend. For Sibeal, like Reyna, knew too much of hurt and hardship, and not enough of joy and pretty things.

Now, however, Reyna's greatest challenge was to calm her own raging thoughts and pounding pulse. She realized with equal measures of horror and self-loathing that she was trembling all over. For Sibeal had touched a raw nerve with her words of prophecy. To think that the thrall had said she would soon stand at wedding—with her enemy!

Reyna would fight that fate with all the strength in her body and soul. She would obliterate every weak, feminine instinct that somehow drew her to her despised adversary.

Still, a sobering truth daunted her: Sibeal's visions were never wrong.

FOURTEEN

"Come ahead—give me your worst," said Viktor.

Three weeks later, Viktor and his warriors were again gathered on a rise above the village for combat practice. He noted that the weather was bleak and overcast, but at least it wasn't raining as it had on so many recent spring days. All around them, yellow, purple, and blue wildflowers were sprouting up on the mossy green tundra. A flock of noisy kittiwakes streaked across the gray skies, and a rabbit watched from behind a basalt outcropping. From the village below, the sounds of lambs bleating drifted up as the herdsmen sheared them.

Since the day Viktor had visited Wolfgard's village and made his pact with the enemy, he had been honing his warrior skills to a razor's edge, spending every free moment with his men practicing swordplay, archery, and wrestling, even the delicate and deadly intricacies of spear catching. The sessions had been brutal, and Viktor had spent almost as many hours soaking bruised muscles in the hot-spring bathhouse as he had practicing warfare. But he knew he had made great strides, and soon he would attempt to capture Reyna. So far, he had not told his warriors of his intentions or his pact with Wolfgard—they thought they were practicing each day so Viktor could lead an attack against Wolfgard. Privately, though, Viktor realized that his passion to seize Reyna had become a fire in his heart, and he knew he would not rest until he had captured this wild, magnificent creature, tamed her, and brought an end to the feud.

Today the warriors were focusing their session on wrestling. Viktor had just dared Orm, Rollo, and Canute to tackle him—all at the same time. Over the past weeks, he had gradually built up to grappling with more than one warrior at once. Now he stood ready for the assault—his body taut, his legs spread, his knees slightly bent, his arms extended wide, his long fingers curled for a strike.

However, the men Viktor had challenged appeared perplexed and hesitant. Canute squinted at Viktor through his one eye; Rollo scratched his crotch; Orm chewed his whiskers.

"But, jarl," Rollo protested, "we cannot all three of us attack you at once. Yea, you have greatly improved your skills over the past days, but we would still be taking unfair advantage."

"If I am to defeat Reyna the Ravisher," Viktor replied, "then throwing down three of you at once may pale by comparison."

Now he had insulted the men, and his comments were met with low growls and glowers on the part of the challenged, and with mocking jeers from the rest of the warriors.

"Are you saying three of us are not equal to one puny warrior woman?" demanded Canute.

"No, no, of course not," Viktor hastily amended. "But are you not aware that this woman, when riled, becomes a she-troll with more than a hundred heads?"

The tension eased, and the men chuckled to one another. As Viktor well knew, there was no disgrace for even the fiercest warrior to need assistance in capturing such a fearsome monster.

"Yea, jarl," agreed Orm with a grin. "The Ravisher is a she-troll straight from Jotunheim. Mayhap you will need Thor himself to help you take her down."

All the warriors threw back their heads and laughed.

"An apt observation," replied Viktor, "but since I cannot count on Thor to make his appearance at the proper moment, I must do everything in my power to become prepared. Now attack—all of you!"

The challenged men exchanged cocky grins and did as their jarl bade. Bellowing battle yells, the three charged

Viktor. After weeks of intensive practice, Viktor reacted like
a precise, well-oiled machine. His foot kicked out to jab
Canute in the knee, sending him doubling over in pain. Then
he grabbed Rollo in mid-flight, threw him over his shoulder,
and sent him crashing to his back with a great groan. Losing
no momentum, Viktor spun about in time to take down Orm
with a skilled over-the-hip throw.

Within seconds it was all over, and the warriors who had
served as spectators could only gape at their jarl in awe.
Viktor stood triumphant, grinning, while all around him,
Orm, Canute, and Rollo grunted and groused and rubbed aching muscles.

Svein came forward with a proud grin. "You have done it,
jarl. After weeks of practice, your skill with the sword is un-
surpassed. You are deadly accurate with the spear and arrow,
and a master at hand-to-hand combat. You are now ready to
lead us into battle against Wolfgard and the Ravisher."

"Yea, I agree," Viktor replied. "And tonight we will convene our war council."

Svein's features lit up with anticipation, while the other
warriors hooted a mighty cheer . . .

Above the men in her concealed position behind the rocks,
Reyna watched in mingled awe and horror as three fierce
warriors charged Viktor . . . and he took down all three in the
space of mere seconds! He was so magnificent as he moved,
like a mighty stallion charging at a horse fight, his muscles
gleaming and rippling, his vigor and agility wondrous to behold.

Reyna's stomach churned and she felt sweat breaking out
on her upper lip. Viktor had grown so splendidly skilled, his
body so strong and hard, kindling in her forbidden desires to
see his strength at close range, to touch those glistening muscles, to feel his raw virility. He radiated such power—

He was preparing to come for her, she realized with a sick
feeling mingled with a mutinous thrill. He would surely try to
capture her soon, just as he had vowed to Wolfgard. Merciful
Jehovah, what if he could master her now?

Never! her pride declared fiercely. Never would she become the pawn of Viktor's will, the slave of his desires.

Damn him to Hel, and damn the traitorous excitement he stirred. If he came for her, she would slay him . . . That, or she would surely lose herself.

"Men, I have something of great importance to tell you."

That night Viktor was gathered at "war council" with his retainers—Svein, Orm, Canute, Ottar, and Rollo. Seated at the large table in the dining hall, the men had just feasted on roast salmon, mutton stew, bread, and mead. Iva was walking around with a jug, refilling the men's oxhorns, and Viktor noted the slave and Ottar exchanging shy smiles. Recently he had spotted the two walking the tundra together and he was pleased to see this evidence of a courtship developing between them.

The warriors seemed in mellow, approachable humor, with their bellies full and their spirits lightened by alcohol. The central chamber itself was more comfortable than ever now that it was smoke-free. Soon after his visit to Wolfgard's village, Viktor, with help from several of his men, had constructed a stone chimney to vent the fire. He had even built a similar device in his bedroom. Crudely shaped but soundly built, the freestanding fireplace was loosely patterned after the adobe ones he had often seen in Santa Fe. The entire village had come out yesterday to marvel at the fabulous invention in the dining hall, and to watch the device draw smoke upward through the roof. Since then, every family in the village had demanded one of the remarkable contraptions, and Viktor intended to see that a chimney was eventually built in every home.

As Iva slipped from the room, Orm urged, "Speak your mind, jarl. We all hunger to hear you are ready to attack Wolfgard, carve out his blackened heart, and kill the Ravisher."

Viktor struggled not to shudder at these grisly images, which more than demonstrated that his men were still every bit as bellicose as Wolfgard himself. Calmly, he replied, "I have conjured a way to end the feud."

"Yea, by slaughtering Wolfgard and all his people," put in Canute eagerly.

"Nay," said Viktor.

"*Nay?*" repeated the other five in unison.

Viktor stared at their stunned faces and gathered his fortitude. "There is something I have not told you. It is the reason I have been practicing my warrior skills . . ."

"So you can slay Wolfgard," finished Svein.

"Nay." Viktor drew a heavy breath. "The truth is, when I went to Wolfgard's village, I made a pact with him."

To Viktor's chagrin, roars of rage shook the table, and mighty Canute bolted to his feet with sword drawn. "Why, you filthy whoreson! You have betrayed us!"

Viktor also surged to his feet. "Nay! I did no such thing."

"Then explain yourself, jarl," beseeched a wild-eyed Svein.

Viktor stared at the others, who appeared equally shocked and angered. "Wolfgard and I made a bargain concerning his stepdaughter. He agreed that if I can capture Reyna, tame her, and make her give me a son, he will end the feud."

Mutterings of incredulity flitted down the table.

"And you believed the villain?" asked Rollo.

"Yes," said Viktor.

Orm slammed his fist down on the table, rattling the dishes. "You have made a pact with Loki himself!"

"Wolfgard made the vow in front of witnesses," Viktor argued. "If I fulfill my part of the bargain, he will have no choice but to honor his word and end the feud."

The men fell into glowering silence.

"But, jarl," protested a clearly disappointed Rollo, "we have no desire to end the feud."

"You mean you wish to continue to watch your kinsmen die?" Viktor demanded.

His question prompted his retainers to glance at one another in confusion. "But 'tis a great honor for a warrior to die in battle," said Rollo.

"And if the feud should end," Orm put in, "what will we do?"

"Why, you could start by improving the quality of life for our own people," Viktor replied.

"What means this 'quality of life'?" asked a frowning Svein.

Viktor gestured toward the table. "For one thing, have you men never given a thought to the high-fat diet all of you consume? I mean, boar meat, bacon, eggs, whole milk, and cheese—why it is all loaded with cholesterol and will put you in early graves."

The warriors stared at one another, utterly perplexed.

"We need to plant more cereal staples," Viktor continued. "Perhaps in time we can even travel to Ireland or England to secure the proper seeds and plantings to start more vegetable crops and fruit orchards."

"You would end the feud so we all may become farmers, jarl?" scoffed Canute.

Even amid cynical laughter, Viktor replied feelingly, "I would end the feud to keep you, my brothers, from dying—from leaving your wives to weep and your children to grow up fatherless. If I can only capture Reyna the Ravisher and tame her, then all of the peoples on Vanaheim can live together in harmony."

The warriors appeared little moved; although no one protested outright to Viktor, much grumbling and headshaking alerted him to their continued resistance.

At last Svein whispered, "You truly intend to proceed with this madness, jarl?"

"Of course." Hoping to appeal to the men's vanity, he added, "Besides, the warrior woman insulted me horribly. She spit at me. I would like to see her put in her place."

Again there was dead silence.

"What is wrong?" cried Viktor.

"Jarl, we do not understand," said Ottar.

"Understand what?"

"If the woman has so insulted you, you should slay her," growled Rollo.

"Kill a woman?" Viktor said in disbelief.

"Yea, even a female has not leave to spit in the face of a king," blustered Orm.

"But if I were to do this terrible deed, then we would have no way at all to stop the feud!"

Again silence reigned.

"Don't you want peace?" Viktor asked, flabbergasted.

The men consulted among one another for a moment; then Rollo answered for the group. "Nay, jarl. We do not."

"Is that what say all of you?" Viktor demanded.

Five heads nodded.

Viktor could have shouted his frustration. Instead, he shook a fist at the lot of them and spoke with determination gleaming in his eyes. "Listen well, you dimwits. Whether you like it or not, I am king, and this is the way it is going to be. I am going to capture Reyna the Ravisher, bring her back here, and tame her. And you, my kinsmen, are going to help me. Either you are with me or you are against me. Choose now."

Another silence ensued. Svein glanced at each sober-faced warrior in turn, then spoke for the group. "We are with you, jarl."

"Good. We go tonight."

"Tonight?' echoed Ottar.

"Yea. I have decided we will make a daring midnight voyage up the fjord and snatch this banshee woman from her bed."

The others mumbled to one another and exchanged glances of mystification.

"What of Wolfgard's warriors?" asked Canute. "Surely he will not leave his village unguarded, knowing of your plans."

Viktor nodded. "We will surprise the sentries, knock them out if need be. But we will avoid the taking of any life at any cost. Is that clear?"

Never had Viktor seen a group of men look so horrified—or so disappointed

"You mean we cannot slay them?" asked a crestfallen Orm.

"Out of the question," Viktor replied firmly. Hoping to further sway them, he argued, "Think of it this way. Wolfgard may not miss a mere woman, but if we kill his warriors, he will be certain to retaliate."

The men appeared no less discouraged. "Can we not at least bring back a few of Wolfgard's kinsmen to torture?" asked Canute in an uncharacteristic whine.

"Torture?" Viktor repeated in a barely audible tone.

"Yea, jarl, we need to plan a fitting diversion for the Shieling feast," put in Orm with a persuasive grin. "We generally roast a live enemy or two whenever the festivities hit a lull."

Oh, heaven help them all! thought Viktor with a sinking feeling. "Do not worry, I will help you devise more suitable entertainment for the Shieling feast," he snapped. "Otherwise, kindly forget about slaying Wolfgard's warriors. As I'm sure you will agree, capturing the woman alone will be more than enough challenge for us all."

No one could argue there.

FIFTEEN

Eerie dark clouds, backlit by the moon, stretched above the swollen, swiftly running fjord. Staring out into the obscure, chill night, Viktor stood next to Svein, who was serving as helmsman, navigating the longship through the treacherous waters toward Wolfgard's wharf.

Only Viktor and his retainers had come, for he had argued that the smaller the raiding party, the less likely they'd be detected. Staring up at the brooding heavens, he said a silent prayer that they would accomplish their purpose without undue violence or loss of life. After all, the goals of this mission were to save lives and to bring the two warring tribes together.

As for the little Valkyrie herself, she would be fit to be tied when they wrenched her from her bed, Viktor mused. And tied she would be, for he had brought along several lengths of rope fashioned from walrus skin to restrain her, as well as a long sash of clean white linen—cleaner than her filthy tongue deserved!—to gag her waspish tongue. As the pièce de résistance, he had also brought a pile of wool blankets to wrap her in—partly to keep her warm during the return voyage, partly to stifle her screams and limit her struggles. His men were armed with ropes and gags in order to restrain the guards.

The wisdom of their preparations became evident as the longship approached the wharf. Spotting Viktor's ship, two enemy sentries rushed forward, while a third man ran off up the trail, evidently to rouse Wolfgard's camp. As Viktor's ship thudded against the wharf, slipping in beside Wolfgard's *drakar,* one of the guards yelled, "Who goes there?" as both men hauled out broadswords.

Orm and Rollo jumped down and charged the sentries, while Ottar and Svein raced off after the man who had escaped up the trail. In a brief scuffle on the pier, Orm and Rollo rendered two of the guards unconscious; a moment later, Svein and Ottar dragged back the third sentry, who had also been knocked cold.

"Are you pleased, jarl?" Rollo called up with a grin.

"Yea—we did not slay them," added a proud Orm.

Viktor hopped down with the mooring rope, securing it to a post. He glanced ruefully at the three insensible men. "It would have been helpful to question them first."

A breathless Svein answered, "The sentries put up too much of a struggle, jarl. But do not fret—we shall likely encounter more of them along the way."

After Orm, Rollo, and Svein had bound and gagged the guards, Viktor grabbed a stack of blankets and ropes from the vessel. With all of his kinsmen assembled, he ordered, "Canute, remain behind to guard our ship."

The one-eyed man appeared crestfallen. "But, jarl—"

"You are our mightiest warrior, the only man we can trust to stave off additional sentries should they patrol the wharf,' Viktor interrupted firmly. "Without you here, our mission might well be doomed."

Glancing up at the deserted hillside, Canute seemed to realize they were in little danger of being attacked by more sentries here. Nonetheless, he grudgingly replied, "Yea, jarl."

"Good," Viktor said, relieved that his most bloodthirsty fighter would be left behind. He tossed a folded wool blanket to each of his four other warriors. "All right, men— remember, we must stay together, in the shadows. If you must communicate, try to use hand signals, or whisper—and only when needed. And heed my warning—no bloodshed unless it is absolutely necessary."

Amid a light mist that had begun to fall, the five left the pier and moved stealthily up the hillside. They followed the trail over the cliffs, all constantly alert for signs of more sentries. When they met with no resistance, Viktor was left wondering if perhaps Wolfgard was easing the way for him, welcoming his kidnapping of Reyna. It wasn't until they had crested a rise on the outskirts of the village itself that Viktor at last spotted two more guards. Blessed good luck! The two appeared to have shirked their duties; they were squatted beneath the eaves of a wattle-and-daub cottage and sipping from oxhorns.

Viktor held up a hand to stay his men, and all crouched behind a low basalt boulder.

"Let me take them," whispered Orm, wiping moisture from his craggy face.

"Yes, you and Rollo," Viktor answered in a hushed voice. "And remember, do not kill them, or even knock them out this time. Bring them back so I may question them."

"Yea, jarl," Orm whispered. "To slay such miserable cretins would be no better than to steal milk from a babe."

"Then be about it. Quickly. And quietly."

As Viktor, Svein, and Ottar waited tensely, Rollo and Orm crept up behind the sentries. At first, seeing both men unsheathe their daggers, Viktor feared his orders had been betrayed. His apprehension turned to relief as he watched his men grab the guards in choke holds and press knives to their throats. Within seconds the sentries were dragged over to Viktor at knifepoint.

"Ask your questions, jarl," said Rollo.

Viktor stared at the two guards, who appeared wild-eyed and terrified. One was so frightened that he had already urinated on himself. Viktor hated having to subject the men to such brutal tactics—although, in the long run, his strategies would result in less loss of life for all the peoples of Vanaheim.

"Listen to me, men," Viktor began earnestly. "You will not be harmed if you simply answer a few questions."

The guards observed him warily.

"Where are the other sentries in the village?" Viktor asked. Neither answered.

Rollo emitted a low growl of rage and tightened the pressure of his dagger. "Answer our jarl, or I will carve out your entrails."

Before Viktor could raise a hand in protest, the guard stammered, "Th-there are n-no other sentries!"

"Why is this?" demanded Orm.

The man shrugged. "Our jarl has grown careless—confident there would be no attack from Viktor the Valiant."

"You are certain of this?" Viktor asked.

"Yea, we are the only guards."

Viktor turned to the other man. "Where does the Ravisher sleep in Wolfgard's longhouse?"

This man resisted, too, until Orm brandished his dagger in the man's face and growled, "Spill it out, man, or I will make a eunuch out of you!"

Already sounding much like a eunuch, the man shrilled, "She sleeps in the northernmost part of the house, not far from the outdoor cattle byres."

"Good," said Viktor. To Rollo and Orm, he added, "Tie and gag them."

"But are you not forgetting something?" said Orm.

"Yes?"

Rollo leaned toward his jarl, jerked his head at the captives, and asked in a low, tense whisper, "What if they are lying?"

Staring at the two frightened enemies, Viktor ground his jaw. It was a logical question, and one that must be addressed. "Are either of you lying?"

Two heads shook vigorously.

"I believe them," Viktor told his warriors.

"Jarl!" protested Rollo. "We must be certain, or we could all risk death. Verily, these fools could be leading us straight into a trap. Pray let us torture them a little, to ensure they are not playing us falsely."

Viktor gazed from his men's eager faces to the sentries, who blinked in abject terror. "If either of you is lying, I give my men leave to come back and slaughter you—in whatever manner they choose. Be advised, as well, that they still haven't completed the roster of entertainment for the Shieling feast."

The two captives exchanged frantic glances.

"Well? Do either of you care to amend your stories?" Viktor demanded.

Again two heads were shaken.

"They are telling the truth," Viktor informed the others.

After the guards were bound and gagged, their bodies hidden behind a nearby haystack, the small raiding party crept on to Wolfgard's longhouse. They entered with surprising ease, for there was no sentry posted, no bar on the door. Leaving Svein posted at the portal, the other four tiptoed into a smoky foyer lit by a steatite lamp. With Viktor leading the way, they proceeded through several more deserted chambers—a looming room, a kitchen, a storage closet—and then past an alcove in which the woman thrall whom Viktor recognized as Sibeal lay asleep on a pallet. They stole toward the northernmost corner of the house, where, as the sentries had informed them, they found Reyna's room.

Just outside the chamber, Viktor assigned Ottar to guard, then he, Orm, and Rollo crept inside. Although the room lay in deep shadow, a small lamp had been left lit near the cot, and Viktor could clearly see Reyna on the bed. Asleep, she appeared as innocent as an angel, her lovely countenance peaceful, her golden hair spread out, a polar bear pelt tucked up to her chin. She looked as beautiful and untouched as Sleeping Beauty, and he felt tempted to awaken her with a kiss.

But, given her prior, ruthless behavior, he was not about to act in such a naive, even stupid, fashion. Still, she was asleep, and there was no need to frighten her out of her wits. Gesturing to his men to hold their places, he tiptoed across the room, knelt beside her, and gently placed his hand over her mouth.

"Reyna. You must awaken and come with us," he said quietly but firmly.

He might as well have just roused a badger from its burrow. Reyna's brown eyes flashed open, brilliant with rage, and then her teeth sank viciously into Viktor's hand. He instinctively lurched to his feet, waving his hand helplessly and struggling against an instinct to shout out in agony and thus awaken the entire household.

In the meantime, the Valkyrie had popped to her feet and aimed a lethal kick straight at his groin! He tried to feint, but she still managed to deliver a painful blow to his mid-thigh that left him doubling over.

Then the demon sprinted straight for the door, past the two mighty warriors, Orm and Rollo, who at the moment appeared utterly mystified, while Ottar stepped inside and froze at the sight of the advancing Fury.

"Stop her!" Viktor forced out.

Orm and Rollo sprang into motion, grabbing the female, who was as wild as an unbroken horse—kicking, biting, gouging both warriors until they released her with bellows of pain—

Shoving past Ottar, she made a nosedive for the door—and for the broadsword that rested near it!

Viktor leaped into action, vaulting across the chamber. In the nick of time, he managed to grab Reyna around the waist. His entire body exploded with torment as she kicked and screamed and pelted him with her fists.

"Valkyrie from Hel!" he roared.

Staggering beneath her blows as he recrossed the room, Viktor flung her down on the bed and hurled his body on top of hers. Even as her pained gasp informed him that the wind had been knocked from her lungs, he felt remorseless. Rage at her vicious attack gave him a strength he had never known before. His hard frame pinned hers to the bed and his strong thigh muscles held her legs immobile. He grabbed both her arms and restrained her wrists high overhead with one of his determined hands. As she at last caught a sharp breath, he forced his other hand over her mouth so she could not scream out. But this time he was wise enough to grip and lock her entire jaw so she would not savage him once more with her lethal teeth.

At last she was restrained beneath him, and ah, it was a splendid sight. Her body trembled with frustrated anger; her eyes shot venom at hm.

And then a curious thing happened. Viktor realized that during their struggles Reyna's nightdress had become hiked up almost to her waist. Her generous breasts heaved against his chest; her soft, supple thighs were bared. And he was aroused—more aroused than he had ever felt in his entire life, as if a log were suddenly lodged in his leggings. Had there not been others present, he would have felt sore pressed not to take her, right here and now. At that moment, Viktor was appalled and fascinated to find himself feeling every emotion a true Viking warrior felt—the rage and the passion, the obsession to plunder and possess. He was left struggling between the enlightened, sensitive man he had left behind in the twentieth century and the Viking fighter who had arrived here in the Dark Ages to confront this warrior woman from Hel.

Ultimately, the caring man won, for Viktor knew he must not take Reyna in the heat of anger, however badly she had provoked him. Yet *his* she would become—this glorious little spitfire—and he savored the thought of that eventual, sweet triumph. Considering the level of his outrage, he couldn't resist taunting her a bit. He arched against her slightly so she could *feel* his victory, and he smiled at her look of wide-eyed horror.

He winked down at her enraged countenance. "You're not on the pill, are you, love?" he teased.

SIXTEEN

IN THE NEXT INSTANT, VIKTOR'S BODY WAS HURLED OFF
Reyna's. Her strength astounded him, and he grunted in pain
as his huge body crashed to the floor.

Struggling to his rise, he paused, jerking his head upward
at the sound of her outraged voice.

"What is this pill you speak of, Viking? Do you seek to
charm me with your poisons? Whatever this potion is, may
you gag on it and die!"

Dio, where did this little demon get her spunk and fortitude? Viktor wondered dazedly from the floor. He had to be
close to double her weight, and the little tigress had flipped
his body off hers as if he were a flapjack!

Heaving a mighty groan, he was up—

But the Valkyrie was up, too, her gown torn to reveal one
creamy shoulder, her hair streaming in wraithlike disarray
around her face. She looked like an enraged ogress as she
faced him down with fists clenched and fire blazing in her
eyes.

"Come give me your worst, Viking!" she screamed at him.
"I will kill you with my bare hands, filthy whoreson!"

Viktor heard his men catch sharp breaths behind him, and
he knew he needn't turn around to see that their expressions
were appalled. For a moment he considered asking for their
help to tackle her, then immediately vetoed the impulse. If he
was to make this Valkyrie his bride, he would have to learn
how to handle her himself. Perhaps in time the two of them

could become equal partners living together in mutual love and respect. But for now, he had to communicate to her on a level she would understand—he had to show her who was master. So far, she was claiming that place for herself, and it was high time to stage an overthrow—

Without any warning, Viktor hurled himself at Reyna, grabbed her around her slim waist, swung her high, then flung her down to the bed again. He landed on top of her, pinning her down.

For a moment she stared at him, evidently too caught off guard to spout another blasphemy. Viktor felt shockingly unrepentant, given the pounding he had just endured.

"You were saying, Valkyrie?" he asked mildly.

She would have screamed out her rage once more, except that his hand again descended on her mouth. She bucked wildly, trying to throw his body off her, but this time Viktor was prepared and not about to become an easy victim. Feeling as comfortable as a cowboy riding a mechanical bull, he hurled out orders to his kinsmen.

"Rollo! Orm! Quit gaping like a couple of simpletons and come help me tie up this dragon lady!"

The men leaped into action, and with the strenuous efforts of all three, the Valkyrie was subdued. First, with Viktor still holding her down, she was gagged, and her flailing feet were bound. Only then were they ready to flip her writhing body over and secure her hands behind her. Viktor couldn't repress a grin as he watched Reyna's shapely buttocks thrash against her nightdress as she struggled helplessly against her bonds. He would live for the day when that beautiful behind would squirm in his hands—but in pleasure as he filled her with his passion.

Now the men began wrapping Reyna in the blankets—until she looked about as appealing as a mummy, totally bound up, save for her red face and her eyes, which still burned brightly with malice.

Viktor scratched his jaw and stared at the defiant captive on the bed. " 'Tis done, then. Let us get her back to the village."

All three men froze at the sound of a female voice behind them. "A moment, my lord."

Simultaneously, Viktor, Rollo, and Orm whirled to see the slave woman Sibeal standing in the archway. Appearing deadly calm, the woman held a dagger at Ottar's throat. Viktor groaned at the sight of the lad, who stood there in horror with a knife poised to end his life in a split second.

Rollo and Orm looked to Viktor for guidance.

"What do you want, woman?" he asked.

Her green eyes gleamed with lethal determination. "For you to release my mistress," she said quietly.

"Jarl, do not listen to her!" pleaded Ottar bravely. "I have disgraced you by deserting my post and allowing a female to best me. I will give up my life now, but you must not release your captive."

Viktor felt caught between a rock and a hard place. He decided to try reasoning with the slave. "Woman, we have no desire to harm your mistress. Indeed, we are bearing her off to a better life—"

"Trussed up like a swine?" she demanded.

"The wench is obstinate, as you well know," Viktor replied. "But the truth is, I intend to make Reyna my bride and the queen of my people. Once she becomes biddable, I promise you I will treat her with the greatest respect."

Hesitation mingled with lingering suspicion flitted across the slave's face. "How can I believe you, Viktor the Valiant?"

"I will make this woman my queen and protect her with my life," Viktor assured her earnestly. "I vow it, before God."

Even as Orm and Rollo exchanged astounded glances, the thrall demanded, "You are Christian now?"

"Yea, I am Christian."

She studied his face for a moment, then cried, "Oh, I do not know what to believe! Swear it before Odin as well."

Viktor did not hesitate. "I swear before Odin that Reyna will become my wife."

"And may a curse take you if you lie!" the slave added fiercely.

"May a curse take me if I lie," Viktor repeated solemnly. Still the woman held her knife at Ottar's throat.

"Will you release the lad now?" Viktor beseeched.

"On one condition. I accompany my lady, to care for her and to ensure that you honor your word, Viktor the Valiant."

"I agree."

"And I shall keep my dagger, to kill you in your sleep if you harm milady."

Viktor hesitated, and Orm said warningly, "Jarl, do not be fooled. This woman is an Irish sorceress, and can summon druids to slay you."

Viktor smiled. "Should I forsake my word, I will doubtless deserve such a fate." He nodded to Sibeal. "You may keep your dagger and come with us, woman."

The slave released Ottar, who staggered away from her heaving a huge breath of relief. Sibeal replaced her dagger in the sheath at her waist and nodded to the men. "Follow me, and bring my mistress. I will help you leave without detection."

"What of Wolfgard?" Viktor asked. "Why hasn't all of this clamor awakened him?"

Sibeal snorted. "He sleeps the sleep of the dead. Still, we must hasten. Wolfgard's thralls are up before first light to prepare his repast. We must not risk detection, as I will not raise a hand against my own."

"We understand, woman," said Viktor. "It is not our desire to harm anyone here, only to fetch my future bride"—he paused to slant a rueful glance at the still-writhing, mutinous Reyna—"so that, in time, this feud may end."

"That is a day we all shall welcome," said Sibeal feelingly. "And for the sake of your own soul, Viktor the Valiant, you had best not be playing us falsely."

"I am not. Let us be about our escape."

Viktor and Rollo hoisted Reyna over their shoulders like a rolled carpet, and, with Sibeal in the lead and Svein rejoining them, the small party exited the longhouse and crept back down the path to the fjord. A steady rain had begun to fall, impeding their progress and soaking the blankets binding Reyna. Canute, upon spotting them coming down the wharf, hopped out of the longship and rushed over to cut the lines on Wolfgard's *drakar,* setting it adrift in the stormy waters. Viktor noted this with an admiring grin.

The party boarded and pushed off. Viktor stood near the mast, while the bound Reyna lay on the deck, with Sibeal sitting nearby to attend her.

Viktor clapped Canute on the shoulder and nodded toward the drifting ship, which was already well down the fjord, being battered by rain and gusts, carried by the swift current toward the open sea. "Good thinking, my friend."

Shaking moisture from his beard, the one-eyed giant grinned. "Yea, Wolfgard will have a bit of shipbuilding to do ere he can pursue us." He gestured toward the trussed-up woman. "So the Valkyrie is yours now?"

"Yes, and we brought along her lady-in-waiting to attend her," answered Viktor proudly.

Canute chuckled, then leaned closer to confide behind his hand, "Just ride the wench vigorously a few times, and she will gentle to your dominance."

Viktor glowered back. "I will not rape her, Canute. I will persuade her to become my bride willingly."

Canute threw up his hands. "Then we have come on a fool's errand. The Valkyrie will never consent to become your bride."

On the deck, Reyna—cold, drenched, and miserable—had overheard the exchange and was thinking she totally agreed with the warrior named Canute, much as it rankled to be in accord with an enemy. Rage churned within her at the helplessness of her plight—to be captured, trussed up like a war trophy, and borne off into the night.

Reyna felt furious at herself as well for having allowed this to happen, after she had known Viktor would come for her. To add insult to injury, her servant, Sibeal, had betrayed her, giving her allegiance to Viktor and believing his lies.

A blight on Sibeal and her visions, which were no excuse for her perfidy. Twisting about in her uncomfortable bonds, Reyna tried to direct a righteous glare at the woman, but found that Sibeal was staring ahead, serene even amid thunder and rain, her hands folded in her lap as the oarsmen propelled them down the turbulent fjord. As for the hated Viking himself, he stood proudly at the helm with his back to her, lightning emblazoning his tall figure. His drenched garments clung to his broad back, hard buttocks, and long legs, and his wet hair whipped about his head. Staring at his muscled thighs, she remembered the strength of them, like iron, press-

ing into her body—as well as *another* part of him that had
felt harder still.

Even though Reyna could not see Viktor's despised face,
his stance clearly bespoke arrogance and triumph. Cursed Viking! How foolish she had been to hope Viktor the Valiant
was different. He was clearly a typical Viking—all he really
cared about was conquest, subjugation, and winning.

Why her enemy still audaciously assumed he could wed
her, Reyna did not know. She suspected his claim was bravado, and that he would in truth torture and kill her back at
his own village. Verily, she preferred that plight to the
thought of becoming Viktor the Valiant's bride. She would
burn in Hel before she wed him willingly—

In a sense, she already was in Hel, forsaken by her own
traitorous female instincts. When Viktor's massive body had
crushed hers, pinning her to the bed, when she had felt the
heat of his vast maleness crushing into her pelvis, the raw
lust and unbridled passion streaming through her had shocked
and horrified Reyna to her very core. Only her outrage at her
body's betrayal had given her the strength to thrust Viktor's
body off her. And then the Viking had taken her down again,
proving that physically, he could master her—

Humiliation burned in Reyna at that defeat. Mayhap he
could overwhelm her body, but her spirit he would never violate. She vowed this fiercely, even as a traitorous tear welled
up to prove how vulnerable she truly felt.

But what most haunted Reyna was a nagging doubt, at the
back of her mind, that now arose to torture her. If her stepfather, Wolfgard, hated Viktor the Valiant so much, then why
had her enemy been able to penetrate the longhouse tonight
and capture her with such ease?

SEVENTEEN

SHE SCREAMED ALL NIGHT LONG.

Back at his village, Viktor chose to confine Reyna in the small hut that served as the village smokehouse. He selected the structure because it was one of the few in the village made entirely of stone. With a strong bolt on the heavy door, the little building provided a stout fortress. He ordered his men to remove the slabs of salted beef and pork, and to bank the fire at the center of the chamber. They left Reyna on a pallet on the packed dirt floor, with only the fire, a steatite lamp, and a chamber pot to keep her company throughout the night.

She screamed and screamed.

Viktor stood outside in the cold, damp darkness with Svein, listening to Reyna's bloodcurdling cries, remembering the savage look in her eyes when he and his men had rolled her out of her drenched blankets onto the floor, untied her feet, and retied her hands before her.

He turned to Svein with a grin that was mostly bravado. "She roars like a dragon, does she not? Quite a little banshee we have captured, my blood brother."

Svein grimaced and shook his head. "She sounds like a berkserker straight from Hel. Let me go in and gag her foul mouth, jarl. 'Twill be my pleasure."

"Nay," said Viktor. "She is like a she-wolf caught in a lair. She will cease her howling when she grows hoarse and realizes no one will come to set her loose."

"She will be loose herself in no time, jarl," Svein warned.
"You should not have tied her hands before her—she will
surely gnaw through the bonds with her teeth—"

"You speak of her as if she is some rodent," Viktor
scolded.

"She is no better than the squirrel Ratatosk, gnawing away
at the World Tree."

"If I restrained her hands behind her, she could not see to
her needs," Viktor argued.

"So let her lie in her own filth," Svein retorted. "She de-
serves no further consideration."

Viktor was dismayed by the depth of Svein's contempt toward Reyna. Convincing his people to accept this Valkyrie as
their queen would not be easy, he mused.

"Do not fret, my blood brother," he said in reassurance.
"Even if she gets loose, what can she do, penetrate walls of
solid stone?"

Svein shuddered as a particularly harrowing scream rang
out. "She is cable of anything. When provoked, the Ravisher
is more powerful than Fenris the wolf."

"She must grow accustomed to her restraints, just as a wild
horse will at first kick against a corral."

"The kick she inflicts will be square in your face, jarl,"
Svein told him.

Viktor clapped a hand on Svein's shoulder. "Go get some
rest, my friend. You well need it, as I do. Then tomorrow I
will go a-courting."

Svein was still shaking his head as the two men parted
company.

"Good morning, sweetheart."

Feeling rested and equal to the challenge of confronting his
future bride, Viktor thrust open the door to Reyna's prison.
Sunlight spilled across the floor, outlining the girl as she lay
crouched on her pallet, watching him warily. Her hair was disheveled, her gown dirt-streaked, her eyes bright and feral.
She appeared a totally wild and captivating creature.

Gathering his fortitude, Viktor flexed the hand Reyna had
so savagely bitten last night. He had scrubbed the laceration
well with soap and then had bound his hand, yet still the

wound throbbed. He would have to pray that infection did not set in.

As Svein had predicted, Reyna had broken the bonds on her wrists. At least she had ceased her screams. Indeed, she now seemed to be giving him the silent treatment.

"You rested well, I presume?" he asked, hoping to rouse some comment from her. Instead, he observed her calculating gaze flicking to the spike of sunlight that hovered between his body and the doorjamb. No doubt she was assessing her chances of escape.

He crossed his arms over his chest. "You wish to leave, Reyna?" He grinned. "You have only to get past me."

That roused her—and stunned him! With a raging howl, the Valkyrie was up, vaulting across the room. Viktor was at first so taken aback that she almost succeeded in sailing past him. Then he reacted, thrusting out his broad arm and grabbing her around the waist, wrenching a stunned gasp from her as he clamped her writhing body against his hip.

She began to struggle in earnest. Grimacing, Viktor bore her flailing body across the hut and hurled her onto her pallet. She landed on her belly, flipping over to glare up at him.

Calmly, he strolled back to the doorway, turned, and grinned at her. "Round two, milady?"

The Valkyrie was game! With a demented cry, she sprang to her feet and hurled herself at him. Seizing her again and battling to contain her, Viktor was amazed by her strength, courage, and tenacity. Three more times she tried to get past him ... and three more times Viktor bore her resisting body back to the pallet and flung her down. Finally, panting from her exertions, she rose to her knees with fists doubled up and regarded him with blazing hatred.

Viktor was feeling utterly perplexed when he heard Sibeal speak behind him. "Master, I bring nourishment for milady."

Viktor stepped aside to allow the woman to enter. "By all means."

Sibeal swept inside with her tray. "How fare ye, my lady?" she asked.

Reyna totally ignored her servant and would not even look at her.

Sibeal set the tray down beside Reyna and turned to leave

Observing the thrall's troubled countenance, Viktor touched her arm. "She will come around in time," he whispered.

Reyna had evidently heard him. After Sibeal left, a loaf of bread sailed across the hut and hit Viktor squarely in his mid-section. With a grunt, he caught the missile, then turned to regard the little she-devil.

"You should not be so careless with your food, my lady," he taunted. "If you seek to defeat me, you must take nourishment, and conserve your strength."

She said nothing, but her eyes were eloquent with malice.

Viktor tossed the loaf back at Reyna. She caught it, tore off a chunk with her sharp white teeth, hurled another glare at him, and began chewing.

Stifling a chuckle, Viktor lounged against the doorway and watched her, taking a certain perverse pleasure from her defiance. "You are a little hellcat, Reyna, but you will be tamed in time."

That remark won him a savage glower.

"Your courage rouses my admiration," he continued, then winked at her. "But you might be well advised to remember that your feistiness also stirs my desire."

For a moment, still staring at him, she went motionless, though her nostrils flared slightly, as if she were sharply catching her breath.

"We will marry, milady," he said with calm determination, "and together, we will end this feud."

Her eyes smoldered and she began chewing viciously.

"We shall have a good life together," Viktor pressed on, now rather enjoying the one-sided conversation and having her as his captive audience. "In time, we will improve the quality of life for all our peoples. Once peace comes to Vanaheim, I will build greenhouses and grow more fitting delicacies to tempt you with—lush fruits and tasty vegetables."

She ripped at the bread with her teeth.

"You know, Reyna, you are quite beautiful, even in your current disarray," he mused. "One day we will have beautiful children together."

Still Reyna did not speak, but this time a spoon, encrusted

with porridge, sailed across the room to hit Viktor on the thigh. He picked it up and smiled.

"You put up a good front, Reyna," he remarked. "But I know what you are really like." He gazed into her eyes. "I know you, you see."

Her eyes flared with emotion.

Encouraged by her response, he continued earnestly. "I know how truly vulnerable and fragile you are inside. You've had to erect strong barriers to shield yourself against a brutal world. But you will not need those barriers with me."

Just when Viktor hoped he was meeting with success, she hurled a tankard full of buttermilk at him.

Although he managed to sidestep the missile, his leggings were spattered with the sticky liquid. He ground his jaw. "Your manners are atrocious, Reyna. A less patient man might thrash you. But perhaps I shall be kinder, and gentle you with my kisses."

This time, following an enraged roar, the entire tray was flung at Viktor. He leaped back, dodging flying dishes and spewing food as best he could. The bowl of porridge and the tray crashed to the earth behind him—

He turned to glare at the little vixen, and at last the Valkyrie spoke, while waving a fist—

"Son of Nidhogg! Never will I wed you so you may triumph in your bargain with my evil stepfather! Never will you subjugate me or make me your pawn to end this feud! And verily, you will never get close enough to kiss my feet, you foul pig!"

Now Viktor was furious, too. "Oh, but I shall, Reyna—you hellion! I'll kiss your feet if I choose to—and any *other* part of you that I desire to touch. Indeed, I think I shall demonstrate—now."

He charged across the room to grab Reyna, but she was ready, heaving herself to her feet and kicking out at him viciously. Jerking back with a cry of mingled pain and rage, Viktor grabbed his wounded shin and glowered at her. She stood just inches beyond him with her fists raised, and was smirking at him vindictively—

"You were saying, Viking?" she asked with poisonous spite.

"You little bitch," he ground out as he straightened. "I should strip off that shift and soundly beat your bottom."

Not in the least daunted, she hauled back a fist to punch him. He ducked the blow, grabbed her around the midsection, and tried to heave her over a shoulder, only to stagger beneath a rain of vicious blows. Viktor howled curses and grappled with the unholy terror. At last he managed to dump her once again on her pallet. He landed on top of her and forced her writhing body down to the mat. She struggled and screamed deprecations. He seized her wrists and pinned them high over her head. Her body wiggled frantically, ineffectually—and in an unconsciously sensual manner that all at once set Viktor's blood on fire. Driven to ruthlessness by her defiance, he felt more determined than ever to kiss her and teach her a lesson. Even as his conscience tried to rise to stop him, his wounded male ego cried out that she had *asked* for this.

"You were saying I would not touch you, Valkyrie," he told her with fury and triumph. "Well, you are not so smug now, are you? I vow that sooner or later, every inch of you will know my touch—and love it!"

She screamed her outrage. Viktor silenced her lips with a savage kiss. Even as out of control as he was, the touch of her soft mouth, the feel of her curves squirming against him, aroused him terribly. Lust mingled with anger hardened his loins; he yearned to part her sweet lips and thoroughly plunder her mouth.

Then her teeth sank into his lower lip, and he pulled away amid a roar of pain.

"Daughter of Hel!" He drew back his hand and realized he was within a hairbreadth of slapping her haughty face. Even in the face of this threat, she betrayed no fear, only cruel satisfaction.

He grabbed her face with determined hands, holding her immobile beneath him. "It's a damn good thing I was caught up on my tetanus shots before I came here," he forced out fiercely. "Hear this, Reyna. I am going to kiss you again—now—and if you bite me, I am going to sink my teeth into your pretty behind until you scream for mercy."

For once, he had managed to shock her. Reyna's eyes went

wide, and her mouth fell open on a gasp. "You would not, Viking!"

"I will!" he vowed. "And I swear to you, I will leave a mark you will carry to your grave."

He watched an intense struggle grip her features—consternation, anger, and finally fear. At last Reyna glared at him in trembling bravado, and Viktor knew she believed him. Thank God, he thought, since he never could have followed through on such a cruel threat.

She would let him kiss her! The very prospect drove him mad with desire. Perversely, he wanted to stretch out the moment, to torture her for having abused him so. He drew his index finger teasingly over her cheek, her rebellious lips, smiling at her low gasp, the hot emotion blazing in her eyes.

Leaning closer to the fuming girl, Viktor brushed his lips across hers; she flinched as if a flame had stroked her. He deliberately took his time, lightly caressing her mouth with his, instinctively knowing that a more subtle approach could prove far more devastating to this proud girl than a brutal kiss.

Although Reyna might be as untamed as a wildcat, Viktor found the taste of her was sweet. He kissed her gently, nuzzling and cajoling rather than ravishing. She held her lips tight, immobile, but she wisely did not bite him.

Her resistance further fueled Viktor's passions. "Open your mouth, Reyna," he whispered, still coaxing her with his lips.

Her eyes, now huge, defied him. "Nay!"

"Yea."

As Reyna would have protested again, Viktor seized his advantage, locking his mouth on hers and thrusting powerfully with his tongue. Her eyes flew open and strangled, incoherent sounds rose in her throat—

Viktor opened his eyes, too. He and Reyna stared at each other, eyeball-to-eyeball, sheer defiance meeting fiery determination, with his tongue all the while deep in the hot, wet velvet of her mouth.

The intimacy of the kiss, the starkness of their eye contact, were both incredibly sexy; heady lust engulfed Viktor. Then he felt her teeth close on his tongue, if tentatively—

He pulled back and spoke hoarsely. "Bite my tongue,

woman, and both of your pretty cheeks will bear the mark of my ownership."

She appeared horrified. "You would bite my face, Viking!" she gasped.

He laughed heartily, and pinched her behind to drive home his point. "Those aren't the cheeks I'm referring to."

She froze in shock. "You call my nethers cheeks? You are depraved!"

He grinned. "Yea, I suppose I am."

He leaned toward her again, while she lay beneath him warily. Inhaling the dusky scent of her hair, he licked her soft, warm cheek with his tongue. A sound much like a sob rose in her, and she thrust her face away. He followed, tickling her chin and the corner of her mouth with his teasing tongue.

Reyna clenched a fist and pounded it helplessly on the floor. "Nay . . . nay," she pleaded.

"Yea," Viktor whispered perversely.

When her eyes beseeched him—wild, desperate, but also passionate—he claimed her lips again. She whimpered, her sweet mouth trembling on his, and this time he knew she was responding! He gentled his kiss and thrust slowly with his tongue. She writhed, making a desperate, drowning sound, but he did not retreat. Pressing a hand to her warm thigh, Viktor seduced her with deep, deliberate strokes of his tongue until he felt her fists uncoiling against his chest—

He pulled back and grabbed her hands. "Kiss me, sweetheart. Wrap your lovely arms around my neck. Love me, angel."

She stared up at him, bright-eyed and uncertain.

"Jarl!"

Svein's voice at the portal jerked Viktor to awareness. At once he rolled off Reyna and stood.

"What is it?" he called with ill humor.

Svein glanced with obvious embarrassment from his scowling jarl to the flushed, disheveled girl on the pallet. "Orm and Rollo are fighting over a misplaced broadsword. You must come settle the dispute or blood will flow."

"Tell them I will be right there," Viktor snapped.

Svein coughed. "Yea, jarl."

After his man left, Viktor turned back to Reyna. "We will finish this later."

She had recovered herself and was glaring at him with loathing. "We will finish nothing. I would just as soon kiss a swine as kiss you, Viktor the Valiant."

He lifted a brow. "That is not how it seemed a moment ago."

"I only cooperated to keep you from savaging my nethers with your teeth," she retorted.

He grinned. "You will grow accustomed to my touch, Reyna—and my kisses. There will be no escaping me, I assure you." He drew his gaze over her meaningfully. "As to your lovely, firm nethers—they will enjoy my caresses, too."

She waved a fist at him. "Pig! You lie, evil son of Loki! I shall escape you—when my stepfather comes to rescue me and carves out your vile heart!"

"So Wolfgard will come, will he?" Viktor mocked. "You know, Reyna, last night when we took you, we made enough noise to wake the dead, but no one came to defend you. There were only a few scattered sentries posted at the wharf and outside the village. Most foolish of Wolfgard, and most odd. Your stepfather must have been eager to be rid of you, don't you think?"

She said nothing, but her eyes were bright, her lower lip quivering. He had gotten to her, and in a way, Viktor was glad. The sooner Reyna accepted her destiny, the better.

He left, slamming and barring the door.

Striding off to go settle the dispute between Orm and Rollo, Viktor was not entirely pleased by his behavior with Reyna. True, the Valkyrie had taunted him remorselessly, but his reaction had perhaps been too close to the edge. He realized he could far too easily revert to a primitive man and become a Viking indeed. Of course, he could have some fun with this physical courtship, provided he did not take things too far—

He grinned as he remembered the kisses they had shared. Ah, it was glorious, especially when Reyna had responded that first little bit.

The Valkyrie was a creature of splendid, intense passion. She might hate him with all her heart right now, but one day she would love him with equal strength. And that was the day he would live for . . .

In the hut, Reyna trembled on her pallet. She felt confused by the feelings the hated Viktor had stirred in her. When he had kissed her, her breathing had quickened, her heart had thumped wildly, and she had felt such a strange, wild fluttering in her blood, in her nipples, even between her thighs. She recognized this as the primal urge to mate—the same twinge she had felt last night when Viktor's hard, heavy body had landed on hers, and previously when he had stolen her ankle bracelet.

What had the Viking meant when he had claimed he "knew" her? They were strangers, and yet, ever since he had returned from Valhalla, she *had* felt some sort of mystical bond with him—partly physical, but also spiritual.

How could she continue to feel such traitorous yearnings for her enemy? If she could not trust her own body, her own instincts, what could she trust? The hated Wolfgard and his clan had deserted her—she could depend only on herself now.

She must escape the Viking—or kill him—before this mysterious frailty he stirred in her brought her to ruin . . .

EIGHTEEN

"FATHER, REYNA IS GONE! I HAVE SEARCHED THROUGHOUT THE village, and she is nowhere to be found! Her pony is still in the stable, and I fear she is lost to us! Sibeal is missing as well!"

Wolfgard was seated on the floor, eating his porridge, when Ragar burst into the dining hall, his face stricken with anxiety.

Wolfgard snorted, not bothering to wipe the gruel dribbling down his whiskered chin. "Your half sister is missing, you say?"

"Yea."

"I already suspected as much myself. It appears Viktor the Valiant has made good his promise and has taken the Ravisher off with him."

Ragar's jaw dropped. "How can this be? How could Viktor have come into our village undetected?"

Wolfgard shrugged. "I stationed the usual sentries—three at the wharf and two outside the village."

"The usual sentries?" Ragar repeated, appearing aghast as he stepped forward. "But, Father, how could you not have doubled the watch, knowing of Viktor's treacherous plans?"

Wolfgard slammed down the tankard of whey he had been sipping. "Do not presume to tell me how to protect my own village, my son—especially when you are unprepared to see to the task yourself!"

Ragar lowered his gaze. "I realize I am not the warrior you

wanted, my father. Yet, under these circumstances, simple logic would seem to dictate—"

"Get ye out of here—and your logic with ye!" Wolfgard cut in nastily. "Verily, I am relieved to have the Valkyrie out of my hair for a time. Yea, I shall relish this respite. I predict that soon enough, Viktor the Valiant will send her packing, once he tires of her waspish ways."

"But you cannot mean to leave Reyna there, at the mercy of our enemy?" Ragar exclaimed.

Wolfgard laughed derisively. "Mark my words, my son. 'Tis our enemy who will need mercy ere long."

Ragar drew himself up with pride. "If you are determined to abandon my sister, I cannot stay you. But I shall lead a rescue mission in your stead."

Wolfgard surged to his feet, sending his dishes flying and scowling ferociously at the boy. "You go on a fool's errand. We have no ship."

"Verily, why?" Ragar demanded.

Wolfgard had the grace to appear embarrassed as he coughed and glanced away. "Egil informed me he found the *drakar* missing at dawn, and the sentries bound and gagged at the wharf. According to the guards, Viktor and his kinsmen overwhelmed them last night and later set our ship adrift in the fjord."

Ragar threw up his hands. "So there again, you left us all but unprotected."

"The deed is done," Wolfgard growled. "And it may be months before a new war vessel can be readied."

"Then I will mount a campaign on land."

"On land?" Wolfgard scoffed. "Do you not realize that with the spring thaw and seasonal rains, there will be no crossing the fjord now? You will be impelled to travel high into the mountains and circle the river's head."

"I am prepared to do so."

Wolfgard's craggy features twisted in utter disbelief. "You are willing to risk the vengeance of Surt—or to drown in a bog of boiling mud?"

"I will do whatever is necessary to rescue my sister."

Wolfgard stepped toward the boy, his battle-scarred face for once mirroring genuine concern. "Son, 'tis true you are not all that I had hoped for. Yet you are my sole issue. You are no warrior. Do not risk your life for this ungrateful wench."

"The 'ungrateful wench' is my sister, Father," Ragar answered with quiet determination. "I have no choice but to stand up for her. 'Tis a matter of honor now."

"Bah!" Wolfgard waved him off. "There is no honor in rescuing a female."

Ragar spoke through gritted teeth. "I will do no less for my own blood." He turned and left the chamber amid Wolfgard's guttural curses.

Wolfgard paced the room, frowning savagely and making frustrated sounds under his breath. When he had allowed Viktor to take the cursed Reyna with ease, he had not figured on the boy's reaction. Now his son was making a fool of himself. Yet if Ragar was determined to embark on this doomed mission, Wolfgard could not stay him, or else make the lad look like even more of a milksop to his men.

A pox on the Valkyrie, Reyna! The chit had brought him naught but grief! He should have abandoned her back in Loire. The only satisfaction he had was the thought of the retribution Reyna would wreak, in such generous measure, on his enemy, Viktor the Valiant.

Wolfgard grinned with sadistic pleasure at the thought. Verily, he could not wait to hear the first report from his spy in the enemy village.

Outside, Ragar sought out his retainer, Harald. He found his friend on the tundra, practicing archery, with a dwarf willow serving as target.

"My kinsman, I must speak with you," Ragar greeted him.

Releasing an arrow—which smartly met its mark—Harald turned to Ragar. "You are worried about Reyna?"

"Yea." Ragar scowled. "You have already heard of her abduction?"

Harald pulled an arrow from its quiver. "After breaking our fast, Cuellar and I discovered the village sentries, Rolfe and Thorald, bound up and hidden behind the haystack. They informed us of Viktor's raid last night."

"And you did not so advise me at once?" Ragar asked indignantly.

"I made the attempt, but by then you had already left your chamber."

Ragar nodded morosely. "Yea, I was searching for my sister. My father seems unconcerned over her plight. I need your help to organize a rescue party."

Harald considered this for a moment, then said, "My friend, I understand your fear and suffering over Reyna's kidnapping. But Odin knows we would be fools to pursue this madness."

"Why?"

Harald moved closer and spoke with regret. "By now most of the village is aware of your half sister's fate. No one mourns her loss—and all will be reluctant to join our cause."

"Then I must speak my mind to them all!" Ragar retorted.

"You know I would lay down my life for you or Reyna," Harald continued earnestly. "But I am also sworn to protect you. How can I allow you to embark on a mission that will surely mean your death—and mayhap Reyna's as well?"

"We must try. I am not afraid."

Harald sighed. "My friend, we have no way to rescue her. Our ship is lost—"

"Yea, I am aware. We will have to proceed overland, and circle the head of the fjord."

Harald lifted a brow in amazement. "You are saying we will journey high into the mountains and surely rouse the anger of Surt?"

"Should we allow fear to stay us, as if we are all women and not warriors?" Ragar argued passionately.

Harald shook his head with sadness. "My friend, I must speak my heart. Our warriors fear the ghosts and trolls that lurk in the moors. They will not be eager to join this cause."

"I will proceed my own self, if need be," said Ragar.

Harald expelled a heavy, resigned breath. "Verily, I am with you, then. I will try to raise a small band of warriors, but you must give me time. 'Twill not be easy convincing our men to risk their lives for a woman who has naught but insulted them."

"This I know," said Ragar grimly. "But do not delay raising our forces—else I shall be about the mission alone."

* * *

Viktor stood in front of the barred door to Reyna's small prison. A day had passed, and he dearly hoped time had eased the Valkyrie's violent temper. But, in fairness to Sibeal, who would soon arrive with the girl's breakfast, he would test the waters first himself, to see if her fiery disposition had cooled, or remained boiling hot—

He removed the bolt and slanted open the door. Sunshine spilled across the dirt floor—

She was gone!

He stepped inside. "Reyna?"

A split second later, she landed full against his back, the shock of her taut body almost knocking the wind from him. He realized too late that she had lain in wait for him behind the panel. Her knees locked at his waist, she howled the scream of a banshee and began beating on his head with her fists—

Mercy, she was behaving like a madwoman! Staggering beneath her vigorous blows, Viktor managed to reach up and grab her wrists. Stumbling across the room while still struggling with her, he finally yanked her off him and flung her back onto her pallet—

She stared up at him, appearing momentarily stunned. Good Lord, Viktor thought, she even *looked* like a madwoman with her hair tangled wildly around her, her eyes bright and fierce, her face and shift smeared with dirt.

Then her features clenched with rage and she charged him again!

This time Viktor was fully prepared—and damn angry to boot! With one strong arm he grabbed Reyna around her waist and bore her, screaming and kicking, back to the pallet. She landed with a thud and flipped over, as lithe and feral as a pugnacious cat.

He crossed his arms over his chest and glared down at her. "Shall we try for round three today?" he asked calmly.

She was silent, staring at him with caution mingled with hatred.

"My, but you are in a raging temper this morning," he muttered, rubbing the back of his head, which throbbed from her punches.

She smiled with malicious pleasure.

That smirk invited retaliation. "Tell me, does this little demonstration of your esteem for me arise out of my kissing you yesterday?"

With a howl of rage she was up again, this time making a dive for his knees! Realizing the little termagant sought to trip him and bring him down, Viktor sidestepped the lunge, caught Reyna low at the waist, flipping her in the process, and straightened with her dangling upside down against his side, her arms and legs flailing wildly and her shift lifted to the tops of her delectable buttocks.

Viktor could not help himself. With his free hand he smartly whacked that adorable, squirming behind—

She froze, and he glanced downward, grinning as he caught a glimpse of her red, mortified face. "That's better," he murmured.

She began wiggling again in earnest. He whacked her once more, and making a sound of repressed rage, she again stilled her struggles. He crossed the room and unceremoniously dumped her on her belly. The action sent her shift hiking up over her curvaceous bottom, and Viktor greedily caught a glimpse—

Then she was yanking down her nightdress, her face as red as a tomato. Viktor was sorely tempted to laugh, but managed to restrain the rash impulse, knowing that to do so would only provoke another ferocious outburst.

"You know, Reyna, you are being most difficult," he scolded.

"Then send me back to my people!"

"Ah, so the she-troll has a voice after all?" he mocked.

She glared at him.

"And now Wolfgard and his company are your people?" he continued with an air of amazement. "That certainly comes as a shock to me."

"Why do you not let me go, Viking?" she demanded furiously. "You know we despise each other, you and I."

"Do we?" he inquired mildly. "Well, I must admit you are certainly inviting my contempt at the moment. But it won't work, Reyna. I am still going to marry you." Looking her over slowly, he chuckled. "Though frankly, you don't make a very appealing bride at the moment—your hair is as charming as seaweed, and you are filthy from head to toe."

"Because you have kept me like a animal!" she blazed.

"Nevertheless, you are quite a sight." He lounged against the doorway and winked at her. "So I think I shall not kiss you today, much as I know you'll be disappointed."

"Disappointed?" she screamed. "I would just as soon kiss an asp!"

"That hardly seemed your attitude yesterday."

"Only because you overwhelmed me with brute strength!"

"I'm pleased to hear you acknowledge that I do have that ability," he drawled.

"Rot in Hel!"

He sighed, growing weary of her unmitigated scorn. "You have only to act more reasonable, Reyna, and I will give you more freedom—"

"Freedom to become your wife?" she scoffed.

"Yea." He grinned. "But we might start with freedom to leave this cozy little jail, to take a bath . . ." He looked her over again and raised an eyebrow. "Which you do sorely need, my dear."

"Take your freedom—and your bath—and choke on both, Viking."

He shook his head. "Reyna, you are your own worst enemy. And you will stay locked up here, like the spoiled brat you are, until you learn to be reasonable."

"Never!"

"Never?" he repeated, his voice rising slightly. He strode closer to her and spoke with low menace. "You know, Reyna, the only time I have seen you display the least respect for me was when I whacked your pretty behind. A few more demonstrations of this defiance, and be warned—I am prepared to blister it thoroughly."

"A plague take you, filthy whoreson!" she screamed.

"And to hell with you."

His patience exhausted, Viktor left, slamming and barring the door. He strode off, grinding his jaw and mumbling to himself, not even acknowledging Sibeal and Svein as they passed, the slave bearing Reyna's meal. Had he truly bitten off more than he could chew with the hellion Reyna? Her hatred for him seemed unremitting and absolute. Worse yet, she was capable of provoking him to a level of anger that frightened him—and to a degree of lust that was every bit as staggering. Had the woman no fear at all, no regard for her own safety? For now, he could only hope she would mend her ways and become more biddable before he strangled her! Provoking the primitive man in him as she so skillfully did, she often made him forget he had ever been a gentleman ...

Inside the hut, Reyna thought about the confrontation with Viktor and trembled in anger and mortification. Why did the hated Viking have to remind her of her body's betrayal? Even as they had struggled, she had felt those appalling stirrings again, especially when his hand had smacked her bottom like a stamp of ownership, when his burning gaze had raked so hungrily over her bare thighs and the exposed tops of her buttocks. How could she feel such cravings for a man she so hated?

Suddenly Reyna's thoughts scattered as the door again opened. She tensed, presuming Viktor had returned, then glowered at Sibeal, who stood at the portal with a tray of food. Behind the thrall loomed one of Viktor's kinsmen.

Reyna continued to glare murder at the woman. Sibeal, undaunted, crossed over with her tray and knelt, setting the repast down beside Reyna.

"Milady, you must take some nourishment," she said worriedly.

"Do not dare to speak to me, traitor!" Reyna hissed. "You could have saved me two nights past, yet you let my enemy take me!"

Sibeal's expression mirrored turmoil and compassion. "Milady, I allowed Viktor to take you because I truly believe your destiny lies with him."

"Do not try to sway me with such foolish prattle, woman," Reyna argued furiously. "'Tis no excuse for your perfidy!"

"Milady, I beseech you, be more reasonable," Sibeal pleaded. "By rebelling against your fate, you are only aggravating your own misery—"

"'Tis you who have magnified my misery through your betrayal!" Reyna raged. "Now leave me before I strangle the life from you!"

Releasing a frustrated sigh, Sibeal rose and left.

Afterward, Reyna glared at the food. How had Sibeal dared implore to her to be more reasonable! How had Viktor dared to insist on the same, as if everyone had forgotten that *she* was the one who had been cruelly snatched from her bed and taken captive by her enemy! Spitefully she decided to leave her breakfast untouched, thereby demonstrating her utter contempt for Sibeal, Viktor, and all of his people.

Verily, she would starve herself rather than submit to his will.

For the next few days Viktor tried again and again to reach Reyna. He stood in the doorway of the hut and talked with her calmly, at length, about what it would be like when they were man and wife. She glowered, hissed deprecations, and hurled dishes at him. At times when she so maddened him, he knew he made some of his comments more to taunt her than to coax her cooperation.

"You may hiss like a tigress now, Reyna," he said one morning, "but you will purr like a kitten when we are man and wife."

She hurled a handful of dirt at him.

"We will have beautiful children together," he told her the next afternoon.

She spit at his feet.

"You will cease being stubborn as a donkey, Reyna, or I will yoke you to a plow to teach you some respect!" he raved the following day.

She bared her teeth and actually growled at him.

Viktor soon dismally concluded that there was no getting through to the obstreperous wench. Within a few days he was in such a foul temper that he could not trust himself around the girl. Because Sibeal fretted continuously that Reyna did not eat or drink enough, Viktor sent his kinsmen with the thrall to take trays to the girl twice daily. He did caution the warriors that he would allow no mistreatment of her, no matter how badly she provoked them.

His retainers fared no better than he had with the waspish Valkyrie. One evening Rollo barged into Viktor's chamber in a terrible temper, his face streaked with mutton stew and a bruise already forming on his forehead.

"The girl threw her victuals at me, jarl!" he declared angrily. "And she called me a fleabrain! I will eat my own sword before I attend the witch again."

"Very well. I thank you for trying," said Viktor. "Next time I will send Orm."

Orm confronted Viktor soon after breakfast the following morning. He was sporting a bad limp, a very red face, and his fists were clenched in fury. "The Valkyrie kicked me in the groin and called me a swine! Let me slay her, jarl."

Viktor groaned. "Go soak your wounds in the bathhouse. Next time I will let Canute deal with her."

That night Canute charged into the dining chamber in a roaring temper. Never before had Viktor seen his mightiest warrior actually trembling in fury. "That she-troll called me a shrivel prick!" he roared, slamming his fist down on Viktor's table. "She horribly insulted my manhood! Let me take her to the tundra and slit her throat! I would sacrifice her to Surt, but the volcano would gag on her loathsome entrails and spit her up!"

"Dammit!" Viktor surged to his feet. "Will the little hellion never cease her defiance? Enough, then!"

Viktor stormed out of his longhouse and down the path to Reyna's prison. He spotted Sibeal waiting outside the stone hut, a tray of food at her feet. She was wringing her hands.

"Jarl, I am worried about my mistress! She was in such a rage that Canute and I were forced to flee her presence. I am distraught because she will no longer eat or even drink!"

Viktor was too furious to be concerned. "You are distraught? I'd advise you to save your concern for others far more deserving! Reyna has practically been the death of us all! It is time for that little, spoiled brat to be taught a good lesson—and do not attempt to stop me, woman!"

Sibeal stepped back, biting her lip.

Viktor ripped off the bolt and kicked open the door. He glanced inside warily, expecting the Valkyrie to leap out at him. Then he spotted her on her pallet. She sat up slowly, but, given his temper, Viktor did not immediately note her sluggish reactions.

"You," he thundered, shaking a finger at her, "are about to be taught some manners—a painful lesson for you, and a pure pleasure for me!"

He stalked across the room, knelt, and grabbed her. She did not resist. He started to throw her across his knees, then at last noticed how red and drawn her face was. He scowled and instinctively pressed a palm to her forehead.

"My God, woman—you are burning up with fever!" he cried.

NINETEEN

IN THE NEXT MOMENT, SIBEAL RUSHED INSIDE THE HUT. WHILE still holding Reyna, Viktor demanded over his shoulder, "What ails your mistress?"

Sibeal knelt beside them. "I tried to tell you, my lord. She has stopped eating and drinking entirely—and the room is overwarm."

Glancing at the fire in the pit at the center of the small hut, Viktor realized Sibeal was right. "It *is* too hot in here, and if Reyna has stopped drinking, she may be dehydrated."

Sibeal gasped in alarm. "What is this dire malady?"

"She may be drained from the heat, and from no drink or nourishment," Viktor clarified. "We will pray she is dehydrated and not actually ill—or I don't know what I will do."

"Nor I, my lord," said Sibeal.

"Bring drink," Viktor commanded.

The woman rushed outside, returning momentarily with a tankard of mead. Viktor pressed the cup to Reyna's lips, only to find they were tightly closed as the girl glared up at him in relentless mutiny.

"Did I not tell you, my lord?" asked Sibeal. "My lady will not cooperate."

"She will," replied Viktor obdurately. To Reyna, he said with soft menace, "Little Valkyrie, you will open your mouth and drink all of this—*now*—or I will summon Rollo, Orm, and Canute to hold you while I pour it down your throat— whether you choke on it or not. In any event, my kinsmen

171

will be witnesses to your total humiliation. Well, what will it be?"

Reyna opened her mouth and began to sip slowly, still glaring at him.

He smiled at Sibeal, then glanced at Reyna's ragged, filthy garment and hoyden hair. "She is so filthy."

"This hut is not a fitting abode, my lord," replied Sibeal. "My lady's bed is on the floor, which is itself no better than caked mud."

"I agree," said Viktor. "I will move her to my chamber at the longhouse. But first, I will take her to the hot spring and bathe her—"

Sibeal's hand flew to her open mouth. "My Lord, you must not! 'Tis not fitting for you to attend my lady!"

Viktor stared from the appalled Sibeal to Reyna, who appeared equally aghast at his intentions. "I must see to the task myself. After all, Reyna is to become my bride. And if I trust her with a woman such as you, you know she will escape."

Sibeal sighed. "Yea, my lord, you speak the truth. Verily, my lady has brought this calamity on herself through her defiance. Go see to her cleansing, and I will go to your longhouse and bid your housekeeper find milady a suitable garment."

Sibeal swept out. As soon as Reyna had downed all the mead, Viktor stood with her still tightly clasped in his arms. He left the small hut, proceeding through the frigid night toward the bathhouse.

"You little fool," he muttered under his breath. "Now I must save you from your own recklessness."

Staring up at the grim-faced, determined man who carried her, Reyna was feeling astounded by all that had transpired, as well as dizzy and very confused. She wondered why Viktor the Valiant had not simply killed her and been done with her. How could he still insist he would make her his bride, as much as she despised him? Why did he treat her with this confusing combination of sternness, gentleness, and humor? Did he not know he could never win her heart, much less her loyalty?

Reyna would have loved to have slain Viktor now, but she was far too weak. For that she had only herself to blame.

Sometime during the past few days, she had simply given up and decided that if she could not escape him, she would starve herself and die before she gave in to his demands.

But even this perfidy Viktor would not allow—he had forced her to drink the mead, damn his eyes. Now she would no doubt live, though the fermented libation had left her feeling weaker, more defenseless against him than ever.

And he actually sought to bathe her? Rape her, far more likely! she thought with fear. Thanks to her own folly, she could not stay him if he decided to force apart her thighs.

Yet Reyna feared something far more than Viktor's ravishment—she feared herself, her own desires. She feared that Viktor, instead of raping her, might arouse her to passion once more with his devastating combination of tenderness and teasing. She feared he would melt her resistance with his pretty blue eyes and the strange, soulful words he sometimes used to woo her.

By the saints, being close to him this way, with his body so hot and hard against hers, with the night wind chill on her feverish face, was torture enough! One of Viktor's strong arms was clamped under her knees, another braced against her back, and her hip bounced intimately against his hard belly as he strode along. She could smell his male scent, could feel his warm breath tickling her hair and the heat of his body radiating into hers. He was her enemy, yet she felt oddly cherished, held in his strong arms. For the first time in her life, Reyna wondered what it would be like to stop fighting, to turn herself over to a tender warrior who would fight her battles, protect her to the death, and make her his queen.

Oh, what was happening to her? He must be a sorcerer, this man. Perhaps he had been granted special powers in Valhalla, for he inspired thoughts that could seduce her straight into the madness of self-betrayal and surrender, subjugation and defeat . . .

Viktor kicked open the door to the bathhouse and carried Reyna inside. The hut was lit by two whale-oil lamps. Ottar and his younger brother, Tyre, both damp-haired and wearing just leggings, popped up from the bench where they had been drying themselves with towels. Both lads stared wide-eyed at the sight of Viktor holding the filthy Reyna in his arms.

"Jarl!" cried Ottar, staring at the disheveled girl. "What are you doing?"

"Please leave us and see that no one else disturbs us," came Viktor's gruff response.

"Yea, jarl," said Ottar. He and Tyre quickly gathered their gear and left.

Viktor set Reyna down at the edge of the bubbly pool, so that her toes dangled in the effervescent water. He watched her flex a shapely foot and stare at the bathing pond longingly.

He plopped down beside her. "Why did you try to starve yourself, Reyna?"

Staring ahead with her jaw clenched, she did not answer. He reached out to smooth down her tousled hair, and she flinched, hurling him a glare.

"Do you find my touch so loathsome?" he asked.

She jerked a glance toward him, her bright eyes telling him in no uncertain terms that she did.

He chuckled. "You may have lost your common sense, but not your spirit, eh, milady?"

She crossed her arms over her chest and ignored him.

"The silent treatment again?" he asked. He studied her haughty profile thoughtfully, noting the slight quivering of her proud chin. "You know, Reyna, you put on quite a show—quite a warlike facade you have. But a true warrior woman would never starve herself, but stay prepared to defeat her enemy. I suspect, then, that you are a little more moved by me than you want to admit."

Still she said nothing, although her hands curled into tight fists at her sides.

"You are so fierce, Reyna, that sometimes it is hard for me to think of you as feminine, or fragile, or vulnerable," he continued quietly. "But you are all of those things, aren't you? And that's what scares you so much that you want to starve yourself—because in time you are going to *be* all of those things with me. We will share everything together as man and wife."

Now he had roused her wrath. She turned to him and spoke with eyes burning and fists raised. "You lie! I will wed Loki himself before I become your bride! And I will yet smite you for your treasonous tongue, Viktor the Valiant!"

Viktor whistled, then grinned.

Reyna attacked him with both fists. Viktor grabbed her wrists, easily holding her defenseless.

"Let me go!" she demanded.

"You should not battle me when you are so weak, little kitten," he taunted her.

She screamed deprecations and tried to wrench her hands away, but ultimately ceased struggling against his superior strength, although she continued to glare at him.

Only then, with another chuckle, did Viktor release her. He casually pulled off his tunic and smiled as she stared wide-eyed at his naked chest. He caught her glancing downward, at the outline of his aroused manhood straining against his leggings. He winked at her. Her face flamed and she hastily glanced away.

Still, Viktor couldn't resist commenting on her delicious lapse. Leaning toward her, he whispered intimately, "Don't worry, Reyna. You will have it. I'm hoping it will soon become your most treasured plaything."

She tried to glower at him but could manage only an uncertain frown, and he noticed to his delight that her eyes had gone beguilingly wide.

He spoke in low, firm tones. "Take off your shift. I'm going to bathe you now."

She was horrified, her spirit recovered. "Nidhogg take you, Viking!"

But Viktor was not about to be thwarted. Without warning, he grabbed Reyna's wrists and wrestled her down beneath him at the edge of the pool. Again he easily subdued her.

"Let me go, Viking!" she screamed.

"Nay, Reyna, not while you're still this filthy."

Restraining both of her wrists with one of his hands, Viktor drew out his dagger. As she gasped, he made a neat slit in the top of her garment. He replaced the dagger in its sheath, drew back, and rent the cloth from neck to waist.

Reyna stared up at him in appalled silence.

He gazed unabashedly at her body—at her lovely, firm breasts falling and rising, at her quivering belly. "You are so beautiful," he murmured, his hand touching the side of her breast through the ragged edge of cloth, and straying dangerously close to her taut nipple.

Reyna cried out incoherently at his daring touch; when she tried to bolt away, he rolled his hip over hers to stay her. A wince of shock and desire escaped her, and she found she could no more summon the will to fight him. Viktor felt so solid, so crushingly good against her, and his intense blue eyes were wreaking havoc with her heartbeat, her emotional equilibrium, even as the heat of his hard arousal on her pelvis pushed a powerful, raw pulse deep between her thighs. The throbbing need was exquisitely pleasurable, and more potent than ever before.

"You shame me, Viking!" she cried.

"I do not," he replied fiercely. "There will never be shame between us, Reyna. I will know your body, and you will know mine, and we will both glory in the intimacy and discovery."

Hearing his words, Reyna struggled to control her own ragged breathing as she very much feared he had spoken the truth.

He caught her face between his hands. "Do not try to convince me that you do not feel what I feel, Reyna. We know each other already."

Reyna felt confused and traitorously touched by his words and the emotion in his gaze. He was regarding her with a strange reverence, not the lust or brutality she would have expected from any other Viking conqueror. And just as she had feared, having Viktor behave with such gentleness toward her was far more devastating than bearing the brunt of all the savagery his magnificent body could have unleashed on her.

"What say you, Viking?" she asked warily.

He spoke in a mesmerizing whisper. "I am saying we are linked, Reyna. Linked in our souls. You must feel it, because you are part of me. Our being together is preordained, inescapable."

"Destiny," she murmured with a pensive frown, remembering Sibeal's usage of this word.

A smile lit his eyes. "Yes, destiny. I am saying I know you, Reyna—and you belong to me." He lovingly swept his hand

down her side, curling his fingers around the sleek curve of
her hip. "I know this body." When he glanced back up at her,
his smile grew very sad. "It's strange to feel you are mine,
yet have you denied to me by your will."

"Why say you I am yours?" she asked quietly.

He was silent for a long moment, then whispered, "Because I have loved you in another life."

Reyna looked up at him in utter awe, her stunned words
barely audible. "You have lived another life, Viking?"

When he stroked the curve of her jaw with his fingers, she
did not pull away. "Lived it—and loved you there."

Despite herself, Reyna was fascinated. "Did you live this
life when you went to Valhalla?"

After another hesitation, he replied, "Yes."

"And I was there with you?"

He leaned toward her until his lips almost touched hers.
"You were in my arms, in a tub very much like this, and I
was inside you. Very deeply inside you."

She gasped, her cheeks very hot, but not from fever.

He brushed her lips tenderly with his, then pulled back.
"As I said, it is destiny. You can fight it, Reyna, but you can't
win."

She was silent, yet appeared very intrigued. She started to
say something, then evidently thought better of it, clamping
her mouth shut and regarding him warily.

Viktor felt a stab of disappointment at her emotional retreat. "Likely I should not have told you that, should I?" he
asked with a trace of bitterness. "Now you will use the
knowledge as a weapon against me, won't you, little warrior?"

"Not that," she admitted, surprising him. "I would not."

He stared deeply into her eyes. "Why wouldn't you?"

She met his searching gaze fully. "Because such a gift
from the gods is most sacred. And because—"

He leaned closer, until she could feel his warm breath on
her cheek. "Yes, Reyna?"

Shocking even herself, Reyna admitted breathlessly, "Because your eyes were sad when you told me, Viktor the Valiant. I know of such sadness."

"Do you?"

Pride flared on her lovely face, and Viktor could literally see Reyna marshaling her defenses, pulling up barriers to shield herself from his further probes into her soul.

"But that does not mean I will be yours—ever, Viking. Or ever trust you. Or ever . . ."

"Yes?" he prodded.

"Be wife to you!"

"Even if it will stop the bloodshed?" he asked passionately.

She raised her chin. "I have no desire to stop it."

Hurt and determination tightened his jaw. "Fair enough. Then I'll simply have to change your mind, won't I?"

She did not comment.

He tugged on her garment. "For now, I'm going to bathe you."

She clutched the ragged edges for dear life. "You will not!"

"I will."

Viktor slipped down into the pool. Reyna made a token fight as Viktor hauled her into his arms. But all her resistance faded the instant she was enveloped by the bubbly warmth. The water felt effervescent and marvelous; the strength of Viktor's body surrounding her felt even better, she had to admit.

Gaining the advantage of her brief lassitude, he pressed his mouth to her ear. "Take off your shift, Reyna."

That titilating remark propelled Reyna from her lethargy. She squirmed out of his embrace, sinking into the chest-deep pool, her toes contacting the rocky bottom. Facing him defiantly, she cried, "Nay!"

"Nay?" he repeated, lifting a brow. "You say that word much, milady. I may just have to kiss a few more 'nays' out of you."

"I will not give up my garment!" she retorted, again clasping the frayed edges. "Even though you have ruined it, Viking."

Viktor laughed. "Reyna, quit being such a stubborn chit. Your servant is bringing you another dress. You cannot put it on until you take off that rag—and why not get yourself really clean in the meantime?"

Reyna was silent, seeing Viktor's logic but still afraid to

trust him—or herself—once the garment was removed. She very much feared that once she abandoned her shift, she would abandon what remained of her inhibitions as well.

As she continued to hesitate, Viktor reached for the cake of soap the others had left on the stone ledge above them. With determination he moved toward her; she gasped as he easily tugged the shift from her shoulders with his free hand. Even in the warmth of the pool, gooseflesh convulsed Reyna at his bold touch. She felt very vulnerable standing next to him in the water, now totally nude, his splendid, muscled chest and arms also bare—and so temptingly close.

He reached out to smooth the soap across her shoulder— Reyna flinched, as if burned. "Please," she pleaded.

"You do not want to be clean?" he teased tenderly.

"I will see to the task myself."

He chuckled, placing the cake of soap in her hands. "See that you do, Reyna."

Relieved, she caught a sharp breath. He moved off a few paces, crossed his arms over his chest, and stood watching her audaciously. Lathering her hair and running the soap over her body, Reyna wondered what was worse—having Viktor touch her, or having him devour her with those bright blue eyes as he was doing now. When he had slit her gown, she had fully expected him to ravish her. Instead, he had touched her with kindness, respect even, and despite her claims to the contrary, she had not felt shame. Indeed, damn her traitorous desires, she had gloried in it, especially when he had spoken his soulful words and looked at her with such painful longing. She had actually felt the link between them then, just as she felt the potent physical need for him in her breasts and deep between her thighs. Had she let him bathe her, she doubtless would have freed that nice bulge in his leggings and made her own disgrace and treachery complete.

Still he watched her, his smoldering look making her heart roar in her ears. She tilted her head back and rinsed her hair. She looked up to see him grinning.

"We are finished now?" she asked with a telltale quiver.

"Nay." His words came out huskily. "You did such a splendid job of cleansing yourself, Reyna, that I would have you wash me as well."

"Rot in Hel, Viking!" she replied tremulously, yet she felt more tempted than she ever would have believed.

"Then at least come give me the soap," he coaxed huskily.

She edged closer to comply, then became thoroughly intrigued when Viktor did not grab her. He appeared so glorious and solemn, so wet, gleaming, and sensual as he continued to devour her with his eyes. Why was his lack of aggression so very debilitating?

And what madness had possessed her? For now Reyna went to him and shamelessly ran the soap over his magnificent male chest. With a growl of pleasure, Viktor hauled her close. The soap slipped through her fingers as Viktor claimed her lips, thrusting powerfully with his tongue and forcing explosive heat deep inside her—

Reyna whimpered, drowning in pleasure, unable to bear the savage sweetness of Viktor's kiss. He kissed her with such desperate need, such urgency, as if they were indeed two souls wrenched apart and he was determined to bring them back together again. His lips were warm and skilled, his tongue deliciously bold and rough. Never had Reyna experienced such shattering intimacy with a man; she felt the communion, the joy, to her very soul. The feel of his hard, satiny chest against her tingling breasts was pure paradise. She could *feel* his desire straining against his leggings, branding her pelvis with his heat. When his large, firm hands slid down her spine and cupped her buttocks, nestling her closer to his glorious erection, she thought she would die of pleasure. Traitorously, she found herself reaching for the ties on his leggings—

The door burst open behind them, sending a chill sweeping in, and both sprang apart, slightly dazed as they turned toward the portal.

"My lord," Sibeal called. "I have brought garments for my lady."

Reyna glanced breathlessly at Viktor, and he winked at her. Oh, what was happening to her? Rather than being insulted—as she well should have been—she felt weak as a kitten, and appalled by her own defection. Had Sibeal not come, she would have given herself over to her enemy—and eagerly so!

* * *

Half an hour later, Viktor tucked a very clean, very bemused Reyna into his bed. The wolves had already been banished to the next chamber. Viktor had forced Reyna to eat
gruel and drink more mead, had felt her forehead and fretted
over her until he was satisfied that she had been merely
"dehydrated"—whatever that odd term meant—rather than
genuinely ill.

"You are comfortable, my lady?" he asked, lounging
against the portal.

"You are not joining me?" she scoffed.

"Is that an invitation?"

"Burn in Hel!"

"I certainly feel flattered to be asked," he teased, ignoring
her outburst. "And I'd like to oblige such a winsome creature
as you. But actually, I'm saving myself for marriage."

She glanced at him in perplexity, evidently not understanding his humor at all.

"And you look so very disappointed," he added with a
chuckle.

That insult Reyna understood! A whalebone comb sailed
across the chamber to hit Viktor in the stomach.

With a grunt, he caught the object, crossed the room, and
handed the comb back to her. "I told you to use that comb on
your hoyden hair—or must I see to that task myself as well?"

Reyna yanked the comb through her hair and glared at
Viktor. "Touch me again and die, Viking!"

"That hardly seemed the case in the bathhouse."

"Because I was weak and exhausted—and dizzy from the
mead you forced down my throat. But you were right on one
account, Viking. From now on, I will build my strength so I
may slay you."

"Good girl," he rejoined solemnly. "I'm pleased to see you
recovering your spirit." He glanced around the chamber, then
pinned her with a stern glance. "And you know I am trusting
you, allowing you to stay here in the longhouse."

She grinned. "That is a mistake, Viking. You should never
trust me."

"Would you prefer being confined in the smokehouse
again?" he inquired mildly.

"My preference is to be set free."

"To go where? You owe no allegiance to Wolfgard."

"Yea. Because he captured me and carried me away against my will."

"So he did. Why must you hate me as well?"

"Because you did the same, Viking!" she raged through clenched teeth.

Doggedly, he persisted. "I repeat, Reyna—if I released you, where would you go?"

"To Loire!" she cried.

A thoughtful frown puckered his brow. "Ah, yes, I've heard some of my kinsmen refer to it as the country of your birth. But I am afraid your going there is out of the question now." He grinned. "I'm too impossibly smitten, you see."

Her face burned. "Then quit taunting me with that which I cannot have, and leave my presence!" she retorted in trembling tones.

He sighed. "Gladly." He suspiciously eyed her belligerent countenance. "Will you promise not to come next door and murder me in my sleep, or must I tie you to the bed?"

She smirked again. "No promises, Viking."

"Then I will make a vow—and give you a warning." He caught her chin in his hand and spoke fiercely. "I'll be next door all night long, Reyna, with my three faithful wolves—and be assured that the four of us are all very light sleepers. You cannot escape without going past us. Show up in my bedchamber—for any reason—and I will assume you are ready to share my bed. You will find yourself a wife by morning, and long before the vows are said. Is that clear?"

Glaring at him, she nodded, but when he left, she quivered. She would not go to his room tonight and attempt to kill him. In truth, she was not sure she *could* slay him—but she did know she would melt when he touched her again.

She wondered what he had meant by his soulful words in the bathhouse when he had told her how they were linked, that he had loved her in another life. Whatever his true meaning or purpose, his sorcerer words had momentarily decimated her defenses. She had been fascinated, touched, and hard pressed not to insist on more details. And she had felt so close to him, as if there were truly a deep bond between them. The sadness in his eyes when he had spoken had moved her greatly.

She hurled down her comb and cursed. Oh, she did not want to feel these things for him—feelings that would ultimately defeat and humiliate her. Best to keep her distance from this confusing Viking until she found an opportunity to escape him.

In the chamber next door, with his wolves dozing, Viktor felt restless. Reyna had given him a good scare tonight, and had stirred a hunger in him that would no doubt burn in his loins all night long.

Why did she have to remain so defiant? At least he knew now that she wanted him—and that knowledge warmed him. In his arms in the pool, she had definitely responded. But would her stubborn pride ever allow her to give in to the passion they both felt? He hoped so, and hoped it would be soon—before he died from unmitigated lust!

He almost wished she would come in during the night and try to slay him—so he could make good on his vow, haul her delicious body close, and end this torment for them both.

TWENTY

A HORSE SNORTED IN THE NIGHT. RAGAR, HARALD, AND THEIR company had ridden high into the back country and were now navigating a rocky embankment by the light of the full moon. After a day filled with rain, the night had at last emerged chill and clear.

To the east of them rushed the deep, silvery fjord, which had gradually grown narrower as they had proceeded north over the past week, although the river was still too swollen to ford. In the distance loomed the craggy volcano, Surt, a haze of red surrounding its sharp peak as it sputtered menacingly.

Grimacing at the ominous sight, Harald nodded toward the line of seven men who remained in the company. "Had we not best stop for the night?" he asked Ragar.

"Yea, as soon as we can find a suitable camp."

"And pray to Odin that our lodge holds no terrors this eve."

Ragar nodded ruefully, recalling how they had already lost nearly half their ranks on this mission. Harald had initially raised a force of twelve, albeit most had volunteered reluctantly, with only the promise of a generous portion in gold enticing their cooperation. All of the men were superstitious about traveling this far north and risking the vengeance of Surt or an encounter with the ghosts or trolls that legend held lurked among the moors and mountains.

On their first night in camp, one of the warriors had claimed to have been attacked by just such a demon. Nord's shouts had awakened everyone. The warrior had jumped up, trembling, insisting he had been tapped on the shoulder by a shape-changer. Observing a small, silvery shape streak past, Ragar had been sure the apparition was only a foraging fox—but convincing Nord of this had been impossible, and the frightened man had defected, fleeing for Wolfgard's camp.

The next eve, just as they were making camp, a misty fog had drifted in, so white and thick that the warriors could barely see one another. To make matters worse, an eerie wind had blown through the hollow, whistling among the stunted trees and raising an inhuman howl. Two other warriors, thoroughly spooked and claiming ghosts were on the prowl, had fled for home.

Then yesterday at noontide, amid a drenching rain, Otto had gone prowling for berries. He had stumbled into boiling mud and almost sunk completely into the seething abyss. At the sound of the man's rending screams, Ragar and the others had rushed to his rescue, and thanks to the heavy leggings and boots Otto wore, his wounds had not appeared mortal. Nevertheless, Ragar had been compelled to spare another warrior to bear the ailing man back to Wolfgard's village. The fact that he kept losing his company did not bode well, and the remaining warriors were growing all the more anxious and wary the farther north they proceeded. Only today, they had been impelled to dodge several sliding boulders that had come hurtling toward them, released from glaciers by the spring thaw.

The group now descended into a valley dotted with birches and willows. Ragar reined in his horse, bringing the procession to a halt. "We rest here. Tomorrow we should reach the head of the fjord, and then we can turn southward."

But before Ragar could dismount, he heard the scream of a horse behind him. He maneuvered his own mount around, to see a steam geyser erupting almost directly beneath Cuellar's mount. Spooked by the emission, the small, nutmeg-colored horse sidestepped, reared mightily, and threw its rider, who crashed to the earth with a cry of agony.

"By Odin, what calamity has visited us now?" Ragar cried in disgust.

He dismounted and, with the others, rushed to the fallen

Cuellar, who was shrieking on the ground and clutching his calf.

Ragar knelt beside the warrior. "Be still, man, before you do yourself more damage."

Cuellar subsided into piteous moans, trembling and gnashing his teeth. Ragar knew before gently examining the twisted limb that it was broken—even at Ragar's careful probing, the man howled again in torment.

Ragar could have cursed his frustration aloud. "Thorald, go find a branch for a splint," he ordered. "The rest of you, use your axes to chop down yon birches. We will need the trunks to fashion a travois. I will have to assign a man to drag Cuellar back to the village."

"We must all turn back now, Ragar," cried one of the men.

"Yea, the gods have already bespoken their displeasure that we have disturbed their sanctuary," said another, his eyes bright with terror in the night. "Surely if we advance further, Surt will cover us with boiling rock and ashes—"

"Or render us vapor with his breath of steam," added a shrill voice.

Ragar stared at the frightened group and knew their fears were genuine. Still, he would not abandon his sister. "Men, we must continue. I cannot allow Viktor the Valiant to hold Reyna hostage—"

"But we cannot go on," argued one of the warriors. "Our numbers are too few."

Now Harald spoke up angrily. "And what of Viktor the Valiant? The sentries informed me that our enemy, with only a handful of his kinsmen, abducted Reyna in the night."

"Yea, because he is a rainbow warrior now," the man argued.

Harald scowled. "What mean you by 'rainbow warrior'?"

"That is what the men call Viktor," the man explained. "He returned along the Rainbow Bridge to Midgard, as no living man has done before him. The gods have blessed him with magical powers in Valhalla. He is now much more than a mere mortal, and our small company will never defeat him."

"Yea," put in another, "and he will be prepared for our attack, expecting Wolfgard to retaliate."

Losing patience, Harald drew his sword and faced down

the mutinous group. "I tell you, Viktor is only a man, as all of you are men. Any one of you who would take the coward's path must first defeat me."

The warriors grumbled for a moment, then went about their assigned tasks. Harald took Ragar aside. "I do not like the look of things, my friend. What men we have left are consumed with fear, and will surely desert us when the opportunity arises."

But Ragar was not swayed. "We shall go on, just the two of us if need be. If Viktor can steal into my father's house to carry away my sister, surely you and I can perform the same feat in his village."

Harald did not comment, but watching his friend trudge off to attend Cuellar, he could not share Ragar's confidence.

On that same eve, Viktor sought out Sibeal. He found her standing in the sewing room of the longhouse spinning wool thread with her distaff. He stared in fascination at the rhythmic motions of her hands as she set the distaff to work and the weighted thread was stretched, spinning, toward the floor. She spotted him and gathered up her gear, ceasing her activity.

"Jarl." She bowed and stuffed her distaff into the belt of her garment.

Viking flashed her a kindly smile. "Please, do not stop on my account."

Sibeal's expression remained guarded. "How may I serve you?"

"I would talk with you about your mistress."

"So you may better subjugate her?" Sibeal asked with a trace of bitterness.

Viktor drew a heavy breath. "I hope not to subjugate Reyna, only to win her trust." When the woman did not reply but continued to regard him warily, he gestured toward a bench. "Would you sit with me for a moment?"

"As you wish, jarl." Sibeal went to the bench and shoved aside a stack of snowy fleece. Both of them sat down.

"I am trying very hard to understand Reyna," Viktor confessed. "One moment she seems to warm to me, and the next she tries to kill me. And this stunt she pulled by trying to starve herself—frankly, that has me most worried. Since then, she has eaten, but her temperament has not improved."

Sibeal nodded. "Reyna is most proud. She will not bend easily to your will, my lord, nor will she trust you before you have won her loyalty—a feat even you will be hard pressed to accomplish, Viktor the Valiant."

"Woman, I am trying," he replied in exasperation.

She raised a dark brow. "Threatening her with beatings is not the way. She has heard that too oft from Wolfgard, and it serves only to raise her hackles."

"I realize this." He gestured his frustration. "But at times the risk of retribution seems all she can understand." He flashed Sibeal an earnest smile. "And you must believe I will make a good husband for her, woman, or you never would have cooperated."

Sibeal laughed bitterly. "You are saying that I—a mere thrall—could have stayed you, milord?"

"On the night I captured Reyna, I would not have allowed you to slay Ottar—and I think you knew this at the time."

"Yea, I knew," Sibeal admitted, "and that is why I allowed the deed to be done, Viktor the Valiant. I knew then 'twas true what the others had been saying—"

"Which was?"

"That you became transformed in Valhalla."

He eyed her thoughtfully, impressed by her wisdom. "Then you must know that I would never harm Reyna."

Sibeal smiled. "Yea—though milady hardly feels so kindly toward you."

"Will she never trust a Viking?" Viktor asked.

Sibeal's sad gaze met Viktor's. "You must understand. As a small child, Reyna saw Wolfgard pillage her kingdom. She watched as her father was slain, her baby brother abandoned to die. Should it happen to you, jarl, whom would you trust?"

He scowled pensively. "A good point—but I did not do these things to Reyna."

"Yea, but you are Viking, my lord, and 'tis all Vikings milady has chosen to blame and hate. Verily, you stole milady away by force, just as the hated Wolfgard did."

"So Reyna has reminded me," Viktor conceded, "but I

acted as I did to serve the ultimate good and bring peace to
Vanaheim."

Sibeal's smile was ironic. "Convince a captured bird that
its cage is for its benefit."

"You sound bitter yourself, woman."

"Mayhap because I have known the same anguish as milady, and I understand her feelings."

"Explain that."

A faraway, melancholy look gripped Sibeal's lovely visage.
"My husband was an Irish king, and our *tuath* lay in southern
Ireland along the River Shannon. When I had been a bride
but two winters, Wolfgard plundered our kingdom. He and
his band of murderers scaled the walls of our dun, slaughtering my husband, his warriors, and even our poet and harper,
who would have harmed not a lamb. Wolfgard took me, my
ladies-in-waiting, and many of our freemen to Iceland to
serve as thralls."

"My God," said Viktor. "So you went from being a queen
to being a slave?"

"Yea."

"But it did not destroy you."

She shrugged, her expression impassive. "I have learned
better than to battle the fates."

"But Reyna is different."

"Yea, albeit she knew the same loss. She was once Princess of Loire, before Wolfgard took all away from her. Her
wounds go deeper than mine, even though her status did not
fall as far—her place as Wolfgard's adopted daughter has always been an exalted one."

"Not according to her," Viktor commented cynically. "I
wish I could understand her better. She is Christian, is she
not?"

Sibeal hesitated.

"Please don't avoid the question," he urged. "I have seen
Reyna in the mountains, praying with Pelagius."

Sibeal sighed. "Yea, milady is Christian, as I am. Still, I
think she has a fear of the Viking gods, after hearing so oft
the legends and myths—and she also reveres the Irish druids,
dragons, and fairies I have told her about over the years."

Viktor touched the woman's sleeve. "How can I reach her, Sibeal?"

She studied his face closely. "What is your purpose, my lord?"

Viktor's reply was earnest. "Only to make her happy, and to stop this obscene feud that has taken so many lives—although I realize that in the short run, Reyna must suffer some for it, until she adjusts to our destiny together."

Sibeal nodded. "I want to believe your motives are true, jarl. But if it happens you have played us both falsely, I vow I will make you rue the day you were born."

"Fair enough," he said. "Now tell me how I can get through to your mistress."

Sibeal smiled. "Long ago, my young husband brought home a puppy that had been abused by peasants. He wanted to drown the bedraggled thing, for it would do naught but snarl and bite."

Viktor chuckled and stroked his jaw. "Who does that story remind me of?"

"Still, I took the foundling under my wing, and would do naught but pet and feed it—even though my hands knew the vengeance of many nips and even gouges."

"What happened?"

Sibeal grinned. "In time it made a marvelous lapdog."

Viktor laughed heartily. "So you are saying I should kill the little termagant with kindness, are you?"

"Mayhap, jarl."

Viktor scratched his jaw. "A smart strategy indeed—if I can only survive milady's sharp teeth in the interim."

TWENTY-ONE

TAKING SIBEAL'S ADVICE, VIKTOR STRUGGLED OVER THE NEXT several days, to maintain his patience with Reyna. She did eat and drink, and seemed to be regaining her strength. She did not again attack him physically, although her tongue remained as waspish as ever. She continuously insulted Viktor as well as his kinsmen who guarded her while he attended to his other duties. Soon all of his warriors despised the proud, haughty captive.

Hoping to improve her spirits, he decided to take her out riding. Each afternoon he placed her on a shaggy black pony, with her hands bound before her on the pommel to discourage an escape attempt. He bade Svein and Ottar come along as guards in case the Valkyrie should grow too feisty. As the procession of four went down the main street of the village, Reyna and Viktor's warriors inevitably exchanged insults.

"Ogress!" Rollo would call from the door of a slave hut.

"Whoreson!" Reyna would yell back.

"Ravisher!' Canute would taunt from the well.

"Brute!" Reyna jeered in return.

"Bitch!" yelled Orm from outside the storage shed.

"Cur!" retorted Reyna.

Meanwhile, Viktor, listening to the invective, could only groan. He had tried without success to stop the verbal assaults between Reyna and his warriors, and had finally consoled himself with the thought that perhaps having the opposing sides vent their spleen in this hostile though nonphysical manner would forestall actual bloodshed—foolhardy though he had to concede that possibility was!

The woman was equally abusive toward him, when she did not coldly ignore him; thus Viktor was sorely tested in his new plan to follow Sibeal's advice and employ kindness and patience with Reyna. He made a practice of dining with her at night, and she violently rebuked his every overture.

"Would you like some bread, Reyna?" he would ask.

"Rot in Hel, Viking!" she would retort, then grab the loaf.

"Would you care for some wine?" he would offer generously. "Svein tells me the warriors got it when they went a-Viking to Scotland last summer."

"Choke and die on it, Viking!" she would retort, then grab the silver chalice from his hand and gulp heartily.

Almost perpetually, his hands itched to give the stubborn wench a good shaking—or worse—and his jaw ached from the continual gnashing of his teeth.

One evening he dared to address the impasse. "Reyna, would it not be much easier if you ceased this show of contempt? You know I must hold you captive until you agree to marry me. There is no other way to end the feud."

"I know what you want, Viking," she sneered. "You want to make me your bride, to get me fat with child so you may gloat to Wolfgard that you have tamed me. You will burn in Hel before that day comes—for I will never become your vessel to win the peace."

"Why, Reyna?" he reasoned. "Don't you want peace?"

She hurled him a glare of defiance and gulped her wine. "Nay, Viking. My fondest wish is to kill you."

"Is it?" he countered with thinning patience. "Then was I having delusions that night in the bath hut when we shared our hearts? We were good together, Reyna, and you damn well know it!"

"You shame me with that!" she whispered, her face hot.

"There was no shame and you know that as well."

"I was sick and weak, and you took advantage," she accused.

"*You* know I did not!"

"I know we are enemies! I know I despise you, and there

will be no peace between us until one of us is dead or you release me."

As the days passed, Viktor began to believe her, and to despair of ever taming her. He also knew time was running out. Wolfgard had lost his dragon ship, but Viktor did not fully trust the enemy jarl not to attempt a rescue of his stepdaughter, even if over land. Thus he kept sentries posted along the fjord and north of the village. Surely within weeks Wolfgard would have a new vessel prepared and could launch a fullscale attack—then what would he do? Instead of drawing Reyna closer to him, she seemed to be slipping through his fingers . . .

Although she would never admit it, Reyna the Ravisher was actually feeling more drawn to Viktor the Valiant with each passing day. Ever since the night he had attended her so tenderly at the bathhouse and they had shared such sweet intimacies, she had found herself falling increasingly under his spell. Since then, the Viking's kindnesses toward her had left her confused and vulnerable, terrified she would again give in to the powerful passion he stirred and then lose herself entirely. When he smiled at her, lavished her with a compliment, or seemed to stare straight into her soul with his pretty blue eyes, she went all giddy and weak inside, longing to be swept into those strong arms again, to surrender, when surrender itself was an alien concept to her. Viktor was right, she realized ruefully: where he was concerned, her emotions had no shame. Thus she defended herself in the only way she knew how—through spite and rage.

Nevertheless, her captor continued to fascinate and perplex her. And while Reyna was grateful to have left her smokehouse prison, living in Viktor's house now, in such close proximity to him, was even worse torture. Although he slept in an antechamber, he was in her presence far too much, stopping by to check on her several times a day. When she scorned him, he would oft pace the chamber and glower like a temperamental lion, and she would find herself mesmerized by his handsome scowl, the way his tight leather leggings pulled at his powerful thighs. She was tempted to soothe him, to let him unleash all his passion and frustration on her own eager body. He was so handsome, with his thick blond hair

and huge, muscled body, too splendid a creature to be merely
mortal. Sometimes she half believed Viktor truly was a god
now, and if so, how could she, a mere mortal woman, ever
hope to withstand him?

The more disarmed by him she felt, the more she railed at
his dominance, although she knew she was really fighting
herself. Her conviction deepened that she must escape Viktor
before he made her defeat absolute.

On the day before the planned Shieling feast, Viktor was
out on the hillside with Svein, the two men selecting rocks to
build a chimney in Eurich's blacksmith forge, when Rollo
and Orm rushed up. Rollo was rubbing a forehead that
sported a goose egg, and Orm was staggering slightly, one
hand braced at the back of his head. Both men appeared cha-
grined.

Viktor dropped the rock he had just chosen onto a nearby
pile, dusted off his hands, and faced his kinsmen with a
scowl. The men had been assigned to guard Reyna, and their
appearance here did not bode well.

"What has happened to you two?" he demanded. "And
where is Reyna?"

"She has escaped, jarl!" cried Rollo.

Exasperation burst in Viktor. "Escaped? How in the name
of Valhalla did she get past you both?"

The men exchanged sheepish glances, then Orm admitted,
"Mayhap Rollo and I became too involved in our game of
chess, jarl. The last time we checked on her, the Valkyrie was
napping. Then, in the blinking of an eye, she crept in and
knocked us both over the head with an iron tankard."

"Damnation," muttered Viktor. "Do you have any idea
where she might have gone?"

"She would go to the fjord, jarl, would she not?" put in
Svein from behind them.

"That seems logical," Viktor agreed. "She might try to
steal a boat and cross over to her own people."

"We must go after her—now," said Rollo urgently.

"Yea, jarl, let us come along and strangle the little witch,
then set her out to sea for the sharks to devour," added Orm
with a feral snarl.

Viktor was appalled and not about to take along these two, with their battered pride and thirst for revenge. "I shall go after the Valkyrie myself. You two nurse your wounds."

"But jarl—" protested Rollo.

"Are you saying I cannot handle one female alone?" Viktor demanded.

At the pointed remark, the two warriors lowered their heads.

"Jarl, let me help you," offered Svein, stepping up.

Viktor adamantly shook his head. "This must be settled between Reyna and me."

He raced down the hillside toward the stable. Had Reyna managed to steal a pony? he wondered. If so, there would likely be no stopping her—she was in a vessel by now and already crossing the fjord.

Inside the stable, he ran across the slave, Nevin, who with a younger, teenage lad was shoveling out the stalls.

"Have you seen Reyna?" Viktor demanded.

"Yea, jarl, she came in here to steal a horse," Nevin replied.

"And?"

"I chased the Valkyrie out with my pitchfork," said the younger slave proudly.

"Then she has no mount?" Viktor inquired with a surge of hope.

"Nay, jarl," answered Nevin. "She has no mount."

"Good," said Viktor, tossing the younger slave a look of gratitude, then tearing off for Sleipnir's stall. If Reyna was on foot, there was a chance he could catch her before she left the wharf.

Moving with feverish haste, he saddled and bridled Sleipnir and led him from the stable. Seconds later, Viktor was galloping across the tundra toward the wharf, vehemently praying that he could still catch Reyna in time. Damn the little Valkyrie and her defiant pride! When would she realize that she could not fight her destiny—*their* destiny to unite and bring peace to all of Vanaheim?

Well, he was done allowing her to thwart his wishes and deny the love that was meant to be between them.

Soon Viktor was carefully navigating his horse down the

rocky fell toward the fjord. His heart rang with new hope as he spotted Reyna in the distance striding down the wharf toward a small moored boat.

He dismounted Sleipnir and raced the rest of the way. Even though his boots were made of soft leather, his footsteps thudded across the creaky wharf. Just as Reyna was preparing to board the vessel, she evidently heard him and whirled to face him.

He felt pleased by the panic in her eyes. Too late, she tried to jump down into the boat. He reached her and caught her around the waist in the final split second. She fought like a madwoman, shrieking curses, kicking, and pummeling his chest with her fists. He tried to heave her into his arms but could not contain her in her fury. His wool cloak fell to the wharf as they careened wildly on the unstable wharf—

In the next second, as Reyna's entire body corkscrewed against his, Viktor lost his balance and they both tumbled into the ice-cold fjord! The shock of the frigid water was exquisite, and as it sucked him under, Viktor lost his grip on the mutinous Valkyrie. He fought the powerful undertow, surfaced, and caught a convulsive breath. He spotted her nearby, flailing about, the currents tugging her downriver, a look of horror on her face—

He swam toward her frantically, at last grabbing the sleeve of her garment. The hellcat began fighting him!

"Stop it, Reyna!" he choked out.

"I cannot swim!" she cried.

"Then stop fighting me or we both will drown!"

She ceased her struggles, and somehow Viktor managed to tow her back toward the bank. Exhausted and quivering with the cold, he dragged them both out of the freezing river, and they staggered up the craggy hillside together.

And then—as violent shivers racked him—Viktor noticed Reyna's dripping body. She was clad only in her thin linen garment, her boots having been lost in the fjord. The cloth was near-transparent, clinging to her shapely breasts and tautened nipples, her flat belly, even outlining the nest of curls between her thighs—

Despite being within a hairbreadth of hypothermia, Viktor felt arousal sear him. With her breasts heaving as she gasped for air, Reyna was a magnificent ice queen, and suddenly he burned to melt her.

"My God," he muttered, staring at her with raw lust—

In the next instant, Reyna's doubled-up fists slammed into his jaw. It hurt like hell!

For the first time in his life, Viktor totally snapped, Reyna's unremitting scorn sending him over the edge. He caught the wet mop of her hair in a wrenching grip, heedless of her cry.

"You little brat!" he roared. "Is there no end to your defiance? You have insulted me, insulted my men, thrown contempt into the face of my every kindness. Now I have saved your worthless hide—at the risk of my own life, I might add—and you dare to strike me? I tell you, now I know why men in the Dark Ages behaved like animals—it is because the women *drove* them to it! Well, you, my lady, are about to learn a lesson you will remember for the rest of your life!"

Grabbing her wrist and moving with ruthless determination, Viktor dragged Reyna's resisting body to a rocky ledge. He sat down, hurled her across his knees, and brought his hand down on her bottom, hard. Only the sound of her low sob stopped him, wrenching him to his senses—

God, what was he doing? He was all but behaving like the brutal primitive man he was determined never to become. He had nearly crushed Reyna's spirit—something he had never wanted to do.

As angry at himself as he was frustrated with her, he muttered a blistering expletive and hauled Reyna up on her knees beside him. Her eyes were bright, yet still defiant. Her trembling lower lip revealed her vulnerability.

"Why tears now, Reyna?" he asked hoarsely. "I thought you were unreachable."

Convulsively, she whispered, "Wolfgard used to—"

Patience at this point was totally beyond Viktor. He caught her face in his hands and demanded, "Used to what?"

"To thrash me with a whip."

Viktor groaned, wanting desperately to pull her close and comfort her, but feeling for the moment unworthy, and fearing she would still resist him. "And now you have brought me to his level. Or have I done that to myself?"

She stared at him, appearing anguished and uncertain. A

tear slid down her cheek as she whispered, "I did it to you, Viking."

Her honesty touched him, but could not assuage his feelings of hurt and alienation. Staring at her starkly, he asked, "Reyna, Reyna, why do you fight me so when all I want is to love you?"

"I fight what you make me feel, Viking," she admitted.

He pulled her closer, until their foreheads touched and their breath mingled. "Why must you think of me as your enemy when I only want what is best for you and all our peoples? When will you realize that I am truly your friend, that I am on your side, that I yearn to become your husband and lover?"

She drew back slightly, staring up at him with tear-filled eyes. "I do not know how to believe it."

"Then I will show you, love."

The emotion in Viktor burst as he pulled Reyna onto his lap and kissed her with all the pent-up passion in his body. He felt her stiffen in his arms and could not bear her resistance, her fear—whatever barrier it was that still held them apart. Desperate, he forced his tongue between her teeth, plunging into her sweet mouth, thrusting and retreating again and again until at last she whimpered in pleasure and surrender. Then she was responding in kind, curling her arms around his neck and pushing tentatively against his lips with her own tongue. The trusting innocence of her kiss made Viktor's chest ache with emotion.

"Yes, darling," he murmured coaxingly into her mouth. "Kiss me just as I've kissed you."

With a low cry, she complied, latching her lips on his, pushing her tongue into his mouth, until pleasure and raging lust totally swamped him. His arms crushed her closer and his lips and tongue claimed and plundered.

His heart pounding with fierce need, Viktor pressed her down beneath him on the ledge and began unfastening the ties on her bodice. Momentarily uncertain, she tried to stay his hands, but he only slowly kissed each of her lovely, resisting fingers while she watched, fascinated. When he pushed her hands aside and resumed undressing her, she did not resist, and the sound of her labored breathing was glorious to his ears.

He freed her breasts, staring greedily at the ripe mounds. He fingered the taut pink nipples, his manhood throbbing in tortured readiness as he watched the little peaks grow even harder.

"You want me," he whispered.

She did not reply, but her expression was eloquent, her eyes so languid, her cheeks so adorably flushed with expectation. He kneaded her breasts with his large hands, and she moaned and laced her fingers through his in an unconsciously sensual gesture. A moment later, his hands pressed hers down on the rock, his mouth took her breast, and she moaned in delight. He tongued the nipple and she arched against him, panting softly.

By now Viktor was so ravenous for Reyna he could not bear it! Never mind that the day was chill, and both of them drenched and cold. The fires of their shared passion kept them warm as the distant sun. Soon Viktor's mouth was on Reyna's again, mating brazenly, demanding all she could give even as he felt shudder after sweet shudder seize her. His impatient fingers raised her skirts, his strong thighs spread hers—

At first she tensed, her eyes wide. But when he stroked her in just the right place, finding and teasing her tiny bud, she writhed beneath him. He slid his finger lower, entering her, and she gasped in mingled pleasure and pain. He touched her insistently, and she tried to wiggle away. He braced his free hand at the small of her back, creating a gentle upward pressure, and continued to torture her gently with his finger, sliding in deeper. She was so tight, so warm and wet! His lips drowned her incoherent moans, and when he felt her strong fingers caressing his shoulders, her mouth melting into his, her hips arching provocatively, he knew she was ready.

Easing his finger out of her, he freed his stiff manhood and pressed against her. He stared down into her eyes, and she pushed to take him inside her, then cried out as his thrust was met by the resistance of her maidenhead—

Her sob reached him, and all at once Viktor pulled back. Good Lord, what was he doing? There was too much at stake for him to take her now, even as desperately as he wanted her. He would not—could not—settle for having less than all of her. He had made that mistake once with Reyna's counterpart back in the present. He would not make the same mistake again with her here.

"No," he said, and began fastening his leggings.

"Nay? Why say you nay?" she cried with frustration and bewilderment.

Although Viktor was literally trembling with unassuaged desire, he managed to stand. He yanked down Reyna's skirts and spoke fiercely. "Not until you are my wife."

She sat up, furious. "Your wife? You care only for the bargain you have made with Wolfgard! You care only for winning!"

"That is not true!"

" 'Tis true!"

Viktor's expression was unyielding. "You will marry me, Reyna, and then we will make love."

"Then I say nay, Viking! Nay! Nay!"

He hauled the recalcitrant vixen to her feet. "Reyna, you are beyond maddening. First you vow you'll never marry me, and now you're furious because I won't bed you. Why don't you decide what in Hel you want!"

She looked him over insultingly, her gaze lingering on the straining bulge in his leggings. Her tone was consummate with contempt. "I want to mate with you, Viking. You have tempted me sorely now—worse than Loki himself—and I find you pretty enough to take the pleasure you have offered. Afterward, I will cheerfully slay you."

Viktor saw red. Here he had thought the little witch could not possibly insult him further! Now she was telling him in her own inimitable Dark Ages style that she wanted to use *him* as a sex object.

"So you would use me for your pleasure, then kill me, would you?" he snapped. "At the moment, woman, I am within an inch of throttling *you!*"

She flung a hand outward in fury. "Then slay me, Viking! Do it!"

"If I don't take you back to the village right this minute, I surely will!" he retorted.

Viktor grabbed Reyna's arm and dragged her to Sleipnir. Using a long length of leather rope, he bound her hands with one end and tied the other to his saddle pommel. He quickly retrieved his cloak from the wharf, tore off strips from it to wrap her bare feet in several layers, then draped the remainder of the ragged garment around her shoulders. They proceeded to the village with him riding slowly and her tugged along behind. It was, of course, a deliberate attempt to humble her—and to keep her from escaping on his mount. Nevertheless, had she proved the least bit biddable, Viktor would have gladly offered her his horse. At least she had the warmth of his cloak, such as it was, while he was still wet and shuddering from the chill of the waning day.

Night was breaking by the time they entered the hamlet. At once Viktor's attention was seized by a large glow at the center of the village. Dozens of men and women were gathered around a fire, and Viktor could hear jeering and shouts of bloodlust.

Near the crowd, he dismounted, untied Reyna's hands, and led her toward the blaze. Even in their agitated state, the villagers stepped aside to allow them to pass. When he and Reyna emerged near the fire, Viktor immediately saw what the uproar was about. Restrained at sword point were two captives—Reyna's half brother, Ragar, and another young warrior from Wolfgard's tribe. Both men had their hands tied behind them, and appeared battered, with bruises and blackened eyes. Both were ashen-faced and clearly terrified.

Reyna spotted the prisoners as well. "Harald! Ragar!" she cried, starting toward them.

Hearing threats of retribution from the mob, Viktor caught her arm and held her back. "If you value their lives," he whispered intensely, "you will let me handle this."

Reyna surprised him when she did not resist his order, but she held her ground, her own face white with fear.

Viktor glanced at his men. "What is going on here?"

Canute turned away from the fire and stepped forward, grinning broadly and holding an iron rod with a glowing red tip. "Jarl, we are glad to see you have returned and recaptured the Ravisher—for we have snared her kinsmen!"

As a spiteful cheer went up from the other warriors, Viktor

gazed at the two frightened young men. "This is all who came to rescue Reyna?"

"The others fled when the sentries converged on them north of the village," explained Orm. He stared with raw hatred at Reyna. "Now we will torture the Ravisher's kinsmen and let the little bitch watch!"

Viktor saw sick terror fill Reyna's eyes. Rollo waved a fist and cried, "Yea, we shall burn gouges on the soles of their feet, and carve out their entrails before their very eyes!" Another cheer of vengeance erupted from the crowd.

Viktor was fearful that this situation could well be beyond his recall. All around him, his warriors were howling like animals and shouting insults, demanding the torture and death of both captives. Never had he seen his men so rabid with bloodlust!

As the frenzied mob began to converge on the prisoners, Reyna turned frantically to Viktor. "Please, you must stop them."

Viktor addressed the gathering. "Men, wait!" When there was no response, when a cruelly laughing Canute extended the glowing rod toward a wide-eyed Ragar, Viktor bellowed at the top of his lungs. "All of you, stop this instant!"

At last the warriors paused, turning to regard their jarl with rage and mistrust.

"Why do you stay us, jarl?" demanded Orm.

"I realize you are angered," Viktor said calmly, "but it is wrong for you to vent your ire on these innocent men. I refuse to allow this atrocity, and insist you release the prisoners at once."

Shouts of mutiny and fury spewed from the men. Torches were waved and swords drawn.

Canute charged up to Viktor, swinging his iron rod. "You are wrong, jarl, and to stay us, you must fight us all." He turned his wrathful gaze on Reyna. "Are you going to allow a woman to dictate your will?"

"If you bow to the Ravisher, you are no better than a female yourself!" declared a furious Rollo.

As the other warriors added their own fierce endorsements, Viktor turned beseechingly to his blood brother. "Svein, please make them understand that this is wrong."

But Svein only shook his head. "Verily, you are in error this time, jarl, and I cannot stay your warriors." He stared hard at Reyna. " 'Tis the Ravisher's own fault for insulting and provoking your men. They take their vengeance out more on her than on her kinsmen."

Viktor glanced at Reyna. Although he realized Svein was right, his heart ached at the stark terror on her face.

"Please," she pleaded.

He turned to the others. "Will you give us a moment?"

More loud resistance followed.

"I beg you," Viktor beseeched his men.

"Only if afterward, you will make the Valkyrie watch!" yelled Canute.

As the warriors stood waiting in frustration, Viktor hastily pulled Reyna into the shadows. Tears were streaming down her face, and he felt utterly helpless against her terrible fear.

Viktor brushed a tear from her cheek. "You love your brother, don't you? I suppose it is good to know you care about someone."

"Please," she begged brokenly, "you must not let your men slay Ragar or Harald."

"What can I do, Reyna? Svein spoke the truth about the way you have taunted my men. If I try to stop them now, they will kill us both. Give me a reason that will convince them to spare Ragar and Harald."

She hesitated for only a moment. "Tell them I will marry you."

"What?" he cried.

"I will marry you," she repeated vehemently.

For a moment, sheer joy filled Viktor's heart. At last he had Reyna where he wanted her—as much as he deplored the circumstances that had brought them to this pass. Then fear and mistrust assailed him. "Do you mean it, Reyna?"

"Yea."

"You will marry me?"

"Yea—to save Ragar and Harald."

"Is that the only reason?" he asked bitterly.

She glanced away.

"Hell, I don't suppose it matters, with the lives of two innocent men at stake," he muttered, looking at the captives. "But will the ploy work?"

She nodded. "Is it not what your men have wanted, to see me humbled?"

"Is that how you see becoming my wife?" he asked sadly.

She hung her head and was silent.

Viktor groaned. "Very well, you will become my wife and then we will work things out. Right now we must act, and pray your concession will placate my men and save your brother and his kinsman."

Viktor caught Reyna's hand and pulled her back inside the circle of men. "Reyna has agreed to become my queen, making it totally unacceptable for you to slay her brother and her brother's kinsmen," he announced.

The warriors, clearly astonished, eyed Reyna dubiously and mumbled to one another.

"No, Reyna!" her brother protested. "I will not allow you to sacrifice yourself for me!"

"Nor will I!" said an indignant Harald.

Reyna faced the two men with unflinching determination. " 'Tis done! I have already given my word! I will not allow either of you to die for me!"

Viktor's warriors had grown broodingly silent, observing the tense exchange.

Viktor stared down his men. "I insist you release Ragar and Harald at once."

The men moved into a huddle to consult; then Svein spoke for the group. "The men are not appeased."

"Why not?" Viktor demanded. "Think of the advantages. Reyna's capitulation will bring great shame to our enemy, Wolfgard, and eventually may bring our two tribes to peace. Isn't that what we all want?"

"Nay, the Valkyrie's consent is not enough!" cried Canute.

"Then what?" Viktor asked in exasperation.

Canute came forward and grabbed Reyna roughly by the shoulders. "On your knees, woman!"

To Viktor's utter amazement, Reyna did not hesitate; she slid immediately to her knees and bowed her head.

"Humbly beg my pardon for ever insulting my manhood!" Canute roared.

"I—I humbly beg your pardon," she whispered.

"Pardon is given—though reluctantly," Canute barked. "Now swear your fealty to King Viktor and all his kinsmen. Vow you will never again lift a sword against any of us, and may Odin smite you if you lie."

Woodenly, Reyna repeated, "I swear my fealty to King Viktor the Valiant and all his kinsmen. I vow I will never again lift a sword against any of you, and may Odin smite me if I lie."

At last Canute threw his iron into the fire, then nodded to Viktor. "The Valkyrie's kinsmen may live."

As the somber silence of the other warriors bespoke their own acceptance of Canute's concession, Viktor noted with gratitude the expressions of intense relief on the faces of Ragar and Harald. Yet, staring at his still-bowed future bride, he also realized that one more step was necessary to make their coming union work. He hated to force Reyna to endure any added humiliation, but he knew this was the only way to ensure her loyalty.

He went up to her and said quietly, "Swear your fealty before God, Reyna."

While the others looked on in hushed fascination, Reyna stared at Viktor with eyes stark and bright. The emotional struggle on her face was exquisite in its intensity.

"You know I am Christian," she gasped.

"Yes—and I am Christian, too." He touched her cheek. "Now swear your loyalty to me before God. I'm afraid it is the only way."

"I swear my fealty to you before God," she whispered brokenly, then solemnly crossed herself.

A cheer went up from the people.

Viktor assisted Reyna to her feet. To the others, he said, "Now, my kinsmen, go to your homes, and I will see to our captives."

"You will not release them?" cried Orm.

"It is the only honorable course," replied Viktor. When the others would have protested, he lifted a hand. "But first, the captives will be our *guests* at the wedding—so they may fully apprise Wolfgard of his own disgrace."

At this pronouncement, several warriors cheered, and relief

surged in Viktor as he realized that the crisis had at last been averted.

"When will be the wedding, jarl?" demanded Canute, staring arrogantly at Reyna.

"Yea, when will the little Valkyrie be shown her proper place as wife?" asked Rollo, while several warriors added bawdy comments.

Viktor actually felt sorry for Reyna, who stood with her gaze lowered, helpless against her own indignity, when he dearly wished she could feel only joy.

Wearily, he replied, "The wedding will be performed tomorrow, right before the Shieling feast."

TWENTY-TWO

Morning brought a flurry of activities at Viktor's longhouse. The women were busy cooking for the night's feast; Sibeal's nimble fingers flew as she sewed a white silk garment for Reyna to wear at the wedding. Out in the village proper, the festivities had already begun; most of Viktor's warriors were swilling mead or ale and occupying themselves in games of archery, wrestling matches, or chess tournaments. At Canute's insistence, Ragar and Harald were being guarded at a shieling cottage in the hills; but on Viktor's orders, they would be brought down tonight to witness the wedding.

Viktor went into his chamber early to check on his bride-to-be. He first spotted Sibeal, sewing in a corner by the lamp, and then Reyna, seated on the bed scowling as she petted the female wolf, Hati. Hati's tail was wagging, her nose resting on Reyna's thigh. The males, Geri and Thor, lay crouched nearby on the floor, their expressions forlorn as they covetously eyed Hati's revered place. Viktor whistled to the male wolves softly, and the sleek beasts bounded up and rushed over to his side. He petted them affectionately while winking at Reyna.

"Good morning," he began cheerfully. "I'm pleased to see you have warmed to at least one of my pets. Geri and Thor no doubt feel slighted, though I can understand why you aren't feeling too kindly toward the male of the species at this moment."

Her expression pouty, Reyna said nothing, still stroking the female.

Viktor turned to Sibeal. "Has she been such a fountain of goodwill all morning?"

Sibeal shrugged and did not comment.

"What is bothering you, Reyna?" he asked quietly.

Her eyes flared mutinously. "You can ask that after you forced me into marriage?"

"I did not force you," he pointed out with forbearance. "You offered yourself to save your brother and Harald from my men."

She clenched her jaw and glowered at him. " 'Tis no different. Had you not kidnapped me, Viktor the Valiant, then Ragar and Harald never would have come to rescue me, thus subjecting themselves to your treachery—*and* forcing me to offer myself to you to save them."

Viktor groaned. "Reyna, let's not split hairs over this." As she frowned, obviously not comprehending his figure of speech, he went on earnestly. "There are far more important considerations at stake now. However resentful you may feel about it, the decision has been made, and will be for the good of all of Vanaheim. We will marry tonight, and you had best start accepting the finality of that."

She was silent for a moment, her shapely fingers sifting through Hati's thick fur. With unaccustomed tentativeness, she asked, " 'Tis true what you said last night?"

"What are you referring to?"

Her challenging gaze met his. "Are you Christian, Viktor the Valiant? Or did you lie?"

Both Reyna and Sibeal regarded him with great interest.

"It is true," he said solemnly. "And I have never lied to you, Reyna."

"Then why would you wed me in a pagan ceremony?"

"Do you think my people will accept our marriage otherwise?"

"Mayhap not." She set her jaw stubbornly. "Still, I would have a Christian ceremony as well."

"How, Reyna?" he asked, his patience waning.

"There is a Christian monk, Pelagius, who lives in the

hills. I would fetch him to the village to say a wedding mass tonight."

"And how do you think my people will feel about this?"

"I care not!"

"Well, you had best start caring—if you want your monk present tonight. It is not going to sit well with my warriors, our traipsing off to the hills at the last moment."

Reyna got up and came over to stand before Viktor. "Only you and I must go to fetch Pelagius."

"What?" He laughed, astounded by her brazenness. "Is this some kind of trick, Reyna?"

"Nay!" she denied. "But I will not reveal to your warriors the location of the monk's cottage. They would go there later to torment him—possibly even to torture and kill him."

Viktor smiled. "You mean you are trusting me not to harm your friend? I am amazed at your faith in me."

" 'Tis not faith!" she snapped, regarding him with scorn. "For I know you have not the courage to harm Pelagius—or a lamb, methinks."

Viktor muttered an infuriated curse. Reyna's words were deliberately cruel, and he was not immune to them. He grabbed her arm and spoke vehemently. "Don't mock me too much, Reyna. You'll regret it. But if you think it takes a real man to harm a servant of God—or a lamb—then you are right that I *never* want to be such a man!"

As the two glowered at each other in a continuing battle of wills, Sibeal surprised them both by lurching to her feet and moving toward them.

"You shame yourself, my lady," the thrall whispered fiercely to Reyna. "You insult the kindness of your future husband."

Sibeal swept out of the room, and Viktor found to his astonishment that Reyna appeared shamed, her head lowered, her teeth chewing her bottom lip as she obviously considered the servant's scolding.

"Well, Reyna?" he demanded.

"Sibeal is right," she muttered with surprising humility, still not meeting his eye. "I spoke out of turn. In truth, I wish you to come with me to fetch the monk because I know you will not harm him."

"And you see that as a weakness, Reyna?"

Her voice came very low. "Nay. 'Tis a strength that none other of your warriors possesses."

His pride still not completed soothed, Viktor spoke with irony. "Yes, and if you and I go alone, Reyna, it will be far easier for you to escape me—won't it?"

Angered, she flung a hand wide. "How can I escape you, Viking? You have Ragar and Harald as hostage—the reason for our nuptials in the first place."

"The *only* reason, Reyna?"

She ignored that. "If I manage to escape you, Viking, I will only ensure the deaths of my brother and his kinsman, and thereby defeat my own purpose. Besides, I swore my fealty to your clan—"

"And to me," Viktor reminded her firmly.

"Yea, to you, Viking, before God, albeit unwillingly," she retorted. "Still, I take solemnly my pledge."

"I'm relieved to hear you take something seriously, Reyna," he drawled. He considered the matter for another moment, then nodded. "You and I will ride alone for the hills to fetch your monk. Are you happy now?"

She hesitated before saying, "There is another matter."

"Yes?"

She tilted her chin proudly. "I must have a dagger with which to defend myself."

Viktor almost howled with laughter. "Woman, you are unbelievable! Do you actually think I'm going to hand you a knife so you may hurl it into my back?"

She gestured angrily. "I have sworn fealty to you—I cannot slay you!"

"And it's driving you crazy, isn't it?" he replied nastily.

She spoke through clenched teeth. "Besides, were I to kill you, I would do so to your face."

"You respect me that much, do you?" he asked in feigned amazement.

"I respect my oath!" she cried, stamping a foot in her exasperation. "I cannot kill you because I have sworn fealty to you, so we are arguing over naught!"

"Yes, I must agree that this entire exchange strikes me as

nonsense." Absorbing her fierce glower, he sighed. "Why do you want a dagger, Reyna?"

Her hand again sliced through the air. "We are going to the moors! There could be wild animals lurking about, or even ghosts or trolls. Indeed, what if Wolfgard has dispatched more warriors, not to rescue but to slay me? And verily, your men . . ."

"Yes, Reyna?"

She lowered her gaze. "You know they do not respect me."

Viktor stared at her for a long moment, then decided that her concerns were real, her fears genuine. "Very well," he agreed wearily. "You may have your dagger."

She grinned, looking all winsome—and devious—vixen.

Eyeing her transformation, Viktor didn't know whether to throttle her or demand a kiss. Ruefully he shook his head. "Let's get out of here before I change my mind. I'm either demented or the worst kind of fool."

It was afternoon by the time the two approached Pelagius's pitiful sod cottage up in the hills. The early summer day was mild and sunny, the tundra brilliant with blooming heather and wildflowers, but their mood was hardly festive. They had traveled mostly in silence, and Viktor was well aware of his bride-to-be's haughty facade as she rode before him astride her pony, the skirt of her long garment bunched between her thighs.

Back at the village, Viktor had given Reyna a dagger in its sheath, though he wisely hadn't turned his back on her since then. Still, there was definitely a bur in her saddle now—for, just as Viktor had feared, before they had left the hamlet, Svein and several other warriors had spotted them on horseback and bidden them pause. All of the men had taken issue with the prospect of their jarl riding off alone with the Valkyrie, especially with Reyna carrying a dagger. When Viktor had refused to cancel the expedition, Rollo had savagely warned Reyna that if the two of them failed to return before nightfall, or if she in any way harmed or betrayed their jarl, he would personally slit the throats of Ragar and Harald. Reyna had accepted the ultimatum in seething silence, tossing her mane of hair and spurring her pony. Yet Viktor realized the warning had had its desired effect—while not in the least measure endearing the stubborn girl to her bridegroom.

Observing her clenched jaw and mutinous eyes, he wondered if she would be able to remain so aloof and defiant when he made love to her tonight. He regretted the fact that physical intimacy in their marriage would obviously have to come before emotional rapport could follow. Nevertheless, he was determined to bring them together tonight, not only because he was burning with desire for this feisty wench, but also because there was altogether too much pride and anger still looming between them, poisoning their relationship. It was high time to start pulling down some of those barriers. Besides, the fate of all peoples on Vanaheim was at stake here; together, they must end both their personal antagonism and the larger war that had too long consumed and threatened the entire island.

At last they paused before the yawning doorway of the monk's ramshackle abode. Dismounting, Viktor grimaced at the sight of the sagging thatch roof and the scrawny garden off to one side. As a derelict chicken limped past the front door, Reyna motioned to Viktor to follow her through it.

"Pelagius?" she called softly. "Are you here?"

"Obviously not," said Viktor.

He glanced around the tiny, gloomy expanse. A crude table held but an iron cup half filled with water, a few berries, and a bowl of soggy seaweed. Obviously an edible variety, Viktor mused, shaking his head at the monk's paltry diet. In one corner jutted a platform of stone where the monk no doubt prayed and slept. A tiny desk held an inkwell, a plume, and a half-finished vellum page from an illuminated manuscript. Viktor took a moment to admire the artful Gothic inscriptions.

He glanced at the walls, on which several bulky leather bags hung from pegs. "What are those?" he asked Reyna.

"The Gospels Pelagius has inscribed," she replied. "He reads to me from them frequently." She nodded toward the desk. "And he frets that soon he will exhaust the supply of parchment he brought with him on his voyage."

"Where did he come from?"

"Inishmore, in the Aran Islands. He came to Vanaheim fifteen summers past, in a curragh with three other monks. Pelagius was the only one to survive the voyage."

"And now he lives the life of a hermit?" Viktor asked.

"He subscribes himself to the rule of St. Enda, and spends his days in labor or at prayer."

"He sleeps on a bed of stone?"

"According to the Rule, salvation comes through deprivation. Pelagius has no fire, eats the most meager, austere diet, and sleeps in a hair shirt on a bed of stone." A smile played over her lips. "He calls the Viking custom of sleeping without garments the gravest sin."

Viktor had to struggle not to laugh. If memory served him, all of Europe went to bed naked throughout much of the Dark and Middle Ages.

But not Reyna, he recalled with a smile. "Tell me," he teased, "is the monk's example the reason you wear a shift to bed?"

"You are crude, Viking!" she snapped in a fit of temper.

"I am to be your husband, Reyna," he stated. "If you find that crude, just wait until tonight."

"You are no better than the others!"

That comment brought a scowl to his face. "Why are you so defensive regarding what you wear to bed? I know you said Wolfgard used to beat you. Did he or his warriors every try to . . . abuse you?"

"Do you fear your bride is sullied, Viking?" she scoffed, and stalked out of the hut.

Bemused, Viktor followed her and caught her arm, not releasing her even when she pivoted to hurl him a mutinous glance. "Reyna, we are to marry. If someone has harmed you previously, I have a right to know—and I'll kill the bastard."

She regarded him with pride. "No one has misused me— though not for want of trying."

Sympathy for this brave girl surged within Viktor, and he flashed her a compassionate smile. "It must have been a very difficult life for you, always having to be on your guard, even as you slept. All of that will change once you are my wife."

"Yea—then I will have just you to battle!"

"If you are still determined to fight me, that is your choice,

Reyna," he informed her, "though your life will be much easier if you work with me, not against me."

"We are enemies!"

Uttering a curse, he seized her shoulders, pulling her closer. "Nay—we are going to be husband and wife." Hoping to lighten her smoldering expression, he added teasingly, "And be assured, Reyna, that I shall soon divest you of your habit of wearing clothing to bed."

Her mouth dropped open. "You would let me freeze, then?"

He threw back his head and laughed. "Hardly. My lady shall be toasty warm, even her toes curling in delight."

She stared at him, her face darkening by shades with each second that passed. She evidently thought it best not to pursue the subject.

"Let us find Pelagius," she ground out, stalking away from him.

"By all means," he agreed.

They searched the nearby hills and valleys for the monk, at first without success. Then, drawn by the sight of ravens swirling in the distance, they climbed a craggy precipice and spotted the monk standing at its edge with his back to them. A stark figure clothed in a tattered dark robe, he loomed perfectly still at the edge of the cliff with only his staff to support him. Coal-black birds perched on his head and outstretched arms, while other ravens cawed and dived around his body. Viktor mused that the man looked like an ancient scarecrow.

"By the saints, he is doing it again!" Reyna cried worriedly.

"Doing what?"

"Standing cruciform. He does it for days at a stretch, and all throughout Lent."

"What is his purpose?"

She stared at Viktor as if he had lost his mind. "To achieve a state of grace through his suffering, of course."

"Ah, I see." He winked at her solemnly. "Have you ever considered seeking such a state yourself, Reyna?"

She bared her teeth at him.

"You might even benefit from it."

Her response was glowering silence as they slowly approached Pelagius. While the monk stood absolutely still, Viktor could hear a rhythmic moaning. Reyna softly tapped his shoulder. Pelagius at once jerked, whirled, and wielded his staff, prompting his visitors to lunge back out of harm's way, amid a screech of flying ravens.

"Who goes there?" he demanded.

Viktor stared at the monk, who appeared as congenial as a madman. Pelagius was tall and gaunt, with a heavy beard and long, wild hair streaked with what Viktor suspected was bird droppings. His nose was red and runny; his eyes darted furtively beneath bushy brows. His skin was coarse and leathery from exposure to the elements—his age difficult to judge.

"Pelagius, it is I, Reyna."

Lowering his staff, Pelagius glanced from Reyna to Viktor. "You have startled me at my meditation, my child. Why are you here?"

"I come to bid you perform a wedding. I am to marry Viktor the Valiant."

The monk hacked out a cough and stared suspiciously at Viktor. "Speaks she the truth, Viking?"

"Yes. We are to marry tonight, and we would be happy to have you there to attend us."

Wiping his nose on his filthy sleeve, Pelagius scowled at Reyna. "You cannot marry at Lent, my child."

"Lent is done," she replied with surprising gentleness. " 'Tis now Shieling time."

"Ah—my mind plays tricks on me."

"Will you marry us?" Reyna repeated wistfully.

The hermit monk solemnly shook his head. "I cannot, my child. I am not ordained."

"Then will you at least say your blessing for us?"

Pelagius jerked his thumb toward Viktor, then asked Reyna in a tense whisper, "You would live in sin with this heathen?"

"I have no choice in the matter," she confided bitterly. "Viktor the Valiant's warriors have taken my brother and his kinsman hostage. They will be slain if I do not wed Viktor. And besides"—she glanced with some resentment at Viktor—"my husband-to-be is Christian now, or so he avows. Mayhap he saw the light when he went to Valhalla."

Pelagius gazed at Viktor with some awe. "You rose from the dead, my son?"

"In a manner of speaking."

"And are you Christian now, Viktor the Valiant?"

"I am."

His expression skeptical, Pelagius turned back to Reyna. "Think you he lies?"

"I know not. But will you come to bless our union?"

"Yea, I will come," said Pelagius wearily. He raised a craggy brow at Viktor. "I will bless your union with Reyna, as she has asked me. But verily, if you lie, Viking, I will curse you."

"Fair enough," said Viktor amiably.

Pelagius refused the offer of Viktor's mount. As they headed back to the village, he walked behind them, mumbling prayers in Latin, a gnarled hand curled around his crosier.

Viktor frowned at Reyna. "I wish he would have ridden my horse. We may miss our wedding at this rate."

"Pelagius has embraced total humility," explained Reyna. "To ride a beast of burden would be placing himself above one of God's creatures."

"Figuratively as well as literally," Viktor quipped. He stole another glance at the monk. "Too bad he has never heard that cleanliness is next to godliness."

Reyna appeared astonished. "Where hear you that, Viking?"

Viktor was silent, while answering to himself, *From John Wesley, seven centuries forward in time.*

Reyna was now regarding him with amusement. "You know, you take a terrible risk, Viking."

"In what way?"

Her eyes were twinkling with repressed merriment. "Pelagius has vowed to curse you if you lie. His curses are remarkably effective."

"Tell me about them."

"A summer past, three of Wolfgard's warriors discovered Pelagius's cottage. They went there to taunt him, and even ripped apart his finest manuscript. Pelagius cursed the lot of them, and one by one, they perished."

"How?" asked Viktor, fascinated.

"One fell into the fjord and drowned, another went mad and impaled himself on his sword, a third erupted in boils and warts that rendered him blind, and he died ere long."

Viktor whistled. "And you speak about it with such relish—bloodthirsty wench."

"Yea," she said, unrepentant. "Then there was Thorstein—"

"Dare I ask?"

"Wolfgard wed me to him, and Pelagius cursed him. That night, Thorstein could not raise his thing to make me wife. It drove him to such a rage he would have throttled me—but first I hit him over his head with his sword hilt."

Viktor grimaced at the apt symbolism. "And the reason for this little lecture now, Reyna?"

She smirked. "If you lie, Viking, your little thing will turn black and fall off."

He chuckled. "I told you, Reyna, I never lie. Besides, my thing *isn't* little—but then, I suppose we'll just have to wait and see how *big* your eyes grow tonight when I make you my wife, won't we?" And he winked at her lecherously.

"Your tongue is filthy, Viking!" she shot back.

"And yours is not?" he countered.

As she fell into tempestuous silence, Viktor grinned to himself, suddenly feeling very glad they had come to fetch Pelagius. Even giving Reyna the dagger had proved an inspired touch, and the ferocious wench hadn't slain him—yet.

Still, the concessions had restored Reyna's feisty spirit; she was back to being her old sadistic self again, and why this cheered him so, he wasn't entirely sure. But he knew he hadn't liked seeing her so defeated and humbled last night.

Taming her without crushing her spirit would be the challenge, then, he mused. He looked forward to their wedding night with great anticipation.

TWENTY-THREE

Iᴛ ᴡᴀs ᴀ ᴍosᴛ sᴛʀᴀɴɢᴇ ᴡᴇᴅᴅɪɴɢ ᴄᴇʀᴇᴍoɴʏ ɪɴᴅᴇᴇᴅ, Vɪᴋᴛoʀ
mused.

That night in the central chamber of his longhouse, he and
Reyna drank the toast of bridal ale to mark their nuptials in
the pagan tradition. As his warriors and their wives, as well
as Ragar and Harald, stood witness in solemn silence behind
them, Reyna sipped first from the silver chalice. When she
passed the cup to Viktor, he stared intently into her eyes and
deliberately placed his lips where hers had been. He watched
unguarded emotion flare across her lovely face—anger, mistrust, vulnerability—as he handed the chalice back to Svein.

With the pagan rite performed, Pelagius solemnly stepped
forward and bade the bride and groom kneel before him and
clasp hands for the Christian blessing. On his knees beside
his bride, Viktor struggled not to betray his slight amusement
with the monk as the bizarre man mumbled over them in broken Latin and rang his bell. Catching a whiff of Pelagius's
rank odor, he fervently hoped that flakes of bird dung would
not flutter down upon his and Reyna's heads.

Viktor glanced at his bride. She looked so gorgeous in her
long, sleekly fitted gown of white silk, which was held together by the gold ceremonial brooches he had given her
earlier as a wedding present. Her shining blond hair was
twisted in one glorious plait interlaced with wildflowers. Her
visage was stoic, but Viktor could tell from the slight trembling of her fingers in his that she was not unaffected by the

proceeding that bound her to a man she still claimed to hate. How it must rankle for her to be impelled to stand before witnesses and accept him as her husband.

Still, they would be wed now, and with that union came hope, both for them and for all of Vanaheim. He prayed this marriage would succeed. He knew that he loved this defiant, proud beauty. He loved her strength and spirit, even as he understood and admired her more vulnerable, feminine side—an aspect of her psyche he was determined to awaken and nurture. If only one day she could care for him half as much. What was she thinking?

Like Viktor, Reyna felt consumed by uncertainty and tumultuous feelings. Her bridegroom looked altogether too beautiful and tempting kneeling beside her, with the light dancing in his thick blond hair. His jade-green silk tunic and tight leather leggings showed off his broad shoulders and muscular thighs to perfection. Remembering the intense emotion in his eyes when he had taken the chalice and placed his mouth where hers had been, she felt desire wash over her in devastating waves. Viktor's gesture had proved more provocative, more intimate, than the most fervent kiss. With their hands clasped, she could feel the heat and strength of his fingers flowing into hers, as if there would be no escaping the bond between them.

It badly chafed her pride to be forced into wedlock with him. But more than that, Reyna was truly frightened, fearing that the strange tenderness, the vulnerability that Viktor the Valiant inspired in her would make her his for the taking. Viktor's concessions today in letting her have a dagger and helping her fetch Pelagius had touched a heart Reyna had always assumed was impervious to emotion. Again she reflected on how his very gentleness could defeat her. Indeed, seeing the vague bruise along his handsome jaw, where her fists had savagely pounded him yesterday, she was awed by the power of that gentleness. Any other warrior would have killed her for such an insult; instead, Viktor had only smacked her bottom once, then had stopped immediately when she had broken down and sobbed. Afterward, they had kissed and caressed with such sweet, desperate passion— verily, they had all but mated! New, potent need swept her as she remembered Viktor's hard member pushing into her tight womanhood, hurting her . . . And yet she had welcomed the invasion. When Viktor had abruptly withdrawn from her flesh, vowing he would not take her until they were wed, she had burned with frustration and unassuaged longing.

Now he was making her his bride; later, when they lay together, he would not stop until he had buried that delicious hot shaft against her virgin womb. Emotionally, she feared the intimacy just as much as physically, her body craved it. And she sensed that following the consummation, she would never be quite the same.

At last Pelagius ceased his mumblings. Although no further action was required to seal the troth, Viktor stayed Reyna with a hand on her shoulder when she tried to rise. As she glanced at him in bemusement, he removed from his wrist the copper bracelet he had previously stolen from her, leaned over, and replaced the circlet on her ankle. She stared at him, feeling even more perturbed. Then he rose and pulled her to her feet. From his garment he removed an amber ring, took her left hand, and slipped the ring on her third finger.

As she lifted her questioning visage toward his, he murmured, "I take you as my wife, Reyna, and swear to you my heart, my loyalty, and my protection."

He kissed her lips, quickly enough so as not to mar the solemnity of the occasion, fervently enough to stamp her with the heat of his possession.

Reyna felt slightly dazed by Viktor's unexpectedly tender, touching ritual. There was a moment of reverent silence as the others waited for her to respond. At last she whispered, "I take you as husband, Viktor the Valiant."

Amid cheers from the assemblage, they turned. Viktor flashed Reyna a smile and felt heartened when she half smiled back at him. One by one, his kinsmen came forward to offer their blessings—Rollo, Orm, and Canute pounded Viktor across the shoulders, and Ottar and Svein wished the couple lifelong happiness.

Viktor noted that Ragar and Harald hung back, both frowning grimly along the sidelines. At the first lull, he moved off to speak with Reyna's brother. "Do not worry about your sister," he assured Ragar. "I will take good care of her."

When Ragar did not immediately reply, Harald spoke in his stead. "See that you stand by your word, Viktor the Valiant, or you will have both of us to reckon with."

"Fair enough," acknowledged Viktor. He smiled at both men. "And tomorrow I'll assign an escort to take you back to your village."

Ragar shook his head. "Nay, Viktor the Valiant. I prefer to stay for a time, to ensure that my sister is well treated."

"As you wish," Viktor readily conceded. He gestured toward the long table, on which a lavish meal had been laid out. "For now, please, both of you must remain as our guests at the feast."

Viktor and Reyna played host and hostess from opposite ends of the table, which was laden with loaves of bread, baskets of berries and nuts, bowls of stew, and platters of mutton and pork. As the guests ate and drank heartily, Nevin refilled chalices and oxhorns with mead. In one corner Quigley recited a series a verses to honor the occasion, while another Irish thrall played a haunting ballad on a lyre. A couple of the serving women danced, and one of the village youths amused the gathering by juggling spoons.

Soon bellies were soothed by food, tongues loosened by liquor. One by one, Viktor's kinsmen rose to propose toasts to their jarl's nuptials. Unfortunately, all of the salutes insulted Reyna in one manner or another.

"To King Viktor, who has now tamed the Ravisher," announced a jocund Canute, and several warriors cheered and joined the toast.

"And who will reduce the spitting cat to a purring kitten ere the night is out," added Orm, to a new round of gulps and hurrahs.

"May he get a son started on her before Haymaking month," proposed Rollo, his words seconded by an earsplitting roar and more swilling of mead.

"Yea, may her belly soon be thick, her stepfather disgraced," put in a sardonic Eurich.

" 'Tis the only way to keep our new *queen* at heel," finished a sneering Canute.

Glancing worriedly at his bride, Viktor noted her flaming

face and blazing eyes, while nearby, her brother and his kinsman sat in outraged silence. He surged to his feet.

"That is enough," he said firmly to his kinsmen. "Reyna is my bride and I will not hear her insulted in this manner!"

"But, jarl, we are but savoring our victory," protested Orm.

"Not at the expense of my wife's feelings!" Viktor snapped. "You will cease."

At their jarl's dictate, the men grumbled and only partly obliged. They leered at Viktor's bride and mumbled slurs behind their hands. Viktor overheard enough to realize that his men were still mocking Reyna, as well as making wagers on how soon she would be "breeding." From the violently mutinous expression on her face, he knew she could hear the insults, too, and he could have cheerfully throttled a few of his kinsmen. But he could not think of a way to intervene again without making matters worse. If he chastised his men too much, they might revolt and try to harm Reyna, Ragar, or Harald. The freely flowing liquor only made the warriors all the more dangerous and belligerent.

To Viktor's dismay, his unwed warriors, notably Rollo and Canute, soon began to pinch and fondle the serving wenches. The married warriors, noting the mortified expressions of their mates, quickly gathered them and left, which made Viktor's bachelor kinsmen grow bolder. Watching Canute heave a buxom female into his arms and carry her to a bench, Viktor surged to his feet.

"Not in front of my wife," he ground out furiously.

With the wench straddling him and his hands reaching for the hem of her skirts, Canute howled with scornful laughter. "She is not your wife *yet*, jarl. Mayhap the Ravisher could use a demonstration of what pleasures a man."

"Yea," added on insolent Orm, tossing a sneer at Reyna. "Why not take the little Valkyrie now for our amusement? The bench is plenty wide enough for both you and Canute to fondle your women!"

Viktor was ready to charge over and punch out both men when Sibeal rushed up to him, tugging on his tunic and whispering frantically, "Master, 'tis time for milady to take her leave to prepare herself for you."

Viktor heaved a grateful sigh and nodded to the woman.

He offered Reyna a conciliatory glance, but she only glared in return.

To Sibeal, he said, "Yes, please get my bride away from these obnoxious boors before I string up the lot of them."

Sibeal drew Reyna from the room a mere second before Canute hiked up the skirts of the serving wench and copulated with her brazenly while the others hooted cheers.

In Viktor's chamber, Reyna was pacing in a fury. She could still hear the bawdy yells, and the serving wench's wanton cries, coming from the dining hall.

"They are pigs, all of them! Pigs!" she exclaimed.

"Yea, my lady," said Sibeal.

"I overheard them making wagers on how soon I would be breeding—the filthy whoresons!"

"I understand your outrage, milady," Sibeal soothed. "But you must forget their taunts and prepare yourself for your husband."

"To Hel with him as well!"

"Milady, he is not like the others—"

Reyna turned on the woman. "He is! Forcing me into this union!"

"And saving the lives of your brother and Harald," Sibeal reminded her in an admonishing tone.

Reyna released an exasperated breath and continued pacing.

"Milady, Viktor's kinsmen will soon bring him in to you—"

"Over my slain body, they will!"

"My lady, you know that, according to the tradition, your husband must be brought to you by witnesses—"

"I will cast the lot of them from the room!" she declared, gesturing furiously. "I will dispatch all of them to Hel."

"And then Viktor the Valiant's kinsmen will go directly to slay Ragar and Harald," Sibeal pointed out with forbearance. "Is that what you want, milady?"

Reyna made a sound of exquisite frustration.

Sibeal moved cautiously toward her. "Here, milady, let me unbind your hair."

Reyna whirled. "Nay."

Sibeal smiled. "Your husband will not want your hair bound."

Reyna's chin came up. "How know you that?"

"I know." Deep sadness shone in Sibeal's eyes. "I was wed once, milady. Do you not remember?"

At once the girl became contrite. "Yea—and I am sorry to remind you of your loss."

" 'Twas not intended," Sibeal said generously, releasing the bindings on Reyna's thick tresses, sending wildflowers tumbling to the floor as her locks spilled free. "Now you must take off your leggings and gown and get into bed, to await your husband."

Reyna's eyes went wide. "Naked?"

"Yea."

"Nay!" she gasped.

"But, milady—"

"I will wear a shift," the girl insisted. "Fetch it now."

"Nay, milady," Sibeal replied. "Verily, I have never questioned your wearing a garment to bed, for I knew you never felt safe with Wolfgard's kinsmen harassing you. But you are a married lady now—'tis not done that way."

"Tell me no more of what married people do!" Reyna raved, anger and fear making her heedless of Sibeal's feelings.

"Milady, you will know yourself ere morning," Sibeal informed her gently. "Your husband will see to the task."

Reyna's reply was unintelligible.

Sibeal quelled a smile as she watched the girl pull off her leggings, then go to the bed, flouncing down while still defiantly wearing her wedding dress.

"Think you that will last long?" Sibeal scolded.

Reyna pulled the covers up to her chin. "Leave me now, pray."

Sibeal stared at her with compassion, started to say something, then sighed. "Good night, my lady."

After Sibeal left, Reyna sat tensely on the bed and struggled with her own roiling emotions. She could still hear the sounds of revelry coming from the dining hall, and she knew that before long, Viktor's kinsmen would bring him to her. Indeed, the bed smelled of his own special male scent, reminding her that he would soon come to seek his due. And as Sibeal had pointed out, she had no choice but to submit, or else see Ragar and Harald slain.

Still, she would not ease the way for Viktor, not after his kinsmen had so insulted her! Not even as much as she secretly, traitorously, wanted him, illogically yearning for *him* to comfort the hurt for which he was at least partly responsible . . .

All too soon she heard the loud sounds of the men approaching, including her husband's voice as the group passed through the next chamber.

"Is this parade really necessary?" Viktor muttered in exasperation as Canute and Rollo escorted him toward his chamber. Both men were staggering, quite drunk, and kept banging Viktor into walls—which did not improve his own temper in the least.

"Yea, jarl," Orm slurred. "You must be brought to your bride by witnesses."

"What next?" Viktor demanded, fully aware of how his recalcitrant bride would receive this latest assault on her dignity.

A second later, the three crashed into Viktor's chamber. Rollo straightened first, and glowered at the girl on the bed, spotting a bit of white silk protruding from above the fur pelt.

"Your bride is still clothed, jarl!" he cried. "She insults you on your wedding night!"

Viktor hastily glanced at the horrified Reyna. "It is none of your affair. Now, if you will both please leave—"

"Let us strip her, jarl, and beat her as well," offered an equally belligerent Canute. " 'Tis time the little hellion learns respect for her jarl and husband!"

Had Viktor not been assured of a drunken brawl erupting in his wedding chamber, he would have slammed his fist into Canute's arrogant jaw. Instead, he ordered murderously, "Get out of here, both of you, and do not dare come back or insult my bride again."

While Canute glared back at his jarl, Rollo seemed to find humor in the situation. "Verily, we do not need to strip her," he informed Canute, then nudged Viktor with his elbow. "Ye need only to raise the bride's skirts, eh, jarl?" he taunted, and rocked with laughter.

Viktor felt intense sympathy for his humiliated bride, and even greater fury toward his two drunken kinsmen. He forced his words through gritted teeth. "You have done your duty—you have brought me to my bride. Now *get out of here,* you besotted fools, or I will kill you both—now!"

At this, Canute and Rollo exchanged cocky grins, and the two left amid much staggering and new howls of mirth.

Viktor turned contritely to his wife. Studying Reyna's tempestuous expression, he felt even more helpless rage toward his kinsmen. His bride had not deserved such mistreatment, and the freeswilling oafs had certainly not eased the way for him tonight with their relentless taunts.

He spoke gently. "Reyna, I am sorry about my men's obnoxious behavior. I'm sure they will settle down in time—and I do plan to call all of them aside once they are sober and insist they treat you with greater respect."

She flounced up from the bed to face him with eyes blazing. "You think their respect is something I crave?" she spit out. "Or yours, Viktor the Valiant?"

Despite her defiance, the sight of her barefoot, in the virginal white gown, stoked Viktor's passions. He moved closer and offered a smile. "Reyna, I know you have endured inexcusable insults tonight. I know this marriage is not of your choosing. But can't we make the best of things? Can't you see that there's much more at stake than simply you or me?" He reached out to stroke her flushed cheek and spoke soulfully. "Tonight, we unite our bodies and hearts. Tomorrow, our union will bring all our peoples together."

She shoved his fingers away. "You only want to use me to bring your craved peace!"

He continued to speak with patience and vehemence. "Reyna, have you ever considered that every time a warrior dies, a sister or wife must cry, just as you cried yesterday when you thought you would lose Ragar?"

She turned away, blinking rapidly. "Now you shame me with that?"

He caught her chin with his fingers, forcing her to meet his searching gaze. "There is no shame in loving another, or in standing up to save him."

She blinked away tears. "Do not hope I will ever feel that love for you, Viktor the Valiant," she said, her voice trembling. "You have forced me to become your bride, but you will never win my loyalty, my trust, or my heart. I tell you, I will not be your vessel to stop this war."

He dropped his hand, and his voice was very low and ominous. "Just what are you saying, Reyna?"

Although her eyes were suspiciously bright, she faced him with pride. "I have fulfilled my end of our bargain. I have wed you. But I will not lie with you tonight unless you force me."

Fury welled in Viktor at her callous betrayal of their pact. His words were just as ruthless. "Reyna, you have *not* fulfilled your end of our bargain, and you damn well know it!"

She held her ground, although her chin quivered.

"Do you realize that if my warriors knew of your refusal to grant me my husbandly rights, they would kill you—and likely Ragar and Harald as well?"

She hesitated for a moment, then whispered, "You would bring me to that just to bed me?"

"No," he stated with contempt. "I will not reduce myself to your level."

"And I will not submit," she hissed back.

A murderous passion burned in Viktor's eyes. He shook a fist at the infuriating Valkyrie. "A true marriage is not about submission. In a true marriage, a husband and wife give themselves to each other in love. We will both of us be dead from this feud before I rape you, Reyna."

He stormed from the room.

TWENTY-FOUR

Reyna sobbed in Viktor's bed. She held the fur cover to her face and tried to smother the wrenching sounds. She felt hellishly guilty for sending him away from their wedding chamber. Yea, his men had insulted her terribly, battering her pride, but that had not been Viktor's fault. Indeed, the blame had been largely hers, for goading his warriors so remorselessly in the first place.

In truth, her husband had lived up to his end of their agreement, saving the lives of Ragar and Harald, and she had tried to weasel out of her own responsibilities in a most cowardly fashion. Yet she felt deeply shaken by her desire for Viktor—a near-desperate need to possess her enemy, to *be* possessed by him. Her new husband had an uncanny ability to connect with her emotionally, to perceive her feelings, to make her feel vulnerable, and Reyna recognized this awesome power as an even more compelling reason to deny him. She feared that the consummation between them would strip her, not just physically but also spiritually, that she would become his pawn, a vessel of his will. Still, no matter what her motives, her refusal had been wrong, just as Sibeal had scolded; by all rights she should be lying with her husband now . . .

Viktor paced in the next chamber. His emotions seethed in turmoil; he felt hurt and betrayed. By God, what did it take to reach this woman? He had tried everything in his power, yet Reyna seemed to possess a heart of stone. Would she never trust him, never let him inside her armor—even just a little? If not, the love he now felt for her—as well as the future of the island of Vanaheim—would be doomed.

And then he heard a low sound—like a fevered gasp—coming from the next chamber. He could not believe it! Was Reyna actually crying? Could she possess a heart and a conscience after all?

For a moment, he struggled between wounded pride and welling passion. His passion proved far more fierce—that, and his intense desire to comfort his bride. He strode back inside the room to observe her shuddering on the bed. She was facing the wall, curled up in a fetal position. A surge of tenderness shook the buttresses of his anger. As much as this woman had maddened him, it killed him to see her suffering now.

He crossed the room and lay down beside her, curving an arm around her waist. At first he felt her stiffen, but she did not resist. Encouraged, he nestled her back snugly against his chest, emotion welling inside him anew when she relaxed against him, a gesture of trust that gladdened him. He moved aside her hair, kissed her soft nape, and felt her shiver. He was profoundly conscious of the warmth and shapeliness of her woman's body cuddled against him, her firm bottom nestled against his heated loins, her lush thighs pressing against his. The scent of her, along with the virginal sensuality of her thin white silk garment, incited his passions even more. Although he knew too many barriers still loomed between them, at least she was allowing him to touch her—how he gloried in that! . . .

Next to Viktor, Reyna was also drowning in deep emotion. By rights Viktor should have raped or beaten her for her defiance. Instead, her bridegroom was comforting her, inundating her with tenderness, and the effect was devastating. Her heart responded with joy and love, her woman's body with painful need. Beside her, Viktor felt so hard, so warm, so close—and her own garment was so thin. She burned everywhere his magnificent body touched her, especially where her bottom was cradled against his hot, solid arousal . . .

Viktor pressed his lips to Reyna's ear and smiled at her soft sigh. "Must you hate so, Reyna?" he whispered. "Even me, on our wedding night?"

She twisted about to face him, her features stark with conflicted emotion, her cheeks stained by tears. "I do not hate you nearly as much as I should, Viking."

Shocked and touched by her admission, he could not help but chuckle softly, for her expression was so earnest. "God help me should you ever truly despise me, then."

She lowered her gaze. "I do not despise you."

"Really?" he chided, remembering past events. "Not even on the day you spit in my face?"

She reached out to toy with the brooch binding his tunic, and the innocence of the gesture twisted his heart. "You did not see how Wolfgard's fiercest fighter, Egil, was about to thrust his spear through your back."

"Ah," he murmured, feeling both amazed and moved. "And that is why you stopped the warriors from battering me?"

She nodded, but still would not meet his eye.

"Why did you spit in my face, Reyna?" he pressed.

Now she did look up at him, biting her underlip. "I had to convince my father's kinsmen that you were beneath contempt, beneath killing. I could not let them see how your courage moved me. I could not trust you then—and I do not trust you now."

"But you're in my arms, darling," he pointed out gently, brushing a tear from her eyelash. "And you're weeping."

She sniffed. "Yea. I weep because I dishonored my word."

Viktor would have laughed had Reyna not appeared so sincere. "So your word to me means something after all?" he asked, unable to hide a trace of bitterness.

The old spirit flared in her eyes. "We had a bargain, Viktor the Valiant. That I do not take lightly."

"Then why did you send me away just now?" When she glanced away guiltily, he grasped her chin and forced her to look at him. "Tell me the truth, Reyna. I'd say it's high time for some honesty between us."

She was silent for a long moment, obviously struggling within herself.

"Why did you send me away, Reyna?" he repeated.

"Because your kisses move me," she confessed. She met his probing gaze fully. "You move me, Viktor the Valiant. I am not pleased by that, either."

Viktor could have shouted his joy at these admissions. "You aren't pleased that my kisses move you, or that I move you?" he teased gently.

"By neither, Viking."

"But you feel the same passion that I do, don't you, darling?"

"Yea," she admitted in a trembling whisper.

He groaned with pleasure. "And you want me."

He watched uncertainty mingled with panic fill Reyna's eyes as she struggled between her desire to be honest and her fear of revealing herself. He ended her torment by kissing her. At her smothered sob, he almost pulled away, but his doubt faded as she kissed him back with such sweet innocence and curled her arms around his neck.

"Oh, Reyna, Reyna," he murmured, pressing his mouth to her soft cheek, her adorably stubborn chin. "Are you ready to give yourself to me?"

"Yea."

"Why?"

"Because you are very beautiful," she answered, tracing a finger along his jaw. "And very kind, even if you are Viking. I will honor my vow to become your wife."

Viktor felt troubled by her motives. "You do not have to give yourself to me just because of our bargain."

He could have sworn he spotted hurt flaring in her eyes. "Then you do not want me, Viking?"

He grinned. "Of course I want you."

She smiled back. "If you truly wanted me, you would hold me to our bargain. No warrior worth his salt would do less."

Viktor had to struggle not to laugh, not wanting to risk shattering the fragile rapport they had established. Instead, he stroked her mouth and teased, "Oh, so are you such an expert on men now, darling?"

"Nay—but Sibeal warned that I will be by morning."

"And is Sibeal always right?"

She looked him over with a thoroughness that heated his blood. "On such matters, always."

"Then far be it from me to spoil her perfect record," he murmured, and hauled her closer.

That little sob escaped Reyna again, but this time Viktor recognized the sound as one of desire and need. Her lips were soft, honeyed, and trembling so, they set him on fire. He felt as if he had waited for her forever, and he burned to have her warm and naked against him. He reached for the hem of her gown and began gently tugging, all the while kissing her passionately.

At first he was bemused when she pushed him away and sat up. "What are you doing?" he asked hoarsely.

" 'Tis not your task to remove my gown," she replied breathlessly. "Sibeal scolded me for that—for not preparing myself for you."

Viktor avidly watched her pull the rich silk garment up her lovely legs. "Perhaps it is not my task, but it would be my pleasure."

She roved her gaze over him hungrily. "See to your own task, then."

"And what is that, darling?"

She tugged the garment over her head and tossed it aside. "Will you make me wife with you leggings still on, Viktor the Valiant?"

Would he indeed! Viktor's gaze was riveted on Reyna's glorious, naked flesh, his pulse roaring in his ears. She was an enchantress, her long hair spilling across her creamy neck and smooth shoulders; her breasts high, shapely, and proud; her belly flat; her legs long and sleek. His fevered gaze lingered on the mound of delectable, downy curls at the joining of her thighs. All at once his leather leggings felt entirely too tight.

Despite her maiden state, she showed no shame at all at her own nakedness or her husband's heated perusal. How he loved her for that!

"You are incredible," he whispered.

Her words came just as tremulously as her hand touched his. "Then make me wife."

Viktor pulled off his tunic, tossed it aside, and pressed Reyna down beneath him. He groaned as her firm breasts, with their tight nipples, contacted his bare chest, stoking his desires like the lick of a flame. Reyna sighed with pleasure and caressed his strong shoulders with her fingertips. Beneath him, she felt soft, yielding, unbearably eager.

Viktor prayed he would be able to maintain his control, to arouse his wife slowly, completely, to hurt her as little as possible with his passion. In truth, he felt he knew her already, knew her body, yet she was also brand-new to him, a virgin and untried. The anticipation of rediscovering this woman he knew, but somehow did not know, made him mad with desire.

He wooed her with thorough kisses, tantalizing her with the leisurely dance of his tongue in her mouth, encouraging her to mate her mouth with his in the same uninhibited fashion. When both of them were reeling, gasping between each hot kiss, he began drawing his lips down her shapely throat, to her breasts. She writhed as he gently tongued the pink, taut nipples.

She pressed her fingers to his nape and held his mouth to her breast. Tears filled his eyes at the sweetness of her possessive gesture, and he sucked greedily at each breast in turn, wrenching incoherent cries from her.

A moment later, he rolled over, bringing her lush nakedness on top of him, wanting to feel her swath of silken hair falling across his face, to see her lovely brown eyes staring down into his, mindless with desire.

His fingers caught her nape and he brought her lips down for another drowning kiss. The way she responded— trembling against him, opening her mouth wide to his passionate possession—stirred him unbearably. He ran his hands provocatively over her back, then cupped her firm buttocks and began a rhythmic rocking.

"Do you want more, darling?" he breathed into her mouth.

She nodded vehemently, catching a ragged breath, then kissing him back. Growing bolder, she reached down between their bodies, touching him through his leggings, wrenching a delighted grunt from him. Abruptly she pulled back, and Viktor caught her around the waist, half fearing she might flee. He glanced up in confusion to see her staring at him, wide-eyed, hot-cheeked—and then she caressed him again, so skillfully.

" 'Tis so large!" she gasped.

He grinned, reaching up to stroke her flushed cheek. "It will hurt a little the first time," he said gently. "Did you know?"

She shook her head solemnly. "Are all men so big?"

He chuckled. "Believe me, darling, I don't go around asking—and I sure as Hel better never catch *you* doing so."

Her sensual giggle was soon her undoing.

Viktor rolled her beneath him, kissed her rapaciously, and stroked her mound of curls with his fingers. As she gasped and writhed, he gently insinuated her thighs apart, caressing her tender little bud. She whimpered, bucking against him like a strong young mare, and he had to hold her down, fearing he might hurt her otherwise. More than anything, he longed to possess her with his mouth, to drown her in her first, blinding climax. But he reminded himself that this was all new to her, that he must slowly teach her such brazen intimacies.

Meanwhile, the bride herself seemed to be growing most impatient. Arching into his touch, Reyna wrenched her mouth from his and gasped wildly, "Viktor, pray, I want—"

"I know, love," he murmured, working loose the ties on his leggings. "Be patient. You'll soon get what you want."

He touched her lower, sliding a finger inside her womanhood, glorying in how snug and slick she felt. He gazed into her fevered eyes. "Is this what you want, darling?"

Her expression was taut with desperation. "Yea, 'tis where I want *you.*"

Viktor moaned in ecstasy, burying his face against her soft throat. Never had he expected his proud bride to respond so sweetly, so fully to him! She reached down again, boldly curling her fingers around his naked, engorged shaft. He sucked in his breath in an excruciated gasp and thrust against her fingers.

As she continued to massage him, Viktor caressed her narrow passage, easing his finger in and out, in a brazen mimicry of the consummation soon to come. When her breathing grew fierce, when she chewed her bottom lip and tossed her head in abandon, he heightened the stimulation, pushing two fingers inside her, probing gently at first, then more insistently, stretching her until she cried out and dug her fingernails into his shoulders.

"Sorry, darling, there's no other way to prepare you," he whispered, nudging her thighs farther apart and continuing the firm stroking. "Relax and it will go easier for you."

She did his bidding with a shuddering sigh, and he plied her taut flesh until her moans were only those of pleasure. At last, satisfied that she was as ready as she could be, he withdrew his fingers and pressed the tip of his manhood to her throbbing wetness.

At his first penetration, she cried out in both pleasure and pain.

Viktor's voice was tortured. "Reyna, do you want me to—"

"Nay, do not stop."

Shuddering with emotion, Viktor stared into his wife's eyes and pressed more powerfully to make them one. She sobbed as he breached her maidenhead. His mouth seized hers in a tender kiss and he pushed in as deeply as he dared, groaning as her warm, snug sheath tightly encompassed him. At last they were one, and it was glorious!

"How does that feel, darling?" he whispered.

Reyna was indeed in pain, but the burning pleasure of being joined with her husband made all discomfort pale by comparison. She felt with Viktor the very physical and spiritual bond she had dreaded, yet the joining itself had banished all fear and brought instead a wondrous wholeness and shattering ecstasy.

"As if I am wife," she murmured through her tears, and stretched upward to kiss him.

Her words and the fervent mating of her mouth stirred Viktor profoundly, particularly when she moaned an incoherent cry of surrender. He began to move gently within her, trying not to hurt her, even as her velvety constriction was making him demented. When she sucked his tongue inside her mouth, his passions broke free. His kiss smothered her moans as he plunged vigorously, again and again, until she melted into his final deep thrust and he shuddered exquisitely inside her.

Viktor tenderly held his bride, his heart pounding, his

breathing labored. At last he reached out to wipe the tears from her eyes, and eased himself slowly from her taut flesh. Hearing her low wince, he flashed her a contrite smile.

"I'm sorry I had to hurt you, darling."

"I am not," came her unabashed reply. " 'Twas beautiful, though it did smart badly, especially at first."

"It won't hurt like that again," he promised solemnly.

"Verily?" she asked, then surprised him again by smirking. "Mayhap we should do it again?"

"Minx," he teased, kissing the tip of her nose. "You may want to give your body at least five minutes to recover."

She looked him over, and even her gaze made his manhood throb back to life. "And what of your body, my husband?"

He grinned. "My body—and I—are both feeling very glad we have brought you pleasure."

She snuggled contentedly against him. "I did like the feeling. It made me remember . . ."

He caught her hand and kissed her lovely fingers. "What, Reyna?"

When she didn't reply, he stared at her. She appeared wary again, but her eyes were bright.

"Tell me, darling," he coaxed. "Don't hold back after we've shared so much. Tell me what our lovemaking made you remember."

A tear spilled from the corner of her eye. "Happiness. It has been so long since I felt it, a lifetime mayhap."

"Oh, love." For many moments Viktor held and kissed her. "Has it been that long, darling?"

She nodded. "Since I was a princess, picking flowers in a meadow in Loire." Emotion choked her voice. "You made me remember that, Viktor the Valiant, for the first time in so many years. For that I must thank you, my husband."

He clutched her closer and pressed his lips to her brow. "Darling, it is I who must thank you for all the joy you've brought me, and there is no greater delight than knowing I have pleased you."

"I thought the happy soul I once knew was dead forever," she admitted poignantly.

"You can find her again, Reyna."

"Can I?" she asked wistfully.

"Yes. We'll find her together."

She frowned. "In truth, I sometimes do not know. I was content so long ago. But afterward ..." She turned away, shuddering.

He slipped his arms around her and nestled her back against his chest. "I know, Reyna. Sibeal told me of all you lost."

"Did she?"

He locked his forearms across her belly and kissed her shoulder. "Your suffering can end now, if you'll only let it. I want to help make you very happy."

She turned in his arms. "Why?"

Because I love you. Staring into her dark eyes, Viktor was sorely tempted to say the words, but something held him back. He realized he could not yet tell Reyna of his love, because he still feared she would use his feelings as a weapon against him. Yet she had bared her heart a little, and so would he.

Sincerely, he confided, "Because I understand. You see, I, too, have lost loved ones."

She appeared fascinated. "Have you? Who?"

Viktor's visage twisted with sadness. "A mother, father—a sister."

Reyna's mouth dropped open. "When was this? When you lived your other life?"

"Yes."

"You must tell me all about it," she urged.

"I will, darling, but not tonight. I don't want to let anything cloud our joy." His expression turned solemn. "Do you think there is hope for us, Reyna?"

She regarded him with regret and turbulent emotion. "You must understand, Viktor the Valiant—I do not know anything except hatred, death, and revenge."

"But you felt happy when I loved you?"

"Yea."

He laced his fingers through hers. "Then there is a chance for us, darling."

She smiled. "Mayhap there is."

"And if our loving brings you happiness, then perhaps I should make love to you all the time," he teased.

"Mayhap you should, Viking." She stretched lazily, then coiled her arms around his neck. "Now would be most pleasing."

"Anything my lady desires," he replied gallantly.

With a grin, Viktor pressed Reyna beneath him. As his strong thighs spread hers, he glanced down and hesitated as he spotted the streaks of blood on her inner thighs. "Perhaps we had better not try again so soon."

"Let me judge that, my husband," she replied, abruptly flipping him onto his back and straddling him with her knees.

He scowled ferociously. "Where did you learn this, wife?"

She smirked at him. "Think you I never saw what the warriors do to the females on their benches?"

As she slid upward to mount him, he stayed her, bracing his hands on her inner thighs. At her curious glance, he spoke sternly. "But with us it is different, Reyna. This is not an act of lust."

She scowled for a moment, evidently considering his words. Watching her, Viktor realized he had set himself up to be hurt. Reyna could wound him badly now by denying his words and cheapening the magic they had just shared.

Instead, she filled his heart with gladness when she whispered, "Nay, 'tis an act of happiness."

Viktor could have wept then. He hauled his wife close and kissed her with desperate love. By the time she moved back once again to mount him, her eyes were dazed, her lips wet and parted, her breath coming in pants.

The rest Viktor watched in fascination. Reyna arched up slightly, and her fingers curled around his manhood. Closing her eyes, she rubbed the tip of his throbbing arousal against her intimate recesses with an unconscious, provocative sensuality that submerged him in madness. At last she located her own warm center—

Viktor clenched his teeth and fought for restraint. With an impassioned whimper, she began taking him inside her, inching herself down upon his engorged shaft. Groans and shudders seized him. The warm tightness of her was so glorious that he struggled mightily not to grab her around the waist and impale her fully with his heat. Reyna let nothing stop her, not even her own breathless cries, as she eased lower until the constriction of her flesh stopped her.

At last her eyes flew open on a gasp.

"Easy, darling," he soothed. "Don't hurt yourself. You'll adjust to me in time."

"What do I do now?" she asked, half frantic.

"Darling, you've already done it. Just relax and enjoy your ride."

Viktor thrust upward, setting the pace. Reyna moaned and rocked with him as the sweet convulsions seized them both. His hands grasped her breasts, crushing them gently. Her breath came in delirious gasps. When she rolled her hips, he could not bear it—he caught her at the waist and held her to the wrenching strokes that hurled them both to ecstasy and tore a demented cry from her lungs.

"Reyna . . . Reyna, darling," he whispered fiercely.

Viktor pulled his wife close for a tender, shattering kiss that sealed their act of joy.

Across the fjord, Viktor's enemy was contemplating an act of lust. With knees spread and the front of his leggings bulging painfully, Wolfgard sat on his bed, staring lecherously at the female thrall he had just summoned, a young woman of two and twenty summers who cowered before him.

It irked Wolfgard that women invariably trembled in his presence, and when he spread their thighs and took his ease, they sobbed piteously, or suffered in silence. Even his wife had lain beneath him for many winters as dispassionate as a slab of meat, with only his occasional cruel thrust drawing a pained moan from her.

Sometimes he wondered if he would gain just as much pleasure seeking his release alone, by his own hand. But it was not his place to service himself, and verily, he liked subjugating a female and forcing sounds from her. Now that he had passed so many winters, he sometimes resorted to very rough measures to ensure that a female responded. When a woman sobbed or shrieked or pleaded, it drove him quickly to violent release.

He eyed the timid wench with contempt. "Take off your garment, slave, and kneel between my thighs."

She began to shudder in horror. "Pray, master, do not make me—not again—"

"Do it or I will slit your throat!" he roared.

The woman's trembling fingers moved to the brooch binding her modest garment, and Wolfgard licked his lips in anticipation and reached down to stroke himself. He paused, scowling, as Egil abruptly entered the room, a dark figure following him.

"Jarl, your spy is here."

"Damn it, man, have you no sense of discretion?" Wolfgard exploded to his kinsman.

Egil gulped in fear, but stood his ground. "I beg your pardon, jarl, but your man has an important message."

Wolfgard glowered at the two, then snapped his fingers at the slave. "Leave us!"

The terrified woman needed no encouragement to flee.

Wolfgard jerked his head around to the spy. "What news have you, man?"

"Your stepdaughter has married King Viktor," he replied.

His visage livid, Wolfgard surged to his feet. "I shall strangle the little traitor myself."

"Jarl, she married Viktor to save the lives of your son and his kinsman."

Making a sound of frustrated rage, Wolfgard stalked forward. "What is this? Tell me of my son!"

"Ragar and Harald were captured by Viktor's men. The warriors were prepared to torture and kill them when your daughter intervened, offering to wed Viktor if her brother and his kinsman were spared."

"And what of my son—the fool!" Wolfgard growled.

"I understand he will shortly be released."

"That is all?"

"Yea."

Wolfgard paced for a moment, still wearing a ferocious frown. He nodded to Egil. "Pay this man for his troubles and see him safely back across the fjord."

"Yea, jarl."

As the two men made to leave, Wolfgard called after them. "A moment."

Both men turned.

"Is the bride happy?" Wolfgard asked sardonically.

"I know not," the spy replied.

"Come back and report to me when you know."

The man bowed. "Yea. I will."

After the others left, Wolfgard sat brooding, staring into the fire. His witless son! Through the boy's foolishness, they had all played right into Viktor's hands.

Now Reyna was Viktor the Valiant's bride, and she must be slain. Whatever the girl's motives in wedding Viktor, Wolfgard must ensure that the girl never bore his enemy a son. If she did, he would lose his pact with Viktor, be impelled to end the feud, and suffer a terrible loss of esteem with his people.

Damn the little Valkyrie! A curse on Reyna!

Deep into the night, Wolfgard plotted how he would accomplish his stepdaughter's murder. He wanted her to suffer for her betrayal, but more than that, he wanted her slain; thus he realized his thirst for revenge must defer to the need to secure her expedient death.

Wolfgard would have summoned back the woman to service him, but for now, his anger far overshadowed his lust. 'Twas just as well for the thrall, he mused. In his current temper, he would use the wench badly, mayhap even beat her dead. Slaves served their purpose, and he could ill afford to slay them all.

TWENTY-FIVE

Viktor awakened well before dawn and stared at his wife sleeping beside him. Reyna appeared as serene and lovely as an angel, her warm body snuggled against him, her hair falling away from her exquisite face in a golden cascade. What joy she had brought him last night, giving herself to him so sweetly. She might not completely trust or love him yet, but that depth of feeling would come in time, he vowed. For now, he was content to be close to her, loving her, building their future—and, he fervently hoped, starting their baby together. Surely a child who was a part of them both would draw them closer and bind their lives and destinies together. He shut his eyes in delight at the image of beautiful Reyna sitting on his bed with his baby at her breast—

When he opened his eyes, he found her awake, staring solemnly at him, almost as if his thoughts had stirred her. "Good morning, wife," he said huskily, leaning over to kiss her.

He was stayed by a glimmer of uncertainty flaring in her eyes. He could almost see the wheels of her mind turning, as if she were remembering the still-unsettled issues between them and questioning her own passionate surrender last night. After all the rapture they had shared, he could not bear her withdrawal from him.

"Don't," he whispered, touching the tip of her nose with his finger.

"Do not what?" she asked in bewilderment.

His hand caressed her bare spine. "Don't pull away from

242

me, Reyna ... Or I swear I'll bury myself in you until I
watch all the doubt fade from your eyes."

Her mouth fell open on a tiny gasp, and Viktor could not
resist claiming those trembling lips in an ardent kiss. Joy
surged in him when she kissed him back with equal intensity.
Moaning with pleasure, he drew her closer and cupped his
hand around a lush breast, wanting to shut away the world
and all their problems for a few more blissful moments and
start the day savoring the woman he loved. Ah, she was so
warm and tasted so good. He hungered to taste her all over—

They jerked apart at the sounds of yapping, and seconds
later, three wolves bounded onto the bed, licking and chewing
them.

"Hey, you guys have a terrible sense of timing," Viktor
scolded, while affectionately petting Hati, who had landed on
his thigh.

Reyna was giggling as Thor licked her face. "Mayhap your
wolves seek to protect me from you, my husband."

"Protect you?" Viktor repeated with a scowl. "You, my
lady, are the one who has been trying your best to slay me,
ever since I brought you to this village."

She fought a smirk. "Did I slay you last night, my lord?"

"Did you ever." He leaned over Geri's squirming body to
kiss his wife's impudent lips. "Why don't we go for a picnic
today?"

"A picnic? What is that?"

"We'll pack up some food and mead and spend the day
picking wildflowers on the tundra."

She appeared intrigued but also bemused. "For what purpose?"

He grinned, then playfully nibbled on her breast. "To enjoy
each other, darling."

An ecstatic sigh escaped her. "Will the wolves come?"

Viktor harrumphed and straightened, gently pushing Hati
aside and hopping out of bed. "I think not." He winked at
Reyna lecherously. "I'm a newlywed, you see, and I just may
find myself feeling amorous toward my new bride."

As Viktor went to retrieve his leggings, Reyna could not
help but stare at his glorious, naked body. She feasted her
gaze on his sinewy shoulders, the smooth lines of his back,

his hard buttocks, and his muscled thighs with their covering of coarse hairs. She remembered those strong thighs drawing hers so widely apart last night, just before he had impaled her with his rigid, hot member. Oh, it had smarted, but so sweetly, and such incredible pleasure had come in the wake of the pain! Heat suffused her cheeks at the memory, and excitement throbbed in the very places where she still ached from her husband's fierce possession. Verily, she was shameless, but some traitorous part of her gloried in the fact that this man was hers, that she was now his bride.

Yet on another level, these potent new yearnings, this sense of emotional exposure, left Reyna uncertain. She still doubted Viktor's motives in wedding her; she still feared he was using her to end the feud. And how could she have forgotten her own vow never to let any man have such power over her, never to become the creature of a warrior's will?

Yet when Viktor had touched her, something elemental in her had been stirred and moved, and she had surrendered eagerly. Her pride, indeed the price his passion demanded, had seemed not to matter. Now she was left off-balance, perplexed, and feeling closer to him than she had ever wanted to feel.

She watched him bend over to retrieve his leggings, and a sigh escaped her. Then he turned to don them . . . Staring at the front of him and seeing how aroused he was despite their night of passion, Reyna felt even stronger tingles of desire deep inside her. She squirmed on the bed, her fists clenched. Viktor had said he would likely feel "amorous" today. Reyna wasn't entirely certain what that word meant, but she had a strong intuition that she would be feeling much the same, and this scared her as much as it excited her.

Observing him grimace while tying his leggings over his distended manhood, she chuckled. "Need you assistance, my lord?" she called.

Viktor grinned back at her. His wife was avidly watching him, her lips parted, her hair falling over her shoulders, her breasts bared. She looked sexy, disheveled, and primitive, especially surrounded by the three eager wolves. He hungered to plunder her body thoroughly—but not while three ninety-pound monsters were bounding all over them!

His voice sounded very raspy. "Get dressed and let's get out of here—before I am well beyond help."

Viktor had finished dressing quickly, and while his wife completed her toilette, he went to fetch them bowls of porridge and tankards of buttermilk. Bringing their breakfast on a crude tray, he spotted Reyna seated on the bed, wearing a long garment of brown wool and soft leather boots and drawing a whalebone comb through her shiny hair. He sat down next to her and balanced the tray on their laps.

Reyna eagerly gulped her buttermilk. "What of Ragar and Harald?" she asked anxiously. "Will they be going back to Wolfgard's village?"

"I offered them escort home this morning, Reyna," Viktor answered carefully, "but your half brother wants to stay for a few days to ensure that you are well treated."

Reyna frowned, and Viktor knew she was again recalling the unpleasant realities that had prompted their marriage. "Mayhap Ragar and Harald could come with us on the picnic."

Disappointment stabbed Viktor. "Do you really want them along?"

"I must know they will not be abused while we are away."

"They will not be, Reyna," he told her. "I'll make sure my blood brother, Svein, guards them while we are gone. And they will both be invited to dine with us tonight." He regarded her earnestly. "Satisfied now?"

"Yea," she answered, flashing him a smile.

Moments later, they rode out of the village, Viktor on Sleipnir, Reyna astride a black pony. The morning had brought a cool breeze and bright sunshine.

Watching his wife wiggle in her saddle, Viktor chuckled. "Sore, milady?"

"Yea," she admitted ruefully.

"We won't go far."

"Yea—you will not want to spoil me for your pleasure," she quipped.

"No, I'll want to spoil you *with* it."

They rode up into the foothills, passing the monk Pelagius,

who barely acknowledged their greeting with a distracted
wave of his staff as he trudged along, mumbling and crossing
himself.

Just beyond the monk, Viktor raised an eyebrow at his
wife.

Reyna chuckled. "Do not mind Pelagius."

"I know—he is seeking a state of grace."

They stopped in a large meadow, where Viktor spread a
wool blanket and set out their repast of mead, dried cod,
bread, berries, and nuts. They reclined together in the midst
of a tundra brilliant with wildflowers—white arctic cotton,
purple heliotrope, and numerous small pink and yellow
blooms. Above them, a hawk circled in the perfect cloudless
sky.

Viktor fed his wife berries and bread and offered the mead
from his oxhorn. He felt intensely grateful for the beautiful
day and the pastoral interlude they were sharing—for once,
without anger in a spirit of tenderness and exploration.

Reyna experienced the same surge of gentle feelings at being pampered by her new husband. Never before had any
man hand-fed her a repast, much less licked the mead from
her lips! She was still afraid to love and trust Viktor, fearing
he would eventually dominate her just as her mother had
been subjugated by Wolfgard. Still, her bridegroom greatly
intrigued her, for he was in so many ways a mystery to her—
strong yet tender, passionate yet elusive. She wanted to know
him better.

The hints Viktor had given about having lived another life
continued to tantalize her. Had he acquired his compassionate, endearing qualities in that other life? He had obviously
known a world she had never seen, one she yearned to ex-
plore, if only through his sharing.

Where, for instance, had her husband learned of this delightful custom, the "picnic"? And why, at their nuptials last
night, had he replaced the circlet on her ankle and slipped his
ring, with its lovely, square amber stone, on her finger? She
had meant to ask Viktor about these odd rituals last night, but
she had become distracted by his kisses.

She smiled as she watched the light play off the ring he
had given her. She glanced at him curiously, watching him tilt

his head back and sip the mead. "During our nuptials, why did you place this ring on my finger—and the bracelet back on my ankle?"

Lowering his oxhorn, he considered her question. "The ring is a tradition where I come from. It's called a wedding ring—the bridegroom places it on the bride's finger as a symbol of their troth. As for the bracelet"—he paused to wink at her—"it *is* yours, my love."

"Yea, but you stole it!"

His grin was unrepentant. "I know, but you had sorely tried my patience, as I'm sure you'll recall." He nudged the circlet with his boot. "Nevertheless, it's your possession, and I've been meaning to return it to you." He chuckled. "Besides, the anklet may prove a convenient device for me to grab you, should you try to leave my bed."

She lifted her chin saucily and sipped the mead. "Think you I will attempt that soon, Viking?"

"You will not succeed if you try," he teased back, then pulled her close for a kiss.

After a languid moment, she murmured, "Tell me of your other life, my husband."

Brushing a strand of hair from her eyes, Viktor regarded Reyna curiously. "What do you want to know?"

She straightened the sleeve of his tunic. "I want to know where you learned such outlandish customs as wedding rings and picnics . . . and being amorous."

He kissed her chin, then licked a droplet of mead from the corner of her mouth. "You mean people are not amorous in this age, Reyna?"

She shrugged a shapely shoulder. "As you know, my experience before you is as naught. But no, I would reckon we know not of being amorous here—only of mating."

"I find that very sad."

More insistently, she urged, "Tell me of where you came from. Of where you lived after you journeyed to Valhalla." Tentatively, she added, "I saw you, you know."

"Saw what?"

"On the day you died, I secretly watched your warriors launch you to Valhalla; then I later discovered you had returned from the dead."

"I thought you knew I had returned from Valhalla!" he exclaimed with a grin. "So you spied on me even then?"

She dodged his question with one of her own. "And you lived your other life before you returned to us?"

He nodded.

"But how could you have lived another life so quickly?"

He considered for a moment. "There's much I can't explain, Reyna. I just know it happened."

"Where did you go after Valhalla?" she pressed.

Again Viktor hesitated, wondering how much she could accept and understand—and how much of his former life he could afford to trust her with. "I went to the world of the future," he said at last.

"The future!" she gasped. "I have never heard of this world! Is it a tenth world, then?"

"What do you mean, tenth world?"

"Vikings believe in nine worlds," Reyna explained. "There is Midgard, the earth, where we are now. There is Jotunheim, where the trolls and giants live, and Vana Heim, the realm of the Vanirgods, after which our island is named. There is also Hel, the world of the dead, and Valhalla, the hall receiving the souls of slain warriors, where you have journeyed—as well as several other worlds." She grinned at him winsomely. "Now it seems there is also a Futuregard."

"Futuregard," he repeated. "Yes, I like the sound of that."

"Tell me of this Futuregard. Is it there you learned to talk so strangely?"

"Yes. But I'm not sure . . ." He flashed her a contrite smile. "Reyna, the world where I lived my other life could prove difficult for you to understand."

A scowl wrinkled her brow. "Think you I am witless?"

"No, of course not. It's just—"

"Tell me of this Futuregard. I will understand."

Observing her determined visage, Viktor believed she would. He drew a deep breath and began. "The world where I lived my other life is very advanced, with buildings made of concrete and steel—"

"What means 'concrete'? What means 'steel'?" she interrupted eagerly.

He wagged a finger at her. "Ah, but I thought you said you were going to understand."

She glowered.

He held up a hand. "Very well. I'll attempt to explain."

Proceeding slowly and patiently, Viktor tried his best to make Reyna understand how steel was forged and concrete mixed. She seemed to grasp the concepts best when he compared steel with the Viking custom of pattern-welding and concrete with the stone and mortar Vikings used for constructing some of their buildings.

After listening raptly, she insisted, "Tell me more!"

Viktor chuckled. "The future is a time of marvelous inventions, with machines that do everything from thinking to cleaning garments to flying through the air."

Reyna appeared amazed. "You are saying a device can fly like a bird?"

"Yes, and take people up into the air with it."

Reyna fell silent, scowling fiercely while conjuring an image of a giant bird with several people clutched in its talons. "Verily, it sounds dangerous to fly through the air in this remarkable manner."

"It can be." A sudden, painful memory brought a frown to his face.

Reyna touched his arm. "You look sad, my husband."

He nodded. "That is how my family died. They were flying in a plane—"

"What means 'plane'?" she demanded. Before he could explain, she snapped her fingers and rushed on. "You are saying the bird dropped them?"

Viktor would have smiled at her unschooled description had his memories not been so hurtful. "Yes, in a manner of speaking, the bird dropped them. The plane crashed into the mountains with my mother, father, and sister on board."

"And they all died?" she asked, crestfallen.

"Yes, they all died." He clutched her hand. "That is why I told you last night that I have known loss just as you have, darling."

Suddenly Reyna appeared wary, avoiding Viktor's eye, as if his sharing had probed too close to her own pain. "That was long ago," she muttered, "when I was but three summers old. But still it smarts."

"I know it does, darling."

"When was your loss in Futuregard?"

His smile was ironic. "Try a thousand years from now."

"Verily?" she cried.

"Verily."

"Nay!" she gasped, but still appeared wholly fascinated.

"Yea," he said with a grin.

She clapped her hands like a delighted child. "Tell me more."

At Reyna's insistence, Viktor complied. He outlined in broad terms the progress of mankind over the centuries, telling her of the development of machines, new technologies, new intellectual awareness, and the medical discoveries that had eliminated many diseases. She listened intently but interrupted often, demanding that he define every outlandish term he used. What most amazed Viktor was how readily his wife seemed to accept his bizarre stories. Then he reminded himself that they were living in the Viking age, when people were highly superstitious, believing in Jotuns and trolls and elves and fairies, in rainbow bridges and monsters rising from the sea. Surely the tales he spun seemed no more incredible to Reyna than the Viking myths and legends she had heard all her life.

On and on they talked. Viktor deliberately kept his discussion upbeat, not telling Reyna of mankind's weapons of mass destruction, of the wars of the future, and the possibility of nuclear obliteration. She continued alternately to listen, wide-eyed, her chin propped in her hands, and to interrupt with impatient questions.

When at last he paused, she was gazing at him as if seeing him for the first time. Quietly, she asked, "And you loved me in this world, Viktor the Valiant?"

"Yea."

"That is what you told me at the bathhouse."

"Believe me, darling, I haven't forgotten."

Her expression grew petulant. "But if you loved me in Futuregard, why do I not remember?"

"Perhaps because you haven't lived that life yet," he suggested gently.

She scowled, considering his words. "What was I called?"

"Monica."

"What manner of woman was this Monica?"

He grinned. "Very liberated."

"What means 'liberated'?"

Viktor had to chuckle, for all of her questions were so endearingly earnest. "You were devoted to your career as a movie actress."

"What means 'movie'?"

It took Viktor quite a while to make Reyna understand the concept of a picture, much less moving pictures. They went over, under, around, and through the concept, until at last she seemed to grasp a tenuous perception.

"So I loved these moving pictures more than you?" she asked.

"You wanted to be a star."

She glanced at the heavens. "Which star?"

He fought a smile. "No, darling, what I meant is you wanted to be recognized for your talents as an actress."

"And you loved me?" she repeated.

He stared her straight in the eye. "Very much."

At the fervency of his words, his gaze, she actually blushed. "Then why did you leave me, Viktor the Valiant?"

"Because you broke up with me."

"What means 'break up'?"

"You ended our relationship. You didn't want to get married and have a child with me."

She frowned at that, pride tightening her features to a cool facade. "Mayhap I am not so different now."

Hurt by her withdrawal, Viktor pulled her into his arms. "Reyna, don't shut me out. Not after we've drawn so close."

He bent to kiss her, but she held him at bay, bracing her hands on his broad chest. "How did you arrive here, my husband?"

Viktor groaned. He was tiring of her incessant questions, especially since he very badly wanted to make love to her again. "You mean, how did I physically arrive back in time a thousand years?"

"Yea. I saw you launched, but I did not see you return."

"My arrival here was bizarre," he concluded wryly. "You see, in the future, I was starring in a movie about a Viking named Ivar the Invincible."

"Nay!" she cried.

"Yea. And you—that is, Monica—played my faithful bride."

She giggled, appearing astonished and enthralled.

"The movie ended with a scene in which Ivar was launched to Valhalla in a burning boat, in the tradition of the Viking king, Viktor the Valiant. Anyway, I was in the flaming ship, I closed my eyes, and the next thing I knew, I was here on Vanaheim and I *was* Viktor the Valiant."

Her mouth dropped open. "You returned here in a flaming boat to become your old self again?"

"Yes." He scowled. "Although I don't remember being Viktor previously."

"You lost your memory in Valhalla—or in Futuregard?"

"Perhaps. On the other hand, maybe I never actually *was* Viktor, but was sent back here in his place."

"Why?"

He stared at her poignantly. "To bring our peoples together. To bring *us* together, Reyna."

At his impassioned words, a series of emotions crossed her face—uncertainty, awe, vulnerability. Her softening expression provided all the encouragement Viktor needed. He pressed Reyna beneath him and kissed her tenderly. The sharing had made him feel closer to her—especially when she had so trustingly believed him—and he longed to draw them closer still. He kissed her cheek, her mouth, her neck, and when she shivered against him, he knew she was responding.

Then he felt a wet nose nudging against his cheek—and it definitely wasn't Reyna's. Bemused, he glanced up to see that her little arctic fox had wandered over and was staring at them both curiously. Viktor grinned. The animal was utterly precious, now in its short brown-and-gray summer coat. The creature was barely two feet long, with tiny paws and large gold eyes.

His wife thrust him away and sat up, her eyes filled with panic. She shooed the fox frantically, waving a hand at it and scolding, "Go away! Go away!"

The little animal stared at Reyna in confusion, then let out a string of chirplike barks, protesting coyote-style.

Viktor was amused by his wife's antics and the little fox's tenacity. "Reyna, what are you doing? Why shoo the vixen away? Surely you don't think I devour foxes for dessert?"

Evidently she did, for the next thing Viktor knew, he was hurled down to the tundra, Reyna's knee was braced on his chest, and she was holding her dagger against his throat.

"Kill the fox, Viking," she said in a lethal voice, "and I will slit your throat."

Viktor emitted a low whistle, feeling utterly bewildered by his Valkyrie wife's sudden, violent outburst. "But why would I kill your pet?"

At his words, Reyna gasped and backed off, her features pale, the dagger slipping through her fingers. She felt shocked at herself as well as ashamed. Already she regretted her savagery toward her husband, which had been sheer reflex. She almost apologized, then bit back the impulse as she remembered what Viktor had just said.

"You knew!" she cried, aghast.

Viktor sat up, rubbing his neck and feeling intensely relieved that his throat had been spared. "I watched you one day on the tundra with your fox." He reached out to pet the vixen. "And later with Pelagius."

"You spied on me!"

"And you didn't on me?" he chided, raising an eyebrow. "At least I didn't try to kill you."

She smiled guiltily. "But you watched."

He caressed her hip through her dress. "You'll have to forgive me, darling. You fascinated me."

She appeared to be relenting.

He sighed. "Reyna, why did you think I would kill your vixen?"

She struggled for a moment, lowering her gaze and blinking rapidly. "Wolfgard's warriors—if they had known I had a pet, they would have seen it as a sign of weakness. Verily, they would have slain the fox just to spite me."

At her touching admission, Viktor's heart went out to this proud yet fragile girl. He lifted her chin and stared into her confused, turbulent eyes. "Oh, Reyna, I'm so sorry for all you've had to suffer. It must have been hell for you, being raised in Wolfgard's camp."

Her gaze darkened with bitterness. " 'Twas worse for my mother. I watched all the heart in her die as Wolfgard broke her spirit."

He took her hand. "I'll never do that to you, darling."

"Will you not?" she challenged. "You seek to make me the object of your will."

"Not like that," he replied feelingly. "I didn't marry you to enslave you, Reyna. Don't you understand? You can be free with me—free to be a woman, and free to have pets, or whatever else strikes your fancy. You can trust me."

Could she? Staring at her husband, Reyna felt terribly torn. She knew Viktor was not like Wolfgard, yet he still sought to dominate her in other, more subtle ways; and, treasonously, she longed to give in . . .

She watched him pet the fox, while the vixen shamelessly rubbed her head against his hand. She suppressed a smile. Could any female withstand her husband's charm?

Viktor glanced up, noting his wife's intent expression. "What is she called?"

At last he coaxed a smile out of her. "Freya."

He ran his hand along the animal's flank. "She is pregnant, you know."

"She is?" Reyna leaned forward, stroked the vixen, then grinned. "You are right. Freya has a mate—I sometimes spy them together, up in the hills. But he never ventures down with her when she comes to see me."

"From the size of her, I would say she will become a mother very soon." He glanced proudly at Reyna. "You are very protective of her. You will make a good mother, too."

Reyna's eyes flashed with resentment. "Yea—to win your bargain with Wolfgard."

He offered her a look of entreaty. "Reyna, why do we have to be so caught up in our pride, and in examining our motives?" He leaned toward her, kissing her stubborn chin. "I want you, darling. I want you to have our child."

She was silent, her hands clenched in her lap.

He stroked her cheek. "You spoke last night about how you were once a happy little princess. Let us bring that same happiness and peace to all of Vanaheim. Let us have a little prince—or a little princess—and make him—or her—very happy, too."

At last Reyna regarded Viktor with yearning and anguish. Oh, how this man could move her with his pretty words and beautiful images! How long had it been since she had allowed herself to dream of joy and peace? She had been consumed by hatred and her thirst for revenge for a lifetime. But this gentle man did indeed make her remember the innocent soul of the lost child who had once daydreamed so blissfully in Loire. And that scared her, because it made her vulnerable, because it threatened the ironclad convictions that had driven her. Verily, she did not know how to readjust her thinking as her husband urged her to do. She did not know how to give up her warrior heart, which was all she had to protect herself from a brutal world—and mayhap from Viktor the Valiant himself. Yea, he tempted her mightily—tempted her to surrender to his bidding. But nothing they had shared really changed the fact that their lives and destinies were at cross-purposes.

Best to take greater care with her emotions—and her heart, Reyna mused with regret. Viktor might promise happiness, but at a price she still found too dear.

As these sobering realities hit home, her visage hardened, and she watched Viktor's expression of tenderness fade to one of regret.

" 'Tis time we start back," she stated tensely. "I fret about Ragar and Harald, left alone with your warriors."

"And you fret about yourself, lingering alone with me?" he challenged.

"Mayhap," she conceded. She stroked the fox, leaning over to nuzzle her cheek against the animal's soft fur. "Farewell, little vixen. I dislike leaving you alone so near to your birthing."

"Then bring her along," suggested Viktor.

She glanced at him, eyes wide. "You would allow that?"

"Of course."

"But what of your wolves? Will they not want to eat her?"

Viktor chuckled and kissed the tip of Reyna's nose. "I'll keep them at bay."

While I worry about keeping my new husband—and my own emotions—at bay, Reyna added to herself.

TWENTY-SIX

Vıĸᴛᴏʀ ᴀɴᴅ Rᴇʏɴᴀ ʀᴏᴅᴇ ʙᴀᴄᴋ ᴛᴏ ᴛʜᴇ ᴠɪʟʟᴀɢᴇ sʟᴏᴡʟʏ, ᴀʟ-
lowing the fox, Freya, to trail behind them. Although Reyna
was often impelled to make clucking sounds and otherwise
coax the vixen along, she felt grateful that the little creature
followed them at her bidding—and even more grateful to her
husband for offering to take the animal to their home. Freya
would soon drop her litter, a fact that would make her and
the pups vulnerable to other predators. How much safer she
would be back at the longhouse, having her pups by the
warm fire.

Again Reyna marveled at the kindness and tenderness of
her new husband—traits she had never expected in a Viking,
qualities that endeared Viktor to her and lowered her defenses. She reminded herself again that she could not afford
to forget what her husband truly wanted from her. If she did
not take greater care, she would soon be totally tamed, her
belly thick with Viktor's seed, and he would thereby use her
to gain the victory he craved. Much as she felt herself softening toward her bridegroom, her warrior-woman instincts
protested against such a humiliation . . .

As he watched Reyna cajole the fox, Viktor's thoughts
were both tender and troubled. He remained flabbergasted by
his bride's reaction when she had pinned him to the tundra
and pressed her dagger to his throat. What a cruel life she
must have endured, and how deep her emotional wounds
must go, if she felt she could not even trust him around an in-

256

nocent fox, and feared he would seize upon any vulnerability she diplayed as a sign of weakness. He realized that he still had a long way to go to win Reyna's trust and get her to lower her defenses. He hoped that his offering to take in the fox would be another step in bringing them closer.

When the two entered the foyer of the longhouse with the little fox at their heels, they were at once confronted by the three wolves, who bounded into the entry chamber and snapped and growled at Freya. The little fox yapped in fear and hid behind Reyna's skirts. The wolves, undaunted, let out savage howls and charged.

Viktor sprang into action, struggling to grab all three of the snarling beasts at the same time. "Stop it, you monsters! Heel, I tell you! Is this any way to treat a guest?"

Meanwhile, Reyna, alarmed, heaved her trembling, yapping pet into her arms and joined her husband in chastising the wolves, who were now jumping on her, their bared teeth aimed at Freya. "Down, Geri! Down, Hati!" she scolded. "No, you may not eat my fox!"

The wolves barked ferociously and continued to lunge at Reyna, trying to wrest the fox from her arms.

"Enough!" cried Viktor, flinging open the front door and vigorously shooing the wolves with swats on their rumps. "Out of here, all of you! And don't come back until you have learned some manners!"

At last the rambunctious pack was chased out the door. Viktor turned apologetically to his wife and petted Freya. The little animal's ears were perked, her gold eyes wide, and she was still quivering.

"I'm sorry. I hadn't counted on the reaction of those mutts."

"Mutts?" Reyna repeated confusedly.

Viktor chuckled. "Is your pet all right? I'll be very upset with those uncouth mongrels if they've scared Freya into premature labor."

Stroking Freya, Reyna smiled. "She seems fine, if shaken. I had not realized bringing her here would so upset the household."

Viktor winked at his wife. "'Milady, don't you know by

now that you have already turned this household—and the entire village—on its ear?"

Reyna fought a smirk.

Bringing along Freya, the couple headed to the dining chamber, where Orm, Rollo, Canute, Ottar, and Svein had already gathered for the evening meal, along with the captives, Harald and Ragar. All glanced with interest at the little fox in Reyna's arms.

"What have we here, jarl?" Canute greeted Viktor insolently. "Did you bring back a live morsel to add to the evening's stew?"

As a wild-eyed Reyna clutched her pet possessively and Rollo and Orm chuckled, Viktor leveled a glare at Canute. "We brought home my wife's pet fox, which will be staying with us from now on—and will be well treated by you all."

"Why 'tis no more than a scrawny mouse," mocked Orm. "We should put the mite out of its misery and skin off that pelt."

Hearing Reyna's cry of dismay, Viktor spoke adamantly. "The fox is pregnant, and any man who dares to harm such an innocent creature will have me to reckon with. Is that clear?"

Rollo, Orm, and Canute grumbled to one another, but did not further challenge their jarl. Tossing her husband a grateful glance, Reyna headed toward her place with the vixen still in her arms. She paused by Ragar's chair, leaned over, and whispered in his ear.

"Are you and Harald well treated?" she inquired tensely.

Ragar smiled and reached out to pet Freya. "Yea, we are fine, my sister, though bored spending our time locked in the shieling cottage. But 'tis you we fret about."

"Do not worry," she replied. "My husband has been kind." She nodded to Harald. "I want both of you to leave this village before Viktor the Valiant's warriors lose patience and harm you. My husband has told me you are both free to go."

"We would prefer to stay and make certain you are safe," Harald insisted.

Reyna heaved an exasperated sigh. "Do not concern yourself—I am in no danger," she replied firmly, and moved off to take her seat.

As everyone began the meal of stew, bread, and mead, Reyna set Freya down, and the little fox amused most of those gathered by roaming around the table begging for morsels. When she nudged her head against Canute's leggings, he started to backhand her, then evidently thought better of the impulse as he caught Viktor glaring at him.

Cutting off a scrap of mutton with his knife and tossing it to the animal, he drawled, "Your lady's fox is well tamed, jarl. Tell me, is the Valkyrie herself just as docile after the wedding night?"

At Canute's bawdy jeer, Orm and Rollo roared with laughter, while Svein, Ottar, Harald, and Ragar all appeared embarrassed, and Reyna angry.

Viktor ground his jaw. "That's none of your damned affair."

Canute shrugged and swilled his mead. The fox moved on to Rollo, who leaned over and petted her, then looked up with a leer. "Tell me, jarl, is the lady now breeding like her fox?" he asked.

Amid more ribald mirth, Viktor surged to his feet and pounded his fist on the table. "Stop it, all of you! I have put up with your taunts toward my bride long enough! Reyna is now my queen and I will not have you insulting her in this manner! You will treat her with respect!"

"Mayhap the Valkyrie needs to earn our respect," sneered Canute.

"She has pledged her fealty to our tribe," Viktor argued. "She no longer taunts any of you, and you will treat her with equal deference. And, by Odin, any man who thinks otherwise may step outside with me to settle this—now."

Rollo, Canute, and Orm received this dictate in smoldering silence.

Svein sought to defend Viktor. "Our jarl speaks the truth. We must listen to him and honor our new queen."

"Yea," seconded Ottar. "To insult our jarl's bride is to insult him."

Viktor's other three kinsmen consulted among themselves; then Orm spoke for the group with surprising humility. "Jarl, 'tis true you have won our esteem anew by wedding and taming the Valkyrie." He stared pointedly at Reyna. "You are

right that we should treat with greater respect the woman who
will bear your son—and thereby help defeat Wolfgard."

At this new, more subtle insult, Viktor groaned, and Reyna
stared daggers at Orm. Abruptly the tense moment ended as
Viktor's three barking wolves bounded into the chamber and
lunged for Reyna's fox. Pandemonium erupted. The wolves
howled with bloodlust, and the terrified fox jumped on top of
the table, landing in the serving bowl of stew. The wolves
pursued the vixen, all three animals vaulting onto the table,
sending dishes and tankards crashing in all directions. Freya
dug in her paws, flailing about in the huge, greasy bowl and
spewing meat, vegetables, and gravy all over the flabbergasted supper guests. At last the vixen leaped off the table,
barely escaping the wolves' descending teeth and digging her
claws into Rollo's shoulder as she sailed over him. Rollo
yelled his outrage, only to freeze in horror as the wolves followed the fox's lead, bounding over his head and shoulders.

The wolves continued their furious chase. Rollo, Orm, and
Canute bellowed cures and wiped stew from their faces.
Ragar and Harald appeared transfixed, amazed. Reyna, frantic, tried to grab her pet. Viktor tried to corral the wolves,
only to get scratched by their claws and showered with more
stew.

"Who in Hel let these beasts in?" he cried, making a dive
for Hati.

In answer, a wild-eyed Sibeal dashed into the dining hall.
"I am sorry, jarl. I was leaving the longhouse to shake the
rugs when the three beasts raced past me."

"Never mind!" Viktor cried, struggling to hold a slippery,
squirming Hati. "All of you—help me corral these monsters
before milady's pet becomes the next dinner course."

There followed much confusion as everyone sprang up to
pursue the wolves, overturning chairs and sliding on the
greasy floor. Rollo and Orm crashed into each other while
trying to nab Thor; Freya ran under Canute's feet, tripping
the giant and sending him crashing to his buttocks. Harald
and Ragar struggled to contain a spitting, snarling Geri. By
the time Freya was safely in Reyna's arms, and Geri, Thor,
and Hati hustled out the door, the chamber was in a total
shambles, the supper guests seething.

"Jarl, your lady's fox has demolished our peace!" shouted Canute as he rubbed his sore backside.

"Yea, the Valkyrie's pet has provided naught but vexation!" seconded Rollo.

"We are all wearing our supper, and verily, we are still hungry," complained Orm.

Viktor, also at his wit's end, snapped back, "Don't tell me three mighty Viking warriors can be defeated by one tiny vixen? I thought fearless warriors such as yourselves laugh in the face of adversity."

Glowering silence followed his comments.

"Jarl, we are all unharmed," said Svein. "And we can survive one night without our supper. Attend to your lady, and the other warriors and I will see that everything is set to rights."

"Thank you, Svein."

Leaving the others to nurse their wounds and straighten the furniture, Viktor escorted his wife and her pet to their chamber. Looking at the two of them, their faces and bodies speckled with stew, he had to chuckle. He went to the basin and wet a cloth.

"Now hold still, both of you," he said, and began blotting Reyna's face and arms, then dabbing flecks of food out of her hair. Once his wife was reasonably clean, he wiped the sticky mixture from the fox.

"Verily, we *have* upset the peace in your household," Reyna murmured drolly, watching her husband wash Freya.

"We shall all learn to get along in time," he replied with determination. Having tidied the fox as best he could, he took the animal from Reyna's arms, grabbed a blanket from the nearby bench, wrapped Freya in it, and set her down near the fire.

Reyna fetched another cloth, wet it, and went over to Viktor. "Now you, my husband. There is stew on your face and in your hair." She stretched on tiptoe to cleanse his face, then scowled. "You are too tall. Sit down."

"Your wish is my command."

Viktor folded his frame onto the bench, enjoying his wife's attentions as she wiped stew from his face, hair, and arms. He also enjoyed the view of her shapely bosom, and soon grew impatient, grabbing her around the waist and hauling her onto his lap. While she struggled to cleanse him, he pawed her breasts and tried to raise her skirts.

"Stop this," she protested in a trembling tone.

"I am just trying to be cooperative, putting your delicious person in closer proximity to my own so you may attend me." He nibbled at her lovely throat and ran a hand possessively over her bottom.

Reyna squirmed. "You are brazen, my husband."

"Yea."

Meanwhile, the little fox, curious, came over to watch the two grapple. When Reyna slapped away her husband's roving hands, Viktor moved her hair to one side and perversely blew on the back of her neck.

Reyna wiggled out of Viktor's lap. Her expression haughty, she tossed the damp cloth at him. "Here, finish the task yourself. You seek to take advantage of my kindness."

"Your kindness and a lot more," he rejoined, raising an eyebrow wickedly.

She thrust her tongue out at him.

Viktor chuckled, wiping stew from his face and cleansing his hands. He watched his wife pick up Freya and take her back to her place by the fire, carefully rewrapping her in the blanket and speaking to her soothingly.

As Reyna straightened, Viktor came over to lay a hand on her shoulder. "You are going to make a wonderful mother."

She eyed him mutinously.

"What did I say now?" he asked. "Are you still upset about the wolves?"

She shook her head. "Nay. 'Tis only instinct for a wolf to want to devour a fox."

Grinning, Viktor pulled her close. "Just as it is instinct for me to want to devour you."

She stiffened in his arms. "Yea, so you can get me breeding—just as Orm said."

Viktor groaned. "Darling, I'm sorry my warriors goaded you again tonight. In time, I'll convince them to cease their taunts, for I'm determined to ensure that you'll have the revered place you deserve among our people." He sighed. "In the meantime, please don't let their crude comments come between us."

His wife, blinking rapidly and clenching her jaw, appeared unconvinced. "There is still much looming between us, Viktor the Valiant."

He ran his finger over her pouty lips and spoke huskily. "Then come to bed. We'll get very naked—and very intimate—and tear down some of those barriers."

At his titillating words, she blushed and caught a sharp breath. Yet she moved away, her mien proud.

He followed her, touching her arm and pulling her against him. "What is wrong, Reyna? I want you terribly, you know. Don't you want me?"

She pivoted to face him, her eyes gleaming with hurt. "I want to be wanted for myself—not to stop the feud."

Viktor sighed again, his heart twisting with compassion for this proud girl. "Darling, do you really think I don't want you for yourself?"

Her voice rang with accusation. "When you spill your seed inside me, you do so to bring our peoples to peace."

"Hardly, Reyna," he replied. "When I make love to you, I do so to bring you and me closer, my love. And if our union provides a child for us to love, and a greater peace for all of Vanaheim, then so be it."

She was silent, still appearing uncertain.

He tilted her chin with his fingers and stared into her bright, confused eyes. "Reyna, I want us to be as intimate as a husband and wife can be. And don't you think a child will bring us even closer?"

The sudden softening of her features told Viktor that his wife was clearly wavering, her emotions torn.

Bitterness darkened her gaze. "A child to end the feud."

"A child to give us both happiness," he corrected her solemnly.

She fell silent.

"Don't you want my child?"

Glancing up at him, she bit her lip. "If we were a world away and this feud did not exist, if you and I were not enemies, then mayhap I would want your child. But a child only for you and me, Viktor the Valiant—not to be used to provide the peace."

He drew his wife into his arms and kissed her troubled brow. "I wish we could have such a world, Reyna—and perhaps we can, when this feud ends."

She pulled away, moved toward the fire and stared down at the little fox dozing contentedly in her blanket.

Viktor followed, touching Reyna's shoulder. Encouraged when she did not move away, he slipped his arms around her and nestled her against his chest. "Do you want me to leave?"

She was silent, but shivered when his hands cupped her breasts and his mouth nibbled at her throat.

His voice came out taut with longing. "Reyna, tell me the truth, please. Do you want me to leave? Because if I stay—"

"I want the pleasure you bring me," she confessed quietly. "But I do not want to be used as your device, your pawn to bring the peace."

"Darling, that is the last way I see you," he protested plaintively.

"I am not convinced."

His expression perturbed, he turned her in his arms. "And what if I can bring you pleasure without spilling my seed inside you? Would you want me then?"

Her face grew hot. "I do not know what you mean."

But Viktor knew, and the very possibility filled him with powerful excitement. "Then I will show you, love. For I think you are correct about something. You have every right to be wanted for yourself. And I do want you—so much that I'm more than willing to give you pleasure without taking mine."

"But how?"

He pinned her with an earnest glance. "You'll just have to trust me. Will you?"

She hesitated for a moment, then whispered, "Yea."

"Then come with me, milady."

Reyna remained confused, but also eager and curious, as Viktor took her hand and led her to their bed. She reclined first, and she felt longing suffuse her as Viktor gently covered her with his large, hard body. For a long moment he merely

stroked her hair and stared down into her eyes, his gaze probing hers deeply, as if he were trying to meld their very souls.
Reyna could not bear the intensity of it and soon glanced
away. At once Viktor's fingers grasped her chin and he turned
her face to his.

"Viktor, pray—"

"No," he cut in firmly. "Look at me, darling."

"Why?" she cried in anguish.

"It's part of the sharing."

Reyna still would have glanced away, but Viktor's fingers
at her chin forbade her from withholding even this part of
herself. She found herself again pierced by his gaze, drowning, riveted by his incredibly blue eyes as he slowly lowered
his face toward hers. Soon she was breathing in pants, and
when their lips at last touched, she was set on fire, moaning
deep in her throat. He kissed her with incredible, devastating
tenderness, again and again and again, until she was mindless. Then, just when she was certain she could endure no
more, his kiss abruptly went from sweet to savage. He ground
his mouth into hers and drowned her with his thrusting
tongue. Reyna was swamped by sensations so shattering, they
frightened her. Yet her torment had only begun. Pulling his
lips from hers, Viktor undid the ties on her bodice and freed
her breasts. Again, for an infinite moment, he simply stared
at the smooth globes, burning her with his fiery gaze. Reyna
could feel her nipples tightening painfully without her husband's even touching her.

Soon she felt ravenous for that touch. She gasped, "Please
. . . please," and drew his face down to her breast.

With a groan of delight, Viktor obliged her, nibbling, sucking, blowing at her breast, then drawing the nipple into his
mouth with fierce hunger. Reyna writhed and raked her fingers through his hair. She pulled his chin up and kissed him
fervently.

He smiled and began tugging up her skirts, until her hands
stayed his. She glanced at him, still uncertain how he meant
to bring her pleasure without taking his own.

He smiled at her and stroked her lush cheek. "You do it,
then. Raise your skirts for me."

"So you may take me?" she asked with lingering hurt.

"No. So I may give you ecstasy."

She hesitated, still confused. But his patience, his ardent gaze, weakened her resistance. With trembling fingers she did his bidding, raising her skirts to her trembling thighs.

He stroked her soft thigh and smiled at her. "No. Raise your skirts higher. To your waist."

Breathless, she complied.

He stroked the downy mound between her thighs. She gasped and tensed against his fingers.

"Now spread your legs," he whispered.

"Why?"

"So I may look at you there, too. It's part of the magic, darling."

Viktor's words and the sexy images they evoked were driving Reyna wild. She eagerly spread her legs, and thought she would die of the rapture when he feasted his gaze on her so thoroughly, yet with such reverence.

"You're beautiful, milady," he whispered. "Do you know how it felt to be inside you last night?"

She shook her head. By now she could barely speak. "Nay. Tell me."

She could have sworn his eyes were stroking her now, for she felt the heat that deeply.

"As if I were a part of you," he whispered. "That's how tightly you held me. As if you would never let me go."

Remembering, Reyna writhed with pleasure. It took all her remaining will not to invite her husband inside her again, not to promise she would hold him there forever.

"How did it feel when I was inside you?" he asked.

"As if we were one," came her feverish reply.

"We *are* one, Reyna," he told her soulfully. "Even when we're not joined physically. There's no escaping the bond between us."

Writhing in rapture, Reyna believed him.

"Now I'm going to touch you," he murmured. "First with my fingers, then with my mouth—"

"You would not!" she cried with equal measures of horror and fascination.

His finger teased the folds of her womanhood. "Just tell me to stop, darling . . . anytime."

His very gentleness made her shameless with desire. "Nay. Do not stop."

He grinned and continued to touch her there, caressing with a single finger, stoking the fires of her desire to a fever pitch. When his finger slipped inside her, pleasure swamped her in wild waves that left her gasping. She squirmed violently.

"That's it, darling. Move against me. Savor it."

She glanced up at him, eager but also curious. "How?"

"I'll show you."

Staring into her eyes, Viktor slipped his free hand beneath her, arching her bottom upward to heighten the pressure of his finger, teaching her the rhythms and movements that would peak her own pleasure. Reyna cried out at the intense stimulation and began to move of her own accord. The pleasure proved too fierce, and still the vise of her rising desire only tightened. When she held back slightly, half frightened of the electrifying sensations streaming through her, his hand was unyielding, pushing her inexorably into a frenzied delirium she could not escape—

When he slipped two fingers inside her, she whimpered, her fingers clawing the fur bedcovers. The pressure was acute, the ecstasy shattering. Again Viktor's hand beneath her lifted her into the exquisite friction.

Reyna was out of her mind. "Viktor, pray, I cannot bear—"

"But you can, darling. You can bear this and a lot more."

"Nay!"

In response, he arched her into his fingers until she screamed in pleasure.

" 'Tis killing me now!"

He only chuckled and drove her far beyond madness.

Just when Reyna thought she would faint from the riotous sensations convulsing her, Viktor leaned down to compound the unbearable torture with his lips—

Reyna panicked, fighting a pleasure so dazzling, so explosive, she feared its very intensity would slay her. Her thighs clenched around Viktor's face, but she succeeded only in heightening her own torment as she unwittingly drove her husband's lips deeper, until she felt his tongue slashing against her sensitive nub. She cried out in agonized joy—

"Don't fight it, darling," he urged, flicking his tongue to and fro and penetrating deeper with his fingers.

Reyna sobbed and beat a fist on the bed.

"Give yourself over to my love. Let yourself feel it," Viktor urged.

Still, he was aware of her holding back, tensing against the building eruption, and he pressed relentlessly, sucking deeply as his fingers twisted inexorably inside her snug sheath. He heard her wail of desperation. Then at last he felt her shuddering, heard her low sobs, and her shattered cries filled him with love. When she threw her knees over his shoulders and arched into his possession, he knew the sweetness of her surrender and tasted her climax on his lips—

Beneath him, Reyna exploded in breathless rapture, trembling violently against her husband's mouth. Viktor brought her to peak after peak of raw ecstasy, making the moment last. She tossed her head and frantically sucked in her breath.

When it was over, when he lowered her legs to the bed, she was still panting, her eyes dark and dilated, focused on him. She saw the tears in her husband's eyes, and the sweetness of what they had just shared hit her with new, blinding force. When he kissed her, she tasted his tears and they touched her very soul.

"There," he whispered, gazing down at her so tenderly. "That's how much I love you, darling. And I do love you, Reyna. I will show you this pleasure for the rest of your life—and never take mine—if it will make you this happy."

Reyna almost wept with him then, so moved was she by his admission of love and the pleasure he had given her so selflessly. Desperate to give him back this wondrous feeling in equal measure, she sat up, tugging at the ties to his leggings, determined to free that delicious hard bulge.

"Take me now. Please," she begged.

Above her, Viktor appeared touched but also uncertain. "Only if you are content to give yourself to me."

She had freed him and was stroking him wantonly, wrenching groans from him. "I give myself to you. Freely. Now take me."

"Are you sure?" came his anguished question.

"Yea, my husband."

Indeed, Reyna now felt as if she would burst if he did not at once fill her with his rock-hard, splendid erection. Frantic with desire, she pushed Viktor back onto his knees and eagerly straddled him.

His hands stayed her, and his voice trembled. "Even if it means having my child?"

His words alone made Reyna quiver with rapture at the thought of Viktor's seed spewing inside her and taking deep root. After all they had shared, her pride, her warrior instincts, seemed not to matter. Truly, in that moment she wanted Viktor's baby—wanted the happiness he offered her—with all her heart, body, and soul.

"Yea, even then," she whispered, lowering herself onto his solid shaft.

As he barely penetrated her, she convulsed in ecstasy once more. Viktor could not bear it. Reyna felt so hot, so wet, the folds of her womanhood swollen so tightly from the intensity of her climax. Just knowing that he had done this to her, and that she was giving herself to him again without reservation, profoundly stirred his emotions and broke his control. He surged powerfully, forcing himself inside her taut vessel, then pulling back at her shattered cry.

"Don't let me hurt you," he pleaded.

What Reyna felt at that moment was not pain but very close to it, so riveting was her pleasure. Kissing Viktor to stifle his cries and her own, she impaled herself on him greedily.

At her eagerness, all of Viktor's remaining control spun away and he devoured his wife's body, lowering her to the bed, where she eagerly coiled her legs around his waist and absorbed his powerful thrusts with abandon. His lips seized hers in an aching kiss. Her soft inner thighs rode his hips, surging higher and higher and taking his essence deeply inside herself, until he came to rest against her womb. They clung to each other, rocking exquisitely as rapture convulsed them both.

TWENTY-SEVEN

THE NEXT MORNING, WITH HER HUSBAND'S PERMISSION, REYNA went to visit her brother and Harald in the little shieling cottage where they were kept prisoner. As she walked out of the village and up the hillside, she recalled her passionate surrender to Viktor last night.

Surrender ... Mere weeks ago, that word had been total anathema to Reyna. In the brutal times in which she lived, there was no kindness, no mercy, and to surrender meant disgrace, subjugation, defeat, even death. Yet in her husband's arms she had discovered new meaning to the word; in surrender she had found joy, tenderness, victory, and exultation. Verily, she had gloried more in giving Viktor *his* pleasure than she had when he had selflessly brought her to rapture.

In his arms she became powerless, and this reality amazed and moved Reyna as much as it threatened all the beliefs to which she had clung over a lifetime. How could she protect herself from a feeling she now so desperately craved?

She set aside her thoughts as she approached the little stone cottage perched on the crest of a rise. Outside the door, Ottar was stationed as guard—although whether he was truly providing security was questionable, Reyna decided ruefully. He did not spot her approaching, and the source of his distraction was plain to see. In front of him stood the thrall Iva; he was leaning toward the girl, stroking her face, obviously flirting.

"Good morrow," Reyna called out.

At once the two sprang apart, wearing matching guilty expressions. Ottar bowed stiffly to Reyna. "Good morrow, our queen. How may I serve you?"

Spotting Iva's red face, Reyna was tempted to tease Ottar about serving himself. Instead, she smiled and replied, "By unbarring the door. My husband has given me leave to visit my brother."

"Of course, milady." At once Ottar removed the bar from the door and creaked open the panel.

At the portal, Reyna paused to wink at the embarrassed Iva. To Ottar, she said, "You may now finish what you were doing."

She stepped inside. As the door shut behind her, Reyna blinked at the darkness and smoke. She spotted her brother and Harald seated near the fire eating porridge. Moving toward the small pool of light provided by the blaze, she noted that both men appeared well rested and the bruises on their faces were fading.

"Good morrow," she greeted them.

"Good morrow, my sister," Ragar replied with a smile. "Will you join us for our meal?"

"Nay, I have already broken my fast." Reyna plopped herself down next to Ragar, crossed her legs under her, and nodded to Harald. "I have come to beg you both to take your leave—while my husband is still willing, and before his men rebel against his dictates and give you their worst."

At his sister's impassioned words, Ragar glanced at his kinsman, then back at her. "My sister, Harald and I have discussed this matter already. We are reluctant to return to my father's camp. Now that you are Viktor's bride, there is certain to be a terrible war. If we rejoin Wolfgard's people, he will expect us to do battle against Viktor and his tribe. But I will not lift a sword against Viktor—not with you here, as his bride."

Reyna glanced at Harald. "Those are your feelings as well?"

"Yea. Your brother and I find our allegiances torn."

Reyna nodded, understanding their dilemma. "Then you had best stay here with us and not return to Wolfgard—"

"How can we, Reyna?" cut in Harald. "What if Wolfgard attacks us while we are yet here?"

"The danger is very real," Ragar declared. "Indeed, for some time Wolfgard has seemed to know of Viktor the Valiant's every move. I have long suspected my father has a spy in this camp."

"Know you who 'tis?" Reyna asked.

"Nay," answered Ragar. "But if Wolfgard attacks, how can we defend you and raise our swords against my father?"

"Yet how can we *not* defend you?" asked Harald.

She scowled. "You must realize I am honor-bound to remain here, unless my husband gives me leave to go. Though it rankles, I have pledged my fealty to Viktor and his tribe in order to save you both."

"That we fully understand," Ragar said, clutching his sister's hand. "We did not want you to give yourself to Viktor to save us, but 'tis done now and we will not try to subvert your loyalties. Only Harald and I . . ." Ragar shook his head. "We find ourselves hopelessly caught in the middle."

Reyna laughed humorlessly. "Verily, we are all caught in the middle."

More than a week passed. Viktor and Reyna had occasional spats, but seemed even more caught up in the wonder of being newfound lovers. Ragar and Harald lingered in the village and gradually, Viktor talked his men into giving the prisoners more freedom.

One night during the meal, the company in the dining hall was astonished when the sentries dragged in two captives, a pair of battered warriors. Both strangers had bloodied noses and blackened eyes; their hands were bound behind them, and they were prodded into the room at sword point.

"What is this?" an astonished Viktor asked the sentries.

Before the guards could respond, Reyna spoke up. " 'Tis Dirk and Garm, two of my stepfather's fighters."

"But—what are they doing here?" Viktor demanded.

"Jarl, we caught these two in a boat at the edge of the fjord," explained the first sentry. "They were trying to sneak ashore under cover of night."

Canute jumped up with features fierce and sword drawn. "Let me slay them, jarl!"

Rollo, too, surged to his feet. "Yea, jarl! But allow me. I swear the slayings will be slow and painful." He drew out his dagger and grinned. " 'Tis my great honor to carve out the hearts of our enemies."

Watching the captives grow ashen-faced at the grisly possibilities, Viktor stood and held up a hand. "Wait a minute. We must keep our heads and consider this matter more carefully."

"For what purpose, jarl?" demanded Orm.

"To begin with, so we can determine why these men have come here."

"Let me torture them for you," offered Canute with an eager, bloodthirsty grin. "Their tongues will loosen once the hot coals are applied to their feet."

Grinding his teeth at Canute's lack of restraint, Viktor approached the frightened men. "Perhaps torture won't be necessary"—he paused to glance meaningfully at the prisoners—"if the captives are willing to tell us the reason for their mission."

Although one of the men remained proudly silent, the other began speaking shrilly. "Wolfgard bade us come here to kill the Ravisher for her treachery."

All at once every set of eyes in the room became focused on Reyna. Magnificent in her fury, she shot to her feet and drew out her dagger. "Then I will kill my stepfather for his perfidy—after I slay the dastardly assassins he has sent to murder me!"

At her spiteful words, Rollo, Orm, and Canute actually cheered her on. With dagger raised, Reyna was marching toward the captives when her husband stepped into her path and caught her wrist. Immediately they began struggling.

"No, Reyna!" he cried, twisting her wrist until she dropped the knife, which clattered to the floor.

Still trying to yank free of her husband's grip, Reyna glared furiously at him. "These cravens came here to slay me—and mayhap even your unborn child—yet you will let them live?"

"We will not kill defenseless men in this manner," Viktor

replied. He nodded to Svein. "See that the captives are guarded at one of the shieling cottages. They may prove useful."

Even Svein appeared skeptical. "Verily, in what manner could they aid us, jarl?"

"What if we can convince them to join our cause?" Viktor replied. "What greater defeat could there be for Wolfgard than to see two of his warriors defecting?" Staring at the captives, he added, "And they may even be able to reveal the identity of Wolfgard's spy among our own."

There was a collective gasp in the room. "Wolfgard has secured a traitor in our ranks?" demanded Rollo.

Viktor glanced at Svein, then nodded to Rollo. "That has long been our suspicion."

"Let us thrash the truth out of the captives!" roared Orm.

"We will arrive at the truth, but not through brutality," countered Viktor firmly.

Although there was some additional grumbling, ultimately Viktor's kinsmen bowed to his dictate that the warriors would be imprisoned and questioned, but not tortured. Rollo even called out generously, "Yea, I am willing to let these two bring disgrace to our enemy, even if it takes more time to secure their cooperation."

Canute stared pointedly at Reyna and said, "Let the two cravens turn traitor to Wolfgard and join our cause, just as the Ravisher has already betrayed her stepfather."

Seeing rage flare in his wife's eyes, Viktor could have throttled Canute. He groaned as Reyna leaned over, grabbed her dagger, shoved it into its sheath, and stormed back to her place. After the captives were led away by Svein and Ottar, a pall descended over the gathering.

Viktor felt highly disturbed by the incident, especially by this proof of an increasing and more imminent threat from Wolfgard. He was equally dismayed by his men's—and his wife's—show of savagery toward the captives. He wondered dismally if he had managed to change the bloodthirsty attitudes of these people at all. At this rate, he might never end the feud, for how could he combat Wolfgard without a terrible loss of life? His men had taught him to be a fighter; how could he train them to become peacemakers rather than predators? How could he tame his own warriors when, so far, he had not even reformed his wayward wife? He must consider these matters at length . . .

Toward the end of the meal, Ragar got to his feet and addressed Viktor. "With my host's permission, I have something to say to this company."

Viktor nodded to the earnest young man. "By all means, speak your mind."

" 'Tis obvious there will be a terrible conflict over my sister's wedding you, Viktor the Valiant," Ragar began solemnly. "My kinsman and I have discussed this at great length. I am no warrior, and if I remain here, I will be hopelessly caught between two warring factions, owing a blood allegiance to both."

Reyna spoke up, her voice taut with alarm. "What are you telling us, my brother?"

"I am saying I have decided to return to the country of our mother's birth," Ragar replied.

"You will go to Loire?" Reyna gasped, wide-eyed.

"Yea. Harald will accompany me. And I wish for you to make the journey with us, my sister." Ragar glanced tensely at Viktor. "Your husband is certainly welcome as well."

At this pronouncement, Reyna turned beseechingly to Viktor.

He in turn frowned at Ragar. "You are convinced this is what you should do?"

Ragar nodded firmly. "As I have already stated, Harald and I have discussed this much over the past days. I feel the pull of my mother's heritage. And if I stay here . . ." He looked at his sister and sighed. "I will end up having to raise a sword against my father—or my sister. I will die before I do either."

"Yea, and so will I," added Harald adamantly.

Viktor felt moved by the sincerity of both men. "I understand. And I will see to it that you are provided a small ship and an escort to Loire."

"Thank you," Ragar told Viktor. Tentatively, he added, "What of my sister?"

Before Viktor could reply, Reyna entreated her husband in a plaintive voice, "May I go with them to Loire?"

As everyone else in the chamber intently observed the exchange, Viktor struggled against his own conflicted emotions. Although he could understand the hurts and longings driving Reyna, it chafed him badly that his wife would so quickly and eagerly desert him.

"We will not discuss this in front of the others," he told her.

Hearing the finality in her husband's tone, Reyna churned in silent frustration. She already well knew what Viktor's answer would be.

"May I go to Loire with Harald and Ragar?"

These were the first words out of Reyna's mouth when she and Viktor entered their bedchamber. Beyond them near the hearth, Reyna's little fox perked up her ears and watched them with interest.

Viktor turned to his wife with regret. "You know I cannot allow you to do that."

"Why?" she demanded.

"Why do you want to go to Loire, Reyna?" he countered.

" 'Tis the land of my people—the land of my birth."

"I know that. And I realize you knew much happiness there. But what you must understand is that your place is here with me. We can find this same happiness together."

"Nay!"

"Why nay?" he asked in anger and hurt. "Why won't you open your mind a little to the possibilities of our future together—here?"

"You are the one with his mind tightly closed, my husband." She stepped closer and spoke vehemently. "You must know I want this more than all else."

"More than me?" he asked bitterly.

In her passion, she spoke without thought. "Yea."

He stormed off moodily to sit on his bench, and she at once regretted her impulsive remark. She followed him and stood before him, twisting her fingers together as he glowered and began untying his boots.

"I did not mean my words as they sounded," she admitted in a small voice.

"Then how did you mean them?" he challenged, eyes

gleaming. "Does what we have shared count for so little with you, Reyna?"

She lowered her gaze. "Nay. It counts for much."

"But you would leave me"—he paused to snap his fingers—"just like that."

She heaved a frustrated breath. "Yea, because Ragar and Harald are sailing for Loire"—she paused to snap her fingers—"just like that!"

Viktor ground his jaw.

"But you can come with me," she added earnestly.

"And abandon my responsibilities here?"

"You care more for those duties than you care for me!"

"That is not true. Our destiny—and that of Vanaheim—are bound together, Reyna."

"How can you know this?"

He rose and looked deeply into her eyes. "I saw it all in a dream I had in Futuregard. I saw the two of us bringing all the peoples of Vanaheim together. We belong with each other, Reyna—here in Vanaheim, not in Loire."

She frowned and considered his words for a long moment. The vision he described sounded quite powerful, and she felt very torn. Still, her obsession to return to Loire pulled at her more powerfully than the temptation of Viktor's dream. All she could see was that here at last was her opportunity to return to the land of her birth—and that Viktor was denying her in this.

Facing him proudly, she asked, " 'Tis true what you said last night?"

"What do you mean?"

"Do you love me?"

"Yea," he whispered intensely. "Very much."

"But how can you say nay if you love me?"

Her ruthless words slashed at Viktor's heart. "Now you are using my own love as a weapon against me. It is because I love you that I must plot a course that is best for you—and for the child we will have together."

Exasperated and confused, she stamped her foot. "Then you still say nay?"

His words were adamant. "I still say nay."

"But you will let Ragar and Harald go?"

"They are both free men who may do as they please. You are my wife, Reyna."

She shot him a belligerent look and began to pace. He sat down on the bench and finished untying his boots. He still felt very hurt that Reyna would not hesitate to desert him to return to Loire. But he also regretted having been compelled to put down his foot so hard with his rebellious bride, even though he really had no choice—he could not let Reyna leave him and go to Loire, since their entire destiny together could be disrupted or even destroyed.

Yet it killed him to see her so frustrated, so angry with him. After the intimacies they had shared, he could not bear the feelings of recrimination and estrangement. Indeed, even as they had argued, he had felt himself becoming aroused, as if his body, too, were determined to end the alienation, to demonstrate to her that there would be *no* wrenching them apart, ever. His wife's feistiness—along with the seductive sway of her hips and breasts as she paced about in such a huff—only further heightened his desires, and his determination not to allow his willful bride to drive a wedge between them.

"Reyna, we are husband and wife," he told her patiently. "My expecting you to stay here with me is hardly cruel and unusual punishment."

From the defiant glare she hurled at him, she evidently thought better of his words.

"Come over here and let's kiss and make up," he suggested huskily.

"Rot in Hel!" she retorted as she stalked past him.

Viktor reached out and grabbed her, hauling her onto his lap. She struggled furiously, but he was much, much stronger. He simply held her tightly against him until she expended her rage and her curses.

He pressed his lips to her cheek. She gasped and fought him anew. He quelled her struggles with a pinch on her bottom. As she seethed helplessly against him, he whispered, "I'm sorry I had to be so stern with you. You'll see in the long run that this is for the best."

"Release me," she snapped murderously.

"No." He nuzzled her cheek and began tugging up her

skirts. "You are my wife and I want to make up with you . . . and then make love to you."

She twisted around in his arms, her visage spiteful. "Do it, then. Hike up my skirts and take me on your bench, as your warriors do with the female thralls. 'Twill make no difference."

Very angry and hurt himself, Viktor shoved her away.

Reyna clambered to her feet, threw Viktor a mutinous glance, and went over to crouch by the hearth, petting her little fox. In truth, she felt very conflicted over her desire to leave him and return to Loire, but she was not about to admit this to him and weaken her own case. And she remained furious at him for telling her nay.

Unfortunately, being pinned down on her husband's lap for so long had aroused much more than Reyna's wrath, and she found her gaze straying irresistibly back to him. She watched him stand and shuck off his leggings, then his tunic. Her mouth went dry at the sight of his magnificent nakedness. As she already knew from struggling on his lap, he was very aroused, his manhood hard and thick. Her fingers clenched in Freya's soft fur as she remembered how that wondrous shaft had felt inside her last night—so hot, big, and smooth, filling her until she was near bursting, then stretching her even more, until the wrenching pleasure had her sobbing.

Her guilty gaze strayed higher, to his flat, hard belly, his muscled chest and shoulders, his strong arms—arms that had held her so tightly last night. She gazed at his mouth, that hot instrument that had tortured her most secret places so sweetly, so relentlessly. She took note of the stubborn set of his chin and wondered suddenly if he felt hurt, too, if it had smarted when she had asked if she could leave him. Caring for someone else's feelings was not a common concern for Reyna— yet guilt gnawed at her for any pain she might have dealt her husband. With awe, she realized that she felt as if they truly were one person now—when she hurt him, she wounded herself equally. Her mouth went dry again as she realized just how she wanted to soothe his hurts, and her own.

She began to tremble, appalled at herself, but unable to contain the overwhelming flood tide of her desires. How could she be so angry at him, so torn and confused, yet still want him so much? Verily, her fury made her desire even stronger!

Evidently, he had caught on to her perusal, for he stared back at her, his gaze bright and fierce. When he spoke, his voice came out low and surly. "What are you staring at, wife?"

"Think you I will lie with you now?" she challenged, struggling to sound defiant.

He sat back down on the bench and began folding his garments. "Why not? It will make no difference, right?"

Feeling a stab of conscience, she offered, "If you will promise to let me go to Loire, I will lie with you tonight."

His head shot up and he whistled. "Feminine wiles! I thought you were above such tactics, Reyna. A knife in my back—or in my heart—is much more your style."

Both intrigued and guilty, she rose and began moving toward him. "Have I put a knife in your heart?"

His voice rang with hurt. "Hah! You want to desert me and go to Loire—"

"I said you may come, too!"

"How generous of you," he snapped, folding his leggings.

She stared at him, feeling even guiltier and weaker with desire, especially standing so close to his tempting body and turgid manhood.

"Will you sit on your bench all night?" she asked in a cracking voice.

"Should I sleep with my wife when it makes no difference to her?" he shot back.

She sat down beside him and reached out to stroke his manhood. "It makes a difference."

Viktor sucked in his breath, but his eyes still gleamed with accusation. "Then you lied."

"I was angry."

"Does it make a difference only because you think you can sway me?" he demanded.

"Nay."

"Nay? Then why does it make a difference, Reyna?"

Shamelessly, she admitted, "Because I want you more than I want my anger."

Viktor helplessly clenched his fists. She knew how to torture a man, all right. She was flagrantly trying to entice him—and it was working! "My, I've really grown in your esteem," he managed to utter. "Now your lust for me is placed a notch above your rage, eh?"

"Verily, sometimes the two feel much the same," she murmured, her words edged in desperation.

Viktor gritted his teeth and shut his eyes. He couldn't answer Reyna, although the truth of her words almost had him exploding in her fingers. He found himself heaving in tortured breaths and even forgetting why *he* was so angry at her.

She continued to caress him skillfully. "I was wondering how you will find ease, my husband, if you do not put this inside me."

He opened his eyes and stared at her.

" 'Twill keep you awake all night, I would reckon," she went on teasingly. " 'Tis so swollen. Does it hurt?"

"My God, Reyna!"

"It hurts where I want you," she told him, meeting his fervent gaze. "And where you touched me last night. My thighs still ache from holding you inside me—and deep in my womanhood, I burn for you even more."

With a raw cry, Viktor crushed his wife close and kissed her rapaciously. Within seconds he had pulled her astride him and raised her skirts. He parted the lips of her womanhood and pushed himself into her tight sheath, to her low cry of rapture.

"Tell me where you ache," he whispered, half penetrating her, rubbing provocatively against the front wall of her tiny vessel. "Is it here?"

"Yea—yea," she cried frantically, tearing at the ties to her bodice and pressing her breast into his mouth.

Sucking on her breast greedily, Viktor continued to thrust against her special, secret place, easing in and out slowly, torturing her, until she begged to feel all of him. His control broken, he buried himself in her, wrenching a broken cry from her, touching the mouth of her womb. He held her there, bracing his hands at the small of her back and tilting her deeply into her pleasure—and his own.

"Is it here?" he whispered.

"Oh, yea!" Her lips seized his in a trembling kiss.

They rocked there for exquisite moments, devouring each other, until Viktor clutched her close and thrust high, bursting inside her even as she shuddered with the force of her own climax.

Tenderly, he carried her to the bed, stripping off her garment and nestling her back against his chest. He ran his hands over her thighs, her bottom, her breasts, and contemplated making love to her all night long.

But as he began to turn her toward him, she stiffened.

"You must understand," she said in a small voice. "I want nothing more than to go home."

Again hurt assailed Viktor. "Reyna, this is your home."

"I want nothing more," she repeated in anguish.

Not even him or their future child. There was no need for her to say the words now, for they were burned across Viktor's mind and heart and filled him with sadness. Despite the intimacy he and Reyna had shared, they were still worlds apart in many ways. He could only pray for the day when his wife would love him and trust him as much as he did her.

For now, his denying her fondest wish had put distance between them. For now, the honeymoon was over.

TWENTY-EIGHT

"Take care, my brother. Godspeed."

The next morning, Viktor and Reyna bade Ragar and Harald farewell down at the fjord. The small group stood on the crude wharf in the chill air. Nearby was moored a long karve; with its square sail emblazoned in diamond panels of blue and white, the small ship would soon bear Harald and Ragar to Loire. The vessel had already been heavily loaded with the necessary provisions and drink; the three crewmen Viktor had assigned to the journey were at their places on board.

Viktor watched his wife clutch her half brother as if for dear life. He noted how young and fragile both siblings appeared, how much the two resembled each other, even down to their melancholy, tear-streaked expressions. He hated having to refuse Reyna's request to go to Loire with Ragar, and he felt deeply troubled, as if he were breaking up a family.

But wasn't *he* Reyna's family now? Didn't he have every right to insist that his wife put their love, their future together, first? How could he make her understand that their destiny truly lay here, on Vanaheim, and not in Loire?

Reyna clung to Ragar and gave his forehead a last kiss. She braved a smile. "May you have fair winds and good fortune, my brother. I will worry about you, out so many weeks at sea."

"We will fare well," Ragar assured her. " 'Tis summer and if the gods smile, the weather should remain mild throughout our voyage." He coughed. " 'Tis you I fret over. There will be a terrible battle to come here on Vanaheim. I wish you could accompany us."

After shooting her husband a resentful glance, Reyna nodded soberly. "Do not worry. As you are aware, I can protect myself. And one day I will join you in Loire. I vow it."

Ragar turned to Viktor, who had listened to the exchange with a scowl. "Thank you for so generously providing for our passage."

"It is the least I can do," Viktor answered. "Take care, now."

Reyna and Ragar shared a last, poignant hug. Observing his wife's heartsick expression as she watched Ragar and Harald board the karve, Viktor felt hellishly guilty, yet still as convinced as ever that Reyna belonged here with him. The vessel slipped into the rushing fjord, and Viktor and Reyna remained there, not speaking, Reyna waving and calling out tearful farewells until the vessel disappeared from sight.

"Darling, we must head home now," he said at last.

She eyed him defiantly, her face still wet with tears. "Nay. I will ride down to the beach and see if I can spot them one last time as they sail into the ocean."

He reached out to brush a tear from her cheek. "Reyna, why torture yourself this way?"

She jerked away from his touch. "He is my brother!"

Viktor drew a heavy breath. "And I am your husband. I'll come with you."

"Nay!" With less vehemence, she added, "I have a need to be alone."

Viktor considered her words, then sighed. "I understand how torn you must feel about Ragar and Harald. But if I let you go to the beach, will you promise you won't try to signal to the ship to take you on board?"

Her laughter was scornful. "Think you your loyal crewmen will eagerly bid me welcome on their voyage?"

"You have a point—but I must have your promise, nonetheless?"

"You have it," she practically spit at him.

"And will you also give me your word that you won't run away, now that Ragar and Harald are no longer hostages?"

She waved a hand in exasperation. "Where would I go? Back to Wolfgard, who now yearns to murder me? Thanks to you, I have no home!"

Losing patience, he exclaimed, "Your home is with me, Reyna!"

"Loire is my home! And there my heart has gone, with Ragar!"

At the vehemence of her declaration, Viktor was immersed in sudden pain, and even wondering if she had given herself to him last night in order to try to change his mind. Part of him yearned to ask her outright, but he feared he couldn't bear hearing her answer.

He gathered his forbearance and spoke patiently. "Reyna, I know this must be very difficult for you. Go on to the beach, but please do not linger long. I worry for you, with Wolfgard's warriors about."

Her hand moved to the dagger at her waist. "I can defend myself—indeed, I would relish slaying a few whoresons at the moment."

No doubt she would, Viktor thought ruefully. "Just take care."

Without another word, his wife was off, rushing to her pony.

Viktor's thoughts remained troubled as he rode back toward the village on Sleipnir. He did worry about Reyna, and she might well be more vulnerable than she thought. Given the appearance of the would-be assassins last night and the warnings Ragar had issued, he was certain now that renewed war with Wolfgard was both imminent and inevitable. How could he hold his bellicose enemy at bay without undue bloodshed?

Near the village, he spotted Ottar and Iva together, kissing beneath the branches of a willow tree. Grinning at the sight, Viktor dismounted and approached the couple. Over the past days, he had continued to spot the two together often, walking the tundra hand in hand or even sharing Iva's chores, Ottar helping her churn butter or comb wool to be spun into thread.

"Good morning," he called out.

The two pulled apart with startled, embarrassed expressions.

"Good morrow, jarl," Ottar replied tensely.

Standing before them, Viktor nodded to the girl. "Iva, if you will excuse us, I would have a word with Ottar."

"Yea, master." The nervous girl hastily bowed and rushed off.

"How may I serve you, jarl?" Ottar asked.

"I have a mission for you." Viktor raised an eyebrow sternly. "But first, I will know your intentions toward Iva. I get the impression the two of you are quite an item now. Indeed, my wife mentioned seeing you wooing Iva recently outside the shieling cottage."

The lad actually flushed. "Jarl, I realize it will not sit well with my comrades, Iva being a slave, but I wish to make the girl my wife." Proudly, he added, "She has told me you will free her."

"Yes, eventually I plan to emancipate Iva, as well as all slaves on Vanaheim."

Ottar appeared amazed. "All?"

"Yes."

"But why, jarl?"

"Because I feel slavery is wrong, and that we can devise a far more equitable system for the land to be worked and all of us to be fed."

"Your kinsmen may not like this," Ottar remarked.

"Yes, and for that reason, I must ask you to keep this our secret for now."

Ottar nodded. "Certainly, jarl. Only when will you free Iva—and the others?"

"I was thinking of emancipating all the thralls as soon as I can end the feud with Wolfgard. Surely that will be the best time to change our system, to dismantle our war machine and convince my warriors to turn their swords into plowshares. In the meantime, I must work on changing some of my men's attitudes toward slavery—and war."

Ottar appeared awed by these disclosures. "Do you really think you can bring peace to Vanaheim?"

"I am absolutely determined to do so."

"And then Iva and I can wed," he said with an eager grin.

"Yes—but not until she is eighteen."

Ottar appeared aghast. "Eighteen! That is almost two summers away, and I am only seventeen myself! Do you not realize that on Vanaheim, a twelve-year-old is considered an adult? Verily, my mother died bearing her fourth child before she was even twenty. What if such should happen to Iva? We will have so little time together! Eighteen is far too long for us to wait! Please reconsider, jarl!"

Viktor stroked his jaw and grinned. "From the way the two of you were just kissing, perhaps I should."

"Please, jarl, I am willing to do anything to change your mind."

"You must love her, then."

"Yea," Ottar replied solemnly.

"I am pleased," said Viktor. "But before the two of you can truly enjoy that happiness, we must end the feud. I do hope you want peace as much as you want Iva's freedom."

Ottar nodded. "Before you returned from the dead, I would not have agreed, jarl. Like the others, I embraced our code of feuds and blood bounties. But your more gentle ways toward all creatures have already begun to change the focus of my thinking, just as loving Iva has altered me. Yea, I would know peace to enjoy my wife and family." He sighed. "Only I am troubled in that Wolfgard still remains a great threat."

"Not if we can outsmart him."

"But how?"

"Let me worry about that. For now, I do have a very important assignment for you."

"I am at your service, jarl."

"I want you and Svein to sneak into Wolfgard's camp tonight. The two of you must take greatest care, for if you are caught, you surely know what your fate will be."

Ottar grimaced. "Yea."

"I want you to report to me on what progress Wolfgard has made on his new ship—and in preparing to do war with us."

"Yea, jarl. You can trust us to get all the information you need."

By midafternoon, Reyna still had not returned, and Viktor grew worried about her. He rode Sleipnir down to the beach with the wolves along to help seek her out.

He traveled the craggy shoreline, galloping between jutting

black basalt cliffs, the seabirds screeching and soaring over-head. For over an hour he caught no sight of his wife, and when the tide began to roll in, impeding his search, his anx-iety increased. He began to despair of finding Reyna, and to damn himself a fool for letting her go off this way. Despite her promise to him, she might well have tried to signal to Ragar's ship to take her on board. Of course, she had been correct to point out that his crewmen likely would not have done so, but it was still a risk he had been foolish to take.

At last he spotted her, sitting at the edge of a cove beneath high cliffs—crouched there with her legs folded under her, her hands in her lap, her eyes closed—and massive waves crashing over her! She did not even flinch as each whitecap battered her. Mercy, had the girl gone mad? Did she seek to die of exposure from the icy breakers lashing her body?

About twenty yards away from her, Viktor dismounted and raced toward his wife, the wolves bounding beside him and barking shrilly. Reyna took no note of their approach, which worried Viktor even more. A frigid wave sluiced over his body as he reached her side. Shivering, he hauled his wife to her feet and yanked her inland, away from the tide's brutal onslaught.

"Have you lost your mind?" he demanded, his voice al-most drowned out by the roar of the surf.

With the three drenched wolves dancing and panting around them, they stood in the shadow of the craggy bluff. Rage welled in Viktor as he studied Reyna more closely. She was trembling violently, her lips were blue, and her body was covered with gooseflesh. Most frightening of all, there was a dazed look in her eyes and she seemed unaware of his pres-ence.

"Reyna, answer me!" he cried, shaking her slightly.

At last she looked up and appeared to recognize him. Her voice came out hoarsely between chattering teeth. "I watched Ragar's ship until it disappeared from sight. And then I lost track of the time—"

"At peril of your own life?" he cried. "With the tide roar-ing in like a demon? Is marriage to me so loathsome that you would risk killing yourself?"

He had kindled a spark of ire in her; her eyes smoldered

with defiance, and she ground out her next words in fury. "Pelagius sits by the ocean for hours sometimes, gazing into the waves and seeking a state of grace." With a sneer, she finished, "You told me once I might even benefit from it."

He gestured furiously at the surf. "Waves like that won't bring you grace, Reyna. They'll bring you death."

"Mayhap they will take me to Loire!" she retorted.

"Try a stunt like this again," he shouted, "and you'll be taken somewhere, all right—to whatever suffices as the woodshed here in the Dark Ages—and you will be kept there until you find a state of obedience—to your husband!"

She glowered at him with bemusement and anger, obviously not fully understanding his words, but grasping the overall import well enough. "Why will you not just leave me be?" she cried.

He hauled her trembling body close. "Because you are my wife and I love you, you little fool! Now we must get you home before you catch your death."

Viktor quickly found Reyna's pony, tethered to a clump of wild heliotrope. He hoisted her onto the saddle, took the reins, and led her toward Sleipnir. He retained her reins as they rode home with the wolves following.

Back at the village, outside the stable, Viktor spotted the lad who worked with Nevin. As Viktor motioned to him, the boy rushed toward them, his expression mystified as he watched his drenched jarl hop down off his horse, then pull his equally soaked bride off her own mount. The wolves were bounding about, agitated and howling, still shaking off droplets of water.

With Reyna in his arms, Viktor jerked his head toward the boy. "See that the wolves and the horses are thoroughly dried off and well fed," he ordered gruffly.

"Yea, jarl," the lad muttered, shaking his head as he watched Viktor stalk off with Reyna.

Inside the longhouse entry chamber, they all but collided with Sibeal. She jerked back and gasped, staring in horror at the drenched and shivering Reyna. "Jarl, what has happened to milady?"

"She's been busy seeking a state of grace," Viktor drawled,

stalking past the woman. "Bring all the blankets you can find."

"Yea, jarl."

Viktor rushed with his wife into their chamber. He set Reyna down on her feet and, with a fluid motion, leaned over to grasp the hem of her dress.

"Nay!" she cried, clutching her skirts and backing off.

Viktor went after her aggressively. "Reyna, you are sopping wet. I am taking off your clothes and putting you in bed."

"Nay! I am not a child! I will see to the task myself."

He laughed mirthlessly. "This from the irresponsible, stubborn vixen who thirty minutes ago was trying to kill herself through exposure?"

"I wanted to be alone!"

"Well, you wouldn't have been alone for long, my love—sucked out by the tide to be eaten by the sharks!"

Purposefully, he grasped her skirt. Again she jerked away.

His patience totally exhausted, Viktor shook a finger at her. "Reyna, jerk away from me again and I swear I will clobber you."

She stared at him confusedly. "What means 'clobber'?"

His words came forth in a snarl. "Believe me, my dear, you *don't* want to find out."

Something in his tone or his gaze must have given her pause, for she hung her head and stared sullenly at her feet.

"That's better." Heaving a sigh of exasperation, Viktor hauled Reyna's gown off over her head, grabbed a linen towel to briskly rub down her body and hair, then wrapped the towel around her head. "My God, you are still all but blue! Get your defiant bottom into that bed."

Reyna dashed off to hide between the covers, just as Sibeal rushed in with a huge stack of blankets. "Jarl, how fares milady?"

"Better, thank you, Sibeal," Viktor replied, taking the stack from her. "I will tend her now."

"Yea, jarl." Tossing a perplexed glance at Reyna, Sibeal swept out.

Viktor unfolded the shaggy blankets and piled them on top of his wife. Then she watched, wide-eyed, as he began to remove his own wet garments. "What are you doing?" she asked.

"In case you haven't noticed," he retorted sarcastically, "I, too, am soaked and freezing cold from wresting you away from your state of grace. So I am coming to bed to warm you up—and myself."

"Nay!" she cried.

He tossed down his tunic and glowered at her. "Why, Reyna? I'd advise you to come up with a really good excuse."

"Because I am still angry at you over Ragar!" she cried.

He began untying his soaked leggings. "Are you indeed? It seems to me you were equally peeved last night. If so, why did you give yourself to me? Or could you have had an ulterior motive?"

"What means that?"

He laughed bitterly. "Don't ask. You're already an expert on the subject."

She glowered, then glanced away guiltily. "I gave up my anger last night, but I do not give it up now. Now Ragar is gone."

"Right. And you didn't accomplish your purpose in seducing me, did you?"

She stared at him in stormy silence.

Hurling down his leggings, he gritted out, "Reyna, we will not use the bedroom as a bartering den. There will be no bargaining or manipulations here, only the giving of ourselves in love. As for your anger toward me . . ." Fully naked, he approached her with his eyes burning. "Whether you like it or not, we are husband and wife now, and when we come to this chamber, we will leave our anger and our pride at the door."

Gazing at him, Reyna gulped. He was so beautiful, so splendidly irate, so intense. Just seeing him thus, she burned to join herself with him again. Oh, why did he always spur such devastating cravings in her! She ached to surrender, but verily, he still demanded too much of her in return—that she give up all that mattered to her and embrace what *he* wanted instead.

In a small, tremulous voice, she said, "You tell me to leave

my pride and anger at our door, but 'tis not so simple for me!
You ask me to give up all I know to protect myself—"

"And what is that, Reyna? Rage? Revenge?" He tore back
the covers and slipped in beside her. "Here we are both vulnerable, and here we believe only in our love."

As he pulled her close, a gasp of desire escaped her. His
massive, warm body felt so good against her shivering flesh,
and she felt so conflicted—torn between what she had always
believed and her deepening feelings for this tender yet determined man who so confused and fascinated her.

His mouth moved to her cheek, his hot breath sending
shivers down her spine. "I'm not by nature a warrior, Reyna,"
he whispered vehemently, "but I'll fight for you, my love . . .
and I'll win."

Before she could catch her startled breath, his mouth covered hers, smothering her, drowning her so pleasurably, while
he rubbed her limbs until her trembling ceased. Before he finished kissing her, she found herself believing that he would
fight for her, and he would win . . .

"Better now?" he asked a blissful eternity later.

"Yea," she whispered tremulously. "You are very hot, my
husband."

He chuckled. "Always for you." He caught her face between his hands and looked at her solemnly. "Reyna, I'm
sorry I had to say no to you today."

With renewed mutiny, she clenched her teeth and tried to
jerk her head away, without success.

"But I had no choice," he continued doggedly, still holding
her captive. "Do you understand?"

"Nay!"

"Then you feel you have no obligation to remain with your
husband?"

"I did not say that! I only said I do not understand!"

"Don't you?"

Again she tried to yank away, but his lips descended to
give her a second scorching kiss that *made her understand* as
much as it set her pulse pounding.

Afterward, as both of them caught their breath, he pressed
his forehead to hers and whispered, "Please promise me you
won't pull a stunt like that again."

When she didn't answer, he drew back to stare into her eyes. "Reyna?"

"Very well," she conceded.

He leaned over to kiss her breast, then kneaded the nipple with his fingers. "You scared me half out of my wits, and I'll become distraught if you get sick over this."

"I am never ailing," she insisted proudly, but now feeling more interested in the delightful sensations he was stirring than in continuing their argument.

He regarded her sternly, touching his finger against the tip of her nose. "Reyna, I know you think of yourself as the indomitable warrior woman, but please remember you are mortal, your body vulnerable to the elements."

"And to you," she murmured tremulously, grabbing his hand and placing it back on her breast.

Viktor groaned. As much as he hungered to devour his wife, a lingering hurt held him back. "Reyna, I must know something."

Frowning, she glanced up at him.

"Last night when we made love, did you give yourself to me because you hoped you could change my mind and that I'd allow you to leave today with Ragar?"

Unexpectedly, he saw her eyes fill with tears. "Nay," she whispered, then glanced away.

He grasped her chin, tilting her face toward his. "Are you telling me the truth?"

She chewed her bottom lip, then admitted, "Mayhap at first I hoped I could sway you when I offered myself in exchange for freedom to go to Loire."

"Reyna—"

"But still you said nay, and then—"

"Yes?"

Her hand moved to stroke him. "Then I found I still wanted you."

Heaving a rough breath, Viktor restrained her fingers with his own, fearing that if he didn't, he would succumb to her and never get the answers he so desperately needed. "If you gave yourself to me willingly, why did you run off to the beach today?"

Her words burst forth with turbulent emotion. "Mayhap because it smarted, after all we had shared, that you would still deny my greatest wish."

His gaze gleamed with hurt. "Aha! Then you did seek to sway me after all."

"Nay!" she said proudly. "Not when we mated."

"Made love, Reyna," he corrected her.

"Made love," she whispered. "Not then."

Staring into her fiercely gleaming eyes, Viktor found he believed her. "But why did you let the elements lash you like that?"

"I do not know!" she cried. "Mayhap because I lost my brother! Mayhap because I did not notice the tide coming in! And because I was confused! Torn between my family, my loyalty, and you." She pulled her fingers loose from his and resumed caressing him. "But then when you touch me, I forget all that. Verily, that is the hell of it."

"And the heaven . . ." Moaning ecstatically, Viktor began touching her just as intimately. "You forget your hatred and your bitterness, Reyna."

"Mayhap." She pressed her lips to his throat. "I only know I forget all but you."

A tender smile lit his face. "Remember when you called what we share an act of happiness?"

She nodded.

He kissed her gently, whispering against her warm mouth, "Darling, you don't have to leave me, to go to Loire, to know that happiness."

Snuggled so close to him, with his fingers teasing so skillfully between her thighs, Reyna suddenly wanted badly to believe him, to hope they could be content together and that he would not violate her trust. As always when he held her, she felt her pride, her anger, receding. And even though she had proudly insisted she did not understand his telling her nay, she really did understand, and was even secretly thrilled by his possessiveness. After all, she was his wife, and for a husband to insist his wife remain at his side was hardly unreasonable. Indeed, the prospect of leaving him had filled her with aching regret, while being in his arms again, locked away from the world and all its troubles, brought such a wrenching joy. The bond between them was irresistible, even frightening. When she was in his arms, she felt that connection to her very soul.

Viktor rolled his wife beneath him, using his free hand to stroke her cheek. "Remember the little princess, darling. Find that love of life in your heart, and let that happy soul out to play again. With me. You can trust me with your heart, with everything you feel."

Reyna stared up at Viktor in awe. Why was it he always seemed to sense her feelings, to know just what she most needed to hear? In his arms, mayhap she could trust. Mayhap she could be young, innocent, carefree again. She had never thought it possible for her, yet Viktor made happiness seem so close, so real.

"How will we play?" she asked with a poignancy that twisted his heart.

He pulled the turban from her hair and combed the damp strands with his fingers. "We will go to the tundra for more picnics. We will frolic in the steam hut. I will tell you more stories—"

"Verily? Of Futuregard?" she asked eagerly.

"Yes. All the stories you want. I intend to spoil you rotten, you see—"

"To make me biddable?" she asked.

"Yes, but not too biddable," he teased. "That would spoil much of our fun."

She bit her lip. "What else will we do . . . to know happiness?"

"When the nights are mild, we will ride together along the beach in the moonlight, sip wine, and watch the stars."

Reyna felt entranced by the images. "But will it be safe, with Wolfgard still seeking to defeat us?"

"When peace comes, it will be."

Her expression turned moody again. "You want peace more than all else."

"Wrong, darling," Viktor whispered, spreading her thighs widely and teasing her with his manhood. "I want *you* more than all else. Even now, can't you feel me trembling for you?"

"Mayhap you are still not completely warm," she gasped

out. "Mayhap there is a part of me that could still use some warming, too—"

Reyna's words broke off in an ecstatic sigh as she felt her husband warming her to the very core.

At midnight in the smoky main chamber of his longhouse, Wolfgard was again meeting with his spy. "What news have you brought?" he demanded gruffly as he paced with his hands clasped behind his back.

The man replied, "Your stepdaughter seems blissful with your enemy, and your son and his kinsman sailed off this morn for Loire."

Wolfgard whirled to glare at the man. "What lunacy is this? You say my son has gone to Loire?"

"Yea."

"But why?"

"I have heard he means to make his home there."

"And never return to Vanaheim?"

The man nodded. "I hear he feels too torn between the warring factions, with his sister now defected to Viktor's camp."

Rage welled up in Wolfgard, and fury spewed from him like a volcano erupting. "The little bitch has lost me my son!"

Uttering vicious curses, he picked up a pottery bowl and hurled it into the hearth, where it shattered explosively and sent hot embers shooting into the room.

Heedless of the shower of fire in his path, and looking much like a demon from Hel, Wolfgard charged toward the guards at the portal and waved a fist. "See that word gets out to all our company! The Ravisher must die! The warrior who fetches me back the little traitor's head on his pike will be rewarded with thirty pieces of silver!"

TWENTY-NINE

Viktor awakened to a man's harrowing pleas for his life. The muffled screams propelled him to awareness, along with his wife's calm, blood-chilling words: "Die, son of Nidhogg."

Viktor bolted to an upright position, blinking to gain his bearings. Instinct told him it was morning, but without the lamps, the room was enveloped in shadow, with only pinpricks of light sifting through the blocks of turf to offer illumination.

On the floor beyond him, he was able to make out the form of his wife. Wearing a linen shift, she pinned a large, stocky man to the floor, her knee at his back, one of her hands restraining both of his wrists, her other hand holding her dagger to his throat. Her expression was one of purposeful rage as the captive cowered and groaned beneath her. The little fox stood tensely nearby, observing the scene in obvious puzzlement.

Heedless of his own nakedness, Viktor jumped out of bed. "Reyna, what are you doing?" he demanded hoarsely.

She jerked her head toward him, snapping, "I am killing this son of Hel who dared to sneak in here and try to murder us in our beds."

"What?" Viktor cried, still rather disoriented.

"Wolfgard sent another assassin to slay us," Reyna explained. "A moment ago as I was playing with Freya, I spotted the villain stealing inside our chamber with his dagger.

The stupid oaf lunged at me and shoved his weapon into the wall."

Viktor stepped closer, spotting the intruder's knife protruding from a block of turf. "My God, why did you not awaken me?"

Cynically, she replied, "Verily, I was hoping not to worry your pretty face, my husband. Go back to sleep now and I will attend to this. The villain will die quietly enough with his throat slit . . . Mayhap he will gurgle a bit, though."

At Reyna's calm, pitiless words, the man emitted a tortured plea for his life, and Viktor sprang over to Reyna, kneeling beside her and grabbing her wrist to restrain her. "No, you may not kill him."

"Then you would let him slay us?" she retorted furiously.

"No. We will take him to be guarded with the others, and later we will decide what must be done with him."

"Nay!" she denied. "I will slay him. *Now.*"

"No," he replied with equal passion. "You will not."

For a moment their gazes locked in a turbulent battle of wills. Then, appearing utterly disgusted, Reyna abruptly released the man and tossed her dagger aside. Viktor was horrified to watch the stranger seize the knife and spring up to attack *him!* He lunged to his feet just as the man roared a curse and raised the lethal dagger.

Viktor, naked and without a weapon of his own, was barely able to grab the assassin's wrist before the dagger could descend to his chest. He was left to tussle with the man while his vengeful bride nonchalantly picked up her fox, strolled over to the bed, sat down, and petted Freya—totally heedless of the two men stumbling around, cursing, groaning, and overturning the furniture. It took all of Viktor's skill to contain the bellicose, foul-breathed attacker.

At last he managed to pin the villain back down on the floor. "Thanks a lot, Reyna," he snapped over his shoulder. "I needed to have the wits scared out of me in order to wake up properly this morning."

From the bed, she eyed him with resentment as she petted the fox. "You have a pretty backside," she said, as if bored with the exchange.

"And I should likely strip yours bare and give it a rosy glow for the stunt you just pulled! Why did you do that?"

She shrugged. "You seem to have developed sympathy for my stepfather's warriors. I thought you might want to see firsthand how deserving they are of your mercy."

"If you expect any mercy from *me*, milady," he retorted, "you had best bring me some strips of linen right now so I can tie up this blackguard."

Reyna complied, though she took her time. Viktor and his wife exchanged not a single additional word as he bound the man's hands behind him, shrugged on his clothes, and led the captive from the longhouse.

Outside on the path to the shieling cottage, Viktor passed Orm and grunted a good-morning.

"Jarl, who have you here?" the warrior asked, scowling at the grim-faced, battered captive.

"Another of Wolfgard's would-be assassins. Somehow he must have gotten past the sentries at the fjord, then sneaked into the house."

"This is most distressing," Orm replied. "Were you—or the Ravisher—hurt?"

"Reyna is my queen," Viktor corrected him angrily. "And nay, neither of us was harmed, though I had to save the villain from my bride's vengeance." He shoved the man toward Orm. "Here, take him to be guarded with the others. I will question him later."

"Yea, jarl." Orm removed his broadsword and used its tip to nudge the captive on.

Viktor returned to the longhouse in a murderous temper. Just inside the door to his chamber, he spotted his wife, still on the bed, petting her fox—as if she had not just tried to deliver him over to his death! He lingered in the archway, fists clenched, afraid if he ventured too close to his maddening bride, he might indeed turn her over his knee.

"What was the meaning of that little trick, Reyna?" he demanded. "I could have been killed, you know."

She smiled poisonously. "The blackguard was such a clumsy ox, I reckoned even you could fell him, my lord."

Viktor was rapidly losing all patience. "You didn't answer my question. Why did you let him have your dagger?"

Her eyes flashing with defiance, she nudged the fox aside and flounced up from the bed. "So you will understand what is at stake here. This is not a game, Viktor the Valiant. This is a life-and-death struggle. Only a fool would show mercy to an assassin."

"I am not a fool!"

She balled her fists on her hips and faced him down. "Then show the strength of a warrior."

He strode over and seized her shoulders. "Strength is not demonstrated through brute force, Reyna. It is displayed through using one's intellect to avoid bloodshed—"

"That is weakness!"

"No, it is strength," he reiterated. "Furthermore, we are all going to learn to live together harmoniously on Vanaheim, without violence. Even you, my Valkyrie bride."

She jerked away from his touch. "Nay! I am a warrior, and I can be naught else. I will never lay aside my sword!"

"Even when you are pregnant?" he demanded. "Will you still do battle then, and risk my baby—*our* baby—inside you?"

Glowering, she began to pace. "How know you we will ever have a baby?" As he lifted an eyebrow meaningfully, she quickly added, "Mayhap I am barren."

He stepped closer and pinned her with an intense look. "Oh, no, Reyna. You are as fertile as Mother Earth herself—"

"Who is this Mother Earth?"

"Never mind." He touched her cheek. "You are going to have my child. Do you remember my dream?"

She frowned. "This is the same vision you mentioned before? The one you had in Futuregard?"

He nodded, and spoke intensely. "In it, I am holding our newborn son in my arms. You are nearby, and all the Viking people are kneeling around us in tribute." He smiled. "You see, the birth of our son will bring peace to Vanaheim."

Reyna felt amazed and moved by these additional details of her husband's vision. The fact that he had experienced the dream while in another world lent credibility to his claims. Such insights from the heavens were most sacred, she knew. But she was still angry at him for not allowing her to slay the assassin, and torn once again between her warrior nature and the more gentle, feminine feelings her husband stirred. More important, she knew that to give in to Viktor, to share his vision, would mean giving up her lifelong yearning to return to Loire. Although she was becoming treacherously fond of Viktor, she missed Ragar and Harald, too, and longed to join them in the country of her birth. The sad truth was, she could not embrace her husband's dream without abandoning her own.

Noting her troubled expression, Viktor pulled her into his arms. "Reyna, I have shared my vision with you. Won't you share your life with me just a little and try to trust me, as I have trusted you with my innermost thoughts?"

Staring at him, Reyna again felt his powerful pull, the potent urge to surrender. But then she recalled how much Viktor was really asking of her: that she give up her will to him, give up her warrior instincts, give up her desire to return to Loire. Verily, *she* was the only one being asked to sacrifice— and sacrifice greatly—and this grim realization made her features tighten in pride.

"You should not trust me," she said, and shoved past him.

Viktor was in a foul mood for the balance of the day, hurt by his wife's scathing words. He had shared with her the details of his vision, and she had thrown his feelings right back in his face.

He understood she was still hurt by his refusal to allow her to go to Loire with Ragar and Harald, and that the warrior woman in her continued to rail out at his dominance. Of course, he didn't *want* to rule Reyna's life like a chauvinist, and he longed for the day when they could make more decisions together. Unfortunately, his bride was not acting particularly mature or reasonable at the moment. Granted, Reyna was not an enlightened twentieth-century woman, but a primitive Dark Ages female who reacted to life in a much more retrograde manner; in a way, the retrograde trait in him could appreciate that quality in her. Nevertheless, he could not allow Reyna to take a course of action that he knew would be wrong for them both; he must insist that she make their marriage her first priority, as it was with him. Toward that end, he obviously had a long way to go in reforming and refining his diamond in the rough.

For now, however, they remained at cross-purposes, and he was still impelled to put his foot down all too often. Reyna drew close to him one minute, then defied him the next. It was maddening—but damned exciting and intriguing in spite of it all.

That morning, Viktor questioned the captured warriors at the sheiling cottage, but was able to get little information from the ill-tempered, taciturn men. He tried to ascertain the identity of Wolfgard's spy in his village, but soon surmised that the prisoners likely did not know who the traitor was—if the resentful, perplexed looks they cast his way were any indication.

At noontime, Ottar and Svein returned from their reconnaissance mission in Wolfgard's village. Both appeared grim-faced. Viktor gathered all of his kinsmen in the dining chamber to hear their report.

"Wolfgard is preparing to do battle with us," Svein announced. "He has already cut the keel of a new war ship from a huge log of driftwood."

As ominous sounds rumbled down the table, Ottar added, "Our enemy's warriors are also busy practicing warfare. Svein and I lingered until daybreak to watch their maneuvers."

Viktor had listened with a scowl. "Another assassin appeared here this morning, sneaking into my bedchamber. Luckily, my wife awakened in time for us to—deal with the situation."

"The Valkyrie slayed the assassin?" queried Rollo.

Viktor coughed in acute discomfort. "No, but we subdued him. He is imprisoned at one of the shieling cottages with the others, and so far, he and the other captives are not willing to talk. But I have decided we must take greater care from now on, and station additional sentries in the village and around the longhouse."

Several of the men nodded agreement.

"How do you propose we deal with the threat from Wolfgard?" asked Svein.

"I am not sure," Viktor answered. "I am still trying to figure a way to end this feud without excessive violence. Perhaps when my wife and I have our first child, Wolfgard will honor his vow to make peace."

This pronouncement was met with skeptical comments. "Jarl, several winters could pass before your wife bears you a son," Orm pointed out. "What shall we do in the interim if Wolfgard attacks? Lay down our swords and die like miserable cowards?"

As Viktor scowled in perplexity, Canute slammed down his fist. "Yeah, jarl. You cannot ask a warrior to be less than a warrior."

"Surely there must be a way," Viktor said. "A way we can win through reason and not savagery."

"Jarl, a lamb will never defeat a lion," Orm contended.

"Yea," echoed several of the others.

Viktor was composing his thoughts when the sounds of barking in the next chamber abruptly postponed further argument. Reyna's pet fox, clearly terrified, bounded into the dining hall, chased by Viktor's three wolves.

As Thor sailed over his chair, Viktor cursed and heaved himself to his feet. This disruptive ritual had been repeated several times lately.

"Damnation! Who let the beasts in this time?" he asked irritably.

His kinsmen were too distracted to reply. Ottar and Svein were already chasing the frisky wolves, while Canute growled at the little vixen, which had just jumped into his lap and was cowering there.

A wild-eyed Reyna raced in, screaming, "Stop them! Do not let them eat Freya!" She made a dive to grab the fox from Canute, but Freya had already scampered off again, with Geri in hot pursuit, the wolf vaulting over the cursing Canute.

Everyone dashed around, clambering into the furniture, overturning chairs and tankards of mead. At last the quivering fox was safely in Reyna's arms, the snarling wolves restrained by Ottar, Rollo, and Orm.

"Take them to the stables," Viktor ordered wearily.

The men dragged out the howling animals. Viktor approached his wife, nodding toward the wide-eyed fox. "Is she all right?"

"Yea—if she does not lose her pups over this!" came Reyna's impassioned response.

Watching his wife toss her head and leave, Viktor groaned. Svein came up, his expression troubled.

"Jarl, you cannot ask your warriors not to battle Wolfgard. 'Tis instinct for a warrior to kill, just as 'tis instinct for a wolf to devour a fox."

"So my wife recently informed me."

In the wake of the incident, Viktor felt morose. Yes, he was battling instincts here on a most primitive level—the instincts of his men to wage war, of his bellicose wife to thwart him at every turn, of Wolfgard and his warriors to kill him. And through it all, he sometimes battled even more fiercely with himself, wondering if the course he had charted was right, or if, through trying to bring these feudal peoples to peace, he might instead be engineering their own doom.

THIRTY

In the bedchamber, crouched near the fire, Reyna fretted over her fox. The creature had been nervous, trembling, pacing around the chamber, ever since her latest encounter with the wolves. Reyna finally coaxed the vixen into lying down near the hearth. For long moments she scratched Freya's ears and spoke to her soothingly.

"You are safe now, little friend," she murmured. "Safe here in the bedchamber I share with my husband, to have your babies and nurse them."

As Reyna spoke, she found herself wondering if she, too, might be safe for the first time in her life, protected by Viktor. It truly was an amazing prospect, for never before in her turbulent life had Reyna known any feeling of security.

At last Freya dozed and Reyna was able to leave her by the fire. As the hours trickled by and nightfall fell, she became perplexed when her husband did not join her. Guilt gnawed at her regarding their argument this morning and her own defiant behavior, but it had chafed against all her instincts when Viktor had forbidden her to kill the assassin. Reyna knew of no code other than the Viking law of swift retribution toward an attacker, of retaliation without mercy. Viktor challenged that set of beliefs, which left her confused, even threatened.

Still, it had been wrong of her to tell him he should not trust her. As much as Reyna missed Ragar, as much as she resented Viktor's refusal to allow her to sail with her brother to Loire, the fact remained that Viktor had intervened to save

305

Ragar and Harald; in return, she had agreed to become his bride and had pledged her fealty to him. Now she would not dishonor her word and raise her sword against him. She had made her bargain and she would live up to it, even if she was not sure just how she might set things right or if her pride would allow her to extend the olive branch.

She stared with sudden longing at the bed. Mayhap when Viktor came to her, they would have another rousing fight, like the one last night, and end up in bed together. Mayhap that was the best place to settle up accounts. Indeed, the mere thought set her aquiver.

But he did not come to her. Reyna was growing most anxious, about ready to go searching for him, when Sibeal brought in a tray of food. "Know you where my husband is?" Reyna asked the thrall.

Sibeal set her tray down on a crude table. "I think my lord is still at war council with his kinsmen. I spied Nevin going into the chamber with a jug of mead to refill the men's ox-horns."

"The threat from Wolfgard is increasing," Reyna murmured with a scowl. "Only this morn, one of my stepfather's warriors stole inside this very room and tried to murder me and my husband."

"How fared ye, milady?" Sibeal asked with alarm.

Reyna shrugged a shoulder. "I overpowered the whoreson and would have slain him, but my husband would not allow the deed to be done. He took the attacker to be guarded with the other captives."

Sibeal studied the grim-featured girl. "Things are not going well between you and my lord."

"How know ye this?" Reyna asked defensively.

Sibeal raised a shapely black brow. "I saw enough yesterday when your husband dragged you in, wet and shivering. Did you try to drown yourself, milady?"

Reyna's eyes gleamed with anger. "I sat on the beach and watched Ragar's ship disappear into the horizon . . . and then I forgot about the tide coming in."

" 'Tis good your husband possessed the prudence to remember the tide and come retrieve you."

"I would rather be in Loire," Reyna burst out petulantly.

"But you are a married lady."

"Yea, I have been forced to become so."

Sibeal slanted the girl a chiding glance. "Viktor the Valiant did not force you into wedlock. 'Twas a choice you made to save your brother."

"But now I am under the control of yet another man who wants to dominate me."

Sibeal's gaze mirrored both sadness and wisdom. "Milady, 'tis not fair that you judge all men by Wolfgard. I know you suffered grievously by him, and your wounds are deep. But Viktor the Valiant is a fine man, and he has never mistreated you like the barbarian who kidnapped you and your mother."

"Mayhap Viktor has never abused me," Reyna conceded, "but too oft he tells me nay."

Sibeal released an incredulous laugh. "What choice do you give your husband? What man would consent for his wife to leave him? Milady, you have always had too much pride—"

"Oh, leave me be and tell me no more of my pride!" Reyna retorted, losing all patience. "Ever since you laid eyes on Viktor the Valiant, you have taken his side in all matters—against your own mistress!"

Sibeal refrained from further comment and left the room.

Reyna muttered a curse, feeling as guilty over her outburst toward Sibeal as she already felt for her angry words to Viktor this morning. She mused that Sibeal was doing an excellent job of acting as her conscience, reminding her of the destructive pride that had already weighed much too heavily on her actions.

Verily, she was almost in a mood to swallow some of that pride, but Viktor still had not come to her. Her worry turned to confusion when she heard someone moving about in the next chamber, where usually no one slept. Curious, she wandered in, and found him—

Standing with his back to her, her husband was naked to the waist, washing himself with a damp cloth. Her mouth went dry at the sight of him.

Seeming to sense her presence, he turned around, the wet cloth lying against his shoulder. His expression was shuttered. "How is Freya?"

"She is calm at last, dozing by the fire."

"Good." He turned away and she watched him run the cloth over a muscled arm, watched the light dance on the gleaming flesh.

Painfully, Reyna cleared her throat. "Why are you here, my husband, and not in our chamber?"

Again he turned to her, and she could see hurt and pride smoldering in his beautiful eyes. "You said I shouldn't trust you. Perhaps I had best spend the night here so you won't slay me in my sleep."

He waited for her response, and Reyna floundered miserably. Her husband's words hurt terribly, especially since she had deserved them. What smarted even more was that Viktor was holding himself away from her, for she felt as if a part of her had been torn away. And she continued to feel hellishly guilty that she had provoked this alienation through her own dishonorable words.

"I would not slay you," she said quietly.

"Ah, so you are trustworthy now?" he asked bitterly.

"I spoke in haste."

"In haste?"

"And in anger."

He fell silent, toweled himself dry, then moved to the bed. Reyna's heartbeat quickened as she watched him remove his leggings. The light played over his thighs and buttocks, the sight of the firm, tanned flesh teasing and tormenting her. She wanted him terribly, and not just in a physical sense. She wanted to close the distance between them, but she wasn't sure how to accomplish this, for never before had Viktor spurned her bed. Her throat aching, she watched him slip beneath the covers.

"Well, Reyna?" he asked. "Is there something else? I'm rather tired—"

"Yea!" Haughtily, she approached him. "You are breaking your rule, my husband. *Our* rule."

"And what rule is that?"

"That we are married and we leave our anger and pride at the door. You have taken it all to bed with you."

He actually chuckled, but his words were obdurate. "Perhaps I should, rather than go to bed with a wife I shouldn't trust."

Exasperated, she began to pace. "Why must you make this so difficult!"

"*I'm* making things difficult?" he asked in amazement.

"Yea! Can you not see how torn I feel? You are asking me to give up all I have ever clung to, to defend myself!"

"Do you have to defend yourself against me?"

"Sometimes I feel I do," she answered honestly. Seeing his jaw tighten in pride, she quickly added, "But you saved Harald and Ragar for me. That I will always remember. That I will always be grateful for."

He turned and punched down the pelts that served as his pillow. "Then maybe your gratitude will keep you warm."

Reyna groaned as he turned his broad back to her, leaving her shut out and uncertain. Through it all, she realized that she truly hated having hurt him, that she had come to care about his feelings. That he had this much power over her emotions was frightening, devastating—and equally irresistible.

At last, in a small voice, she asked, "What do you want from me?"

"I think you know, Reyna," came his muffled reply.

"Tell me."

Flinging back the fur pelt, he turned to look at her, his weight propped on an elbow, his gaze burning into hers. "I want us to share everything—our thoughts and innermost fears, our hearts, bodies, and souls. But we must have complete trust and honesty between us, and you have shattered our trust."

It took great courage for Reyna to go to him then, knowing how hurt he was. But she did, and when she reached his side, their gazes locked for another long moment.

"I am sorry," she said at last.

He reached out to touch her hand, but his expression remained stern. "Just sorry?"

With a sigh, she removed her dagger from its sheath and solemnly placed it in his hand. "You can trust me, Viktor."

He stared at the weapon in awe, knowing just what the surrender of it meant to Reyna. "You're giving me your dagger?"

"Yea." She pulled back the coverlet and glanced lower,

confirming what his eyes had already told her—that he wanted her, badly. "Will you give me yours now?"

In answer, Viktor tossed the dagger aside, hauled Reyna down on top of him, swatted her bottom, and kissed her. "So that is what all this sackcloth and ashes is about! My young wife is feeling horny again."

"What means 'horny'?" She pouted. "I have no horns."

Viktor chuckled as he remembered one of Monica's comments from the faraway present. "You, milady, have horns and a tail." Stroking her, he added, "And a most delightful tail at that."

She snuggled against him. "Verily, I am not just horny, but tired of battling with you. I want to make peace—at least in our bedchamber."

Viktor was amazed. "My Valkyrie bride wants to make peace?"

"I gave you my dagger, did I not?" she asked irritably.

"You gave it to the attacker this morning," he reminded her with a lingering hurt.

She smiled and mussed his hair. "I would not have let him slay you. I had my eye on you the entire time. Had he even nicked your pretty flesh, I would have castrated him, and quickly so. I am very fast and lethal, you see."

Viktor grimaced. "So you are." He rolled his wife beneath him, raised her skirts, and teased her with the tip of his manhood. "Why would you have saved me, Reyna?"

She moaned ecstatically, trying unsuccessfully to impale herself on his tormenting, elusive sword. "Because you are so pretty."

He appeared upset. "Is that the only reason?"

She bit her lip. "Because you are good to me."

"And why else?"

"Because you mate with me so splendidly."

"Make love, Reyna."

"Make love."

"And why else?"

She offered a contrite smile. "Mayhap the other reasons will come in time?"

He was staring at her, brushing a wisp of hair from her

eyes and about to plunge into her, when a yapping sound
directed their attention to the portal.

Gently pushing her husband away, Reyna sprang up. " 'Tis
Freya. She is nervous again."

Viktor also got up, shrugged on his leggings, strode over,
and knelt by the fox, stroking her flank. "Her belly is as hard
as a rock. I'd say she is having contractions."

Reyna's eyes went wide. "Contractions?"

"She's having her pups, darling."

"Oh, merciful Jehovah! We must help her."

While Reyna carried the fox back to the other chamber,
Viktor threw on the rest of his clothes. He knelt with his wife
near the hearth, and together they experienced the miracle of
birth. Both of them comforted Freya when she yowled while
pushing the first tiny silver-and-brown pup out through the
birth canal. They cleaned the tiny blind creature, stroking it
to life, glorying in its first faint cries, setting it to nurse at its
mother's belly. Viktor smiled at Reyna and saw tears in her
eyes. He felt so touched, so close to her, and could not wait
until they shared the birth of their own child.

They had just delivered the second pup when they were
distracted by a scratching and low howling sound near their
chamber, but outside the longhouse. They glanced at each
other in curiosity and some alarm.

"The wolves?" Reyna asked Viktor.

"No, that bark does not sound like a wolf's. Besides, they
are locked in the stables." He leaned over, quickly kissing his
wife's troubled brow. "You mind the store while I go inves-
tigate."

"Yea," she agreed with a frown.

He left, and Reyna was pleasantly surprised when he returned a moment later. But she was puzzled to see him back
slowly into the room, crouching, while speaking soothingly to
someone—or something—she could not see.

"Come on," he coaxed, "you can join us. You don't have
to be afraid, little friend."

Reyna watched in amazement as a gray-and-brown ice fox
crept inside the chamber, furtively observing both her and
Viktor.

"Freya's mate!" she cried.

The fox growled at her.

"Careful," Viktor cautioned his wife. "He is a rather distrustful fellow." He plopped himself down beside Reyna and winked at her.

The fox darted forward slightly, then stopped, staring at Freya, who was far too distracted to take note as she yowled softly and pushed another pup into the world.

Reyna inclined her head toward the newcomer. "What is he doing here?" she whispered to Viktor.

"I imagine it's a matter of instinct," Viktor replied. "I seem to recall reading once that the male fox helps to raise the litter. So you see, my dear, not every male of the species gets the female in the family way and then shirks his responsibility and abandons her."

Reyna chuckled and glanced again at the anxious fox, watching him paw the floor while casting his gaze toward them. "He is staring at us and Freya so intently. What shall we do?"

"Let's just continue with what we're doing and let him get accustomed to us."

Viktor and Reyna helped Freya deliver three more pups as her mate watched warily from across the room, occasionally making growling or chirping sounds, or pacing in a tight little circle. Once all the pups were delivered, Viktor fetched a wet cloth to cleanse Reyna's hands and his, and then he wiped up the afterbirth.

He looked up to see more tears in his wife's eyes. "Why are you crying? And you're trembling, too, darling."

Reyna glanced at the nursing pups, then stared at her husband with her heart in her eyes. " 'Tis so beautiful. It makes me want what you want. And that frightens me."

With a groan, Viktor caught her close and kissed her hair. "Oh, Reyna." Hearing an impatient yowl from across the room, he added, "I think we had best let the new family be alone."

"Yea—'tis time for *our* family to be alone," she murmured tenderly.

Viktor carried his wife to the bed. Cuddled close under the covers, both of them watched, awestruck, as Freya's mate finally approached her and began licking her and the pups. At last the small family settled down together and slept. The sight of it was so poignant, so sweet, that Reyna again wept, and Viktor kissed away her tears.

Reyna and Viktor made love on the bed—two young, strong, splendid creatures, passionate, insatiable, and a little wild. Tightly entwined, they rolled about and made their passion last, first coupling slowly, side by side; then more urgently, with Reyna astride Viktor; then explosively, with her beneath him as he drove them both to a breathtaking climax.

Afterward, Viktor, too, felt tears stinging at the incredible sweetness of what they had shared. He kissed his wife's ear and whispered, "What brought you back to me?" Feeling her hands move to his shoulders to nudge him away, he grasped her wrists. "No, darling, talk to me while we're still one, while I'm still inside you—where I long to stay forever."

She shuddered against him, and he felt his loins throbbing back to life.

"What brought you back, Reyna?" he asked, more insistent.

"Your vision."

He tensed. "But after I told you this morning, that's when you—"

"I know. I was wrong and cruel. It was my fear and pride that spoke."

"Fear of what, Reyna?"

She sniffed at tears.

"What, darling?"

Her words came out choked with emotion. "That you will swallow up my will." With a ragged breath, she explained, "When my mother died, I swore on her grave that no man would ever subjugate me as Wolfgard had suppressed and broken my mother."

Viktor stiffened. "Do you really think that is what I want? To break your spirit?"

"You want to tame me," she argued. "You want to tell me what to do—that I may not kill, that I may not go to Loire—"

"I responded as I did because I believed what you wanted was wrong, darling," he explained patiently. "But I do not like having to tell you nay. When you are more reasonable, we can make more decisions together."

"Reasonable?" she repeated with a skeptical frown. "Verily, you mean when I am willing to think as *you* do."

He chuckled, kissing her brow. "What else are you afraid of, Reyna?"

Again tears filled her eyes. "Mayhap that I *will* want your vision as much as you do."

"Do you?" By now he was kissing away her tears.

She shivered against him. "Yea. Especially after watching the little fox. I want your baby, too—a child to bring us that same special joy Freya and her mate now have."

"Oh, darling."

Viktor's words came in a shuddering moan as he felt himself grow rigid inside her. At her feverish sighs, he withdrew, then sheathed himself again in her tight flesh.

Reyna curled her legs around his waist. "Tell me of your vision again while you make love to me. Tell me of our beautiful son. I would believe in him and you. Tell me more stories of Futuregard. I love your stories, my husband."

Staring into her eyes, Viktor wished with all his heart that she could say she loved him, too. Perhaps for now, it was enough that he loved her as desperately as he did, and that she wanted to believe in him and his vision.

"I'm not sure," he whispered, thrusting deep, "I can talk at a time like this."

"We will go slowly, then," she whispered back, rising to meet him.

But *slow* was hardly on Viktor's mind at the moment, either, as he found himself being propelled toward a second, mind-shattering climax. Afterward, he cuddled his wife close and entranced her for the rest of the night with his stories of Futuregard, his visions of their destiny together.

THIRTY-ONE

Viktor's thoughts were consumed by Reyna.

Early the next morning, he rode Sleipnir across the tundra. The horse's hooves thudded on the loam as a noisy flock of snow geese flew overhead. Viktor knew he needed to clear his head and consider the dangers confronting his people, with Wolfgard surely within weeks of having a new ship readied and potentially mounting a massive attack. Yet his mind was filled with images of his darling bride: Reyna, giving herself to him so sweetly last night; Reyna, listening to his stories, as rapt and eager as a child, but all woman when she held him; Reyna, awakening him in the wee hours, her mouth on his, her fingers touching him intimately . . .

He had told her again of his vision, and new stories of Futuregard: rockets flying to the moon; boats swimming under the water; buildings touching the clouds. She had asked him myriad questions, her curiosity boundless. They had hardly slept the entire night, so insatiable had been their passion, so eager their sharing. And yet he had awakened feeling utterly refreshed and fulfilled.

Never had Viktor felt such passion for any woman. Even the love he had felt for Monica back in the present paled in comparison to the deep bond he enjoyed with Reyna. He now felt connected with her on every level—physical, emotional, and spiritual.

And how she loved the tales he spun! Even after listening to him raptly throughout much of the night, she had awak-

315

ened begging for more. If only his bellicose men could be mollified so easily.

But couldn't they? Viktor scowled in deep thought, recalling the night of the feast, when he had forestalled bloodshed by using his wits and inventing clever yarns. All of his men had been enthralled by his hastily contrived anecdotes of his alleged exploits in Valhalla.

Would they not become even more mesmerized by tales of Futuregard—just as his wife always was? Viktor had always felt leery of telling his men where he had truly come from, fearing that his superstitious, primitive warriors might conclude he was demented or perceive him as a threat. But now that he better understood the Viking society and legends, he was beginning to see things in a different light. Considering how eagerly Reyna had accepted his stories, wouldn't his men, all of whom were even more firmly rooted in the pagan, mythical tradition, embrace his tales all the more readily? Could he not use his knowledge of the future to create parables that would teach his men how to live more peaceably?

Yes, it was possible, and there he must thank his bride for bringing him this valuable insight. In love lay all the answers.

Reyna sat in the stable, in the stall that had been allocated for Viktor's three wolves, Thor, Geri, and Hati. The canines were crouched around her, their heads resting on their forepaws, their light blue eyes moist with melancholy as she petted them.

"My husband has banned you from his house until you learn some manners," she lectured the three. "I agree that you may not eat Freya, her pups, or her mate."

The wolves listened morosely.

"Still, my heart feels sorrow for you all. 'Twas your place in the household first, before I came, and then Freya. How greatly insulted you must feel, as well as jealous. And verily, I know what 'tis like to be a renegade and warlike. Only Viktor, my husband, is most stubborn. He wants peace for us all, and I fear he will not relent until all of us are tamed."

The wolves lifted their ears and began to sniff as, from the pocket of her garment, Reyna took out several scraps of mutton. She grinned as tails wagged and sharp-toothed mouths opened eagerly. She tossed a scrap to each wolf while chiding gently, "Try to think more kindly of Freya and her pups."

Watching the animals devour the tidbits, Reyna smiled. To-morrow she would return with the scent of the pups on her and let the wolves sniff her hands. Doubtless they would be-come confused and snarl aplenty, but when they calmed, she would feed them more treats and rub the scent on them. Then one day soon she would bring in one of the pups and grad-ually train the wolves to accept it. For she was determined that the animals be returned to the household . . .

Reyna's musings scattered as the stall gate creaked open, and the thrall she recognized as Nevin glowered down at her. "What are you doing here, girl?"

Next to Reyna, the wolves growled menacingly. Insulted, she shot to her feet. "Heed my words well, thrall. I am not 'girl,' but your jarl's queen. I will be treated with respect."

"With respect?" the man scoffed. "As you treated your own clan when you turned traitor?"

"I never swore fealty to Wolfgard's clan," Reyna retorted. "I was a captive, like you."

"Yea, a captive who has exalted her position through her treachery."

Reyna was on the verge of losing her temper. "How dare you insult me, thrall, and disturb my peace! What is it you want?"

Nevin jerked a gnarled thumb toward the wolves. "I want those mangy creatures out of my stable."

Reyna's reply was laced with steel. " 'Tis not your stable, thrall, 'tis my husband's. And his wolves are welcome to stay here. See that you treat them with kindness."

"Bah!" Waving her away, the man trudged off, slamming the gate to the stall.

Frowning, Reyna sat back down and soothed the wolves, who had grown more tense during the thrall's intrusion. What a bad-tempered fellow he was, she mused. No doubt he re-sented her exalted position; originally, both of them had come to the North Country as lowly slaves.

She had encountered Nevin here once before, when she had come to the stable to steal a horse before she had run away. As she had dashed inside, the thrall had blistered her

with a look of contempt, but had not attempted to stop her.
Reyna had been throwing open the gate to a stall, about to
grab a pony, when Nevin's assistant had jumped out at her,
threatening her with a pitchfork. Reyna could have disarmed
and brought down the lad, but it went against her grain to
hurt or possibly slay one so young. Instead, she had raced out
of the stable and gone on to the fjord on foot. Then Viktor
had captured her . . .

Mayhap it had all been for the best, though it galled her
that her husband had succeeded in turning her so soft. For
here she was, trying to tame his wolves and bring peace to
his household. His goals were becoming her goals—even to
having the child she now found herself longing for as much
as he did. Viktor had seduced her to his own purposes with
his pretty blue eyes and his mesmerizing stories of
Futuregard.

Ah, she was hopeless! More frightening still, she was
clearly falling in love.

"Men, I would speak to you of an important journey I recently took."

A week later, Viktor made his planned move and met with
his kinsmen in the council chamber. Svein, Ottar, Canute,
Rollo, and Orm sat with him, sipping mead, their expressions
jovial.

Over the past days, Viktor had considered at length what
he would say tonight, and had conjured up the stories he
would spin. He had decided he would tell his men of both the
good and the evil of the future world, of the weapons that
could destroy all of mankind, and of the lessons that had been
learned from wars of the future.

"You are speaking of your sojourn in Valhalla, jarl?" Svein
asked amiably.

"Yes—but I made an important side journey." Viktor drew
a deep breath, then confessed, "I lived another life."

For at least ten seconds there was only stunned silence in
the room as all five of Viktor's kinsmen stared at him.

A clearly puzzled Canute spoke up first. "But how can a
man live more than once, jarl?"

"Don't Vikings believe that brave warriors live at least two lives—one here in Midgard and a second in Valhalla?" Viktor countered.

"Yea, this is so," answered Orm, while the others nodded.

"So I am saying that after I reached Valhalla, I embarked on a third life before returning to you."

Silence again reigned as the men scowled at one another.

"But there was no time, jarl," argued Rollo. "How could you have lived thrice? We launched you to Valhalla after sunset, and you returned to us ere midnight."

"Yea, you had not time," agreed Canute.

"Time as we know it does not exist where I have been," Viktor replied solemnly.

Several mouths dropped open. "But how can this be?" asked Orm.

"I don't claim to understand it all—I only know I lived again before I returned to you."

There was another perplexed pause; then Ottar urged, "Tell us of your other life, jarl."

Viktor drew a deep breath. "I went to a place called Futuregard. It is a tenth world."

Utterings of astonishment flitted down the table. "You mean there are ten worlds instead of nine?" asked a mystified Orm.

"Yes."

"Where is this Futuregard?" asked Svein.

Viktor braced himself, then continued. "Right here on earth—but a thousand years beyond us in time."

A collective gasp was followed by comments of amazement.

"You are saying you traveled across the centuries, jarl?" asked Ottar in an awed whisper.

"Yes—and almost to the year 2000."

"The year 2000!" exclaimed Ottar.

"Yes."

" 'Twas there you found this Futuregard?" asked Canute.

"Yes."

The warriors again consulted among one another in hushed, excited voices. Then, as heads nodded, Rollo commanded, "Tell us of this tenth world."

"It is a true world of the future, a place so advanced it almost defies our imagination," Viktor explained. "There are incredible machines in Futuregard, devices that do everything from digging ditches to flying to the moon."

"How is that possible?" cried Canute. "A machine cannot do the work of a man!"

"But that is not entirely true," Viktor countered. "Even here on Vanaheim, have you not plows and carts to do your sowing and carrying?"

Several heads bobbed in agreement.

"I'm telling you, then, that the process of creating and perfecting such devices continued into the future. Beginning with a time known as the Industrial Revolution, machines became much more advanced and complex. Giant power looms produced huge bolts of cloth in a fraction of the time it takes your women to weave a simple swatch, and giant iron horses, called locomotives, began to carry people and provisions across vast continents."

Viktor's speech was met by utterings of excitement and astonishment. "Tell us more of these marvels!" demanded Orm.

Viktor elaborated on the fantastical machines of Futuregard, at first offering simpler examples such as steam engines and farm machinery, then moving on to more advanced devices such as ships, planes, and cars, and even touching on the amazing twentieth-century phones and computers that could send information shooting through the air. He told the men of "living" stories composed of pictures that moved across a vast screen, and of magical potions and pills that could rescue a life on the brink of death.

All the while the men listened, clearly astounded and entranced, their expressions rapt. Occasionally, they interrupted to ask a question or two. Viktor felt immensely grateful that his instincts about telling the stories had been correct: like Reyna, his warriors readily accepted his strange tales; in many ways the men seemed as guileless and teachable as children. Viktor also realized that it was not critical that they embrace literally his every word, as long as they adopted the overall lessons he intended to teach.

The warriors were sitting on the edges of their seats when Viktor abruptly changed the tack of his lecture. Ominously, he stated, "There are also machines to make war in Futuregard—guns, rockets, and bombs."

"Can we produce these machines here and use them to destroy Wolfgard?" Canute asked eagerly.

"No," came Viktor's firm reply. Ignoring his men's crestfallen expressions, he explained. "For you see, in the future, mankind almost destroyed itself with these weapons. And that is the reason I lived my other life, to bring back an important lesson to you: that in war lies destruction, and in peace, the future of all mankind."

At first, the men seemed skeptical of Viktor's message, so he elaborated on his theme with lengthy parables of Futuregard: he told of two warring gangs in a city that laid down their arms and became guardians of their neighborhood; he told of two battling nations that, on the verge of destroying each other, made peace and created a greater prosperity for all; he told of two brothers divided against each other in a terrible war, of how they laid down their arms on the battlefield and brought their countries back together.

"It is only man's misguided instinct for war that can rob our race of this wonderful future to come," Viktor said in summation.

"You are saying we can no longer wage war?" asked Svein.

"What will you have us do when Wolfgard attacks?" demanded a horrified Canute. "Shall we lay down our arms like lambs and let him slay us all?"

"Nay," Viktor answered. "We will defend ourselves and our families, if need be. What I am saying is that we must change our thinking—to begin to fight with our minds instead of with our guts. I'm saying we can outwit Wolfgard, outmaneuver him."

These words were met by brooding silence.

"Well, men? Will you at least consider what I've said?" Viktor asked.

"Yea, jarl, we will ponder the matter," answered Rollo for the group. Abruptly he grinned. "But first, tell us more stories."

At his men's insistence, Viktor talked well into the night.

* * *

In the bedchamber, Reyna sat by the fire petting the male fox, whom she had christened Freki. Through Reyna's continued patience—and her capturing lemmings and rats for both adult foxes to eat—she had gradually won the trust of the nervous fellow. Next to Freki, Freya dozed as the little brown pups nursed hungrily.

The sight of the mother and pups filled Reyna with poignant emotion and made her acknowledge consciously what she had been sensing for days—that she already carried Viktor's child. Her woman's time was late, and during the past several days she had felt her body subtly changing, her breasts enlarging and becoming tender, her appetite increasing, her need for sleep intensifying. Come next spring, she would bear her husband a child, and if his vision proved true, 'twould be a son.

Wonder filled Reyna at the possibility of having a child who might well enjoy the happy childhood she had been denied. Yet her sense of awe was mingled with fear—fear that Viktor was still determined to make use of her and the child to achieve his own purposes. For this reason, she had not yet shared with him the joyous news.

She frowned, wondering where he was now. He had told her he would be late coming to their chamber, since he needed to meet with his kinsmen tonight. But the six of them had been at council for so long. What matter were they discussing that would keep her husband away this late?

She questioned Sibeal regarding this when the thrall brought her supper. "Know you what my husband and his kinsmen are doing in the council chamber so late?"

Sibeal shrugged. "I know not, milady. No females have been allowed to intrude for the hours they have been in the dining hall."

"You are saying Rollo and Canute have not even fondled the serving wenches?" Reyna asked in amazement.

Sibeal chuckled. "Nay, they have not." She gestured toward Reyna's tray. "Will you eat now, milady?"

Reyna nodded, but her thoughts were distracted, focused on the husband who had been absent too long.

THIRTY-TWO

During the next week, Viktor continued to weave his fables of Futuregard to his warriors as the ranks in the council chamber swelled. Word had gotten around to the other men of the fascinating tales the jarl spun every night, and more and more warriors appeared for the assembly, until there was only standing room left in the chamber.

Viktor was hard pressed to keep inventing parables—and to make certain each tale held its moral lesson of peace. He began weaving bits of fantasy in with reality. He told of the mariner who sailed under the sea in his great whale-shaped ship, and how he taught the giant sea monsters to live together in harmony. He told of the spaceman who flew to the moon in his bird machine, and how he found little green people at war with one another and taught them all to coexist in peace.

In preparation for the day when slavery would be abolished on Vanaheim, Viktor told more realistic tales of slavery in Futuregard, outlining how the cruel institution that had abused millions and broken up families was eventually obliterated from the earth.

Viktor knew he was making true progress the night the guards hauled in two strange warriors. The men cowered as they were dragged over to stand before Viktor.

"Who are these two?" Viktor demanded.

"They are spies from Wolfgard's village," announced a guard. "We caught them listening at the portal."

Viktor stared sternly at the trembling men. "What do you have to say for yourselves?"

"We come to hear the stories!" cried one.

"Yea, we will swear fealty to your tribe if we can only hear the stories!" added the other.

Abruptly the room erupted in laughter as every man, save for the bemused captives, rocked with mirth. "Jarl, you have tamed even the enemy with your stories!" Rollo called out.

Viktor grinned, feeling elated by this small victory, this proof that even Wolfgard's company could be won over by words instead of weapons. He allowed the prisoners to remain, and turned their appearance into a new parable of intellect triumphing over man's base desire for warfare. Before the night was over, the two newcomers swore fealty to Viktor's tribe and swilled mead with his own warriors.

The next night, Viktor followed up on this success by ordering the three other captives brought down from the shieling cottage to hear the stories. Only Dirk listened unmoved; the other two swore fealty to Viktor's tribe by evening's end.

Usually by the time Viktor went to bed each night, Reyna was asleep, and he would rouse her early the next morning to make love to her. She would curl her arms and legs around him, still drowsy but moaning with pleasure. When she questioned his nightly absences, he would say no more than that he was teaching his men to be more peaceable.

On the eighth night of Viktor's sessions in the dining hall, Reyna's patience snapped. Viktor was inventing a parable of two Futuregard knights who solved their differences in a chess tournament rather than in a dueling match, when suddenly one of the sentries pulled Reyna into the room. Viktor paused in mid-sentence as he spotted his wife, her features tight with pride and anger, her eyes shooting murderous sparks at him.

"Jarl! I caught your wife listening at the portal!" the guard announced.

Before Viktor could comment, Canute surged to his feet. "Women are never allowed to attend council!"

"Yea!" growled several other angry warriors.

"Get the female out of here!" roared Orm.

"Reyna, what are you doing here?" Viktor asked.

She raised a fist at him. "You are telling them of Futuregard!"

Viktor stared from his fuming wife to his shocked warriors, then back to his wife. "We will discuss this later," he told her firmly.

"Craven!" she retorted.

Viktor spoke low, through gritted teeth. "Reyna, please, we will not settle this in front of my men."

Even as the guard tried to drag Reyna out of the room, she wrenched herself free of his grip, hurled Viktor a defiant glance, tossed her head, and left.

Viktor concluded the storytelling session as quickly as possible, knowing there would be the devil to pay when he went to his chamber. He was right. Half an hour later, when he stepped inside, Reyna charged up angrily.

"Whoreson!"

Viktor was stunned. "Reyna, what is wrong? Why are you greeting me with such hostility? What have I done?"

She punched his chest with two fingers. "You told your warriors of Futuregard, did you not?"

"Yes," he admitted, still perplexed.

"Traitor!" she ranted.

Staring at her, Viktor was mystified to spot tears in her eyes. "Why am I a traitor?"

Tears spilled from her eyes, and when he tried to reach out to wipe them, she jerked away. "You told them of Futuregard."

"Yes, Reyna, I already admitted that I did."

Her voice catching on a sob, she demanded, "Did you also tell them our vision of our son?"

He smiled tenderly. "So it's *our* vision now, is it, darling?"

She shoved him away. "Call me not 'darling,' and answer my question, son of Hel!"

He whistled.

"I am waiting!"

"No," he said gently. "Of course I did not tell them our vision of our son."

She heaved a great sigh, but still her voice rang with accusation and hurt. "But you told them our stories of Futuregard!"

"Reyna, *why* are you so angry?"

"Because you did not ask me!"

"I should have asked?"

"Yea! They were our own special sharing—and you broke our trust by telling them."

Viktor felt so touched by this evidence that Reyna held sacred the sharing between them that he wanted to pull his proud, magnificent bride into his arms. But when he reached out, she again flinched.

Drawing a heavy breath, he said, "Reyna, I told the stories to bring a greater peace to Vanaheim."

"You did not ask!"

He took in her gleaming eyes, heaving chest, and clenched fists, and realized he could never really make her understand. But he could empathize with her wounded feelings and her sense of betrayal.

"You are right," he said. "I should have asked. And I humbly apologize."

She eyed him, clearly wavering. "The stories are mine."

He smiled. "So they are."

She moved closer. "You are mine, Viking."

"Of course I am." He hauled her into his arms, drew her fingers to the front of his leggings, and whispered devilishly, "Don't forget that *this* is yours, too."

"Do not *you* forget it, Viking."

"How could I?" He nuzzled her cheek and whispered, "Please don't be mad at me."

Exasperated, she tried to shove him away, but he held her fast. She stamped her foot, but he only chuckled.

"Why do you call me mad?" she demanded. "I am not mad—only angry."

"And perhaps a little jealous?" he suggested.

"I do not like being left alone every night," she burst out.

Viktor began rhythmically stroking her spine, smiling when she began to relax against him. "What if you come listen to the stories, too? Would you stop being mad—er, angry—over my telling them?"

She chewed her lower lip, her expression ambivalent. "Your warriors will never abide having a female attend council."

He grinned. "My warriors are being taught a new order. Besides, they will be given no choice. And you will be the only woman allowed."

She hesitated, reaching out to toy with a strand of his hair. "Well, Reyna? If you are there, may I tell the stories?"

"You will not tell of our vision?"

He pulled her close and kissed her trembling lips. "Never, darling."

"Very well," she conceded. "You may tell the stories. But only if I am present."

"Good." He playfully swatted her behind. "Now let's go to bed and kiss and make up properly."

Her expression petulant, she pushed him away. "Nay. I am not yet of a mind to kiss and make up."

He raised an eyebrow. "Weren't you scolding me recently for breaking our rule? Don't we leave our pride and anger at the door?"

Haughtily, she lifted her chin. "You break our rules when the fancy strikes you. So will I. I am not finished being angry."

Pulling her close again, Viktor moved his hand low on her belly and caressed her through her garment. Reyna gasped as the rough wool abraded her wickedly.

"I know a place where you are never angry," he whispered. "Only mad with desire."

Even as she staggered against him, Viktor sank to his knees before her and began lifting her skirts. She squirmed and tried to jerk away until she felt his lips low on her bare belly. She panted and swayed against him, only heightening her own delirious pleasure. Soon she was brazenly holding up her skirts to give him greater ease.

Viktor parted the folds of her velvety flesh and gazed at her in fascination between soft kisses. He saw much more than her moistness, tasted much more than her unique flavor, for he was forever conscious of every tiny change in her body. In the past few days he had noticed that the tender petals of her womanhood had grown darker, as had her nipples, while her breasts had become fuller and more sensitive. Given the fact that she had not bled since they had married, Viktor suspected she was already carrying his child. Did she instinctively know this, too? Would she trust him enough to tell him?

No matter. He loved her so much and was so proud of the miraculous secret they had yet to share. He cupped her bottom with his hands, arched her high, and kissed her deeply . . .

"Oh, Viktor! Viktor!" she cried, her fingers tearing at his hair.

He held her to the exquisite flicks of his tongue, heedless of her cries of pleasure and pleas of desperation. He continued relentlessly until the rapture grew so intense that she collapsed onto her knees beside him, kissing him with fierce love. When she pushed him down on his back and returned the favor with her own mouth, she drove him to even greater heights of frenzied passion . . .

While Viktor and Reyna coupled, Wolfgard received his spy. The two men faced each other over the fire in the central chamber of the longhouse.

"Four of your kinsmen have turned traitor," the man announced.

"You lie!" Wolfgard retorted in fury.

"Nay. King Viktor has mesmerized his warriors with tales of Futuregard—"

"What is this 'Futuregard'?"

"It is a tenth world where Viktor claims he lived another life. His stories are fantastical, and all the men listen, as docile as lambs. The two spies you recently sent stole into the council chamber and, when they were caught, swore fealty to King Viktor just to hear the stories. As for the assassins you sent to kill Reyna, all three were brought in, and after they heard the tales, only Dirk remains faithful to you."

Wolfgard trembled in rage. "And what of Reyna?"

"Viktor has tamed her as well."

Wolfgard uttered a curse.

"You must understand—all of Viktor's warriors revere their jarl. They believe he has been blessed by the gods with supernatural powers, ever since his return from Valhalla and Futuregard."

"He is but a man!" Wolfgard bellowed. "As soon as our longship is readied, we will cross the fjord and carve out the traitor heart of my stepdaughter. And when we return, 'twill be with her husband's head dangling from our mast!"

THIRTY-THREE

SEVERAL WEEKS PASSED, AND MID-SUMMER BEGAN TO EMBRACE Vanaheim with its long days and mild weather, brightly blooming tundra and fully leafed trees. The days of the midnight sun approached, when twilight would linger well into the evening.

Viktor continued to spin stories each night, while the ranks swelled in the council chamber. He found much of his free time consumed with creating moral tales to convince his people to take a more peaceable path.

After some initial protests, Reyna was allowed to attend each session at her husband's side. At first, Viktor's warriors heckled her when she appeared, but she defused their anger by not responding to the baiting, and even thanked each of Viktor's kinsmen for allowing her to remain. One evening when Nevin fell ill and could not replenish the men's oxhorns, Reyna poured mead for the men! Viktor was amazed by these signs of maturity in his wife, just as he was moved by this proof of how much she loved his stories, of the lengths to which she was willing to go to ensure that she was accepted by his kinsmen and could enjoy the tales with them.

Viktor was growing increasingly concerned over the threat from Wolfgard. Ottar and Svein still ventured forth on their spying missions, and informed their jarl that Wolfgard could sail across the fjord almost any day now, since his ship was finished, save for the caulking of its seams. After receiving this daunting news, Viktor again increased the number of sentries stationed at the fjord and outside the longhouse. He also planned strategies for repelling an attack without due violence, and was even designing some machines that could be helpful in this respect. While in college in Italy back in the present, Viktor had belonged to a medieval reenactment society, and he still remembered how to construct crude siege warfare devices such as the petrary and the trebuchet. He intended to use the contraptions in an inventive way that would minimize bloodshed.

When Svein informed him that the time for the annual meeting of the Vanaheim Thing was close at hand, Viktor decided to give Wolfgard one final chance: He would invite his enemy to attend the meeting, there to air their grievances. He decided to send his message with Dirk, the one captive who had remained loyal to Wolfgard.

Viktor went to speak with the man at the shieling cottage where he was kept captive. Stepping inside, he spotted the burly warrior hunched on the floor, unshaven and filthy, eating mutton stew from a crude bowl. On spotting Viktor, the man set down his food and eyed the jarl with distrust.

"Good morning," Viktor said.

Dirk was silent, glowering and taking a gulp of buttermilk.

Viktor stepped closer and crouched near him, grimacing at his offensive odor. "Dirk, I know your loyalty remains with your own people, and that I do respect. However, I am willing to offer you your freedom if you will do something for me in return—"

"I will not betray my jarl!" the man cut in fiercely.

"I do not expect you to do so," Viktor replied calmly. "I realize you must be devoted to Wolfgard."

"Yea!" Dirk retorted. He extended his right hand, and Viktor spotted on his third finger a silver ring fashioned in the image of a spitting dragon. "Wolfgard gave me his own dragon ring for my valor in a previous attack against your clan. I will not forsake my fealty to him."

"I understand, and again, I am not asking you to betray him. I am only requesting that you deliver a message for me."

The warrior's blunt features twisted with lingering suspicion. "What message is this?"

"I want you to extend to Wolfgard my invitation that he attend a meeting of the Thing, several days from now. Please tell him I desire to air our grievances and settle our differences in a peaceful manner."

Dirk's laughter was scornful. "He will not attend."

"Even though his refusal will likely mean more bloodshed for both our peoples?"

Scowling, Dirk was silent.

"Will you at least deliver the invitation, in exchange for your freedom?"

The man considered this for a moment, then nodded. "Yea. I will deliver the message."

Viktor rose. "Good. I'll have a thrall bring you water for bathing and fresh clothing. Afterward, I'll assign a couple of my men to see you safely across the fjord."

As the days passed, the mellow period continued between Viktor and Reyna. They often talked throughout much of the night, he telling her more stories, she asking endless questions. Soon the queries grew more personal, as Reyna pressed Viktor for additional details of his life back in the present. He told her of his childhood in Italy, how he had fished and hiked with his father, how he had traveled and gone skiing with his family. Sometimes they would talk about the loved ones both of them had lost; they shared their grief and comforted each other with tender words and gentle touches. "We are family now, darling," Viktor would whisper, deep in the night. "We are everything to each other . . ."

"Yea," Reyna would answer breathlessly.

Occasionally, she would ask him about the woman he had loved in Futuregard. "Reyna, please don't press me," he would plead. "You know it makes you angry to hear about her."

"Yea, I will go to Futuregard one day and claw out the eyes of the she-troll who dared to touch you," Reyna would respond. "You are mine, Viking."

"Unconditionally, darling. Now say that again, and kiss me . . ."

Ah, it was so sweet!

Viktor's delight with his bride reached a peak the day the Thing met. The gathering—traditionally a day of both peace-making and celebration—was held out on the tundra; the summer day was exceptionally mild, with a gentle breeze wafting through the wildflowers and stirring the sweet scent of the heather. Viktor and Reyna surveyed the festivities from atop a hillside, sitting side by side in throne-style chairs, languishing beneath the splendor of a crimson silk canopy constructed especially for the occasion. Reyna wore a regal dress of blue silk; a necklace of hammered gold charms graced her neck, and a brightly braided headband restrained her sleek hair. Viktor's tunic was of jade silk, pinned together with copper brooches; his leggings and boots were fashioned of soft leather.

The couple had left the foxes at home that day, except for three of the pups, which Reyna had brought along in a basket. At three weeks old, the plump, furry creatures were as frisky as kittens; Reyna spent a great deal of the day either chasing down the rambunctious animals or petting them in her lap. Viktor's wolves had also been brought along and were thoroughly enjoying the outing, racing around the hillside and barking with gusto at one and all. However, Viktor did find it odd that Hati, Geri, and Thor kept their distance from the fox pups, which they normally would have viewed as irresistible hors d'oeuvres.

For the day's entertainment, Viktor's men had wanted stallion fights—a barbaric traditional battle to the death between horses—and equally brutal duels between warriors. Viktor had vetoed the carnage and, through his various parables, had convinced his men to plan more peaceable activities. Now, beneath them in the valley, Rollo and Canute were busy mud-wrestling, while nearby, Ottar and Svein were engaged in an archery contest. Iva enthralled a throng of children as she rode around, crouched on the back of a black pony. Orm amused a group of housewives by juggling iron plates. In the distance, two warriors were embroiled in a mock joist, battling each other with wooden shields and swords. Closer to the canopy, the older children from the village were occupied with everything from a tug-of-war to arm wrestling to egg throwing to chess matches.

Viktor had suggested many of these activities, but Reyna had helped, too. It had been her inspired touch to propose that

Sibeal be invited along to tell fortunes; several people were lined up at the small table where the thrall sat offering her predictions to anyone who stopped by.

Surveying the busy scene and his exuberant clan, Viktor felt deep pride and gratitude that his people could be content to be involved in such peaceful activities. He smiled at his bride, who sat with one pup wrapped around her wrist, while another was balanced on her foot, gnawing on her copper ankle bracelet.

"Happy?" he asked.

"Never happier, my lord," she whispered back, and clutched his hand.

Viktor reached down to grab the third pup as it tried to leap out of the basket. He set the ball of fur on his lap, whereupon the pup began exercising its teeth on the sleeve of his garment.

Inclining his head toward the valley, Viktor grinned. "I never thought I'd live to see the day when Rollo and Canute would be content to sling mud at each other—or Orm to juggle dishes."

"You have tamed even your fiercest warriors, my lord," Reyna replied.

"And what of you, my Valkyrie bride?" he teased, winking at her. "Have I tamed you as well?"

She wrinkled her nose at him and did not reply.

At noon, everyone paused to share the feast of roast boar, mead, bread, and vegetable stew. Reyna and Viktor fed each other berries and nuts and tossed the pups scraps of meat. Viktor gloried in the celebration, but was nagged by a feeling of disappointment that Wolfgard had not appeared, although he realized there had never been more than the slimmest chance that his enemy would attend.

After the meal, the council session began. Viktor's attention became riveted on the long line of village people who stood before him to air their grievances. One villager accused another of insulting his wife, and Viktor settled the matter through the exchange of a small amount of grain. Another man complained that his dog had sired the litter of a neighbor's bitch, yet he had been offered none of the pups. Viktor talked the neighbor into offering the affronted man his pick of

the litter. Most of the grievances were of a highly trivial nature, but Viktor had already learned that in Viking society, the
smallest slight could result in full-scale warfare and loss of
life.

As the day lengthened, he became even more convinced
that Wolfgard would not appear. Hope surged in him toward
sunset, when he watched two strange warriors ride up, followed by three of the guards he had stationed at the fjord.
The newcomers dismounted and strode up to the canopy, and
the first man laid a round wicker basket at Viktor's feet.

"A gift from our jarl," said the warrior. "Wolfgard regrets
he cannot join you today."

Viktor frowned at the basket. "I was hoping your jarl could
attend himself."

" 'Twas not possible," muttered the man.

"Will you at least stay to break bread with us?" Viktor offered.

The two warriors glanced at each other; then the first man
shook his head. "Nay, we are expected back ere nightfall."

Without even waiting to ask Viktor's leave, both men
turned and hurried back to their mounts. The sentries would
have stopped them, but Viktor motioned to them not to inter-
fere.

Watching Wolfgard's emissaries gallop off, Svein rushed
toward Viktor, who was reaching for the lid to the basket.
"Nay, jarl, do not open it! This is surely a trick! Look how
quickly Wolfgard's warriors flee! There could be a poisonous
serpent in the basket."

Reyna, her expression equally alarmed, reached down to
restrain her husband's hand. "Heed the words of your kinsman, my husband. Do not open the basket."

Drawing a deep breath, Viktor nodded to Svein. "You are
right that I should be more cautious under the circumstances.
Come with me, and let us open the basket away from the others."

Viktor gingerly carried the basket to the top of a nearby
rise. After he set it down, Svein, using the tip of his broadsword, nudged the top off.

"My God!" Viktor cried.

Both men stared at a bloody, severed human hand.

"Jarl, what is the meaning of this?" Svein asked.

Studying the amputated member more closely, Viktor ground his jaw in fury. "It is Dirk's hand. I can tell by the dragon ring. I sent him back with an invitation to Wolfgard to attend the Thing and settle our differences. This is his reply! I've heard of killing the messenger, but my God! That bastard Wolfgard would slay one of his own—indeed, his most loyal warrior—just to prove a point!"

"Wolfgard is ruthless, without honor," Svein replied bleakly. "This you should know by now. From what Ottar and I have seen at the enemy village, he will attack again ere long." Svein nodded toward the basket. "Especially after this. A most ominous sign, I think."

"Well, Wolfgard's message may just backfire," Viktor said with grim determination. "For I think I have figured out a way to slow him down a bit."

That evening Viktor stepped into the bedchamber and spotted his bride seated on the bed, petting Freki. At her feet, three of the pups were jumping about, chirping and battling over a ball of yarn. At the hearth, Freya was nursing the other three pups.

Smiling at the peculiar domestic scene, Viktor cleared his throat. "Darling, I must be gone late tonight. Please don't stay up, or worry about me."

Her gaze flashed up to his. "Where are you going?"

"It is best that you don't know."

She thrust her chin high. "I am not some child who must be kept in the dark. I am your wife!"

"Reyna, I realize that. I just feel—"

"This has to do with Wolfgard's basket delivered today?"

"Yes."

"What was in it?" she demanded.

"Again, I think it best not to comment." He crossed the room to his bench, where he picked up and donned his chain-mail tunic.

Reyna watched him, her expression angry and resentful. "You are going to battle Wolfgard, are you not?"

He turned to her contritely. "Darling, I really cannot say."

"Verily, you *will* not say! Do you not trust me?"

"This has nothing to do with trust."

"Bah! If you trusted me, you would tell me!"

"Reyna—"

"Oh, why do you not just leave?" she demanded moodily.

With these furious words, Reyna snatched the ball of yarn from the pups and hurled it at Viktor. The bemused pups barked shrilly as they vaulted across the room to retrieve their toy.

Viktor caught the ball of yarn and tossed it into the pups' basket near the hearth. The pups skidded to a halt at his feet, then leaped off, chirping, after their plaything.

Viktor stepped closer to Reyna, shoring up his patience and offering her a conciliatory smile. "I was surprised when the wolves kept their distance from the pups today. Tell me, is that your doing?"

She spoke through clenched teeth, her visage belligerent. "You do not share with me—I do not share with you."

He groaned. "Now you are behaving like a stubborn child—"

"Do not dare call me stubborn when you are the one keeping secrets!"

Sighing, Viktor went to remove his sword and shield from pegs on the wall. "I guess I had better go."

She said nothing.

But when he began to leave, he heard her call his name, and turned to her. "Yes?"

"Be careful," she said in a grudging tone.

He smiled. "Of course."

After her husband left, Reyna continued to stew in her resentments. She was now certain that Wolfgard had delivered some dire message in his basket and that her husband had gone off to fight him. If so, why would Viktor not tell her what he was about? Had he finally realized that he could not defeat his enemy peaceably, and did pride hold him back from admitting that she had been right all along?

Certainly pride held her back from communicating. Verily, sometimes her throat ached from containing her feelings and the wondrous secret she had yet to reveal to Viktor. But she was no closer to telling her husband that she carried his child, still fearing he would see her news as a victory to be used rather than as a private triumph to be celebrated. Nor could Reyna bring herself to share with Viktor the news of her success in taming the wolves and the foxes: how she took the litter to the stable each morning; how the wolves had adopted the pups; how Hati, the female wolf, even licked and mothered the baby foxes.

Following their spat, Reyna also felt guilty. She missed her husband already and was anxious for his safety. What if he was hurt or killed tonight, with only her bitter words to send him off to his death? She was coming to love him far too much!

Eager to distract herself from these unpleasant worries, she got up, went over to the hearth, grabbed the basket, and began gathering up the remaining pups.

"Come on, babies. We are fretful and bored. Let us all go to the stable and see the wolves."

In the middle of the night, at Wolfgard's wharf, three men bearing wooden mallets stole quietly down the plank toward three sentries who sat near a longship, two of them playing chess while a third looked on, all blissfully unaware of the intruders stalking them. One moment the guards were laughing over a botched chess move; a split second later, amid grunts of pain, all fell unconscious to the pier.

"Good," said Viktor, staring down at the insensible men. "Ottar, gag them and tie them up." He glanced up at the dark, elegantly carved ship straining at her moorings as the powerful currents tugged at her hull. "She is a beauty, is she not? It almost seems a shame to scuttle her."

"Her bulwark appears thick," said Svein. "Why do we not just cast her loose in the fjord?"

"Nay. We are now past the spring thaw, and the fjord is shallow in places," Viktor replied. "She might drift ashore and Wolfgard could recover her."

"Mayhap he will recover her in any event," Svein fretted.

"Mayhap. But we'll not make his task easier."

"We could set her afire," suggested Ottar as he busily bound the ankles of one of the sentries.

"Yes, but the glow of the fire might be spotted from the village," Viktor pointed out.

Svein nodded. "Then let us be about our task."

The two men hopped inside the longship and, using their mallets and large iron bolts, began hammering holes through the dense decking. As soon as he finished tying and gagging the sentries, Ottar joined them. Within half an hour, the boat had sprouted numerous leaks and was filling up with water. The men clambered out and cut the vessel adrift.

Watching the swift current tug the listing ship into the dark fjord, Viktor smiled in grim satisfaction. "Now, even if Wolfgard recovers her, this should slow him down a bit."

Later, exhausted, Viktor trudged inside his bedchamber to a wondrous sight. Reyna lay sprawled on the bed, surrounded by Freya, Freki, their pups—and all three wolves! Viktor actually had to blink twice to make sure his eyes were not deceiving him—but yes, all three wolves were there, as well as eight foxes! Two of the pups were even chewing on Thor's ears, as the latter indulged them with an air of boredom.

Viktor laid aside his sword and shield and stepped farther inside, his expression flabbergasted. Twelve sets of eyes turned to focus on him, and eleven tails wagged.

"What is this?" he asked his wife.

Viktor could have sworn he saw relief spring into Reyna's bright eyes. "So you have survived your mysterious mission, my husband?"

"Obviously. It appears you have been busy, too."

"Yea, we have all become friends," she replied casually, petting one of the pups.

"This is your doing?"

"Yea."

"But how?"

Reyna raised one of the pups and nuzzled it against her cheek. She giggled as the little creature licked her. "Gradually, I accustomed the wolves to the scent of the foxes, and rewarded them with food when they did not snarl. Then I brought one of the pups in to the wolves, and Hati soon adopted it. The rest was easy."

Viktor grinned. "You are amazing."

She shrugged. "You are gone much, I was bored, and so we all decided to kiss and make up."

He winked at her tenderly. "Will you kiss and make up with me?"

She tilted her face at an impudent angle. "I am not sure. Where have you been, my husband?"

"I went to drill holes in the bottom of Wolfgard's longship."

Unexpectedly, she chortled with glee. "That is most amusing." Then her pouty expression drifted back. "But why did you not tell me of your plans?"

Viktor pulled off his chain-mail tunic and tossed it down on the bench. "Because you would have insisted on coming along."

"True. I would have drilled a few holes in Wolfgard's heart." She stretched forward eagerly. "Were you successful in your mission?"

"Very. His longship is history."

"Good." She petted Thor and cooed to one of the pups.

"Er . . . Reyna?"

"Yea?"

He flashed her a crooked grin. "Where will I sleep?"

She tossed her mane of hair out of reach of a determined pup scampering up her arm. "With all of us, of course."

"But . . . how?"

She flashed him a simpering smile. "We will make room."

He pinned her with a meaningful glance. "And what if I *do* want to kiss and make up? That is, if you're ready."

She considered this with a frown, then regarded him saucily. "I am not quite ready, despite your pretty smile and woeful eyes."

"I have woeful eyes?" he teased.

Now she, too, was fighting a smile. "Yea, when you try to cajole me."

"Which I am determined to do right now."

But as he started toward her eagerly, she held up a hand and glowered. "Do not think you have won my favors, husband. Verily, I am still angry at you for treating me like some child who cannot be trusted with a man's business."

He made a gesture of entreaty. "Reyna, it had nothing to do with trust. It was strictly your safety I was concerned about."

"Bah! 'Tis no excuse for not sharing."

"But I just told you what I was doing tonight. Isn't that sharing?"

"Nay. You confessed only afterward. 'Tis not the same."

"And there's nothing you're not sharing with me?" As her guilty gaze darted away from his, he added, "Like now, when you're holding yourself apart from me?"

She tried to glare back at him, but her mouth trembled and her gaze became riveted on the muscles of his naked chest.

"Well, milady? Who's not sharing now?"

Ignoring his query, she watched him untie his leggings and gulped.

His voice was thick and insistent when he said, "Reyna, enough of this. I am tired and you are being deliberately perverse. Must I come over there and make you biddable? You know I'm going to, even if you squirm and fight me every inch of the way."

She sighed, sounding more relieved than acquiescent. "Very well. I will kiss and make up."

"Finally!" Shucking off his leggings and moving closer, he regarded the crowded bed quizzically. "But how can I make love to you in such a tight space?"

She reached out to stroke his manhood and licked her lips. "You do it remarkably well every night."

"Wicked wench!"

She smiled tenderly and took his hand. "Come on, my husband. You do look tired. Come to bed."

Naked, Viktor crawled in among eleven squirming dogs, and finally squeezed in next to his wife. He glanced up at Geri, who was panting in his face, while Thor's wagging tail was whacking the crown of his head. Meanwhile, four of the cubs began to leap about and chirp eagerly at his and Reyna's feet, one of them chewing on Viktor's toes through the pelts.

Viktor scowled murderously. "Reyna, this is ridiculous. I feel like I'm making love to you in a kennel, with eleven dogs serving as voyeurs. This will never work—"

" 'Twill work," she said huskily, drawing him closer. "Come here, my husband, and I will show you how two bodies can share the space of one."

"Hmm . . ." he murmured, already thoroughly enjoying the demonstration.

THIRTY-FOUR

WHEN MORNING CAME ACROSS THE FJORD, WOLFGARD WAS IN A
terrible rage. Cowering at his feet in the main chamber of his
longhouse were the three sentries who had fallen such easy
prey to his enemy last night, allowing his newly constructed
longship to be cast adrift in the fjord. Before sunrise, the relief sentries, upon arriving at the wharf, had found the night
watchmen tied up and lying on the planks.

"How could you have allowed this to happen—you miserable dimwits?" Wolfgard demanded.

"Jarl, we were patrolling the wharf just as you directed,"
stammered the first sentry, imploring Wolfgard with dark,
fear-filled eyes. "But our enemy took us by surprise—"

"How could this be if you were attending to your duties?"
Wolfgard shouted.

"Jarl, 'twas dark," protested another.

"Bah!" scoffed Wolfgard. "Thanks to your stupidity, my
enemy has again managed to thwart me. But Viktor the Valiant should not gloat. We will attack—and slay him—if we
must first swim across the cursed fjord."

"Yea, jarl," the men mumbled in unison.

Another of Wolfgard's warriors charged into the room.
"Jarl," cried Egil, "the sentries lie! They were not attending
to their duties last night."

Wolfgard glanced at the guilt-ridden faces of the men, then
asked Egil, "How know ye this?"

Egil crossed to Wolfgard and handed him a small ivory

341

chess piece fashioned in the image of Bragi. "I found this chessman stuck between the planks of the wharf. Verily, I have warned these fools time and time again not to play chess when they should be attending to their duties."

At this ominous pronouncement, the sentries began quivering with fear and begging their jarl for mercy. Wolfgard was heedless, his battle-scarred face darkening with fury as he fingered the ivory piece. "Find ye the rest of the chessmen?" he asked Egil with low menace.

"Nay." Egil glowered at the men. "Methinks that, even tied up, they kicked the rest of the chess set into the fjord to cover their infamy . . . or mayhap the wind completed the villainous task for them."

"Speaks Egil the truth?" Wolfgard roared to the sentries.

"Nay, jarl, nay!" the men denied.

Wolfgard hurled the ivory piece into the fire, then waved a fist at the kneeling men. "Miserable whoresons! Your lies have sealed your fate!"

Amid the horrified expressions of the captives, Wolfgard charged across the room and hauled a wickedly sharp battle-ax down from the wall. Ignoring the doomed men's pleas for their lives, he strode back to loom over them like the Angel of Death, wielding his ax high. He paused only to wonder if he could still lop off two heads in one fell swing.

He did so, silencing the sentries' cries with a single cruel stroke, then quickly slaying the third man, who had already grown mute with terror.

Dead silence fell in the wake of the terrible carnage, with only the thuds of heads and bodies falling, and the snap of the fire, to fill the awful void. Then, all at once, two more of Wolfgard's warriors, Bjorn and Leif, burst into the chamber.

Paying no heed to the grisly scene on the floor, Leif announced excitedly, "Jarl, we have found your longship beached down the fjord. Viktor the Valiant drilled holes in her bulwark, but she can still be salvaged."

Wiping his blood-spattered ax on the garment of one of the slain men, Wolfgard glanced up, his grin filled with sadistic pleasure.

* * *

Viktor knew that he and his tribe were living on borrowed time, that sooner or later Wolfgard would find a way to attack. Indeed, only a few days after he had set Wolfgard's new longship adrift, he received from Svein the troubling news that several of Wolfgard's men had been spotted repairing the vessel where it had drifted ashore farther down the fjord.

Thus Viktor prepared his men for imminent battle, planning war games that stressed defensive maneuvers. He also kept Eurich and Svein well occupied helping him build the warfare machines he intended to use to repel the siege. All of his warriors were amazed by the stone-throwing and slinging machines Viktor was constructing—although they would surely become stupefied when they learned what he *actually* intended to hurl at Wolfgard. The first time he issued orders to Ottar to begin stockpiling "ammunition," the lad responded, "Jarl, you must be jesting." Viktor's response was a solemn shake of his head.

Reyna, too, took an interest in her husband's fantastical inventions. Late one night when he had not come to bed, she joined him at the blacksmith's cottage, where he was putting the finishing touches on one of his new machines. Just inside the doorway to the small hut, she paused to scowl at the odd contraption filling so much of the room. The large, crudely constructed device was composed of a long, stout frame on four wheels, with an upright brace running its width; behind the brace, shooting out at a low angle, was a long timber with a bowl carved at its tip. The plank was suspended by ropes attached to the upright brace. Reyna's husband stood with his back to her as he tugged on the ropes and frowned in fierce concentration.

She cleared her throat.

He turned and saw her. "Reyna, what are you doing here?"

"What are *you* doing here so late, my husband?" she countered.

"Just performing my duty to protect home and hearth," he quipped.

She rolled her eyes. "You are not where you should be."

"And where is that, my amorous bride?"

"In bed with me."

He chuckled. "Just can't resist me, can you? And after the

marathon session we held last night! Are you trying to kill me, woman?"

"A most pleasurable way to be slain."

His grin was broad. "Agreed."

Smirking, she stepped forward and nodded toward the odd-looking device he was working on. "What is this, my husband?"

"It's called a petrary—a stone-throwing machine."

"Where did you learn of such devices?"

"When I was in Futuregard at college—"

"What means 'college'?"

"A place of higher learning. Anyway, I was a member of a medieval reenactment society, and we constructed machines such as this one for the various events we staged."

She nodded toward the engine. "How does it work?"

He sighed. "I'm afraid it doesn't work at all right now." He leaned over to tug on one of the ropes. "In theory, you are supposed to put a large stone in the bowl, then lash the shooting arm down under the frame." He pointed as he spoke. "Then you adjust the tension really tight, release the beam, and off the rock flies—"

"To land on Wolfgard's head?" Reyna asked eagerly. "Oh, I am in heaven!"

He chuckled. "Well, that's the general idea."

"Then why does the device not work?"

He grimaced. "The problem is the ropes. I cannot even lash the beam to the winch—"

"Wench?" she said.

"Winch," he corrected her, pointing to the device under the frame. "The ropes suspending the shooting arm from the upright brace are way too slack. I'd give my eyeteeth for some strong hemp right now."

"Hemp?" she asked, bemused.

"You see, leather rope is not strong enough, and the walrus-skin type is too elastic. And without the proper tension on the beam from above, the darn thing will never pop up—"

All at once, giggling, Reyna came forward and stroked the front of Viktor's leggings. "Then mayhap we must increase the tension, to make it pop up?"

He grinned. "Wanton minx." As she squeezed him, he stifled a groan. "You see . . . the plank is supposed to be hard and firm . . ."

"Ah, yea. Hard and firm . . ."

He sucked in his breath between gritted teeth. "But right now the darned thing feels more like a teeter-totter."

"What means 'teeter-totter'?"

Moving away, albeit reluctantly, from her titillating touch, he pushed on the beam to demonstrate the slack in the ropes. "See, it goes up and down."

She hauled him close again and continued caressing him. "Hmm . . . Up and down. I like that." And she pushed him toward the petrary.

Viktor regarded his wife in amazement. "Reyna, what depraved act are you contemplating *now?* I mean, having wolves and foxes as voyeurs was bad enough—"

She giggled and shoved him closer to the device. "I am merely trying to help you adjust your shooting arm."

"Which shooting arm?"

She chortled. "You must sit on it, my husband."

"Sit on *what?"*

"On the beam. You must sit on it, and I must sit on you, so we can bounce up and down and stretch out the tension—"

"What tension?" His words were hoarse, barely audible.

"In the ropes, of course." She grinned and slipped her fingers inside his leggings. "Or whatever other tension you may need to stretch taut, my husband."

He moaned in agony.

"Then we can lash the beam to the winch—"

"Wench?" he gritted.

"Winch," she said, pointing to the frame. "And then the beam will pop up."

"Amen."

Viktor needed no further prodding. Trembling, he straddled the beam, propped his back against the upright brace, and pulled Reyna onto his lap.

"Ahhh . . ." Seconds later, Reyna was bouncing on Viktor and panting ecstatically. "I like this teeter-totter, this up and down, this tension."

"I like this *wench.*" Viktor grabbed his erotically bobbing wife around the waist and pinned her deeply in his lap.

She absorbed his powerful thrusts amid soft gasps of ecstasy. "Am I not very helpful, my husband? Can you not already feel the tension getting very tight? Mayhap soon we can lash the beam to the wench—er, *winch*—and verily, then it will pop up entirely—"

"Verily," Viktor grunted, "it already has . . ."

The expected attack from Wolfgard came a week later, on a cool summer night.

Stealing in quietly under oar power, Wolfgard and his company docked their longship at Viktor's wharf. Leading twenty of his fiercest fighters, Wolfgard disembarked by the light of the full moon to find the pier strangely unguarded. Stranger still, none of Viktor's vessels were moored there, and the night was almost eerily still and quiet.

At the edge of the wharf, Wolfgard halted his company and squinted at the rocky fell looming before them. Still he spotted no sign of sentries.

"This is good," he muttered to Egil. "My enemy has grown complacent, thinking he has destroyed my longship and we will not attack."

Egil grinned at him. "Yea, jarl. You have planned your strategy well."

At Wolfgard's signal, his warriors began creeping up the shadowy trail.

They never made it to the top.

Egil was the first to slip on the whale blubber that had been liberally applied to the path. With a howl of fear and surprise, he lost his balance, careened to the ground, and, amid the loud cacophony of his banging sword and crashing shield, rolled back down the trail, knocking two more warriors off their feet before he landed, with a loud cry and an explosive splash, in the fjord.

"What madness is this?" Wolfgard demanded as he fought to keep his own balance on the slick path.

"They have greased the trail, jarl!" cried one of his men, just before he also slipped, fell, and went tumbling into the fjord.

"March around the trail!" Wolfgard bellowed to the others.

Slipping and sliding their way off the path, the men began navigating up the craggy basalt rocks on either side of them, only to freeze and jerk their heads upward as ominous *whooshing* sounds hissed out. Within seconds the attackers found themselves being pelted from above by huge heavings of mud, manure, sticks, and small rocks. Curses spewed and groans were bellowed as, one by one, the besieged men were battered off their feet and went tumbling back down the fell to land in the fjord.

Somehow, Wolfgard staggered upward amid the onslaught, even though his body was soon covered with dung and mud, his advance slowed by the painful pounding of rocks and sticks. At last he spotted his nemesis, Viktor the Valiant, standing atop the hill. On either side of his enemy loomed several bizarre-looking machines being manned by his warriors and spewing out vast quantities of muck.

And the whoreson Viktor was laughing at him!

"Fight like a man, you craven!" he yelled, waving his fist.

A split second later, a pie-sized load of manure landed squarely in Wolfgard's face.

Atop the hill, Viktor was indeed chuckling as he watched Wolfgard and the others retreat and hastily sail off, hoisting lifelines to rescue the warriors still flailing about in the fjord. He turned to Svein, Ottar, and Rollo, who were also watching the rout with broad grins.

"We did it, my friends. Victory without violence," he said proudly.

"As they do in Futuregard?" questioned Ottar.

"Just as they should."

"'Tis provident that Ottar told us Wolfgard recovered his longship," commented Rollo.

"Yes, we were prepared."

"And 'twas also fortunate we hid our own vessels farther down the fjord," said Ottar. "Otherwise Wolfgard might well have retaliated for our recent raid by setting our own ships adrift."

"Yes, I must agree our planning was impeccable, every step of the way."

Viktor left his comrades to keep watch for the remainder of the night. Riding back to the village on Sleipnir, he felt intensely proud of his men, and keenly grateful that they had embraced his system of values and helped him win the day without loss of life.

Moments later, when he entered his bedchamber and glimpsed the petulant expression on his wife's face, his bubble of elation burst.

"What is wrong?"

On the bed, Reyna had been petting their huge brood of canines. On spotting Viktor, the wolves and foxes wagged their tails, but his wife's expression was hardly eager as she rose to confront him.

"The hour is late, my husband. Where have you been?"

He couldn't repress a smile as he watched several of the dogs leap off the bed and bound toward him. "We battled Wolfgard tonight—and repelled him."

Reyna gasped and looked Viktor over carefully. "Were you hurt?"

"Nay."

"But you could have been."

Viktor leaned over to pet the wolves and foxes that were barking and leaping about his legs. "Not likely. You see, we had a few surprises in store for your stepfather. We greased the trail leading from the fjord, and the invaders who didn't go sliding off like pigs in a chute found themselves being pelted with manure, sticks, and rocks. As it turned out, our unwelcome guests could hardly wait to retreat. Believe me, there was no danger."

Her mouth dropped open. "So that is what you used the machines for! But why did you not slay the villains?"

"Because it wasn't necessary."

"Wolfgard fights with swords, not dung," she pointed out heatedly.

"Believe me, he never got close enough to pose a threat."

She moved closer, her expression remaining troubled. "I do not want scars marring your pretty body."

"Nor I yours, milady." He touched the tip of her nose. "You know, I think you are mad just because you didn't get to join the fight."

She spoke vehemently. "You know I would do battle for you, kill for you."

"You can still battle *with* me," he teased.

She heaved an elaborate sigh. "Not *with* you anymore. I am tamed."

He grinned.

Watching pride flare in her eyes, he pulled her close and kissed her hair, inhaling its sweet scent. "Darling, I am delighted you are less warlike, because it will mean greater happiness for you and me—and all our people."

"And what of Wolfgard?" she asked. "He will not give up, and 'tis foolish of you to repel him with the toys of a child. Have you not the courage to kill him?"

"It is not a question of courage at all," Viktor replied firmly, "but a matter of doing what is right. Sometimes I think it takes greater courage to solve problems without violence—"

"Mayhap," she conceded, surprising him, "but Wolfgard does not fight with your puny weapons." She drew herself up with pride. "I am still a warrior. If it goes against your beliefs, my husband, then I will slay him for you."

He smiled at her bravery and protectiveness. "I know you would, darling. But not while you're carrying our child."

She jerked away from him. "You knew!"

He nodded tenderly. "Of course I knew. I could see—and feel—your body changing."

She bit her lip. "Why did you not say something?"

"I was waiting for you to tell me."

Hurt gleamed in her eyes. "So you could gloat to Wolfgard of your victory?"

She moved away, and Viktor followed, placing his hand on her rigid shoulder. "Darling, turn around and look at me."

She complied, her expression guarded and resentful.

"Are you happy about the child?"

A secret smile played on her lips. "Yea. But I am not happy that he, like me, will be used as a device to bring the peace."

"You don't want peace, then?"

She scowled, seeming to struggle with her own torn feelings. Then, with an angry gesture, she burst out, "I do not know! I only know that I want the child and me to be wanted for ourselves."

"Of course you do, darling." He took her hand, placed the soft palm on his cheek, and stared into her eyes. "Believe me, Reyna, you are both wanted—and loved—for yourselves. But the coming of peace will only make all our lives better. Can't you understand by now that our family's destiny—and Vanaheim's—are irrevocably bound together?"

Solemnly, she shook her head.

He reached out to brush a wisp of hair from her eyes. "Reyna, help me build a world for our child, a world of peace where he can play and grow strong. In time, we'll have a daughter, too. A happy little princess, just like you used to be. We will watch her pick wildflowers on the tundra. *Our* tundra."

Viktor felt touched when he saw his wife's eyes fill with tears, and then she caught him against her, her arms trembling around his waist. "Yea," she whispered achingly. "A happy little princess. I would like that, my love."

At her poignant words, Viktor's heart welled with a near-painful joy. "Reyna, please say it," he whispered.

She instinctively knew what he needed to hear. "I love you, my husband."

A tear spilled from his eye and onto her cheek as he crushed her close and kissed her. "Reyna ... Reyna ... you have made me so happy."

Her answering kiss was wet with her own exultant tears.

The next evening, with his wife's permission, Viktor informed his kinsmen of the coming of his and Reyna's baby. "My friends," he announced in the central chamber, "my bride and I will have our first child come spring."

As Viktor informed the others, Reyna sat tensely, anticipating gloating and crude comments from her husband's kinsmen. She could not have been more surprised when an awed silence fell. Then Rollo stood, lifted his tankard, and solemnly offered a toast. "To our queen, Reyna, and the son she will bear our king ..."

A cheer went up from the group, leaving Reyna feeling touched and grateful. She smiled at Viktor, and he winked back. Afterward, the celebratory mood continued: Svein presented Reyna with his own talisman of Thor, insisting she wear it to protect the child; and at Orm's bidding, the skald quickly improvised a verse to honor the occasion.

Reyna blinked at a tear. She had expected scorn and ridicule from her husband's fighters and had received jubilation and acceptance instead. She realized that during the time they had all shared stories together, the warriors' attitudes toward her had changed, just as she had mellowed toward them.

Still, it disappointed her that she remained shut out of the men's discussion of battle strategies to protect the village from Wolfgard. After all, before she had become an expectant mother, she had been a warrior in her own right, and she felt she had much to offer.

The next morning, Viktor and Reyna took their brood of canines out for some exercise on the tundra. The excursion was lively, with the foxes chasing lemmings, while the wolves bounded about, leaping over the foxes and each other. The sounds of exuberant howling, barking, and chirping filled the air. Viktor and Reyna strolled along with the animals, holding hands and laughing.

Reyna still had much on her mind. "What will you do, my husband, the next time Wolfgard attacks?"

Viktor leaned over and picked up a stick. He whistled softly, hurled the twig, then chuckled as all eleven dogs bounded after it. To Reyna, he replied, "Oh, my kinsmen and I still have a few tricks up our sleeves."

"I think you should hoist all of Wolfgard's warriors up by their balls," Reyna said grimly.

Viktor glanced askance at his wife, then went down on his haunches as Geri, with ten other canines on his flanks, returned with the twig. He snatched the stick from Geri's teeth and flung it again.

Straightening, he slanted his wife a chiding glance. "And you wonder why I won't let you in on our strategy sessions."

Stubbornly, she continued. "I think you should fill your fancy machines with knives, boulders, and chunks of iron, and hurl *that* at Wolfgard."

"I'd like to fill all my fancy machines with *you*," he teased her.

She appeared petulant, unmoved. "But that will not repel Wolfgard."

Viktor sighed as the pack returned. He retrieved the stick from Hati and tossed it yet again. Then he asked his wife, "Reyna, haven't you learned anything from my stories each night?"

He regarded her sternly, and noted to his satisfaction that she had the grace to at least *look* guilty.

"You know I love your stories," she replied.

"Yes, but have you *learned* anything from them? Don't you know by now that I'm determined to end this feud without killing people?"

She scowled and mulled this over. "And what if I can suggest ways to defeat Wolfgard without slaying his warriors?"

He hooked his elbow around her neck and gave her lips a quick kiss. "Then I'll happily follow your suggestions, wife."

Reyna frowned and considered the possibilities. Then her pensive mood turned to glee as she watched ninety pounds of gray wolf crash full force against her husband's chest. Caught off guard, Viktor fell to the tundra, just as ten other exuberant canines landed on top of him.

Reyna almost split her sides laughing as Thor dropped the stick squarely between the jaws of Viktor's opened mouth. With tears of mirth spilling from her eyes, Reyna watched her husband clench the twig in his teeth and glower up at her ferociously.

Late the next night, Wolfgard again attacked, docking once more at Viktor's deserted pier. The company embarked amid a thick white fog, but Wolfgard and his men managed to navigate their way up the trail, which this time, blessedly, was not greased.

At the top of the fell, all of the men tensed at the sounds of low, eerie screams. Suddenly several white ghosts loomed toward them from the fog, the apparitions lunging frightfully about and screaming banshee wails.

Wolfgard's company panicked utterly. The warriors screeched with fear, dropped their weapons, and even knocked one another down in their haste to flee. Left alone with the menacing, wailing phantoms, Wolfgard had no choice but to join the retreat. Halfway down the fell, he stumbled and rolled the rest of the way, yelling curses.

At the top of the trail, Viktor, Orm, Rollo, and Canute laughed heartily as they removed the white linen sheets they had worn to disguise themselves as specters.

"It seems my wife has some pretty inspired suggestions after all," Viktor remarked.

Two nights later, Wolfgard made his next move. This time, anticipating Viktor's defenses, he sailed his longship all the way down the fjord to the Atlantic, then landed at midnight at the beach due south of Viktor's village.

Bearing weapons and torches, the long line of armed men proceeded north from the beach, reaching the tundra without incident—until Wolfgard heard a horrible scream. He and his men rushed to the edge of a precipice to discover that one of the warriors had fallen through rushes into a deep lava tube. There the terrified man was being chased by an angry, snorting wild boar.

"Throw in a line and pull him out," Wolfgard ordered with disgust.

The warriors had no sooner hauled the man out and marched on than two more warriors fell into a second pit—this one filled with rats and snakes that had the men shrieking hysterically. While attempting to retrieve these two, Wolfgard sent Egil ahead to reconnoiter the trail, and he promptly fell into a third abyss, in which hundreds of seabirds had been trapped. At the intrusion of Egil's tumbling body, the birds panicked, screeching and flapping about wildly as they sailed out of the pit and defecated all over Wolfgard's bewildered band.

The dung-spattered company at last regrouped and moved forward. Then, from the distance, the frightened men again heard the eerie screams of ghosts—

In the frantic retreat that ensued, Wolfgard was knocked to his buttocks by his panicked men.

"Halt, sons of Loki!" he screamed. "Halt, you miserable cravens!"

When his confused warriors ignored him and continued their escape, and the horrendous wailing of the demons grew closer, a very disgusted Wolfgard could only heave himself to his feet and flee with the others ...

In the distance, watching the retreat with his kinsmen, Viktor again laughed. Chalk up another inventive maneuver to his diabolical wife.

Then a frown drifted in. Wolfgard was very determined to defeat him and his people. As the weeks and months passed, it would require more and more ingenuity to keep Reyna, their unborn child, and his people safe.

The next morning Wolfgard's spy visited him. "Your stepdaughter is breeding," the informant summarily announced.

Wolfgard's face twisted in rage. Damn Reyna and her whoreson husband! Viktor the Valiant had already made Wolfgard a laughingstock among his men, especially by making debacles of his latest attacks. Some of his men had already defected to Viktor's camp, and others now believed that their enemy was truly in possession of supernatural powers. This latest feat on Viktor's part would only hasten Wolfgard's downfall.

"How know ye this?" he demanded of the spy.

"The entire village knows, after King Viktor announced to his kinsmen that his wife is with child. You should see the two of them together, all smiles and kisses as they roam the village with their eleven canines. I have even heard that the Ravisher is now helping King Viktor plan his battle strategies."

"The damned little traitor! So she has allowed Viktor to tame her?"

"Yea. Entirely. She is now almost as docile as a lamb."

From the doorway, Leif called out, "What shall we do, jarl? Once the Ravisher delivers a son to King Viktor, you will be honor-bound to end the feud."

"She has disgraced me!" Wolfgard raved. "And I will kill her with my bare hands. Yea—'tis the only solution. My stepdaughter will die ere she bears my enemy a child!"

THIRTY-FIVE

Summer passed, and then came winter. Wolfgard continued to attack, and Viktor repelled his enemy with a combination of strategy and skill. Several more of Wolfgard's
warriors, developing an awesome respect of Viktor's mastery,
or hearing of the fantastical stories he still wove nightly, defected to his camp.

Much of the winter passed in idyllic fashion for Viktor and
Reyna. On days when the sun all but disappeared, and nights
that seemed to stretch on forever, they languished by the fire,
playing with their eleven animals. Sometimes late at night,
when fierce ice storms did not threaten, they bundled up tight
and stood outside beneath the eaves of the longhouse, watching the dazzling splendor of the northern lights electrify the
midnight skies.

As winter receded, Reyna's stomach grew great with their
child. Viktor often worried about her delivering their baby
here in the past, without modern doctors or hospitals. But
when he fretted over the dangers to her, he would always remember his dream—his vision of the two of them with their
son, bringing peace to Vanaheim.

Spring came, and the snow and ice caps began to melt.
Seals once again frolicked in the fjord; geese, plovers, and
guillemots sailed overhead in the clear blue sky. One morning
the entire ice fox family, including six grown pups, departed
for the tundra, all eight still ensconced in thick white winter

coats. Standing in the doorway of the longhouse, Reyna and
Viktor lovingly bade their pets farewell.

On another fine spring morning the couple received a
shock. They were eating breakfast in the dining chamber
when Orm and Rollo ushered in three captives at sword point.
Viktor noted that all of the strangers were fair, and were
dressed in dark wool tunics and leather leggings. The tallest
man appeared quite young; he was blond, his curly locks
encircling a finely etched, aristocratic face.

"We caught these spies down by the fjord," announced
Rollo with contempt. "Wolfgard has likely sent them to slay
you and our lady, jarl."

Meanwhile, Reyna was staring at the newcomers with an
expression of puzzlement. "These are not my stepfather's
warriors," she informed Rollo. "I have never seen these men
before."

"That is not true," said the tall newcomer, staring intently
at Reyna. "You saw me many years ago in Loire, my lady. I
am your brother Alain."

Reyna shot to her feet, her features white. Viktor, fearing
she might faint, jumped up to grab her arm and steady her.

Reyna stared in shock at the thin blond man, noting his
slight resemblance to herself, especially in the angular shape
of his face and the deep hue of his brown eyes. "But this cannot be! My brother Alain is dead! Wolfgard condemned him
to die of exposure because of a slight deformity—"

"Call off your sentries, milady, and I will show you that
deformity," the man interrupted calmly.

Reyna glanced at Viktor, and he in turn nodded to Rollo
and Orm, who sheathed their swords and stepped back. The
man who called himself Alain went over to Reyna and pulled
off his soft leather boot.

She stared in awe at the six toes on his right foot. " 'Tis
true! You are my brother Alain!"

He smiled. *"Oui,* my sister."

With a cry of joy, she fell into his arms. "Alain! Alain! I
was convinced you were dead! I am so glad to see you, my
brother."

"As I am overjoyed to see you, my sister."

After an emotional moment, the two moved apart, Reyna

wiping away tears of joy and looking her brother over carefully, as if she expected him to disappear again at any moment. As Alain pulled his boot back on, Viktor stepped forward, wrapped an arm around his wife's waist, and smiled at their guest.

"Welcome to Vanaheim, Alain. I must apologize that my men did not recognize you. Can we all sit down and become acquainted? I'm afraid Reyna has had quite a shock, and as you can see, she's in a rather delicate condition right now."

At Viktor's words, the young man stared at his host with cool suspicion, then turned back to Reyna. "This is your husband?"

"Yea. He is Viktor the Valiant."

Alain's mouth twisted into a sneer. "This Viking got you with child?"

Reyna and Viktor exchanged a glance of bewilderment at the venom in Alain's tone.

"Let us all sit down," Viktor repeated firmly and patiently. He nodded to Orm. "See that our guest's kinsmen are found lodging and food."

"Yea, jarl."

Rollo and Orm escorted the other two men from the chamber, and Alain sat down with the couple at the table.

Smiling, Reyna handed Alain a tankard of buttermilk. "My brother, I cannot begin to describe my joy in seeing you again. Verily, I thought I never would."

"*Oui,* I only narrowly escaped death back in Loire."

"You must tell me how you came to live," Reyna urged.

Alain's brown eyes darkened with bitterness. "After Wolfgard abandoned me as an infant and sailed off with you and my mother, some peasants found me in the countryside and rescued me. They were a simple couple—farmers with only a small plot of land to work—but they were good people. They raised me until I was fourteen summers old and could assume my rightful place as Prince of Loire."

"You are now prince?" Reyna asked, her eyes alight with awe.

"Yea. I live in our parents' old castle"—again he leveled a distrustful glance at Viktor—"which the Vikings ransacked when they killed our father and took you and our mother captive. Now I have restored the castle to its former glory, and

I yearn to bring you back there, where you belong, my sister."

Reyna's expression remained enchanted. "But—you must tell me how you managed to find me!"

"Ah, yes. Through our half brother, Ragar. He gave me directions to find you here in Vanaheim."

"You have seen Ragar?" she cried, reaching out to clutch Alain's hand in her excitement. "Then his voyage was successful?"

"*Oui*, Ragar is now living in Loire and has married a lovely young French woman, Mignon." Alain smiled and squeezed his sister's hand. "All of us want you to return there—and live away from these Vikings in their godless, cold country."

At the obvious insult to Viktor, another awkward glance was exchanged between husband and wife. Then Reyna said gently, "Alain, I am deeply thrilled to see you again, and touched by your devotion to me. But I am married to a Viking now. We are to have a child, and I love him."

Alain clenched his jaw. "You love one of the very pagans who was responsible for our mother's death?" At Reyna's confused look, he said, "Ragar told me all about what happened to you and our mother here in the North Country, after Wolfgard kidnapped you."

Passionately, Reyna replied, "Then my half brother told you 'twas Wolfgard who broke our mother's spirit and drove her to her grave. My husband took no part in Wolfgard's infamy, and he is in no way responsible for our mother's fate. Indeed, my husband now holds Wolfgard enemy, and thus will avenge the wrongs done to our family."

Alain laughed scornfully. "Your husband avenges us by making bargains with our enemy over your own fate—and gloating that he will tame you?"

Reyna went pale. "Ragar told you that?"

"*Oui.*"

As Viktor would have spoken out to defend his wife, Reyna held up a hand. To Alain, she said firmly, "My husband made his bargain only to bring peace to all of Vanaheim."

Alain swung his scornful gaze toward Viktor. "If you believe that, sister, then it is no wonder your husband has succeeded in making you his pawn."

At Alain's barbed comment, Reyna gasped, and Viktor at last intervened. "Alain, given all you have suffered, I can understand your bitterness. You are also most welcome to remain here in our home as our guest. However, I will not have you addressing my wife in this contemptuous manner. Is that clear?"

Alain glowered at Viktor.

Reyna gazed plaintively at her brother. "Alain, we are your family here, and most grateful to have you among us. But verily, my husband has spoken the truth. I will not be ridiculed in this manner. And if you are to remain here, I must insist that you treat my husband with respect as well."

Alain jerked his head in a grudging nod, but his eyes smoldered with defiance.

Brother and sister continued to talk as everyone finished breakfast. Largely left out of the conversation, Viktor sat patiently.

Although he felt thrilled for his wife's sake that Alain had appeared, he could not help but feel threatened, especially considering Alain's hostile attitude. Still, when Reyna asked Viktor if he would mind if she and her brother went for a walk alone, he could not object, since he knew they still had so much to catch up on. But the uneasy feeling about Alain's arrival continued to dog him . . .

Outside in the village, Reyna and Alain held hands and chatted as they followed a path up toward the tundra. At first they spoke of the years they had spent apart—Alain's childhood with peasants back in Loire, Reyna's youth with Wolfgard and her mother, first in Iceland, then on Vanaheim.

"Ragar tells me our mother died soon after the clan moved to Vanaheim," Alain said.

"Yea," Reyna replied sadly. "I wish I could take you to see her grave. Unfortunately, 'tis in the village of our enemy, Wolfgard. All my life I have longed to kill him for the cruel way he treated her."

"Mayhap I can slay the whoreson now that I am here," Alain said proudly.

She stared at him in alarm. "Please, you and your two kinsmen must not take on this battle."

He frowned, then nodded. "I will not let the task stay me from my main purpose here, which is to return you to your people in Loire. But if the opportunity arises to slay the bastard, I will make use of it."

Reyna regarded him with regret. "Is your heart so filled with hatred, my brother?"

He laughed incredulously. "And yours is not?"

"Not like it used to be."

He waved her off. "You are a woman, and with child. Your softer attitude is understandable. I only hope there is time to take you to Loire before the baby arrives."

Reyna bit her lip. "That is unlikely, since I feel the child will come very soon. And verily, I cannot leave my husband."

"But he is Viking!"

"Do you so despise all Vikings?"

"Oui."

Reyna drew a heavy breath. "I did once myself," she admitted. "But Viktor is different. He has mellowed my heart. What we have is special . . . *He* is special."

Alain raised an eyebrow. "In what respect?"

Reyna's smile was filled with love. "My husband is a rainbow warrior. Last spring, he died in battle against Wolfgard's company and was launched to Valhalla. From there he lived another life, and then returned to us from the dead."

"Bah!" Alain made a gesture of contempt. "That is pagan nonsense. No doubt Viktor only feigned death to fool you and his people, and to manipulate you to his purposes."

"Nay—'tis true!" Reyna insisted. "My husband really died. From Valhalla he embarked on another life in a tenth world called Futuregard, and there he learned many wondrous things. You should hear his stories . . . And he is a Christian now."

"Would a Christian make a devil's bargain as your husband did with your enemy?" Alain scoffed.

"You do not understand—"

Alain swung about to confront her. "What is not to understand, my sister? Did not Viktor the Valiant vow he would tame you and get a son on you, in exchange for Wolfgard's ending the feud?"

"Yea, that is true."

"And did he not then kidnap you and make you his captive?"

"Yea."

Alain gestured angrily. "How can you swear fealty to a man who so abused you?"

"Viktor never abused me," she retorted.

"Hah! Your belly is now thick with his seed—so he has used you well for his purpose, I would say."

Reyna spoke through gritted teeth. "My husband never forced himself on me. He treated me with respect."

"He forced you into marriage, did he not?"

"Nay. I offered myself to appease his warriors, who would have slaughtered Ragar and Harald."

"Still, he took advantage of what you offered."

Reyna struggled to maintain her patience. "Viktor loves me, and is convinced we belong together, that our union will bring a greater peace to all of Vanaheim—"

"And your baby becomes his device for winning this peace? What if his ploy fails? Will there not be great danger to you and the child? From what Ragar has told me, I would reckon Wolfgard despises you by now."

"Yea, he does," Reyna conceded unhappily. "He has tried many times to slay me."

"And yet you are eager to stay with this Viking who exposes you to such danger?" Alain raved. "If you were a truly good mother, you would take your child away to safety, Reyna."

"Now you are not being fair," she accused hotly.

"I want what is best for you and your child. How can that be anything but fair?"

For a moment Reyna frowned fiercely, lost in thought. Was she being the best possible mother? Was she placing her child's life in peril by remaining here on Vanaheim? "You are right that there is still much danger here. But Viktor is convinced that the child's coming will end the feud with Wolfgard—"

"Then your husband is a fool. Mayhap he does want to

bring an accord to Vanaheim, but at a terrible cost to you, my sister. As for this Wolfgard ... Vikings and peace are about as compatible as fire and ice, methinks. You would be so much safer and happier in Loire. You and the child could live in luxury, supported by our tenants, enjoy the fruits of our fields and drink wines fermented from our own vineyards. Our entire family could be together again."

Reyna felt a strong tug on her heartstrings at the lovely images Alain had spun. It was indeed tempting, the thought of leaving this land of turbulence and war and taking her baby to live safely and prosperously in Loire.

"Ragar is happy there?" she asked wistfully.

Alain smiled. "Most. He and his wife are expecting their first child ere winter."

"I am pleased for them." She sighed heavily. "But I cannot leave my husband."

"Then bring Viktor as well," Alain offered in exasperation.

Reyna twisted her fingers together. After a moment, she pinned Alain with a challenging glance. "If I can convince Viktor to come with us to Loire, will you promise to accept him? He really is a good man."

Alain hesitated. "Verily, I will try. For your sake."

Brother and sister continued walking in silence. Reyna felt delighted to be reunited with Alain, but saddened by the depth of his bitterness. She realized that seeing Alain was like looking at an image of her own former self. His unforgiving attitude demonstrated to her how much she had changed, how Viktor's love had filled her heart and left no room for hatred and revenge.

Still, Alain had raised a valid point. Why bring up her child in Vanaheim, with its many dangers, when they could all live in peace in Loire—and her entire family could be together, Viktor included?

She must speak with her husband.

That night Viktor stood in the bedchamber watching Reyna on the bed. With the coming of milder spring nights and the burgeoning of Reyna's stomach, they had again banned the wolves from the room at night, although Thor, Hati, and Geri frequently came in to visit during the day.

Viktor saw Reyna's hand move to her belly. "Is he moving?" he asked tenderly.

She smiled. "How can you tell?"

"By looking at your face. First a little frown creases your brow, as if you are concentrating intently. Then your eyes fill with wonder and your hand moves to your stomach."

"You know me so well."

"I should by now."

She jumped slightly, then giggled. "Come feel your son. He is really clobbering me now."

"Oh, is he?"

Viktor went to the bed, lay down beside Reyna, placed his hand on her belly, and felt the subtle fluttering against his palm. A proud grin lit his face. "He's going to be a real handful, I'm betting. Is he keeping you awake at night?"

"No." She wrinkled her nose at him. "But wanting you is."

He kissed her pouting lips. "Reyna, I've already explained that to you. You are too close to term. We can't risk harming the baby, or possibly getting germs in your birth canal."

Her eyes widened. "What means 'germs'?"

He grinned. "Just trust me, darling. We want to avoid the little gremlins right now. All right?"

She sighed deeply and nestled against him.

He stroked her back. "It's been an exciting day for you, hasn't it? Alain appearing, when all these years you thought he was dead."

"Yea," she replied feelingly, " 'twas like a miracle. His arrival has been one of the greatest surprises and pleasures of my life."

"Have the two of you caught up on everything now? I noticed you had your heads together throughout dinner, too."

"There is much to discuss."

When she fell silent, Viktor asked, "Reyna, what is troubling you?"

"What do you mean?"

"Come on. As I said, I know you. And there is something on your mind right now."

She stared up at him solemnly. "You are right. Alain wants us to come live with him in Loire."

Viktor groaned. "Reyna, our destiny lies here."

"How know you that?" she asked, her expression torn.

"Remember the dream, darling? You, me, the baby . . . and peace coming to Vanaheim."

"I see no peace!" she flared petulantly. "Wolfgard still attacks us. And our baby could soon be in peril."

He raised her hand to his mouth and kissed her fingers. "You are forgetting that when our son is born, Wolfgard will be required to honor his word and make peace."

She shook her head with terrible fatalism. "I think you are a fool, my husband, if you believe Wolfgard possesses any honor at all."

"Reyna, I know what is best for us. I saw it in my vision. You are simply going to have to trust me. Peace will come."

"But why must we fight this battle?" she asked in anguish. "Why can we not go to Loire, where all of my family can be together at last?"

He reached out to stroke her cheek, his expression troubled. "Reyna, this is our home. This is where our future lies. I cannot abandon my people. As for you . . . I know you love your brother, but you wouldn't want to leave me to go to Loire, would you?"

She flashed him a quick, reassuring smile. "Nay, my husband. I love you more, and my place is with you."

"Oh, Reyna."

Viktor clutched her close. Reyna clung to her husband, but her heart remained troubled.

THIRTY-SIX

Just after dawn a week later, Alain of Loire stood at the bow of the small ship he and his kinsmen had sailed to Vanaheim from their native land. Behind him, his retainers, Gilles and Barde, were busy navigating the vessel up the rushing fjord toward Wolfgard's wharf. The early spring day was chill, with a biting wind pulling at Alain's clothing and snapping at the ship's square sail.

Alain was still exulting in his victory at finding his sister after a seventeen-year separation. But he knew his mission here on Vanaheim was far from complete. During the past days, he had continued to become acquainted with Reyna, and had tried his best to convince her to return with him to Loire—so far, without success. Although Alain had held open his invitation to Reyna's husband as well, privately he recognized that Viktor was the true stumbling block to his purpose—and he dearly hoped that ultimately he could persuade his sister simply to abandon the hated Viking. Outwardly, Alain treated Viktor with courtesy, not wanting to alienate Reyna; inwardly, he felt for the jarl nothing but contempt, lumping him with the other godless barbarians who had overrun Loire shortly after his birth and split apart his family.

Now Alain feared that time would run out before he had accomplished his goal. Just yesterday he had noticed that the baby had dropped low in his sister's belly, which meant she might deliver her child any day now. Surely the young woman would feel an even stronger bond toward her husband once the child was born.

For these reasons, Alain had decided he would visit the jarl of the rival tribe, Wolfgard, to see if Reyna's enemy could be persuaded to join in his cause. In choosing this rash act, Alain feared for his own life, but he had decided the possible benefits outweighed the risk, for he had much to gain if his interview with the rival chieftain was successful. Alain also had a message from Ragar to deliver to Wolfgard, and he was planning to use his possession of the missive as leverage to help ensure his own safety.

He tensed as the ship bumped against Wolfgard's wharf. Before his kinsmen could even hop out to moor the vessel, three sentries charged toward them with swords drawn.

"Who goes there?" demanded the first burly fellow.

"I am Alain, Prince of Loire," Alain replied with bravado. "We come in peace, and would see your jarl, Wolfgard. I bring a message from his son, Ragar, who now lives among our people."

At this announcement, the guards consulted among themselves; then the first man nodded. "Throw us your mooring rope, Alain of Loire, and surrender your arms. We will escort you to the longhouse of our jarl, and he will decide what is to be done with you."

Alain and his men handed over the rope and their weapons, and the three were escorted at sword point to Wolfgard's longhouse. As soon as the small group entered the smoky central chamber of the abode, Alain recognized Wolfgard from Ragar's descriptions; the chieftain sat next to the open fire, chewing on a leg of mutton, his stubbly chin and dark garment streaked with grease. The jarl glanced up with suspicion as the captives were ushered inside.

"Who are these intruders?" he questioned the head guard. "Spies from Viktor's camp?"

"Nay, jarl," the sentry answered. He nodded toward Alain. "This one says he brings a message from your son."

Wolfgard glared at the lad. "Who are you?"

Alain smiled cruelly. "Do you not know, old man?"

Wolfgard hurled down the bone and surged to his feet. He studied carefully the tall, thin young man who had just dared to insult him. He found something about the boy vaguely familiar—and equally irritating.

"Spite me with your tongue again, lad, and I will cut it out!"

Alain revealed no trepidation. "'Tis not within you to kill me, old man. You tried once, and failed miserably."

"What nonsense are you spouting now?"

"Let me remove my boot and you will see."

Wolfgard hesitated, scowling at him.

"Let us slay him, jarl," implored one of the guards. "He clearly speaks with the tongue of madness."

But Wolfgard held up a hand. "Nay, my curiosity is piqued." He nodded to Alain. "Remove your boot, then."

Alain did so, and a couple of the warriors gasped as they viewed his foot with the extra digit.

Alain stared contemptuously at Wolfgard, who had grown pale while viewing the six-toed foot. "Do you recognize me now, old man?"

"You are Reyna's brother?" he asked incredulously.

"*Oui*, I am Alain of Loire," the young man replied proudly. "I was the helpless infant you left to die in the countryside of my native land. But your infamy could not defeat me, old man. I am here now as living proof."

"Verily, I can see that," Wolfgard snapped. "What is it you want from me? You say you have a message from my son?"

"*Oui.*" Alain took a moment to pull his boot back on, then removed from his neck a leather loop with a wooden talisman attached. "Ragar sends you this as proof that I speak for him—and that he is alive."

"Let me have that!" Wolfgard ordered, extending a gnarled hand.

Alain stepped forward, and Wolfgard snatched the necklace from his fingers.

"This belongs to my son, all right," the jarl muttered. "'Tis the talisman of Odin I gave him two summers past." He glanced sharply at Alain. "Where is my son? And what message does he send?"

Alain hesitated, his eyes gleaming shrewdly. "If I give over the message, will you promise safe passage from your village for me and my kinsmen?"

"Why should I honor your request?" Wolfgard scoffed.

"Mayhap so I can convey your own message to your son," Alain countered.

Wolfgard tossed the talisman back at Alain. "You are a poisonous viper, but I will agree to your terms. Now state my son's message."

Alain smiled. "Ragar sends his love. He said to tell you he is very happy in Loire. He has married a young woman, and they are expecting a child. He asks your forgiveness for leaving Vanaheim. He wants you to know he never possessed the heart of a warrior, and he begs your forgiveness for having disappointed you."

Wolfgard received the news in stony silence, though his hands, clenched in fists at his sides, trembled.

"Do you have a response?" Alain asked.

"Yea." Wolfgard's voice came out hoarse with rage. "Tell my craven son to return to Vanaheim ere winter—else he is no longer my son."

"I will convey the message," Alain answered. Glancing at the others in the room, he raised an eyebrow at Wolfgard. "May we speak for a moment alone, old man?"

Wolfgard considered the request with a scowl, then jerked his head in the affirmative. "Yea, but call me an old man again, puny whoreson, and you will leave this village carrying your own head."

Alain smiled slightly. "'Tis understood."

Wolfgard motioned curtly to his guards. "Take our visitor's kinsmen to be guarded in the next chamber. I will speak with this one alone." He scowled at Alain until the others had left the room, then commanded gruffly, "State your business."

Alain regarded the enemy chieftain icily. "First, I would see my mother's grave before I leave this village."

Wolfgard shrugged. "'Tis no concern of mine what you do." He studied the boy with disdain. "Verily, you rather resemble your mother—and most especially, your sister. Even the demeanors match. You have seen the Ravisher since your arrival here?"

"The Ravisher?"

"Reyna."

Alain nodded. "*Oui,* I have spent much time with my sis-

ter. And you must know she is great with child—the child of
your enemy, Viktor the Valiant."

Wolfgard's gray eyes sparkled with outrage. "Yea, I know!
The wench has turned traitor to me, allowing Viktor to tame
her!"

"From what Ragar tells me of your pact with Viktor the
Valiant, once my sister delivers to Viktor a son, you will be
honor-bound to end the feud, will you not?"

Wolfgard charged on the lad, waving a fist in his face.
"Why do you rub salt in my wounds? Yea, I shall shortly lose
face horribly, thanks to your blackhearted, treasonous sister!"

Alain smiled. "Patience, my comrade. Mayhap I can help
you keep from losing face."

Wolfgard's features twisted in a mixture of curiosity and
suspicion. "What do you propose?"

"I am saying there may be a way to thwart Viktor in his
scheme. Mayhap we can help each other."

Wolfgard snorted. "And why would you help me—and betray your own sister?"

"I will cast my lot with you because I hate all Vikings,"
Alain sneered. "Besides, 'tis Viktor I will betray, not my sister."

"But you propose conspiring with another Viking,"
Wolfgard pointed out shrewdly.

"Only because 'twill save my sister from living her life on
this godless island with a pagan husband," Alain retorted. He
looked Wolfgard over with scorn. "For you, I feel no esteem.
Indeed, I hold you responsible for my mother's death."

"Ah—so your malice is out in the open," Wolfgard muttered. "I like knowing the mind of my enemy. Yet I still
doubt your motives. Hating me as you do, why would you
join my cause?"

"Because I am willing to do whatever is necessary to get
Reyna away from Vanaheim!" Alain cried.

"And why should I help you accomplish your goal when I
despise your sister as much as you surely hate me?"

"Because if I can convince Reyna to leave her husband before the baby is born, then you will never have to admit defeat to Viktor."

Wolfgard scratched his bearded jaw and considered the

boy's argument for long moments. "'Tis true. What do you want from me?"

"Your promise that you will not attack my sister—or me—until I can get us both away from this island. And your word that once we are gone, you will never pursue any of us—including Ragar—to Loire."

"Bah! You are demanding that I give up my son?" Wolfgard's tone was thunderous.

"He will not truly be your son unless he returns to you willingly."

"You will allow him to?"

"*Oui.* Once Reyna and I arrive in Loire, I will deliver to Ragar your message. If he chooses to return to Vanaheim, I will not try to stay him."

"But you expect me to allow my traitor stepdaughter to escape unscathed? Why should I cooperate?"

"Because then the thorn in your side will be gone forever," Alain argued. "Reyna's baby will be born away from Vanaheim—and you will not lose the pact you made with Viktor. Afterward, for all I care"—Alain paused to shrug, then finished in a cold, cruel tone—"you can kill the Viking bastard who put his seed inside my sister."

Wolfgard regarded him with an inquisitive scowl. "You seem to take joy at the prospect of Viktor the Valiant's death."

Alain's words were hoarse with bitterness. "*Oui.* Great joy."

Wolfgard grinned. "Then let us speak some more."

Alain held up a hand. "Only with the understanding that my sister will be spared your wrath."

The jarl nodded grimly. "Get the wench away from this island before she drops Viktor's brat, and yea, she will be spared."

The two men continued to converse intently, settling the terms of their devil's bargain. Privately Wolfgard concluded that young Alain was every bit as headstrong as his sister—and even more of a fool. Did the dimwit really believe he would allow both brother and sister to escape Vanaheim unscathed? On the contrary, like a serpent lying in wait,

Wolfgard would study the boy, learn of his plans, then conjure the best moment to strike.

Wolfgard realized he should have slain both of Blanche's brats back in Loire. He had missed his opportunity once, and he would not let the chance slip through his fingers again.

Later that day, Alain walked through Viktor's village, seeking his sister, who had been absent at the longhouse. He spotted Reyna in the distance, sitting on a boulder at the top of a rise. She was petting one of Viktor's wolves crouched at her feet; beyond her, the tundra was sprouting back to life with grasses and wildflowers. His sister appeared quite comely in her long blue dress, although her huge stomach reminded him of Viktor the Valiant's treachery, and of his own determination to take Reyna away from this island.

He would try to love his sister's baby when it came, he vowed, just as he had come to love his half-Viking brother, Ragar; but never would he feel either respect or allegiance toward his sister's husband. Despite Reyna's arguments to the contrary, Alain would never see Viktor the Valiant as anything other than a traitor and a brute, a barbarian who had cruelly subjugated and impregnated his beloved sister, abusing her for his own purposes.

Spotting her brother approaching, Reyna smiled and patted a vacant spot on the boulder. "Come join me, my brother. Where have you been? I sought you out earlier, and fretted when I could not find you."

Plopping himself down beside her, Alain flashed her a conciliatory smile. "I visited our mother's grave today."

Reyna was aghast, her jaw dropping. "You went to Wolfgard's village! How could you have been so careless? You could have been killed—"

He touched her arm to stay her protests. "I am perfectly fine, my sister, as you can see."

"But why did you venture forth so foolishly?"

"I truly yearned to see our mother's grave. And I wanted to meet the man who abandoned me to die so many years ago."

"Why?" Reyna's query was the merest whisper.

"To prove to him that he could not defeat me," Alain retorted with fierce pride.

She nodded solemnly. "Verily, did you meet Wolfgard?"

"Oui. And he is every bit the animal I expected."

She squeezed his hand. "But how did you manage to survive the encounter?"

"In exchange for my safe passage out of the village, I gave him news of Ragar."

Reyna nodded. "That was wise of you." She regarded him curiously. "Was Wolfgard stunned to learn you had survived his treachery in Loire?"

"Oui." Alain's jaw hardened. "If only I could have slain the whoreson today—but such was not my luxury."

"I know, my brother," she murmured sympathetically. "Your wounds go very deep. But I think in time you will be happier to give up this bitterness."

His troubled gaze beseeched hers. "Can you not understand that I will always be embittered until our family is truly reunited? Wolfgard stole not just my mother, but also my sister." He clutched her hand and smiled. "And I want her back."

Reyna struggled with her own feelings. "I know, and I also yearn for us to have a future together in Loire. But 'tis complicated now. I have a husband and a child to consider."

"Oui. You and the child are my greatest concern, and the main reason I spoke with your stepfather today."

"What do you mean?"

"Wolfgard and I spoke openly of our concerns. I do not think you realize, my sister, how thoroughly you have aroused his wrath by defecting to the camp of his enemy— and especially by bearing Viktor the Valiant's child."

"Go on," she urged with a worried frown.

"Wolfgard considers you a blackhearted traitor. He hates you, Reyna. And he does not intend to honor the pact he made with Viktor."

She went pale. "I was afraid of this."

"Especially if you deliver to Viktor a son, Wolfgard will become more affronted than ever, and more determined to kill you, Viktor—and the child."

Her hands moving protectively to her belly, Reyna struggled to her feet. "Oh, I have suspected as much all along! He will not honor the pact, then?"

"Nay. He never intended to."

She spoke with increasing frustration. "But my husband is convinced Wolfgard will live up to his word—and that the coming of our child will bring peace to Vanaheim."

"Your husband is a fool who places his own doomed craving for peace before the safety of his wife and child."

Reyna began to pace. "I will have to convince Viktor that he is wrong—that we must all leave Vanaheim."

Alain sighed. "Try if you must, but mind you, we must leave quickly—tomorrow, in fact."

She turned to face him. "Why so soon?"

Alain stood, gripping his sister's shoulders. "Reyna, I made a pact with Wolfgard—"

"What?" She jerked away. "You turned traitor?"

"Nay. I did what I had to do to save your life and that of your child."

"What is this pact?" she demanded.

"Wolfgard has promised me that if you leave Vanaheim before your child is born, he will not harm you, and that afterward"—Alain glanced away and coughed—"he will live in peace with your husband."

Reyna mulled over this startling bit of information, then laughed incredulously. "Bah! The man lied before when he made a pact—why should I believe him now?"

Alain scowled in exasperation. "You still have no idea how your betrayal has caused Wolfgard to lose face with his people, do you?"

She bit her lip and did not comment.

"Then let me repeat that the man despises you now, Reyna. Some of his warriors have defected to Viktor's camp, as you know. For all of these disgraces, he blames you much more than Viktor, directing his rage toward the woman he feels is plotting his downfall. Now he is willing to go to almost any length to rid himself of you and keep the respect of his warriors—even if this means living in peace with your husband once you are gone."

Reyna frowned deeply. "I must think these matters over carefully."

"Think *quickly,* my sister. And bear in mind Wolfgard's alternative if you do not depart Vanaheim." Alain paused for a moment. "Your stepfather swears to me that if you do not flee before the child is born, if you deliver to Viktor a son, he will not rest until all of you are slain."

Feeling panic encroaching, Reyna again touched her stomach. "Oh, what will I do? What will I do?"

"If you value the life of your child, you will sail with me for Loire tomorrow."

Watching Alain turn and walk away, Reyna felt enmeshed in turmoil. All her life she had wanted to return to Loire. Ragar was there, and Alain was willing to bear her and the child back.

The obstacle was Viktor, and his misguided insistence that they remain on Vanaheim, that their destiny lay here. Why could he not see that he was embracing a fool's dream? And endangering the lives of his wife and child?

Reyna bucked up her spine in grim determination. She would simply have to convince Viktor to leave Vanaheim. It was the only way. But first she needed to speak with Wolfgard and assess his motives for herself. Was he truly centering all his rage on her now? Would he spare Viktor if she left? Would he slay her entire family—including her innocent, helpless babe—if she remained?

Had Alain told her the full truth? Verily, she loved her brother, but something about his demeanor—particularly his hostile attitude toward her husband—she could not completely trust.

THIRTY-SEVEN

On her way back to the village, Reyna encountered her husband's blood brother, Svein.

"Good afternoon, milady," he greeted her. "Did you have a pleasant walk?"

She smiled back at him. She liked and respected Svein, with whom she had become friends over the past months. The two of them had even shared a few games of chess on some cold winter afternoons when Viktor had been busy with other duties.

"Yea—the day is quite lovely."

He fell into step beside her. "And having your brother here—learning he survived—has been a true blessing, has it not, milady? Even though he appears to despise our jarl."

She frowned. "So you, too, have noticed that?"

"The lad's hostility is blatant."

She paused, touching his arm. "Svein, I have a great favor to ask of you."

He bowed from the waist. "I am your servant, milady, as you know."

Reyna took a deep breath, then blurted, "Tonight, I want you to help me steal inside the camp of my stepfather so I may speak with him."

Svein's features went ashen. "Have you gone mad, milady? Such a foolish mission will only mean death for you and your child!"

Yet Reyna shook her head. "I am not afraid, and I know how to infiltrate the village undetected."

"But why would you risk this?"

She ground her jaw. "Because I must judge for myself the motives in my stepfather's blackened heart."

"Explain that, pray."

"My brother Alain has already been to see Wolfgard. He tells me my stepfather has no intention of honoring the pact he made with my husband, and that if I deliver my child on Vanaheim, Wolfgard intends to slay us all."

Svein gazed at her with mingled doubt and horror. "That is terrible, milady. But does not Viktor believe that the coming of the child will bring peace to Vanaheim?"

"Yea, but I feel he is wrong to trust Wolfgard's word. That is why I must go see my stepfather—to discern the truth for myself."

Svein shook his head ominously. "Milady, I cannot support you in this. 'Tis too risky for you and the child. And if our jarl discovered what we were about ... I would not doubt King Viktor would resort to violence toward me in this instance, for exposing you to such peril."

Reyna gripped his arm, her worried gaze beseeching his. "Svein, do you value the life of your blood brother and jarl?"

"Yea—of course, milady."

"Then you must help me. And neither of us must ever tell Viktor." She drew herself up with pride. "You must accompany me tonight ... or I swear I will go alone."

Svein cursed softly. "Milady, I could tell our jarl of your plans," he warned. "Verily, he would order you confined to ensure your safety."

"Tell him, then," she retorted with an angry gesture, "if you do not value his life!"

Svein considered this for a long moment, then sighed. "There is no dissuading you?"

"Not with my husband's life—and that of our child—hanging in the balance."

Svein nodded morosely. "You have defeated me, then, milady. But I must insist we go under heavier guard. There are several among our warriors—particularly Ottar and his brother, Tyre—whom I can trust, whose discretion will be absolute."

"Very well. Gather a guard. We cross the fjord ere midnight."

"We meet again, old man."

That night, Wolfgard came awake to see his stepdaughter hovering over him, malice blazing in her eyes and her dagger pressed to his throat.

"You!" he bellowed, jerking slightly, then freezing as the girl's knife nicked him. His cagey gaze darted around the room, moving from Reyna to her three kinsmen, who loomed in the archway with broadswords drawn. Realizing escape was impossible, he demanded, "What are you doing here?"

"I come to look into your evil heart, old man."

"And you speak with all the respect of your six-toed brother," Wolfgard snarled.

She smiled. "Alain told me of his visit and the pact you made."

"I should have killed him, as I should slay you for turning traitor," Wolfgard hissed.

Reyna chuckled. "You speak boldly for a man with a knife at his throat."

Wolfgard eyed her with contempt. "You have gone soft, stepdaughter, your belly bulging with my enemy's seed. Were it not for the presence of your kinsmen, I could easily overpower you now and carve out your perfidious heart."

Reyna was actually shocked by the depth of malice in Wolfgard's words, the raw hatred burning in his eyes. "So Alain spoke the truth. Now you assign all the blame to me for your loss of face with Viktor."

Wolfgard virtually spit his next words. "Yea, you are the weakling who let him tame you, who spread her legs with the ease of a Hedeby whore!"

Reyna gasped at this diatribe, while Svein surged forward angrily, pointing his sword at Wolfgard. "If you value your life, old man, you will mind how you address milady."

"Bah!" Wolfgard scoffed. To Reyna, he sneered, "Kill me, stepdaughter, if you have the courage to do it."

"I have it, old man!" she retorted. "But first I will give you one final chance to save yourself. I will know if you intend to honor your pact with my brother. If I leave Vanaheim before the child is born, will you allow my husband to live here in peace?"

Wolfgard hesitated for a long moment.

"Answer, old man, or die!"

"Yea, stepdaughter," Wolfgard retorted bitterly, "if you leave Vanaheim, if you cleanse my soul of this terrible disgrace, then I will stop doing war with your husband. But if you remain and have Viktor's brat, I will not rest until all of you are dead."

Reyna tightened the pressure of her knife. "Speak ye the truth?"

"Yea."

"Swear it by Odin!"

"I so avow," he sneered.

"I have my answer, then." Reyna flashed her hated stepfather a cruel smile. "And now I will slit your throat, old man, to stay you from harming my family."

Reyna was pleased to note fear flashing into Wolfgard's gray eyes and his haggard cheek muscles twitching in distress. But before she could slice her dagger across his throat, Svein rushed over to restrain her wrist.

"Stay yourself, milady."

She swung her vengeful gaze on him. "Nay. I will kill this whoreson now, so he may never harm us!"

"You will not," Svein reiterated. "You offered Wolfgard his life in exchange for the truth, and you will not dishonor your own word."

"Tell me not of honor when we are dealing with a whoreson who has none!"

" 'Tis no excuse for our behaving like animals," Svein argued obdurately. "Verily, one lesson I have learned from our jarl is that we do not slay defenseless men."

"Wolfgard is not defenseless! He is a villainous jackal."

"You will release him, my lady," Svein repeated.

The two continued to confront each other, this time in murderous silence, while Wolfgard observed them, wild-eyed. At last Svein pulled Reyna's hand away from Wolfgard's throat and snatched the dagger from her fingers. Wolfgard reared up in bed, then froze in horror as he watched Svein raise his broadsword high over his head. But the warrior merely used the flat side of his weapon to knock Wolfgard unconscious. With a groan, the enemy chieftain slumped in his bed.

Reyna turned on Svein. "Let me slay him!"

"Nay!"

Clutching her wrist in steely fingers, he pulled her from the room.

Back at Viktor's village, Reyna and Svein parted company with Ottar and Tyre, and Svein escorted Reyna home. The two were riding toward the longhouse when Viktor suddenly loomed before them on the path. The horses reacted in fear, neighing and stamping the ground; Reyna and Svein quickly reined in their mounts.

Viktor stared incredulously from Svein to his wife. "Reyna! Where have you been? I awoke to find you gone, and I have been searching everywhere for you."

"I was restless, my husband, and wanted to go for a ride. You were sleeping peacefully, so I started out alone for the stables." She nodded to Svein. "I met your kinsman along the path. When Svein could not stay me from my plan, he insisted on coming along to provide escort."

Viktor continued to regard them both in mystification. "The two of you went riding in the middle of the night, when Wolfgard could attack again at any moment? Have you both lost your minds?"

"We were in no danger," Reyna retorted.

"No danger?" he raved. "You, milady, have no business whatsoever being on a horse this close to your delivery!"

"We rode slowly," she argued.

"That is beside the point." Viktor leveled his glare on Svein. "As for you, my kinsman, I will speak to you tomorrow about your utter lack of judgment in letting my wife talk you into this middle-of-the-night folly."

"Yea, jarl," responded Svein humbly. "I am sorry we gave you a fright. But please know my goal was only to protect milady."

Viktor grunted a response. Moving between the horses, he gently pulled Reyna down off the saddle and into his arms. "Take milady's mount to the stable," he ordered Svein. "I will carry my wife back to the longhouse."

"Yea, jarl."

Viktor started off with Reyna in his arms.

She squirmed. "Put me down. I am not a child!"

"You are behaving like one!"

"And if you stumble in the darkness, you could harm the babe."

That remark stopped Viktor in his tracks. Carefully, he set Reyna on her feet. "And what if your horse had stumbled in the darkness?"

"Mayhap the horse has more sense than you at times, my husband."

He shook a finger at her. "You are one to talk of sense, riding around in the moonlight when you are likely to have my baby at any moment. Not to mention drafting Svein into this lunacy—"

"Verily, cease," she cut in, losing patience. "You have scolded me enough."

To her surprise, he grinned. "My God, what a handful you are."

"Handful?" she repeated, bemused.

"You must be close to term, for you are behaving like a madwoman." He scratched his jaw. "As a matter of fact, I seem to recall my mother in Futuregard telling me that, a day or two before she delivered me, she grew restless and full of energy, polishing all the marble in our villa. My father had a fit when he caught her."

"My dementia is explained, then."

He sighed and wrapped a protective arm around her waist. "Darling, you really do scare me sometimes—and I don't know what I'd do if I lost you."

Beneath the eaves of the longhouse, she turned to touch his arm, pulling him to a stop. "If that is so, if you fear for my safety, then take me away from here."

He sighed in keen disappointment. "Reyna, must we go over this again?"

She nodded, her expression deeply troubled. "I happen to know that your dream of peace is doomed, my husband. I happen to know that when I deliver your son, Wolfgard plans to break the pact and kill us all."

"How can you know these things?" His features suddenly

taut with suspicion, he reached out to grasp her arms. "Don't tell me you went to see him? By God, if you did—"

"Alain went to see him!" Reyna interrupted fiercely, realizing once again that she could not tell her husband of her own reckless mission tonight. "Wolfgard told Alain that if you win the pact, he will slaughter us all anyway." She stared at her husband in entreaty. "Pray, take us away from Vanaheim. Let us all go to live in Loire, with Alain and Ragar. 'Tis the only way our child will be safe."

Viktor shook his head. "Reyna, this is just your fear talking, fear inspired by your brother. I know he hates Vikings—despises me, in fact—but I thought we had moved beyond allowing bitterness to rule our lives."

"I am not bitter! I only want my child to live!"

Viktor stared earnestly into her eyes. "If you do, then you will place our love above the fear your brother inspires. You will believe in my vision of peace for Vanaheim and for our child. Reyna, I truly saw it—you and me together with our son, and all of the people of Vanaheim bowing in tribute, brought to peace at last by his birth."

"That is a fool's dream!" she cried. "Wolfgard will never honor the pact!"

"I believe he will, and that you must stop allowing your brother to drive us asunder—"

"And what of you? You are putting your desire for peace above the lives of your wife and child."

"That is not true," he replied fiercely. "I swear to you, the dream will soon become reality. I swear to you, I saw it all in Futuregard."

Rage and frustration burst in Reyna. "A blight on you and all your babble about Futuregard. You do not care about me or the child, and I do not believe any of it anymore."

"What are you saying?"

She faced him with unflinching determination. "I am saying I will go with Alain to Loire anyway."

"You will not," Viktor stated, his visage equally obdurate.

"You are forbidding me?"

"Yes. I am forbidding you."

As he stood glaring at her, relentless, she gazed at him as if he were a stranger, bitter tears welling in her eyes. After all they had shared, Viktor was still determined to dominate her! Her heart ached with anguish.

"What of sharing?" she cried. "What of making decisions together? You promised me—"

"I promised that once you became more reasonable, we would decide things together. But, Reyna, you are still being totally stubborn and obstinate—"

"According to you! Mayhap I think *you* are the one being stubborn and obstinate!"

He clutched her arm. "No more arguing. It's freezing cold out here. Let's get you into bed."

She shook off his touch. "Rot in Hel!"

But Viktor just hauled his rebellious wife up into his arms and carried her inside.

Later, with her husband asleep beside her, his arms wrapped protectively around her, Reyna found slumber elusive. Ever since he had forbidden her to leave Vanaheim, the defiant warrior woman in her had risen up. She realized now that she could not live with a man who was determined to rule her life so implacably, to give her own feelings no heed. Granted, Viktor was a much better man than Wolfgard, but her husband was still trying to subjugate her, just as Wolfgard had repressed her own mother.

It broke Reyna's heart that in the final analysis, Viktor placed his doomed desire for peace above what was best for their family and unborn child. She could not stay with a man who would not put his wife and child first. At least if she went to Loire, her baby would be safe—and so would Viktor. Hopefully, he would join her and the child there in due course, once he realized she was right.

Her painful decision made, she knew she must inform Alain. It took Reyna a long time to extricate herself from Viktor's embrace, carefully prying away first his fingers, then his hands, then his forearms. Finally she left his bed and lumbered through the house to her brother's chamber.

Gently, she shook him, and when he jerked awake, she whispered, "I will sail with you before the dawn. Yea?"

"Yea, my sister," he replied, smiling sleepily. "You have made the only choice."

Through Reyna knew in her heart that Alain was right, when she tiptoed back into the bedchamber and lay down beside her husband, she shook with silent sobs for hours before falling into a fitful slumber.

Wolfgard sat in bed, glowering at the female thrall who was dabbing at the oozing gash atop his head. At the doorway, Egil stood watching them with a scowl.

"My lord, I must bandage this," the woman fretted. "But first, mayhap you need a stitch or two to bind the wound."

As she probed the cut more carefully, Wolfgard bellowed a curse and cruelly backhanded her. "Begone, wench—you only increase my misery!"

Her hand on her bruised cheek and her eyes wild with fear, the slave stumbled from the room.

Egil stepped forward. "Shall I summon another woman to attend you, jarl?"

"Nay. Females be damned, the lot of them!" Wolfgard lurched out of bed, then groaned at the pain and dizziness that came in the wake of his sudden movement. "To think my cursed stepdaughter invaded my very home!"

"We must retaliate once you are recovered—"

"We will retaliate now!" Wolfgard roared, grabbing his leggings.

"Think you it wise to battle the enemy so soon after your injury?"

"Think you I will let my stepdaughter and her brat escape Vanaheim unscathed after she came here and threatened my very life?" Wolfgard retorted. "Nay, the Valkyrie has pushed me too far this time. I will slay her, her brat, her husband, and all of their people."

"And what of the boy, Alain, who came to bargain with you?" Egil asked with a puzzled frown.

Wolfgard's cold gray eyes gleamed with bloodlust. "That fool? Before the dawn breaks, the dim-witted whoreson will drown in his own screams."

Now Egil's grin was broad. "As you wish, jarl."

"Rouse my men. We sail at once."

Egil rushed from the chamber.

THIRTY-EIGHT

Well before dawn, Reyna awakened and lumbered out of bed. She stretched her lethargic body, then winced. She felt exhausted and the small of her back ached, no doubt from the pressure of the babe.

As she had done throughout much of the night, Reyna again questioned her radical decision to leave Viktor this day. He was her husband and she loved him fiercely, despite their differences. Taking a sea voyage so close to her delivery could also risk injury to her baby.

Yet Reyna remained convinced that a much greater peril to her child loomed if she remained on Vanaheim—for if she had the baby here and rubbed Wolfgard's nose in the disgrace of his own defeat, he would never rest until she and her child were dead. Although she would gladly give her own life for her husband, never would she risk their precious babe!

Moving around slowly and awkwardly, Reyna dressed in a long wool garment, a mantle with a hood, and warm boots. She packed a few essentials in a walrus-skin bag, then dared to glance at Viktor, who looked almost boyishly innocent as he slept sprawled on his side, an arm outstretched where she should have lain.

Love, anguish, and regret welled inside her with painful intensity. How she hated leaving him! How it broke her heart to defy his wishes and even dishonor her wedding vows! But she could not remain and allow his fool's dream to destroy them all; she would put the welfare of their child first, even if he would not.

Tears filled her eyes as she leaned over, gently kissing him one last time. He stirred slightly, smiling in his sleep as her lips brushed his—and that smile was almost her undoing. Her baby's sluggish kick reminded her of what was at stake. Before she could lose her nerve, she turned quickly, grabbed her bag, and left the room.

In Alain's chamber, she found him already dressed and gathering his things.

"Good morrow, my sister," he said cheerfully. "Are you ready to sail for home?"

But this is home, Reyna almost replied, confusion and guilt surging within her anew. "I cannot feel true joy in this day," she replied dismally. "Of course I am heartened to anticipate living in Loire with you and Ragar. Nonetheless, the idea of leaving my husband brings me great heartache. 'Tis only fear for my child's safety that moves me to take this rash step."

"I realize that," Alain said cajolingly. "And you are entirely warranted in leaving Vanaheim. Your baby will be in the greatest danger otherwise, as you know." He touched her arm and smiled. "Now let us hurry. My kinsmen should be meeting us at the stable."

Taking a smoky steatite lamp, the two left the house and proceeded through the chill air toward the stable, moving slowly due to Reyna's cumbersome girth. The smells of animals and manure greeted them as they entered the darkened building. Several of the animals snorted nervously as Alain opened a stall. A stout blond horse jerked up his head and neighed at them.

Scowling, Reyna watched Alain take down a saddle and move toward the animal. "That is my husband's horse," she protested.

Not even hesitating, Alain threw the saddle onto Sleipnir's back, while the horse stamped the ground with a foreleg. " 'Tis no matter. I plan to leave my mount at the wharf before we sail away from Vanaheim."

Reyna stepped forward to grab his hand, restraining him. "Nay. Take another horse."

He turned to her in exasperation. "What matters it if we are leaving?"

"It matters to me. 'Tis regrettable enough I am deserting my husband. I will not have him thinking we stole his horse."

Alain uttered a curse. "I have told my men to gather provisions from your husband's stores. Surely you will not object to that as well?"

"Nay, supplies are necessary. But you may not take my husband's horse."

Hurling his sister a resentful glance, Alain hauled the saddle off Sleipnir's back and moved to the next stall, where he saddled a small brown horse. Reyna proceeded to the stall where her own black pony was stabled. She was stroking the animal when suddenly she felt a presence behind her. She whirled to see a man pointing a knife at her.

"Where do you think you are going, milady?" he asked with a sneer.

"Nevin, what are you doing here?" she replied confusedly. Watching him advance with a cruel smile, she screamed, "Alain!" and reached for her own dagger—

But the thrall grabbed Reyna before she could unsheathe her weapon. He quickly pinned her against him and pressed his knife to her throat. Terrified for her unborn child, Reyna dared not move.

"Reyna, what is the matter?"

At the sound of Alain's alarmed voice and advancing footsteps, Nevin spun around with Reyna still clutched against him. "Halt!" he ordered.

Alain skidded to a stop before them, taking in the scene with a look of horror. "How dare you threaten milady, slave! Release my sister at once."

"So you may help her leave Vanaheim?" Nevin scoffed. *"Oui."*

"Nay!" Nevin replied, his dark eyes burning with malice. "Your sister has heaped terrible disgrace on her stepfather."

"What matter is that of yours?" demanded Alain.

Nevin sneered a laugh. "I would slay her on Wolfgard's behalf, rather than let her flee before feeling his vengeance."

Reyna twisted about, staring at Nevin in realization and terror. "You are the spy, then!"

"Yea."

"But why?"

"Why should I serve those who enslaved me?" he countered harshly. "Your stepfather gives me respect, and pieces of silver for my loyalty." He regarded Reyna with contempt. "He will award me a generous bounty for slaying you. And he has promised to free me once he defeats Viktor."

"To free you?" Reyna mocked. "If you believe that lie, then you are a fool."

Nevin's features convulsed with fury, and he tightened the pressure of the knife. "And your evil tongue is about to be silenced, traitor!"

Glimpsing the lethal purpose in his eyes, Reyna felt panic encroaching. "Please, you would not harm my child—"

"A brat born only to disgrace your stepfather?" Nevin taunted.

"You will let my sister go, slave," Alain ordered.

"Nay."

"If you hurt her, I will kill you afterward," Alain vowed vengefully. "And I swear 'twill be slow."

Nevin hesitated for a moment, his fingers trembling on the knife at Reyna's throat. Then, mercifully, she heard the bang of the stable door blowing open and the thud of footsteps approaching, and she realized with intense gratitude that Alain's kinsmen must have arrived. Even more blessed, the noises distracted Nevin for the split second Reyna needed. She grabbed his wrist, yanking his hand away from her throat.

Even as Nevin howled a protest and struggled with her, Alain leaped forward, quickly wresting the knife away from the thrall and restraining him with the weapon. Reyna lurched away, slumping against the wall of the stall, nauseated and breathing convulsively, her hand pressed protectively to her belly. A dull pain gripped the small of her back, and she grew terrified that the ordeal might have harmed her child.

Alain's two kinsmen appeared before them, quickly taking in the scene. Dropping the sacks of grain and the parcels of dried meat they had fetched with them, Gilles and Barde rushed inside the stall to help Alain.

"Seize him!" Alain commanded.

He shoved the captive toward his kinsmen, who held Nevin firmly restrained as Alain threatened the slave with the knife.

"Not so proud now, are we, thrall?" he demanded, wielding the weapon in Nevin's face.

Though Nevin's eyes were bright with fear, he did not reply.

Alain hauled the knife back and spoke savagely. "This is for trying to murder my sister!"

On the sidelines, realizing her brother's deadly intent, Reyna screamed, "Alain, no!" but it was too late. As she watched, horrified, he brutally thrust the knife deep into Nevin's belly, then just as savagely yanked the weapon out. The thrall's scream of agony lanced Reyna's ears; sickened, she watched him fall, jerking with torment, to the hay-strewn floor.

"He will die slowly," Alain informed his sister with sadistic relish. " 'Tis fitting."

Her features ashen, Reyna stepped forward to grip Alain's arm, the sounds of the thrall's terrible moans making her even more nauseated. "Why did you gut him? You had him trapped and helpless already! Verily, you could have tied him up—"

"He was a traitor who threatened your life," Alain retorted ferociously. "You have gone soft, my sister, and I will hear no more of this. We are leaving now."

Still sickened by the man's cries of pain, Reyna was tempted to ask Alain to put Nevin out of his misery, but was equally afraid of how—or even if—he would honor her request.

A moment later, as the four of them rode out of the stable, Reyna continued to feel horribly repulsed. Alain's show of barbarism had disturbed her greatly, and made her wonder if she really knew her brother at all.

She also felt shocked by how deeply the slave's suffering had affected her, when a year ago the show of savagery would have been meaningless to her. She realized she had dramatically changed: knowing and loving Viktor had altered her heart and soul and conscience, making violence and warfare as loathsome to her as it had always been to her husband. With awe, she recognized that their lives, their feelings and beliefs, had truly melded in every way. They were indeed like one being now, and in leaving him, she felt as if a part of her heart, the essence of her soul, were being ripped away.

Yet how could she turn back and subject her child to life in a brutal world where their enemies would never share their vision?

The journey to the wharf was slow, and the pain in the small of Reyna's back increased as they navigated their way down the craggy fell. What was equally daunting, Reyna had begun to see an unusual red glow in the skies to the south, along the Atlantic horizon. The illumination was alarming and surreal—a sunrise where no sun dwelled. Reyna feared that hell itself was opening up to forbid their passage, and she began even more intently to question the wisdom of her decision.

After they had dismounted and started down the pier, Reyna touched her brother's arm. "Alain, I am no longer completely certain we should leave—"

"Do you want your child to die?" he cut in furiously. He jerked his thumb toward the small sailing ship awaiting them. "Board the vessel. We embark now."

"But look at the sky!" she cried, pointing to the southern horizon. "The red is surely a warning—"

" 'Tis only a reflection of the sunrise," he scoffed, grabbing her arm and tugging her onward.

Reyna had little choice but to comply and climb the gangplank to the ship. After loading the provisions, Alain's kinsmen cut the mooring ties and maneuvered the boat into the turbulent fjord. The rocky motion of the vessel left Reyna awash in new nausea and dizziness. Emotionally she felt very conflicted, tempted to beg her brother to return them to the wharf. Then she glanced northward and spotted a new menace—the ominous bulk of a longship, outlined in the red glow of torches, gliding down the fjord toward the wharf they had just abandoned.

"What is this?" she demanded of Alain, gesturing wildly.

He laughed in contempt. "Most likely Wolfgard, come to kill your whoreson husband."

"What?" she whispered, aghast. "What are you saying? I

thought you made a bargain with Wolfgard regarding my
husband—"

"I did, sister, but I lied to you about its terms."

Reyna stared at Alain. His eyes were gleaming with such
raw malice that she felt as if she were looking at him for the
first time. "Why?" she gasped. "Why would you lie?"

"For your own benefit. Wolfgard promised me that if I
could convince you to leave Vanaheim with me, he would not
attack your husband until after your departure." Alain's voice
softened to a triumphant sneer. "So now you are gone, and
Wolfgard is free to kill the bastard who put his seed in you."

"You betrayed me!" she cried in outrage. "You must take
me back at once!"

"Nay, my sister." He glanced contemptuously toward her
belly. "And if you want me to tolerate Viktor's brat, you had
best start demonstrating a more biddable attitude."

Watching him turn away to speak with one of his kinsmen,
Reyna was horrified. What a fool she had been to allow her
brother to dupe her. Alain's heart was clearly poisoned by
hatred—a rancor that possibly extended even to her unborn
babe!

Reyna realized that, like Wolfgard, Alain was another man
who wanted to control her and dominate her life, while the
man she truly loved, the man to whom she owed her allegiance, had been left to die at Wolfgard's traitorous hands!
Viktor had been right all along to insist that she remain at his
side, but she had grasped the truth too late!

In his dreams, Viktor felt strangely bereft. He came slowly
awake and reached for Reyna. She was gone!

Instantly alert, he bolted out of bed and threw on his
clothes. Perhaps she had just become restless again or hungry,
he mused. Perhaps her labor had begun, and she had sought
out Sibeal.

Yet somehow Viktor knew such hopes were futile; he was
dogged by a sickening feeling that she had left him. His fear
was confirmed when he rushed into Alain's chamber and
found the boy gone as well, his belongings missing.

God help them! Alain must have convinced Reyna to return with him to Loire. And he himself had doubtless pushed his wife over the edge with his unyielding attitude last night.

Viktor ran to Sibeal's chamber and shook her awake. "Have you seen milady?"

She sat up. "Nay, jarl."

"I fear she has left with her brother."

Sibeal's eyes went wide with fear. "This is most distressing! Milady's time is close at hand, I am certain."

"I will go after her at once, and pray I am not too late."

Sibeal clutched Viktor's arm. "Let me come with you, jarl. I have a strong feeling milady may need me. I can sense disaster looming."

As could Viktor! "Meet me at the stable," he ordered, already tearing out of the room.

He hurried to Svein's cottage, roused him, and set him to the task of awakening the other warriors. A moment later, Viktor rushed inside the stable to the sound of moans. He spotted Nevin inside a stall, bleeding profusely from a stomach wound, his features stark with agony.

Setting down his lamp, he knelt beside the thrall. "What happened, man?"

"Your wife's brother slew me!" Nevin gurgled, blood spewing from his mouth.

"Reyna and Alain were here?"

"Yea!"

"But why would Alain have hurt you?"

Nevin snorted in contempt. "Because I would have slain your wife!"

"What?" Utterly panicked, Viktor seized him by his garment. "Did you hurt my wife? By God, if you did—"

"Nay!" the man shrieked between shudders of pain. "Can you not see that I am the one murdered?"

With this, Nevin succumbed to new shrieks of misery, while Viktor heard a quiet voice behind him say, "Mayhap we have found our traitor, jarl?"

Viktor glanced around to see that Svein, Sibeal, and several of his warriors had entered the stable. All stood grim-faced, evidently having overheard most of his exchange with Nevin.

Standing up, Viktor nodded to Svein. "Yea, we have found the traitor—and he even tried to hurt Reyna. We must hurry to the wharf and pray there is still time to detain her and her brother."

"Yea, jarl—the other men are on their way," answered Svein.

Canute nodded toward the agonized man on the floor. "Shall I put him out of his misery, jarl?"

"Nay," Viktor replied. "We are human beings. We do not put down our fellow man as if he is an animal." He nodded to Sibeal. "See if you can help him."

As Sibeal dutifully sank to her knees beside Nevin, Viktor rushed off to saddle Sleipnir. Leading the horse to the door, he again passed the stall where Nevin lay, only to watch, horrified, as Sibeal handed the wounded thrall a dagger.

"No!" Viktor cried.

But his command came too late. Nevin at once thrust the knife through his breast and slumped over, dead.

Viktor rushed toward Sibeal. "Damn it, woman, what were my instructions?"

Rising, she shook her head and spoke with keen regret. "Jarl, there was no hope. Nevin was suffering terribly, and he begged me for the dagger."

Viktor sighed deeply. "Very well. Let us all prepare to ride."

His remaining warriors soon joined them, and within moments the large band was riding for the wharf, with Viktor and his kinsmen leading the charge. Viktor was alarmed to see a bizarre red glow on the horizon to the south of them and he wondered what the light could be. A sickening fear for his wife and child—the same feeling of impending doom that Sibeal had mentioned—threatened him with renewed panic.

As he galloped with the others down the fell, Viktor's heart sank, for he noted that Alain's vessel was nowhere in sight. Worse yet, he found to his mystification that the eerie red light now spewed forth from both the north and the south. Down toward the Atlantic, an unearthly crimson dawn was breaking where no dawn should be! Even more unnerving, closer to them up the fjord, another blot of fire made its way toward them ... Good Lord, it was a longship loaded with torch-waving barbarians! It was like a nightmarish repeat performance of the very night he had arrived in Vanaheim!

"Wolfgard is attacking!" cried Ottar.

"He will reach the wharf before we can board!" added Orm.

"I realize that—but what is the glow to the south of us?" Viktor yelled. "Oh, God! Please don't let Alain's ship be on fire, and my wife on board!"

"The glow is too large to be a vessel!" Rollo shouted.

"Then what is it?"

" 'Tis the vengeance of the gods!" cried Canute.

At the bottom of the fell, Viktor signaled his men to halt. Just beyond them, Wolfgard's frightful longship was gliding up to the wharf. As Viktor and his men dismounted and unsheathed their weapons, he ordered Sibeal to stay out of sight. Then all conversation ceased as they tensely watched Wolfgard's vessel thud against their wharf. Within seconds, dozens of shrieking warriors swarmed down onto the pier and raced toward them with swords waving.

At Viktor's signal, he and the others charged forward to defend themselves against the onslaught. Viktor felt crazed with fear for Reyna, and now he would have to fight his way through this pack of madmen before he could even start after her.

The vengeance of the gods, Canute had said. As Viktor crossed swords with a howling berserker who attacked him with wild lunges and savage thrusts, he wondered if the kinsman had spoken the truth. By now his state of mind was so frantic, the rush of adrenaline so intense, he did not at first notice that the boards of the wharf were shaking beneath his feet.

And then his entire world began to tremble . . .

THIRTY-NINE

Down the fjord, near the ocean, Reyna also was fretting about the distant red glow, as well as the waves that loomed far higher and more bilious than normal. In that same instant she felt warm water gush between her thighs and excruciating pain grip the small of her back. She gasped and pressed a hand to her belly. Feeling her stomach muscles harden, she realized she was in labor, and might already have been in labor for some hours.

Reyna was eaten up with fear for her child, about to be born on the turbulent seas, and for Viktor, left behind to defend himself against Wolfgard. And as each moment passed, she became more terrified of the deepening crimson tide emblazoning the southern horizon like a spreading pool of blood. Again, it was as if they were sailing straight into the jaws of hell!

She could not have her baby amid that!

As a violent spasm gripped her, she turned to grab her brother's arm. "Alain, please, we must turn back," she beseeched. "I can feel the baby coming!"

"Good. He or she will grow strong in Loire."

"But we cannot proceed!" Stifling a moan of misery, Reyna pointed to the ominous horizon. "Look in the distance, at the red glow. There is clearly danger ahead."

"Bah! You are being a silly woman," Alain scoffed. "I have told you already, 'tis only a reflection of the dawn."

Reyna could have screamed her exasperation. "But there is no dawn to the south!"

One of the kinsmen spoke up from the helm. "Alain, we, too, are frightened of the glow. Mayhap 'tis a sign of troubled waters ahead."

"You are turning into a woman," Alain chided Gilles.

A strong wave buffeted the small craft. Reyna, close to panic, pulled out her dagger, grabbed Alain's arm, and pointed the knife at his chest.

"How dare you threaten me, sister!" he snapped, scowling angrily at her.

Reyna spoke with deadly determination. "Alain, you will take me back to my husband's wharf now, or I will kill you."

He only laughed, infuriating her. "You will not slay me. You cringed at the mere thought of my harming the thrall who would have murdered you. You will not kill your own flesh and blood."

Reyna knew he had spoken the truth, and desperation choked her voice. "Alain, pray listen to me—"

"Alain! Look!" cried Barde.

As the vessel again rocked hard, brother and sister jerked around to watch an unfolding nightmare scene. Beyond them toward the southern horizon, the sea was literally boiling! As the company of four looked on in awe and disbelief, the waves churned and heaved; then the waters parted violently to form an abyss ... And out of the yawing cavern spewed huge streams of liquid fire, ashes, and rocks!

Clinging to the bulwark, Alain spoke distraughtly to Reyna. "What is happening?"

At first she was just as confused as she heard the sea roar like a savage demon, watched huge clouds of steam rise as the ocean filled the vacuum, saw embers and large chunks of basalt explode into the sky. And then she realized what she was witnessing—a moment of birth such as she herself was experiencing, the very primal forces that had created Iceland, created Vanaheim—

"'Tis a volcano erupting," she told her brother with fierce triumph. "Now we have no choice but to turn back—or else be boiled in the raging sea ahead of us."

This time Alain had no chance to protest. Hot cinders were

already fluttering down around them, and Alain's kinsmen were frantically struggling to turn the boat against the monstrous waves slamming the vessel . . .

The battle seemed interminable. Viktor chopped and lunged and swung and thrust, fighting desperately to make his way down the wharf to his ship, to go rescue his wife. Even as the path before him at last cleared, his sense of horror and terrible fear increased as he watched a river of fire spew into the sky on the distant southern horizon, while the ground continued to shudder beneath his feet—

Hearing crashing sounds, he whirled to see rocks and small boulders sail off the fell and crash toward the pier. A couple of warriors howled in pain as they were hit by the flying debris. The rumbling of the ground increased, and steam and ashes filled the air.

Dio, the entire landscape appeared like the end of the world. What in God's name was happening? Was Reyna sailing straight into the fires of Hel?

"'Tis a volcano erupting!" he heard Orm shout nearby.

Viktor realized the man was right. As the spewing of fire increased in the distance, the air grew acrid with the scent of cinders and ashes. A red glow crept over the wharf. Then a most curious thing happened. As the warriors of both sides became conscious of the calamity, they ceased fighting, one by one. Several even fell to their knees and faced the south, amid the still-roaring skies and trembling landscape.

A moment later, Viktor stood staring around him, stunned by the lull in the battle. "What has happened?" he asked Svein.

"The eruption is considered a sign from the gods," Svein explained. "The warriors believe the gods are displeased with the battle."

Viktor felt a momentary elation that surged to a blinding sense of relief when he saw Alain's vessel make its way back up the fjord, with Reyna standing at the rail. Thank God! His wife and child had been spared!

No one tried to stop him as he raced down the wharf to meet Reyna. Indeed, when Wolfgard lunged forward with his sword drawn, two of his own warriors restrained him.

Viktor was on the ship before the gangplank could even be extended. "Reyna!" he cried, then almost froze when he glimpsed her white, stricken face and saw the wetness on her dress between her thighs.

"My husband," she gasped, "I am having our child. Very soon, I think."

Viktor lifted his wife into his arms and proceeded steadily, quickly down the gangplank to the wharf. Warriors from both tribes moved aside as he bore Reyna off the pier and up the trail. His kinsmen fell into step behind them to discourage any aggression.

"No, my husband!" she cried halfway up the trail. "I am having our baby *now.*"

Glancing directly overhead to make certain there were no loose rocks or boulders to threaten them, Viktor paused at a ledge and gently laid Reyna down. Sibeal emerged from her position behind some stunted willows and rushed over to join them. Viktor's kinsmen stood in a line facing the wharf to shield the birth.

Sibeal raised Reyna's skirts and gasped. "My lord, she is birthing now. You must turn away."

Viktor would have protested, but Reyna grasped his hands and spoke, staring into his eyes with utter love. "Nay, my husband will watch his son being born."

Tears filled Viktor's eyes at her gesture of unconditional trust and sharing. During the next moments, he actually hurt for Reyna as he listened to her cries and watched her push and strain to bring their baby into the world. At last he saw his son's tiny head push between his wife's thighs. He heard Reyna's primal cry at the moment of birth and felt with her both the pain and the incredible exultation.

A moment later, the squalling infant fell into Sibeal's hands. Using the small scissors from her brooch shaped like a key ring, she cut the cord and tied it off. After cleansing the child with the sleeve of her garment, she extended the naked infant to Viktor.

"My lord, do you accept your son?" she asked quietly.

"God, yes." Viktor removed his tunic and wrapped the infant in it, taking him in his arms. Emotion shook Viktor as he felt his son squirming and heard his lusty cries. The boy was perfect in every detail, his body beautifully shaped and plump, a crown of blond fuzz on his head. Viktor looked down at his bride, spotting the tears in Reyna's eyes and glorying in her expression of sublime happiness.

"Thank you, my love," he whispered.

He leaned over to kiss her lips, and they shared their bliss for a poignant moment.

Then Viktor stood with his son in his arms. Both the skies and the landscape surrounding him were calm now, with a spectacular red-gold dawn breaking, and he realized with awe that the volcano's eruption, and quaking of the ground, had ceased, the sun emerged, at the very moment of his son's birth, as if all the forces of God and nature had been brought into harmony. Glancing beneath him, he surveyed the Viking warriors of both camps, bowed in tribute and united at last. Here, finally, was the moment of his dream, the moment of his destiny. Clutching his tiny, beloved son close, he trembled with painful joy as he realized that in every way, he was home now . . .

Tears rolling down his cheeks, Viktor held his newborn son high for all to see. "My comrades, may I present Eirik the Peacemaker, king of all the Vikings. Just as I have promised, he has come to bring all our peoples together. Go now, and let us make war no longer."

For a moment the warriors of both tribes appeared awed, transfixed. Then, slowly and peaceably, the men began to disperse, murmuring to one another in reverent tones about how Viktor had now won the day and settled the feud.

In the face of his warriors' retreat toward the wharf, Wolfgard sprang forward to confront his company, his sword waving, his face purple with rage. "Do not listen! Fight the whoreson! Do not let him sway you with his lies!"

But even as Wolfgard ranted and raved, his men ignored him and proceeded back to their vessel. After a moment more of futile ranting, Wolfgard, his features ashen with the finality of his own disgrace, sheathed his sword and joined the retreat.

In his father's arms, Eirik began to squall. Viktor knelt beside Reyna, placing the baby on her belly. As he looked on tenderly, she unfastened her garment and nestled the infant against her breast. At once Eirik suckled hungrily and quieted, and Viktor's heart twisted at the beautiful sight. At last he had the family of his dreams!

After Sibeal had cleaned up the afterbirth, Viktor gently lifted both wife and baby into his arms. Slowly and carefully, he carried his small family back toward his longhouse. By now sunlight was flooding the landscape—the dawning of his family's glorious destiny together.

After a lengthy moment, Reyna whispered, "I am sorry."

"Don't ever leave me again," he said fervently.

"Never!" came her fierce reply.

EPILOGUE

"WHAT ARE YOU DOING, MY HUSBAND?"

"I am designing our future home."

"You are tickling me."

"With the greatest pleasure."

Six weeks later, Reyna, Viktor, and Eirik were outside together not far from the longhouse, swinging in a hammock Viktor had designed and constructed between two stout beams dismantled from one of their war machines. He had built the hammock in large part as an outdoor cradle in which Reyna could rock and nurse her son. Eirik was a good-natured baby, but his occasional fretfulness was always soothed by moments like these. Often, Viktor could not resist joining his wife and son, especially now that peace had come to Vanaheim and he had many lovely, lazy days to spend with them.

The little family made an appealing portrait, arranged in spoon-style layers: first Viktor, with his wife on top of him, and then the baby nursing hungrily at her breast. On Reyna's now-flat stomach Viktor had laid a sheet of parchment, and with charcoal he was sketching his dream home—and tickling her.

Beyond them, the tundra was vibrant with wildflowers. Seabirds soared overhead, making their way back to the coast. Viktor smiled as he caught sight of Ottar and Iva strolling together, hand in hand, just to the east. In honor of peace coming to Vanaheim and his son's birth, Viktor had freed all the slaves and given each family its own plot of land to work. Iva was now seventeen, and Viktor had finally consented for her to marry Ottar. The ceremony would be held in early summer at the Shieling feast, on the first anniversary of his marriage to Reyna.

Smiling as he anticipated that day, he kissed Reyna's cheek and thought of how happy she had made him. And he could not be more pleased with Eirik—his golden son with his solid little body, wisps of blond hair, bright blue eyes, and eager, toothless smile. Already Viktor loved the child fiercely, and spent many happy moments walking on the tundra with Eirik in his arms.

Viktor missed his life in the distant future not at all. Eirik's birth had brought to realization his dream of his destiny for himself and Reyna, and had bound them both to the life they were meant to live together—a life of peace, harmony, and love.

"Tell me of this house," Reyna urged. "'Tis most peculiar-looking."

"Well, it is an A-frame," he explained. "Lots of glass and wood." At her frown, he added, "We shall have to go to Europe for the window glass, I imagine. Surely it has been invented. Anyway, we do need to secure seeds, cuttings, and saplings, to help improve our diet here on Vanaheim."

She nodded and scowled at the sketch. "Where is . . . what do you call it? The chimney?"

He grinned. "That's the beauty of it. We're going to build our house on the rise yonder"—he pointed—"over the hot spring. We'll warm the house with pipes heated by the spring. I've already discussed the forging of the metal tubing with Eurich. So, you see, there will be no need for a chimney. We shall have a totally smoke-free environment."

"What of cooking?"

He frowned. "I've been thinking of that. Perhaps we should have a building separate from the main house."

"So I am to freeze when I fetch you your dinner?" she asked indignantly.

"I'll construct a breezeway."

She rolled her eyes.

He chuckled and resumed sketching. "Well, perhaps I

should add at least one fireplace in the bedroom just for fun. Then you can heat up our dinner there on cold winter nights."

"Yea—and you can heat up *me*," she teased.

Grinning, Viktor set down his charcoal and stroked Eirik's soft little fist, which was pressed against his mother's breast as he suckled lustily. "Reyna . . ."

"Yes?" she said dreamily.

He nuzzled his cheek against her. "I'm so happy. Are you?"

She sighed. "Yea. I am happy that peace has come to Vanaheim. And though this may sound unkind, I am happy that Wolfgard died the night after the battle."

Viktor nodded. "His hatred poisoned him, as did his inability to accept the concept of reconciliation or peace. I really think it was his own malice that caused him to expire in his sleep."

"Good riddance," she said feelingly. "And I am glad that Alain returned to Loire without rancor, that he and I parted as friends. He even admitted that he was wrong to try to split our marriage asunder."

"Perhaps in time his attitude will change."

"I hope so."

Smiling tenderly, Viktor added, "We are meant to be together, Reyna. Just think—when you tried to leave me, it caused a volcanic eruption."

"Yea, but now your son has his own small island."

Viktor smiled. Like Vanaheim centuries before, the island of Eirikhelm had been born out of the boiling sea—and on the morn of his son's birth. Recently, Viktor and several of his kinsmen had sailed down to the small, craggy islet that had already become a haven for seabirds.

"Perhaps by the time our son is old enough to be taken to Eirikhelm, wildflowers will bloom there," Viktor mused aloud.

"The island will stand as a monument to our child, to the coming of peace on Vanaheim—and to our love," Reyna declared feelingly.

"And to your never leaving me again?" Viktor asked with a touch of sternness.

She flashed him an apologetic smile. "I left because I thought I was saving our baby's life—and yours."

"I know, darling."

"And I left because you forbade me to go."

"Ah, so the rebellious warrior woman rises up again?"

She glowered at him.

"Well, maybe I was unyielding," he admitted. "But I was frantic concerning your safety."

"Now I realize you were right," Reyna acknowledged humbly. "Right that the coming of our child would end the feud."

"I always believed in our dream," he said, "though I could understand your fear."

She stretched upward to kiss his handsome jaw. "I will not doubt you again."

He raised an eyebrow. "And will you obey me, like a good little wife?"

She uttered an indignant cry. "Never! Not as long as you order me around like your thrall—forbidding me this and forbidding me that."

He teased her soft neck with his lips. "My love, I will never again forbid you anything—as long as you promise never to fight battles or to try to leave me."

She wrinkled her nose at him. "But you are denying me my two greatest pleasures."

He feigned a wounded air. "You mean you enjoy leaving me?"

She giggled. "I love for you to come after me, Viking."

He sighed with pleasure and clutched her close. "Will you truly be content to stay here with me forever, milady?"

"Yea. Forever."

"You know, one day I'll take you and our children to visit Loire."

"Verily?" she cried with excitement. "And to Futuregard as well?"

He scratched his jaw. "My, I have no idea."

They fell into blissful silence, swinging to and fro and watching the baby nurse.

"He's asleep," Viktor murmured after a few moments, noting Eirik's precious expression as he dozed against his mother's breast.

"Yea ..." Shifting the infant slightly, Reyna retied her bodice, then leaned over to kiss his soft cheek. "He is happy, as we are."

"Totally content," Viktor agreed.

"But I am puzzled about something, my husband."

"What?"

She tilted her face up to his. "If I am not to do battle, and you are not to forbid me, how will we settle our disputes from now on?"

He winked at her. "You can always wrestle with me, darling."

"But that is not fair! There you can master me!"

"Then why don't we battle just for fun?"

She nodded. "A winsome idea."

He ran his hand over her thigh. "If you are completely recovered, of course, my lady."

"My health is back at its prime."

Viktor motioned to the couple beyond him. "Ottar! Iva! Come here!" As the two rushed over, he ordered, "Iva, take this baby—good practice for you. Ottar, come take this sketch, and study it well to plan your own future home. Milady and I have decided to battle it out."

Seconds later, as Iva and Ottar stood laughing on the sidelines with the baby, Reyna and Viktor faced each other on the tundra, both of them young, free, and beautiful, full of love and happiness.

"Come ahead, milady," he teased. "Give me your worst."

Reyna gazed at the man she loved with all her heart—at his handsome smile and laughing blue eyes, features her adored Eirik shared. Far from feeling subjugated or oppressed by the vows between them, she had at last found her freedom in their love—and in devoting her life to Viktor and their son.

With an exultant battle cry, Reyna charged him. But instead of tackling her, Viktor delighted his wife by scooping her up into his arms and carrying her inside to their bed.

Now and Forever

Fabio

waits for you

Unforgettable romances by
the sexiest man in the world

VIKING
77048-2/ $5.99 US/ $6.99 Can

ROGUE
77047-4/ $5.99 US/ $6.99 Can

PIRATE
77046-6/ $4.99 US/ $5.99 Can

Coming Soon
COMANCHE

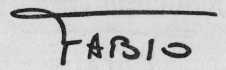

International Multi-Media Superhero
Champion of Romance, Fitness
and Self-esteem, has an

Official Link to his fans—

THE FABIO INTERNATIONAL FAN CLUB

- *Have you wondered what Fabio is all about?*
- *Would you like a glossy photo of him?*
- *Want to know where to write to Fabio?*
- *Curious about Fabio's wants, needs,
  personal philosophy and future plans?*

YES! Then the Fabio International Fan Club is
designed for you...once you sign up, you'll receive

—an 8 x 10 glossy photo...
—newsletter "updates"...
—membership card...and much, much more!

For more information on how to join, write to:
FABIO IFC, P.O. Box 827,
DuBois, WY 82513

FFC 0794